W9-BSG-078

THE ATTEMPTED MURDER
OF TEDDY ROOSEVELT

THE ATTEMPTED MURDER OF
TEDDY
ROOSEVELT

BURT SOLOMON

A TOM DOHERTY ASSOCIATES BOOK

NEW YORK

THE ATTEMPTED MURDER OF TEDDY ROOSEVELT

Copyright © 2019 by Burt Solomon

Map by Jon Lansberg

A Forge Book
Published by Tom Doherty Associates
120 Broadway
New York, NY 10271

www.tor-forge.com

Forge® is a registered trademark of Macmillan Publishing Group, LLC.

The Library of Congress Cataloging-in-Publication Data is available upon request.

ISBN 978-0-7653-9267-1 (hardcover)
ISBN 978-0-7653-9269-5 (ebook)

Our books may be purchased in bulk for promotional, educational, or business use. Please contact your local bookseller or the Macmillan Corporate and Premium Sales Department at 1-800-221-7945, extension 5442, or by email at MacmillanSpecialMarkets@macmillan.com.

First Edition: December 2019

Printed in the United States of America

0   9   8   7   6   5   4   3   2   1

To Nancy,
the source of life
beyond the keyboard

32nd Street

Connecticut Avenue

16th Street

① ②

③

H Street

P o t o m a c   R i v e r

Mason's
Island

T H E

F, G   E

H   Lafayette
Square   D

I   C

J

A   B

WASHINGTON, DC
❦ 1902 ❦

1. Henry Cabot Lodge's House
2. General Miles's House
3. Lafayette Square
4. The US Capitol
5. Pennsyvania Railroad Station

Massachusetts Avenue

Pennsylvania Avenue

B Street

MALL

A. Corcoran Gallery of Art
B. New Willard Hotel
C. US Department of the Treasury
D. Mark Hanna's House
E. St. John's Episcopal Church
F. Henry Adams's House
G. John Hay's House
H. Temporary White House
I. State, War, and Navy Building
J. White House

THE ATTEMPTED MURDER
OF TEDDY ROOSEVELT

PROLOGUE

Big Bill Craig, the president's bodyguard, saw it first. Or heard it. The clanging was insistent, like a boxing gong. The Secret Service man spun in his seat and gazed up Howard's Hill in horror. A trolley car was hurtling down toward them.

On the thirteenth and final morning of Theodore Roosevelt's campaign tour of New England, his horse-drawn carriage was leaving Pittsfield, at the western edge of Massachusetts. The city's church bells had tolled; the factory whistles had rung; the schools and mills had shut down. The president had addressed two thousand admirers from a bunting-bedecked bandstand in Park Square, and his open-air landau was a mile and a half along South street, rolling toward Lenox.

It was ten fifteen.

"Oh, my God!" Craig cried. He reached an arm over President Roosevelt's head. "Look out! Hold fast!"

The sepulchral Governor Crane turned and leapt to his feet and waved his arms. The electric streetcar kept rushing downhill, along the center of South street. At the bottom of the hill the road narrowed and the tracks slanted to the right; this was where carriages ordinarily crossed. To-day the vantage point was crowded with Kodak enthusiasts.

The landau's two lead horses cleared the tracks. The two wheel horses did not. The trolley's metal fender slammed into the nearer wheel horse and the left front wheel of the rig. The carriage toppled over, splintering its sides. Its occupants went flying. Wheels spun unfettered. Horses kicked at nothing. Their shrieks filled the air.

Suddenly, silence.

Governor Crane landed on his shoulder in the roadside twenty feet away, uninjured but white with shock. George Bruce Cortelyou, the president's secretary, suffered cuts to his nose and the back of his head. The carriage driver lay still under the fallen horse. President Roosevelt was thrown thirty or forty feet, into a bank of soft earth, crumpling his silk hat, shattering his spectacles, ripping his frock coat at the elbows, crushing the red rose in his lapel, and covering his patent leather shoes with dust. His right cheek was swollen and blood flowed from a cut on his lip. His bronzed face was splattered with mud.

His personal physician, Dr. Lung, in the nearest carriage, rushed to his side and probed the barrel chest for broken ribs.

"I'm all right." The growl came out as a squeak; the president pushed his doctor away. "Some of the others are badly hurt. Look after them."

Roosevelt jumped up in a rage. The trolley had rolled twenty feet down the track, and by the time he reached it his temper had calmed and his fists had loosened, if slightly. "Where is the motorman of this car?" he demanded.

"Here, sir."

The respondent was a meek-looking man of indeterminate age, short and balding, with rounded features but a defiant crouch.

"Did you lose control of the car?" Roosevelt's high-pitched voice had grown husky.

The motorman looked too frightened to answer.

"If you did, that was one thing," the president bore on. "If you didn't, it was a goddamned outrage."

The passengers gasped.

"You don't suppose I *tried* to do it, do you?" the motorman managed at last.

Roosevelt bit his puffy lip.

"Well, I had the right-of-way, anyway," Euclid Madden, for that was his name, continued. "You had a right to look out for yourselves."

Roosevelt looked like he wanted to punch the man. With a visible effort, he turned away.

That was when he saw what remained of William Craig. The Secret Service man lay under the sharp metal wheels of the trolley. He had been dragged along the track, his mighty torso crushed, his skull split open.

The president sank to his knees. "Oh, poor Craig, poor Craig, poor Craig," he moaned. "Here, some of you, get a blanket and throw it over that body."

He bounced to his feet and stalked off. No one dared follow.

CHAPTER ONE

Y ou should have come, Henry," I said. "You'd have hated it."

Henry Adams had the good grace to laugh. It was a merry sound, so different from the Brahmin breathiness of his chatter. "Labor Day is a silly idea to start with," he said. "Mr. Cleveland's sop to the unions. So, when is Capitalists' Day, pray tell?"

"Every day is Capitalists' Day," I replied.

"You ought to know, Hay," Henry jabbed. Then: "The lawyers lost, you say."

"Eight to two, on Georgetown College's campus. The doctors hit the ball too damn hard. So did the lawyers, but right at someone."

"I find a certain pleasure in that, I must say, old boy."

Henry was well aware that I am a lawyer, though I have had the luck never to have practiced a day. "You don't find pleasure in anything, Henry," I said. "I've never known anyone who enjoyed his unhappiness more. Part of your charm."

"Only a part?"

Our daily stroll usually began in Lafayette Square, in our topcoats and silk hats, around four o'clock in the afternoon. The walks had been Clara's idea—what wasn't?—and not only to keep me, at the venerable age of sixty-three, in (you should pardon the expression) boxing trim. Mainly it was to lure me away from my office, in that sand castle next to the White House, the State, War, and Navy Building, whose architect had killed himself a year after the final geegaw was squeezed on.

Lately, the world had cooperated. It's a pain in the arse to be a world power—how I've missed spending all summer in New Hampshire—but I shouldn't complain. This summer was the quietest since the mid-'nineties, or certainly in the four years since McKinley had done me the dubious honor of making me his secretary of state. (Not that I played hard to get; I just made it look that way.) Theodore, probably against his better judgment, had kept me on.

To-day Henry and I dispensed with our topcoats, for the afternoon was hot and humid—womb-like, in my way of thinking. Henry was wearing his starched frock coat, wing collar, and funereal cravat. He looked even paler than usual, his cheeks thinner. More hair seemed to have migrated from his scalp to his pointed, devilish beard; he looked like the oversize brain that he was. Yet I had never known a man so honest, in his intellect and in his morals.

We glided to a stop, without conferring, along the western edge of the square, in front of 22 Jackson Place northwest. The sturdy brick town house with the pretentious Greek temple pediments over the windows was serving as the temporary White House. The real one was being renovated, cellar to attic, adding a western wing for the president's executive offices.

"You know, Theodore is a stupid, blundering, bolting bull calf," Henry was saying. The diamond stickpin in his cravat caught the afternoon light.

"Tell me, Henry, what do you really think?"

"And he might have arranged this accident by himself. He is capable of it, you know."

"That's cynical, Henry, even for you."

"But plausible. For a president, you know, character is destiny."

"Why on earth would you ever think that?" I teased. Henry's grandfather and great-grandfather had been presidents, of which he never tired of reminding me. But, as usual, Henry had a point. Too often, I made the mistake of judging presidents as people—idiotic, I know, for a secretary of state, but I had befriended enough of them since Lincoln not to be cowed. And in this regard, I had to admit that Theodore came up a little short. (Not that I was pure.) Yes, he had the noblest traits—intelligence, fidelity, passion, sincerity, honesty, a grasp of history, a good heart, not to mention gobs of courage, physical and moral. His undeniable virtues were entangled, however, with a fixation on himself and a belief in his own rightness that scared me. He was warm to his friends (his thank-you notes were sonatas in paper and ink) but quick to belittle his political opponents as aunties or eunuchs. You didn't want him at your dinner table if anyone else had a desire to talk. Here was a man of substance and probity who was still in many ways a child; you had to remember, as his best man said, that Theodore was about six years old. I liked him, I did—I made allowances for youth. Maybe he was stuffed fuller with talents than any mortal could handle with grace.

Cortelyou's wire had come before noon, telling of the collision and the two arrests. The president was "considerably bruised" but not injured seriously, and Governor Crane had escaped without a scratch. But (from Cortelyou, it was probably an afterthought) William Craig was dead. No explanation.

Not Craig! Even now it was hard to believe. What a horror! Nothing like Del, of course, our late and intensely lamented son, but still. What a man Craig was! The man any man wanted to be. An accomplished boxer, wrestler, and swordsman; a war hero, muscled but modest; an invincible man. Yet his pectorals couldn't protect him. And if his couldn't, whose could?

"He loves the drama." Henry was harping on Theodore. "He adores being the center of attention."

"To the point of almost killing himself?"

"Especially then. For a grand exit. But he didn't, did he? A narcissist—that is what that sex-crazed doctor in Vienna would call our well-bred Mr. Roosevelt."

"Henry, I shall never take you seriously again."

"No need to, old boy. I take myself seriously enough for both of us." And at that, Henry squirmed—rather a rarity. A famed historian in his own right, he thought right well of himself. But didn't we all? (Most Washingtonians, you should remember, are self-selected.) But this time, apparently, his discomfort was not about pride. "There is something I need to show you," he said.

Henry bolted across Jackson Place and into Lafayette Park. This was the true center of the nation and more and more, therefore, of the civilized world. The iron fence was gone, a victim of democracy run amok—as Henry would rail—but the maples and elms were still in full leaf. Good ol' Andy Jackson faced us on his rearing horse—the "tippy-toe statue," as Tad Lincoln used to call it. How Henry hated looking from his bedroom window at his grandpappy's rival—twice—for the presidency! Along the east and west sides of the park, in the Federalist-style brick town houses, resided ghosts from the past—of Seward and Sumner, of Webster and Blaine, of Decatur and McClellan. On the third side, to the north, Henry and I had built our houses side by side. (I hesitate to call mine a mansion, but others do.) From my bedroom I could see across the park to the White House, to the second-story room where I had slept in Lincoln's day. Yet the park remained as tranquil as ever. The bowers of trees, the curves of gravel paths, the dawdling civil servants, the benches with courting couples—the place felt removed from the world yet surrounded by it, pressed in by it, like the eye of a hurricane. Beyond Lafayette Square, Henry liked to say, the country began.

I scrambled to keep up. It was rare that Henry outpaced me. I knew where he was going before he got there.

Marcus Alonzo Hanna was living there now, next to the ugly new opera house. The cream-colored brick house had a turret-shaped foyer and a second-floor balcony with a wrought iron railing. The senator from Ohio was the industrialist who had purchased the White House for William McKinley in 'ninety-six, and Roosevelt feared him as a rival for the Republican nomination in 'aught-four. But Hanna wasn't the lure—not for Henry. Of that I was certain. Henry was drawn by a ghost, although not a ghost from the past. Lizzie's ghost. A living ghost, as I understood all too well. Henry had loved her once; now it was my turn. But was it love or infatuation? I had spent far too much effort debating the subject and hating myself for it.

+══+

"Electric cars are the enemies of humanity," Henry Adams pronounced. "So sayeth the kaiser."

"Then it must be true," Clara said, pouring the tea. She knew how

to handle Henry—with gentle mockery. My wife's empathy was abso-
lute, so she was rarely if ever disappointed in Henry, or in anyone else,
including me. Her advantage was low expectations—the secret to hap-
piness in life. I admired that in her. Envied it, in fact. Tried to emulate
it and usually fell short. (But what else was new?) She had only the
highest expectations for herself.

"Did you hear about the electric streetcar that rammed the rear of a
train?" Henry said. "A couple of months ago—you were at the Fells."
That was our lake house in New Hampshire. "Happened in the city here,
on Four-and-a-half street southwest. Threw the trolley from its tracks
and tossed the passengers from their seats. Scared the poor devils half to
death. And just the other day, the frightened horse on Wisconsin avenue
that collided with one of those steam-spewing automobiles. Only by
some miracle was nobody—"

"We are living in an age of miracles," I pointed out, watching the
cream in my tea coalesce into the shape of Luzon.

"And those miracles will murder us all," Henry said. "I should prefer the twelfth century over the twentieth any day of the week. Less
brutal, for one thing. And grander in conception. The finest epoch in
Christian civilization, as the construction of Chartres and of Mont-
Saint-Michel will attest." Henry's forearm swept close to the teapot,
alluding (although never admitting) to his current opus. I happened to
know, by way of Lizzie, that he was just finishing the first draft. "And
compared to what, may I ask? The Kodak, naphtha lamps, rubber tires?"

"How about the dentistry?" Clara cooed.

We were taking tea, as we ordinarily did, in my library. I loved this
room, more than any I had ever called my own. It had plush chairs and
mahogany woodwork and Oriental rugs and a pair of stuffed white
cranes perched near the ceiling, above the carved settees. The fireplace was a yellow marble, the hearth a reddish rock. Books overflowing the shelves piled up on the floor. Clara (and Henry, of course)
thought the room overfurnished, but I found the clutter a comfort. It
swaddled me, and besides, I knew where everything was. I was sitting
in my maroon leather armchair.

"Did he have a family, John?" Clara said. She was still thinking about
Craig.

"He was to get married next month," I replied. "At the White House. To a lovely girl."

The conversation turned to the price of anthracite coal, quadrupled since the miners had walked out last spring, thence to the unending mess in the Philippines, before settling on an issue that mattered more: Should lilies rather than roses decorate the tables at our younger daughter's wedding? Alice was marrying a congressman's son (not exactly a recommendation) at month's end at the Fells. The nuptials promised to be less fancy—and less expensive—than Helen's were (to a Whitney!) last winter. Yet Del, our wise and smiling son, would be absent again.

Clara said, "What do you think, Uncle Henry?" That's what our children called our next-door neighbor and dearest friend.

"I think that Alice will look so beautiful," he replied, "that no one would notice, lily or rose."

Clara beamed. She, too, was beautiful—to me, at least. Her features were blunter than Venus de Milo's; her body, sturdier. The candor of her gaze told you she was nobody's fool. Yet kindness was written all over her face; her deep brown eyes gave root to laugh lines. The bloom in her cheeks made my knees weak. When Clara smiled, she lit up a room. I liked being in that room—loved it, really. Still do. That's what made whatever I was feeling for Lizzie that much worse.

Henry was holding forth on the autumnal troubles of daisies when a perfunctory knock brought James gliding in, a silver tray in his hand. The butler was a slight man with cappuccino-colored skin and a fringe of white hair. "Fer you, suh," he said.

The yellow envelope rested on a silver tray. Few people knew where to reach me in the late afternoon. I used the ivory-handled dagger, a gift from the Abyssinian emperor, to slit open the envelope with a savagery that surprised myself. From Cortelyou, was my guess.

Wrong.

"HAY," the telegram began. Cortelyou would have said "MR. SECRETARY"—or nothing, to save a few cents. "COLLISION NO ACCIDENT. COME HERE TO SAGAMORE HILL."

Cortelyou would have omitted "HERE."

Only one of my correspondents would be so peremptory.

"THEODORE."

I read the wire aloud. "First train in the morning," I announced.

Henry seemed shaken, uncharacteristically groping for words. "I told you," he declared. "*He* arranged it."

I described Henry's surmise to Clara.

"That is nonsense, Henry," she said, "and you know it."

"I know nothing of the sort," Henry replied, his stubbornness engaged. "Indeed, I know nothing about nothing. *That* is part of my charm."

"Yes, we all admire your ignorance, Henry," I said.

"More, my dear Mr. Adams?" said Clara, nodding at his half-empty porcelain teacup.

Henry shook his head. "I wouldn't make it home."

He was rising from the wing chair when another perfunctory knock produced the butler. "Pardon me, suh. Just came."

"More and more, James, the world is like that," I said, reaching for the dagger. "Any bets on who?"

"*Whom,*" Henry said.

"No, *who,*" I replied, a little too pleased with myself.

The telegram, from Oyster Bay, New York, consisted of a single word. "NOW."

The State, War, and Navy Building was experiencing its customary dearth of activity at five forty-five on a weekday afternoon. Alvey Adee, however, was at his rolltop desk—he was always at his desk. The top was crowded with medicine vials, ink bottles, and an orderly stack of paper two feet high. He was writing on a long pad in his meticulous hand—he regarded typewriters as the enemy of thought—while puffing on a corncob pipe. The tobacco smelled sweeter than his habitual blend.

"Adee!" I shouted.

No response.

The steel-nib pen was scratching, and I waited until it paused before stepping to his right ear and shouting again, "Adee, I need you!"

"My four favorite words." Adee looked up. His vast forehead and lush beard lent him a scholarly look, but the sky-blue eyes behind the pince-nez showed a sparkle inside. His face would come alive when-ever his attention turned to something that interested him, which was nearly everything. Born deaf, he had been mute as a boy, before gain-ing a modicum of hearing as a young man. I never figured out how much of that faculty he had, for he was skilled at using his deafness to ignore what he preferred not to hear, an advantage in negotiating with foreigners—and with Americans. I had known him since soon after the war (the real war, not the splendid little one against Spain), when he took my place as the secretary of legation in Madrid. Since the 'eighties, as the second assistant secretary of state, he had learned everything about everything and everyone. My indispensable aide.

"The maharajah has returned." Adee's speech was soft on consonants, elusive on *R*s, and nasal on vowels, as from a mouth stuffed with gauze. Most people had trouble understanding him, but I never did. His lack of embarrassment about his lack of hearing has always charmed me.

"And will be leaving right away," I said. "For Sagamore Hill. I've been . . . summoned." Adee's eyes widened, but he knew not to inquire. "So, what do we have on the boil?"

"The usual pleasantries," Adee said. He reported on the overnight wires from London, from Paris—and the one from Vienna. "Seems it wasn't the Austrian prince of Braganza who was arrested in London without all of his clothes, allegedly in the company of other men, but rather the emperor's heir apparent himself, the Archduke Franz Ferdi-nand."

I couldn't resist a giggle. "Well, live and let live," I said.

As Adee described the kaiser's latest complaint about Venezuela as a deadbeat on German loans, Margaret Hanna slipped into the room and stood behind him. She was a big-boned woman in her early thir-ties—my guess—with mannish features and dark French braids that reached the small of her back. She was Adee's able assistant and, while Spencer Eddy was away, mine as well. She was unrelated to the odious senator, although most people assumed otherwise, which I found an-noying. No sign Adee did. Or Margaret.

"And here she is," Adee announced—"our Miss Riflery of 1902. The Labor Day tourney, she was the victor. At one hundred yards." Margaret blushed. "And speaking of Venezuela, I would like to extend

her correspondence duties to include Central and South America—
the entire hemisphere. If that suits you. She has really been doing it
already."

"Of course," I said.

"And allow *me* to reply to the kaiser's note wishing the president a
full and speedy recovery. Every word of it a lie."

"The task has found its master," I said. "But on this, let him be a liar.
We have our hands full with him as it is. Anything in the Philippines?"

"Nothing for us. Let the fat man handle it." Taft, the governor-
general of the distant islands, had mostly but not entirely quelled the
insurrection by Filipinos who had been foolish enough to believe that
America's conquest of imperial Spain would bring them independence.
Little had they counted on the newest world power's feeling so full of
itself. (I mean us.)

"And the Roumanian Jews?" I reminded him.

"I'll have a draft on your desk by the time you return, Hay. And
when, if I may ask, might that be?"

I shrugged. The answer was not up to me.

+=━━=+

The Pennsylvania Railroad Station always gives me the willies, especially
at night. Not because of anything physical. The building itself, the
square brick tower and the crenellated facade, had a startling elegance.
Its location was beyond compare, at the corner of Sixth and B streets
northwest, amid the trees and winding carriageways of the National
Mall. The problem for me was its history. The bronze star in particular. It decorated the floor in the ladies' waiting room on the exact spot
where President Garfield had collapsed after an office-seeker of shaky
sanity shot him in the back. (I had interviewed Guiteau once myself.
He was as nutty as a pecan pie.) I had stood by Garfield's bier. By Lincoln's and McKinley's, too. I wondered if the common denominator
was *me*.

The high-ceilinged station was dimly lit. My footsteps echoed. A few
passengers sat, mostly by themselves, in the waiting room pews. I gave
the bronze star a wide berth as I rushed through to the platform and
onto the train.

My compartment was in the third car, and I left my valise (I took a perverse pride in not needing a porter) and went in search of the club car. It was unoccupied save for two elderly men with high collars and pinched cheeks—bankers, was my guess—and a dapper young chap with a distracted, melancholic air. I chose a high-backed upholstered chair in the far corner and gazed at the arched ceiling with light fixtures shaped like hard-nippled breasts. I ordered a Dewar & Sons whisky, a double.

An *Evening Star* was splayed across the low marble table. I tidied up the pages and glanced across the front. A prediction by Pennsylvania's vile senators that the anthracite coal strike would be settled within a week—how quickly they would be proved wrong. The missing troop ship from Manila had arrived in San Francisco—Adee had told me that. An unfunny cartoon about the war games off the New England coast. The new limit on automobiles' speed through Rock Creek Park, of twelve miles per hour—so as not to scare the deer, I supposed. (The limit in Baltimore was half that.) I feared that these clattering, smoky machines were here to stay—the gasoline-powered ones, I mean. Or who knows? Maybe the quieter, electrical ones would win the day.

I read that last item twice, scanning for a reason to hope, and only then turned to the leftmost column on the page.

PRESIDENT INJURED
Narrowly Escaped Death in Collision.
CAR STRUCK HIS COACH
One of His Companions Killed
DRIVER WILL RECOVER
MR. ROOSEVELT ONLY
SLIGHTLY HURT.
Others of the Party Severely Shaken Up and Bruised—
Wild Rumors Started.

Wild rumors! That was my bailiwick. Or the president's.

". . . when near the Country Club"—a most avid reader was I—"an electric trolley on the Pittsfield and Lenox street railway was noticed coming at a terrific rate of speed. Mr. Craig signaled for the motorman to stop, but he apparently paid no attention to the warning and the car came plunging on. The President's carriage was literally smashed to pieces. A witness of the accident stated that the motorman was speeding his car in order to reach the club . . ."

I fished Theodore's telegrams from my pocket: "COLLISION NO ACCIDENT."

The whisky arrived just in time.

CHAPTER TWO

Even past midnight, the terminal in Jersey City was noisy. Yawning passengers jostled past me, straggling the hundred yards from the railroad depot to the ferry, jabbering in a dozen tongues, wearing every conceivable garment—yarmulkes and caftans, silk hats and velvet-lapelled overcoats. Too many whiskies, not a wink of sleep, whiffs of the Orient and the Bronx—I could be forgiven a passing acquaintance with nausea. I took a spot in the ferry's prow, where the cold, sharp wind cleared me like penance. I stood by the railing beneath a sliver of a moon and watched the Hudson River and its whitecaps.

What I saw beyond the whitecaps astonished me. Lights. Above the ground. From the skyscrapers—what a poetic word! Not sky*piercers* or sky*punchers*, but sky*scrapers*. I envied the man who coined it. Eight stories, twelve stories, eighteen stories, even thirty stories high. Their lights floated like low-hanging stars, just shy of the clouds, arrayed along Manhattan's—another delightful new word—skyline.

A line of poetry came to me.

A tinkle of bells in the light,

Not bad.

A call to the wild in the night . . .

Not *wild*. This was civilization, or what passed for it. *Tame?* No.

A crashing of bells in the light.
A clashing of minds in the night.

Hmm, maybe. It came perilously close to meaning something. I was extracting my calfskin notepad from the inside pocket of my frock coat when cold water sprayed over the side, splashing my overcoat and drenching my valise. My three changes of clothes were no longer dry. Nor was I.

Hearing metal screech against metal was a relief; we had arrived at the Twenty-third street pier.

Climbing back onto land improved my spirits, not nearly as much as seeing at the end of the pier a strapping man with a square face and a drooping mustache. Theodore!

"Mr. Hay," the man called as I drew near. It wasn't Theodore. His voice was huskier. "The colonel sent me," he said, reaching for my valise. He introduced himself as the coachman. "Franklyn, with a *Y*. Franklyn Hall."

"Hello, Franklyn with a *Y*," I said. "Mr. Hall, the pleasure is most definitely mine."

＋≻═≺＋

The surrey jolted along the country roads and kept me awake. I wrapped myself in carriage blankets and stayed warm enough to think. And so I thought. About Theodore, mainly, with varying degrees of lucidity.

Among my foggier notions was the fear that he had summoned me to Long Island in order to fire me. Maybe almost dying had persuaded him that somebody else should stand next in line to the presidency. I couldn't blame him. He and I got along just fine. Not that we were bosom buddies; Theodore didn't really have any, other than that prig Henry Cabot Lodge. But I had known him well for at least a dozen years now and considered him a friend. I had made acquaintance with his daddy many years before that. Hadn't Theodore Sr. attended the Lincolns' ball the night in 'sixty-two that young Willie took ill? Later he introduced me to his older boy during a Hudson Valley rainstorm. Not that our personal history would matter much, if the younger Theodore was intent on letting me go. Still, I doubted that he was. For all of his flaws, he was neither coy nor cagey nor in any way a namby-pamby. If he wanted me gone, he would say so.

Then, let us assume (*never assume*, my old friend Nicolay used to say) that Theodore had summoned me for the reason he gave. The collision was no accident. The president believed it. Why did he believe it? I expected an earful on that. Did he have evidence beyond his pique? The man was operating on emotion—that seemed pretty clear, and understandable. And not to be pooh-poohed. Emotion, combined with discipline, had gotten Theodore far in life—and quickly. At the age of—what?—forty-three he had already accomplished more than any three men might in a lifetime. Merely thinking about it tuckered me out. Charging up San Juan Hill in his Brooks Brothers uniform put to shame anything I've ever done. (I spent *my* war shuffling papers for Lincoln and wooing Kate Chase.) Into one daunting job after another—as New York's police commissioner, as governor, now as the leader of a turbulent land—Theodore felt deeply about things and, unembarrassed and unrestrained, acted. He worked on instinct; he was rarely in doubt. Lord knows, his judgment was not always right. But more often than not—even Henry would concede the point—it was. In less than a year, Theodore had proved to be a damn good president—bold, unafraid—even in the absence of an economic panic or a war.

I reached into my pocket and fingered his telegrams. I couldn't read them in the dark, but I knew what they said.

COLLISION NO ACCIDENT. COME HERE TO SAGAMORE HILL.

NOW.

"Franklyn," I said. We shared the surrey's soft front seat. "How did you know when I was coming?" I had never specified a time, figuring to hire a hack.

"Been waiting awhile, sir."

"How long?"

"Before sundown, sir. As soon as the colonel told me, I left."

The carriage curved past a thin woodland. The darkness beyond the trees must be Long Island Sound.

Another question kept recurring: Why was he summoning *me*?

About that, I had a sneaking suspicion: Willie Lincoln. Somehow, Roosevelt had learned of my experiences in solving the unlikeliest of murders. Lincoln's eleven-year-old son was only the first. I never spoke to anyone about my occasional forays as a detective (better, I must say, than my record in the ring), but Theodore had his own means of learning what he needed to know.

The surrey took a fork to the right off Cove Neck road. We passed the tennis court in the hollow and ascended the steep, sweeping lane to Sagamore Hill. Even in the scant moonlight, the three-story house loomed high on the hill. It was a grandmotherly sort of house, of a leisurely design, with a wraparound porch and more gables than Hawthorne could count. Lights flickered in the windows.

The carriage drifted to a halt beneath the porte cochere. On the porch, a ghost shimmered in the gaslight. Teeth flashed; a white shirtfront glistened. I climbed down from the surrey and saw the president, still dressed for dinner in a black cutaway, a pearl-gray tie, and a white waistcoat that strained at the buttons. His face was calm, resolute— serene. It was a young face of a young man who took himself seriously, indeed, as I hope any president would. He had a bull neck, a square chin, a muscleman's shoulders, and nary a line in his brow. His girth had grown on the job; he reminded me of a walrus in formal wear. A silk ribbon dangled from his pince-nez. His mustache was assertive but trimmed and under control. The slight smile on his lips suggested he was gazing into a future that nobody else could see.

He leaned down as I mounted the four steps to the porch. His handshake was as strong and enveloping as ever, as if to say, *Nothing is wrong with me.* I noticed his right eye had swollen shut and his cheek was the size of a late summer peach.

"*Dee*-lighted to see you," he said. "Just the very man I wanted to see."

"You look terrible, Theodore," I exclaimed. Only people who didn't know him called him Teddy (he had disliked the nickname since his first wife died, for she had called him that), and I hadn't earned the privilege of addressing him as Roosevelt.

"Don't I look as if I have the mumps?" He snapped his teeth as he spoke, and clamped his jaw. His vitality bowled me over, given his injuries and his usual four or five hours of sleep. "Come in, come in."

The front hall was an altar to the outdoors, paneled in oak and ornamented with the heads of animals unlucky enough to have crossed Theodore's path. The fireplace was ablaze. Theodore led me into the library, on the right. He limped.

The room was dignified yet warm, with its bear rugs and a paneled wall of paintings of the men he admired—Lincoln, of course, and Grant, and at the center, his truest hero, the man whose name he carried. (When his adored father died, he dropped the Junior and insisted that his family call him Theodore instead of Teedie.) Now he was the nation's twenty-sixth president, its youngest ever, rocking at his desk. The gaslight showed the cuts on his chin and the coal-black bruises across the upper right side of his face.

He was oblivious to my stare. "Thank you . . . for coming . . . at this . . . hour." His teeth clacked, every syllable distinct. He pulled the bell cord and offered nourishment, alcoholic if I wished. I knew better than to ask if he would join me. I requested coffee, both for survival and to curry his favor, in case I was too optimistic about his intentions. "And what did you think of my New England tour?"

"A triumph, by all accounts," I replied. The flattery was harmless enough and, by Washington standards, truthful.

He grinned, revealing acres of enamel. "It was, wasn't it?"

"Especially the last day." I nodded at his leg. "Staring death in the face."

"Facedown, I would say," Theodore cackled. "Really, I am not at all badly hurt. In my salad days, I suffered worse injuries at football and polo. I would have been ashamed then to acknowledge that I felt hurt. I wouldn't care a snap of my fingers for what happened, if not for the death of poor Craig."

"How about your boys?" I knew that the two youngest, Archie and Quentin, worshiped the glorious Craig. "Have you told them?"

A portly woman with thin silvery hair entered with a tray of coffee and crumpets. I was sorry to have disturbed the servants from their sleep, but I consoled myself: this was not my doing.

Once the servant withdrew, Theodore went on, "Not yet. Haven't the heart." I noticed a dampness on the president's cheeks. "I hated having a man around me all the time, but after Buffalo it seemed I had no choice." Two days short of a year earlier, an anarchist had entered the Temple of Music at the Pan-American Exposition, draping a handkerchief over his gun. President McKinley took eight days to die. "Rarely have I known anyone like Big Bill Craig. Nothing weak about him. The most faithful man I ever knew. A Scotsman, in the Queen's Grenadiers. Volunteered for the Sudanese war and saved a comrade— wouldn't talk about it. He marched six hundred miles across the desert from Alexandria to Khartoum, in relief of the mahdi's siege, and arrived to find Gordon *murdered*." Theodore's fist shook, as if he were there. "An expert horseman he is—*was* . . ." It tore from his throat. "And a boxer besides. And with a sword! Put an apple between your chin and your throat—not mine, mind you—he would split it in half. He would slice right through a sheep with a single stroke, or so I've heard—and not from him. He has been teaching me the broadsword."

I was aware of the president's penchant for boxing, wrestling, and jujitsu, but his swordsmanship was a new one on me. A hard shake of the head restored a glitter to Theodore's blue-gray eyes. He slurped coffee from a mug. He said, "And I will tell you just how bully I feel. To-morrow, you and I shall spar. To-day, I mean."

"In your condition? I couldn't."

"Of course you could. And you shall."

"You serious? You do have a few inches on me, I must say, and . . . a . . . uh, a few pounds." More than a few. "Not to mention twenty years."

"Sounds like a fair fight to me," Theodore said.

+⊨—⊨+

The roller-skating in the hallway woke me before dawn. Each boyish shriek brought a louder response. Amid flurries of footsteps, a ball bounced, bounced, bounced off a wall. My wall.

I vaulted from my bed into the hallway. The littlest miscreant, the towheaded Quentin, gave me a frank look of disgust—*me*, the wrecker of his game, whatever his game happened to be at the moment. I resisted the urge to apologize, until I succumbed, and the four-year-old accepted with graciousness. I returned to bed and surprised myself when I burst into tears. I hadn't done that in a while.

It was about Del, of course, our older son. Fifteen months had passed—it seemed like fifteen years—since he died. Every word of praise for our dead boy made the grief worse. Twenty-four years old, a tragic death, an accident, everyone said, and I believed it. I had no reason not to. Other than how I had treated him. That wouldn't have explained anything, even if there were something to explain, which there wasn't. That long-ago Sunday in my library, the afternoon sunlight slanting in, after I read his schoolboy essay on the Roman Forum (he asked me to!) and I told him it was sluggish and heavy. *Like you*, I had blurted. Which he was. And wasn't it my fatherly privilege, if not my duty, to say so? You can't fix something if you don't know it's broken.

He was fourteen or fifteen at the time, and of course he took offense, and things were never quite the same between us. But I do have to say that it worked. He had shined at Yale, and President McKinley had just appointed him as his assistant private secretary, the same job I had held for Lincoln—and on Del's own merits, not on mine. Del was six-foot-two, ridiculously taller than I am, able to hold his own in a fight or a council. He was the sort of good-natured fellow that everyone liked on sight. All of that promise, now dust and ashes. I was still learning how much grief a man could endure.

I tried to make my mind go blank, and I must have succeeded, at least this once, for when I opened my eyes again the sunlight was streaming in and the noise—was I imagining it?—seemed farther away. It was a comforting room, despite the narrow bed scraggly with straw. The dark wood of the hearth and furnishings felt sturdy, and the wallpaper had enough pastels to quell a lunatic. My grandfather's pocket watch, on the side table, showed ten minutes to eight. Tardy for country life, but not for Sagamore Hill. Breakfast in the dining room, I understood, was not served until half past eight.

I was relieved to see the bathroom free of children. (The two older boys must be back at Groton.) I did what I needed to do, which took me a little longer than it used to, and put on a frock coat—mostly dry by now—and a baby blue cravat.

When I got to the dining room, I saw my mistake: Theodore was wearing a flannel shirt and knickers, as if dressed for a hunt.

"Morning, Hay," he said. "I trust you slept well."

I lied, then added, "And you?"

"Always," he said. The high pitch of his quavering voice never failed to surprise, coming from the body of a bear. "The harder my day, the better I sleep."

I marveled at a man without guilt or apparent self-doubt. Or maybe he was merely oblivious. Or young—he was bursting with the impetuosity of youth. (The answer was always: all of the above.)

The dining room at Sagamore Hill was a cozy place, with rose-colored wallpaper above the dark paneling, swirling with the aromas of coffee and bacon. The buffet was heaped with beefsteak, waffles, potatoes, blueberries, soft-boiled eggs. Theodore piled his plate high and seated himself at the head of the small oval table, waiting to eat as patiently as a dog would, funneling foodstuffs into his mouth

A whoop brought a barefoot boy bursting past me and into the dining room like an Apache into battle. His impish face was streaked with black—coal dust, could it be?

"Quenty-quee," Theodore called. Quentin was the child who was most like the father, the daredevil nonchalant. I looked across at the president's contorted face.

Archie flew by in full pursuit, his countenance serious below his low blond bangs. The seven-year-old clutched a bow and a real arrow, with a sharp stone point. He was wedging the arrow into the bowstring when he tripped on the wrinkled rug. The arrow went flying past my shoulder and into the eggs. Archie's eyes, searching mine, grew as wide as silver dollars. No reason not to laugh—it *was* funny—and when I did, Archie joined in, less in mirth than in relief.

Quentin whooped again and thrust his hand into the blueberries, glancing sideways to see if his father was watching, which he was. The boy's eyes never left his father's as he popped a fistful of blueberries into his mouth. Theodore roared with laughter. No wonder Quentin was an undisciplined brat; he reminded me of Tad Lincoln minus the lisp.

From the doorway came a trill that might have unnerved a coyote. "And are we having a good time yet?" I recognized the lilt before I looked to the doorway and saw Princess Alice. The president's eldest stood haughtily, as was her custom, neck stretched, chin raised, eyes piercing to the point of menace, all beneath a wasp's nest of hair. In self-possession, Alice Roosevelt was eighteen going on forty. Her face had a marble beauty, feature by feature, albeit crammed together and (for my taste) a little too sharp. "You haven't told them yet, have you, Father?" she said.

"Sister!" Theodore shouted.

"Told me what?" Quentin and Archie said in unison.

"Nothing!" the president said. "Eat your breakfast. You, too, Sister."

"Oh, but I'm not hungry," Alice said. "I merely wished to shake hands with our distinguished guest here. And not with you, Q."

Quentin was licking clean his blue-stained hand.

I knocked heads in pleasant reverie, but instead I bowed and kissed the back of her hand and said, "The pleasure is mine." She laughed, an airy sound. I felt lucky she didn't have a snake around her neck or a revolver in her pocket (though I was assuming the latter).

The boys had filled their plates, and the president ordered Alice to take a seat—to my surprise, she obeyed—so he could recount the travails of their oldest brother. "They sicced the dogs on him," Theodore said. "That's what they did, out in Dakota. For shooting prairie chickens."

Quentin perked up. "Are they like real chickens?" he said.

"Teddy *is* a prairie chicken," Alice said. She and Teddy Jr., who was about to turn fifteen, were close.

"Listen . . . to . . . this," their father said. "'Set . . . Dogs . . . on . . . President's . . . Son'—that's the headline." He spoke in staccato. "And below that, 'South Dakota Populists Treated the Youth Boorishly.'" He was reading from the *Evening Star* I had left with him the night before. "'Because he is President Roosevelt's son, a large number of populist farmers in the vicinity of Arlington, South Dakota, combined to prevent Theodore Roosevelt, Junior, from shooting prairie chickens in their stubblefields.'"

"What's a prairie chicken?" Quentin said.

"The article goes on," Theodore said. "'Scarcely had the party arrived when the farmers' telephone was brought into service, and the news was spread, and the entire prairie was alive with farmers patrolling the fields and posting notices forbidding trespass.'" Alice shrieked with laughter. "Listen to *this*!" the aggrieved father went on. "'Because he was the son of the president'—now this quotes a railroad's vice president in Teddy's hunting party—'these populists, who . . . might . . . well . . . be . . . classed . . . as . . . *anarchists* . . .' In the Dakotas; my beloved Dakotas!"

Theodore's two years as a rancher in North Dakota had shaped his sense of himself—and Americans' sense of *him*.

"Anarchists! Do you hear that? What the devil are they . . . ?"

Quentin said, "What are prairie chickens?"

Theodore thumped his fist on the table, and the breakfast plates jumped.

"Are they like real chickens?" Quentin said.

Archie said, "Told me what?"

+≡+

Everyone else had left the dining room when Roosevelt refilled his canyon-size coffee mug, stirred in seven lumps of sugar, and said, "It was no accident."

"How do you know?"

"I know."

"Do you have evidence?" I was enough of a lawyer to care, and maybe even enough of a detective.

"I don't need evidence. I *know*." He smacked his right fist into his left palm.

"But Theodore . . ." How do you argue with someone so sure of himself? Maybe I wasn't being fair—how he loved to say *On the other hand*. The man knew what he didn't know. Usually. "I would think that anyone investigating this . . ." I looked for a response and got none. "Would need evidence."

"I know who was behind this."

"Who, then?"

"The motorman."

"Of the trolley?"

"Yes, who else?"

"How do you know this?"

"I saw his face. That's all the evidence I need." Theodore turned in my direction but looked through me.

"And what exactly did you see?"

"I saw a man intent."

I waited, then said, "Intent on what?"

"Intent on whatever he was doing, which was ramming into my carriage, broadside. He was standing at the wheel, at the front of the trolley, looking directly at me. I *saw* him. And when I confronted him after the crash, he had the gall, the *gall*"—in full falsetto—"to tell me that *he* had the right-of-way. A damn outrage!"

I don't remember ever hearing Theodore curse before. Was he mad at the collision or at the motorman's defiance? Probably at both. "Why on earth would he want to do that?" I said.

"How should I know? That's your job."

"My job?"

Roosevelt's eyebrows lifted.

I swore to myself. (I did not share Theodore's compunction.) "I'll try," I said, despairingly enough that he might notice. He didn't.

"Actually, I *do* know," he said. "Or *suspect*, as you might prefer, given your ladylike sensibilities."

I laughed. The man was so *obvious*. "By all means, please tell me your . . . suspicions."

"The anarchists, of course. They assassinated McKinley. Why not me?"

I sighed, but he did have a point. "You're saying the motorman is an anarchist?"

"Not saying anything. That's for you to find out. I do know that Emma Goldman was arrested in Omaha not ten days ago for hatching a plot to murder *me*. She was also arrested, you will recall, after Buffalo. That soft-headed Leon Czolgosz listened to one of her lectures."

"And she was released for lack of evidence."

"Which doesn't mean she was innocent," Theodore said.

"Or guilty."

"Only because the evidence was never found, perhaps. Assassinating leaders is what anarchists *do*, my dear John. Finding the evidence is your job."

My stomach tightened. "Starting where, do you suppose?"

"At the top, of course."

"The anarchists don't have a top," I said. "That's why they're anarchists. This isn't the papists, with a hierarchy."

"Nonsense. Every human organization has a hierarchy. Every animal kingdom has a top and a bottom—every phylum, every species, every family of wolves in a den." Theodore was a verifiable expert in nature as well as in naval history, American history, the American West and wilderness, and animal skulls of too many descriptions. "Even anarchists have leaders. You know this, Hay. You just don't want to admit it. Too rough for you."

He was goading me, I knew that, to leave me no choice but to pursue his damn investigation and, not incidentally, to meet him in the ring. Amusement glinted in Theodore's eyes. "Our Red Emma is back in New York, I understand," he said. I was curious how he knew. "You should go see her. If an anarchist was involved, she will know."

"And she will be only too pleased to spill everything to someone she's never met."

"You are a charming man, my dear John. You can open the door to China. You will get me my canal. You can talk a porcupine out of its quills. Surely you can persuade a woman to do what you ask."

I laughed in spite of myself. "That is one thing I have never learned to do," I said. "She is listed in the city directory, I imagine? Under Goldman comma Emma?"

"I couldn't say. No need to. Cortelyou has made the arrangements. You will meet with her to-morrow morning, at eleven."

⊬⊨⊨⊣

"Father, must we entertain that old fart?" Alice said. Her eyelashes quivered—with mischief, I supposed—and her ivory skin looked translucent, surely cool to the touch.

"'Young fart,' if you please," a Russian-inflected baritone boomed from the dining room doorway. Grand Duke Boris, a cousin of the tsar, was coming for lunch.

"Please forgive my daughter, Your Excellency," the president said, standing by the sideboard, examining the borscht. "And may I welcome you, in our rather informal fashion, to my home at Sagamore Hill."

Alice tilted her head and said, "Perhaps Mother will be along."

"Sister!" the president snapped. "Not another word."

I was well aware that Edith was off visiting Theodore's aunt, to avoid meeting the tsar's cousin, who had sipped champagne from a lady's—well, a woman's—slipper while in Chicago. Adee had wired me: "GRAND DUKE BORE-US NOT THE RECEPTACLE FOR CONFIDENCES."

"Meow, meow," Alice said, obeying the letter of her father's dictum.

"You may leave now," her father said, and with a tilt of her head and a switch of her tail, she complied.

The Russian guffawed. "The high spirits of youth," he said. Grand Duke Boris had an unlined, rouged face and a pompadour; his scarlet tunic was covered in medals and featured gold epaulets that would have sunk a shark. He was shorter than I, and when he reached up to tap my shoulder, I imagined a crocodile's chomp. Theodore recoiled.

"It is a pleasure, I must say," Grand Duke Boris said, "to meet both of you gentlemen at once. The two grandest men in your government. An honor for myself, for Tsar Nicholas, and for my country." His gaudy smile left cracks in his rouge. "But let me say, it is rare for the crown prince to be older than the monarch."

Rather gauche, I thought, in referring to our statutory line of succession. In the absence of a sitting vice president, rights to the throne coursed immediately through the cabinet, starting with the oldest department first. Mine. This was not news to me, I assure you. It was a fact of my life, to which I had grown inured, and which affected my life not at all. That must sound silly to anyone's ear, but it was true. For the most part, anyway.

"Ours is a young and vigorous nation, Your Excellency," I replied. "It is right and proper for its ruler to be young and vigorous." A perfect diplomatic response, I must say: sounds profound, says nothing, means less. "I should mention, sir, that my favorite color is gray. Matching my whiskers."

⊹┝═━═┥⊹

The gun room, on the top floor, was clearly Theodore's sanctum. Shotguns were propped up in the corners; books lined the shelves. The ceiling

slanted in eaves, making a cave out of the dark decor. Archie was helping his father push the desk to the wall. I rushed over and kept the
Tiffany lamp from toppling off. The Kodiak bear rug had been shoved
aside. The woven rectangular rug remained. That, plus an oblong of
floor, would serve as the ring.

No good could come of this. I felt certain.

I hadn't sparred in a couple of years. Because of the demands of the
job, trying to keep a disorderly world in line—so I told myself. But
the truth was a lack of desire. Not none, to be precise. I had never
known anything quite as vivid—indeed, life-affirming—as climbing
into a ring and whaling away at someone who was whaling away at me.
Even saving China from Europe's depredations was like a lager next to
a whisky. I loved having sparred, mixing it up with a bloke, making
ourselves vulnerable to each other, proving . . . what? Something fun-
damental. I had done it more times than I cared to count. I had never
been knocked down; I had always stood my ground. Yet there was no
ignoring the fact that climbing into the ring (or, here, stepping onto the
rug) still scared the bejesus out of me. Can't say why, exactly. Getting
hit, even in the face, rarely hurts for long. But scare me it does, and less
and less do I see the point in bashing somebody else's head and having
mine bashed in return. I had proved whatever I needed to prove—
courage, I suppose. Besides, the prospect of sparring with my boss—in
front of his children, no less—eased none of the apprehension.

I wore a pair of Theodore's old boxing trunks, requiring a rope as
a belt to keep myself decent. Theodore had stripped to black trunks
and a sleeveless, lemon-yellow shirt that showed a baboon's shoulders and a buffalo's belly. His right cheek was purple. His jowls were
heavier and his face was lined more deeply than I had noticed before.
His blue-gray eyes, naked without the pince-nez, looked clouded
over.

"You ready?" he said. He seemed nervous, too.

"Always," I replied.

Alice pulled the laces tight on her father's brushed-leather gloves, and
then on mine. She gazed past my right clavicle, never meeting my eyes.
When she stayed on the red and gray patterned rug, I realized with a
thud: she was the referee. Princess Alice probably thrived on watching

people get hurt, possibly including her father. Certainly no exception made for me.

Theodore and I touched gloves and glared at each other in the customary way. For the moment, at least, I meant it. We stepped back into our corners. Alice's forearm fell like a scythe. "Fight!" she declared.

Theodore came straight at me, unleashing two, three, four jabs. I realized that the glazed look in his eyes was near-blindness. (A couple of years later, a young artillery captain mauled blood vessels in the president's left eye.) The man was charging like a rhinoceros, and the best defense was to step out of his way. Theodore rushed past me, stopping just short of the rope on the floor. He swiveled with an agility that belied his bulk and came straight at me again. No angles, no shrewdness, no strategy. Hadn't the man learned anything about boxing as chess, as art? I stepped aside again. The next time he barreled through, I held my ground and socked him in the jaw. He looked surprised—and newly attentive.

He circled around me, his gloves low, almost tauntingly, staring hard at me, as if trying to peer into my soul. That was how I took it, anyway. I figured that my soul (such as it was) was my business, nobody else's, not even his. Now the fight would begin.

I kept my gloves by my temples and, when he circled in front of a corner, I closed in, to annul his advantage in height. I delivered a jab, then a right cross, followed by an uppercut that caught him unawares. His head snapped back.

That enraged him, and he came at me more nimbly than I expected. I was too old, too slow, to move aside. He landed a hard right on my kisser; my upper lip scraped my teeth. I tasted blood.

Now I became enraged. Letting myself be humiliated would only diminish his respect for me, not to mention my own. I stayed away from his injured right side but advanced toward him with a jab and sent a hard right cross to his other cheek, followed by a thump to his jaw. He stumbled back.

I landed another jab and readied an uppercut, when I noticed something at the edge of my sight. A rumpled pile of clothes. At first I didn't know what it was. Then I realized *who* it was: Quentin, doubled over.

Theodore had told him about Big Bill Craig.

My fist halted on its way to his father's chin. I could not hurt another boy like I had hurt Del.

The president showed no such restraint. Spittle flew in my face as he pummeled me with a flurry of fists. My head was knocked back three or four times, and at last I pivoted and watched my opponent dance past. I considered punching him in the temple but held back. It was all I could do not to cry.

❡

The breeze was blowing in from Long Island Sound. I could not see down to the water under the paltry moon, but I smelled the salt and heard the waves whipping up. Or was it the rhythmic drone from Cortelyou's rocking chair, out here on the wraparound porch? The man never sat still, and his pattern never lost its cadence.

The president stood at the far edge of the porch, facing the sound. He had shed his coat and wore his white shirt from dinner. An assassin's target, a shot through the heart. Which would make me . . . hmm, a suspect! Though only if he were shot in the back. And then which of us would be deemed likelier—Cortelyou or me?

Me. I had more to gain.

So everyone said, but I swore it wasn't true. For one thing, I didn't want to be president. Unlike my friend Henry, I never have. I've seen too much of it close up. Batting away complainants and sycophants all day long, dealing with the dolts on Capitol Hill—what I did for Lincoln would last a lifetime. I could never keep on a false smile hour after hour, and I pitied (and distrusted) anyone who could. For me, a fever unfelt, a fetish undesired.

And for another thing, consider Bruce Cortelyou, in the neighboring rocking chair, a man of vast ambition. Frighteningly efficient, brilliant as a bureaucrat, and (best I could tell) deceptive to his core. A chameleon, for certain. Indeed, he *looked* like Theodore—the bristly black hair, the pince-nez, the push broom mustache, the stolid face, the broad shoulders, the deep chest. I thought of him as the Prussian, although he was Dutch. He also looked a little like McKinley, his previous master; I swear I saw a resemblance around the cheekbones. Had he been obese while in Grover Cleveland's employ?

"Justus Schwab's saloon," Cortelyou was saying. "Do you know where that is?"

"Should I?"

"I should hope not. It is an anarchists' redoubt." I had never heard anyone use *redoubt* in a sentence. "On East First street, number fifty, between First and Second avenues, just north of Houston."

"I know New York a little, if anyone can," I said. I had spent nearly five happy years toiling a mile and a half away, writing editorials at the *New York Tribune*. "Who is this Schwab?"

"Was." Cortelyou rocked faster. "Tuberculosis, two years ago. His son runs it now. Rather a lowbrow place, and still a mecca for anarchists and nihilists and socialists and their ilk. Unkempt communists, too, you know the type." I wondered where the kempt communists drank. "Our Miss Goldman was his closest . . . friend." He held the word at a distance, like a wriggling eel. "Or so I understand."

"Closest in what way—or ways?"

Cortelyou trained his gaze on an unseen point past the hollow. "With these people, who can tell?" he said. I noticed the jagged cut along his nose, but Cortelyou always sounded like he was catching a cold. "She received her mail there. And she still—what is the word?—*frequents* the place. I cannot say how often, but often. She will be expecting you to-morrow morning at eleven o'clock sharp."

"I would have guessed that anarchists aren't usually punctual."

"I don't regard this as a matter of amusement, Mr. Secretary."

"When you survive to my stage of life, Mr. Cortelyou, everything is."

CHAPTER THREE

I sat next to the coachman in the express wagon, as Theodore's children called the two-seat, yellow-wheeled surrey. I raised the blanket from my lap to my shoulders and peered to the right. Between the tangle of trees, the sound looked indistinguishable from the sky. Gray against gray. It was that kind of day, chilly and aloof.

Franklyn Hall sat ramrod straight. "We'll get there soon enough, Mr. Hay," he said. "People will be rushing every which way. But ain't it pretty in the meantime?"

"Indeed it is, Frank. I'm enjoying the quiet. I don't get enough of it anymore."

"Oh, this modern world of ours. Always the noise."

"And the hurry."

"Oh my, yes. Used to be, the whole world ran at a horse's pace, no faster than that. That's all a-dyin', sir. Everythin', it's speedin' up."

The village of Oyster Bay still had its leisurely summertime pace. But the pastels of the shop fronts looked somber. Pedestrians sauntered across the street and scattered at an automobile's honking. A horse reared.

The railroad station was a gabled shelter by the tracks. Men crowded on the platform, most of them wearing derby hats or unfashionably late-in-the-season straw boaters. Mine was the only high silk hat.

"This way, sir," Franklyn Hall said, carrying my valise to the end of the platform. He boarded the car and lent me a hand in mounting the stairs. I didn't need the help, but he wanted to give it. When I thanked him for the ride, he said, "I'm comin' with you."

"All the way?"

"To Long Island City, sir."

I was being told, not asked. "No," I said.

"I am under orders."

"Which I am countermanding. I am perfectly capable of doing this on my own. You tell the president I insisted."

Franklyn Hall stood like a donkey caught between two piles of hay.

"Thank you," I said, and nudged him down onto the platform.

In the club car, I sank into the plushest chair, the one with crimson cushions and a latticed back. I was delighted to see that it both swiveled and rocked. A waiter brought me a corn muffin and a violet-and-white fluted cup with steaming coffee. On a side table I found a copy of yesterday's *Tribune*. I unfolded it—I still loved the smell of paper and ink—and scanned the front page. A volcano had erupted in the Caribbean, killing two thousand people, a tragedy without meaning unless a victim was real. The president had agreed to review the Grand Army of the Republic parade, of Civil War veterans, in Washington next month. J. P. Morgan and the Pennsylvania Railroad were gobbling up another line—this time, the Reading. The strong preyed on the weak. The way of the world. Newsworthy, to be sure, but nothing new.

I stared over the top of the newspaper at the woodlands rushing by. The anarchists had a point; I would concede that. An individual counted for nothing anymore. The forces in ascendance—in control—were beyond the scope of any one man. Blame the capitalists, if you like, for spitting on labor, and blame labor for spitting back. The industrial trusts were cornering the economy, but at least Theodore was trying to stand in the way. Not to break them up but to civilize them a little. The anarchists should at least concede *that*.

Yet the president's animus toward anarchists, his obsession with them, evidently his *fear* of them, was something that flummoxed me. An anarchist, for God's sake, had put him in the White House. Maybe Theodore had some deep, dark reason to—

No, no, no. Leave that to the quack in Vienna. Let me think about Emma Goldman. Maybe she did know something. I shouldn't rule it out. Though I had to admit she unnerved me a little. A force of nature, I understood. Lord save me from the like. Theodore was hard enough to handle. But a woman—an obstinate woman . . . Despite Theodore's blithe assurance, my confidence about winning over women had already met its match. In Lizzie.

Ah, Lizzie. Elizabeth Sherman Cameron, a duchess of American history, one of her uncles the Union general who terrified Georgia, another uncle my predecessor plus one as secretary of state. Lizzie carried herself as royalty, and made herself unapproachable, which increased the temptation all the more.

It was an infatuation, nothing more. She was married; I was married. I had no defensible reason to pursue her. Usually I resisted, but sometimes I gave in and tripped on her toes or, more often, on my own. We were dancing a waltz; whenever I stepped forward, she stepped back. When I stepped back, she—Well, you can guess. It was a game. Both of us knew it wasn't serious. It couldn't be. We couldn't allow it to be. But a man could flirt, couldn't he? Up to the edge and no further.

But then why did I feel so guilty about it?

I checked my watch. It was hours too early to order a drink. Besides, I was heading for a saloon. It wouldn't do to arrive smelling of liquor—and certainly not at eleven o'clock!

Through the windows, the woods gave way to scrums of buildings separated by cornfields and barns. We were entering Long Island City. The smokestacks spewed ashes that deepened the gray.

With tremors and screeches we jerked to a halt. The splendid isolation of Sagamore Hill was gone. So, too, was the peace of the club car. I lowered myself onto the platform, into a maelstrom of fishmongers and rude commuters. The valise felt heavier than I remembered, probably because my arms and shoulders ached from yesterday's exertions in the ring.

I weaved my way through the waiting room and onto the ferry. It was a paddle wheel, a whiff of the past. (*Everything* was a whiff of the past, if you paid attention.) The seats inside were crowded with men in derby hats on their way to work in Manhattan. Pinched lips, faraway looks—the human condition, twentieth-century style. The odors of steam, rotting bananas, and male-pattern anxiety drove me onto the deck. I ignored the chill and tried to imagine the wind as my friend, with minimal success.

The ferry landing at Thirty-fourth street was even smellier than in Long Island City. The automobiles and the motorboats by the wharf made it too noisy to think. Not that I wanted to.

I slapped my feet along the grimy boards, into the depot. The vaulted roof had no walls, and I peered under the eaves and saw the clouds, swollen and gray. I stepped around the piles of pig manure (I could still recognize it, sorry to say) and descended into the street.

At the curb, I noticed a brougham with brass trimmings but thought it unwise to arrive in luxury at an anarchists' saloon. I hailed a hansom cab but let a woman with a squirming tot step in front of me—to-day's contribution to the common good. And again for a haggard old man carrying a bulky package; that counted for to-morrow. The third hack's nag looked ready to rear up at a human's sneeze. I jumped into the cab.

The driver was a dwarf with a mop of red hair and a smile that reached his oversize eyes. "Whar to, suh?"

I recited the address.

"Raht 'way, suh."

"Take your time."

A nudge from the whip sent the nag trotting south onto First avenue.

Around Thirtieth street we passed the high iron gates and grimy brick of Bellevue Hospital for the insane. Was anyone more than an absurd act or two removed from an involuntary visit?

The farther downtown the carriage ventured, the more chaotic the traffic. At Twenty-third street, the elevated railway swooped overhead, casting a shadow and pressing down on the taverns, the tailors, the barber poles, and the grocers huddled below. In the roadway, the hacks and drays and rigs and clattering automobiles all claimed their right-of-way. By rights, a collision ought to occur at every intersection, on every block. The older I get, the more I realize how precarious life is, and how dependent we are on everyone else's judgment. *That* scared me.

⊬╾═╼⊩

Turning onto east First street ushered us into a different world, one as tranquil as a summertime pond. A couple walked arm in arm down the center of the road, the woman plucking her long skirt above the muck.

Number fifty was on the left side, almost to Second avenue, across from a macaroni factory and a Chinese laundry. The brick row house had seen better days. Soot covered the windows, and the peonies in the flower boxes were dead, their stalks gray. The saloon was four steps down.

The basement door, its green paint peeling, was heavy, but I pushed it open with ease. Until something—or someone—stopped it. I pressed my shoulder against it and a man grunted inside. My knocking brought a growl, and the door creaked. A pug-nosed giant straddled the doorway.

"I am Hay," I said.

"Heard o' ya. T'is way."

The saloon was smoky and smelled of last month's ale. Men sat at tiny tables, holding tightly to mugs, squawking in languages I did not understand. Polish or Albanian, perhaps. A young man with long, straggly hair and a collarless shirt sat with his back to the bar and examined me as I passed.

Ah, my silk hat. In an anarchists' hideaway.

I grinned at the young man, as if sharing a joke. It *was* funny. To my surprise, he grinned back.

"In he'e," my chaperone said, pointing to a door, ajar. I walked through and the door closed behind me with a *click*.

It took me a minute or more to see much of anything in the windowless room. A bead of perspiration tickled my spine. I sensed a movement in the far corner. The scratch of a match brought a candle to life. A woman sat behind it, at a tiny round table, her face in shadow except for a pursed mouth and a determined chin.

"Mr. Hay!" Her deep voice, accented by Europe, was used to command.

"Miss Goldman," I replied. "Thank you for seeing me."

"My pleasure." Her pince-nez reflected the flame. She half rose, to the height of a fireplug, and just as thick. She wore no corset beneath the dark, shapeless dress. She was smaller than I had expected (like the Alamo), but her handshake was strong. "What did you wish to see me about?"

No offer of a drink, though she was nursing a short, chipped glass that was half filled with a clear liquid. "Euclid Madden," I said.

"Pardon?"

I repeated the trolley motorman's name. Her face registered nothing—my vision was adjusting to the gloom. Her thin, flat lips looked incapable of smiling. Black-rimmed spectacles magnified her eyes, which kept a stern and level gaze. Her features were too masculine to be pretty, but they had a strength, an assuredness—a magnetism—that made it hard to look away.

"Euclid Madden, the motorman in the trolley that collided with President Roosevelt's carriage in Pittsfield, Massachusetts—do you know him?"

"Why should I know him?" she said.

"There is every indication . . . There is *some* indication that Mr. Madden's action in operating his streetcar in . . . an unsafe manner was . . . not an accident. That it was on purpose." I had to be careful about saying too much.

Was that a smirk? "And you want to know if this Mr. Madden of yours has been hypnotized by my irresistible oratory, perhaps, or otherwise enslaved in my brigade of anarchists, who will obey my wishes even if I never express them. Is that what you are asking?"

"That is not how I would phrase it," I replied, "but . . . yes."

"Oh? How would you phrase it?"

"Just as I did. Do you know him?"

"I do not. So far as I know, I have never met the man. Nor did I know Leon Czolgosz, to skip to your next question, although I have no reason to quibble with the government's"—she fairly spat the word—"contention that he once attended a lecture of mine. I have become accustomed to arrests for every crime the police are unable to solve. Now you are accusing me, are you not, of trying to murder another president. Whether a crime has actually been committed or not. Or do I misunderstand you, Mr. Hay?"

"You are most cooperative, Miss Goldman. I am much obliged. It is indeed a pleasure to interview someone who both asks the questions and answers them. It allows me to take a rest from my duties. But if I may be allowed to resume them, *is* there any possibility that Mr. Madden attended one of your lectures?"

"Not that I know of, though I could not say for certain one way or the other. But I will tell you, if you are asking, that I have never delivered a lecture in . . . where did you say? In Pittsfield, Massachusetts. Maybe I ought to. But even if I did, I can't be held responsible for everyone who listens to me, Mr. Hay. Nor am I responsible for what they do."

"There is such a thing as inciting to riot."

"Is that what you are accusing me of?"

"I am not accusing you of anything. I am simply asking a question."

"And I have answered it. Do I know this Mr. Madden? I do not. Are you satisfied now?"

"What are you drinking?" I said.

"Water."

"Nothing for me, please," I said. If asceticism was the game, I would compete. "Tell me, if you would, what happened in Omaha."

"Nothing happened. That is why I am back in New York. They let me go, as surely you know, for lack of evidence."

"That was not my understanding. I was told"—I prayed that Cortelyou's information was accurate enough—"that you were seen in the company of known communists who are skilled as bomb-makers."

Emma Goldman gave rather an easy laugh. "Who told you that *mishegas*?"

"You were arrested for plotting against the president, were you not?"

"The authorities can make up whatever charges they wish. I cannot be held responsible for their literary imaginations. I have said this every time someone has asked me: I do not believe in killing the president. Not because it would be an evil in itself but simply because it would not succeed. The reaction would undo any good that the action might bring. Isaac Newton understood these things. I daresay you do as well, Mr. Hay."

She reached under the table—I froze—and returned holding a cigarette, which she lit by leaning into the candle. She offered me one.

"No, thank you," I said. "Though I would like to reserve the right to change my mind."

"Why should you have that right and not everyone else, Mr. Hay?" She was looking at me oddly, examining me like I was a bug under a microscope. "I have seen you before," she said at last. "At one of my lectures."

I felt like I was blushing. "How did you know?" I said.

"Where was it?" The eyes behind the glasses snapped alive. "Tell me, where? You sat in the second row, in the center."

"In Brooklyn," I said, amazed. "How did you know this?"

A shrug.

I said, "But you have no recollection of Euclid Madden?"

That easy laugh again. "Do you believe me now?" she said. "It is immaterial to me whether you do or not, but let me tell you another reason why you should. Two reasons. If this . . . collision was the work of an anarchist, he would have used a gun, like Mr. Czolgosz did, not a trolley car. He would want a sure thing. *And* he never would have kept the crime to himself. He would have shouted it from the rooftops. Otherwise, what was the point? Mr. Czolgosz confessed his crime. He was proud of it."

"But only because it succeeded. Why brag about failure?"

"You miss the point," she said. "The ease of the attempt reveals the state as vulnerable, and if the state is vulnerable the people can take back their power. I will admit my involvement if that is the truth, and I will deny it when *that* is the truth. I am naive enough, Mr. Hay, to still believe in the truth, and I am even more naive to believe that you do."

+>——<+

"So, what did the old girl say?" The squeal was either the president or the telephone line. I was calling from an apothecary around the corner from the saloon.

"Young girl," I replied. "Well, young woman."

"So, what did the old girl say?"

"She doesn't remember ever meeting the motorman."

"Which doesn't mean she didn't."

"I suppose not." I preferred not to explain why I believed her. "But there is no evidence that she did."

"Your job is to find it."

"I understand that, but I cannot find evidence where it doesn't exist."

"We have been through that, Hay. So you need to look for the evidence where it *does* exist."

"Where is that, would you say?"

"Pittsfield."

The reply I had feared. "On a Friday?"

"No time to waste, John."

My Christian name—he was pulling out the stops. In my experience, a life without time to waste wasn't worth living. But I could never expect an apostle of the strenuous life to agree.

＋━━━＋

"I suspect the world can survive without you for a few days," Alvey Adee said. He was still at the office late on a Friday, married to nobody but the department.

"It hasn't done all that well *with* me," I replied. Margaret Hanna repeated what I'd said.

"We might keep you away indefinitely," Adee said.

"That's a strategy. Anything I need to know?"

"Not really."

That meant yes. "What is it?" I said.

"A letter from Taft. Asking you to support eight hundred more troops in Mindanao."

"Only to cover his sizable derriere," I said. "My apologies, Miss Hanna."

"A fact is a fact," she replied.

＋━━━＋

The depot was thick with men tired after a long week, heading home to unhappy wives. They scurried this way and that, crossing paths but only rarely colliding, their derbies bobbing but never displaced, a marvel of individually regulated chaos. A point for the anarchists!

I bought my ticket at one of those marble-rimmed windows beneath the rotunda. The waiting room at the enlarged Grand Central Terminal, on Forty-second street, in an up-and-coming part of town, was immense. If you wished to feel small, this was a good place to sit. I chose a rocking chair by a fireplace and imagined myself a water bug in the desert.

My third telephone call, to Clara, had not gone as smoothly. Not a cross word was said, but I felt all the things unsaid, having only the faintest idea what they were. I apologized for being called away, and meant it. That usually worked (I think), but not this time. She seemed distant. She *was* distant. My fault, no doubt—it always was. If only I could figure out how.

All for the sake of going to Pittsfield. Lucky me. *Pittsfield.* I waved the ticket in my hand; the faint breeze might keep me awake. What I knew about Pittsfield would fill a worm's ear. A small city at the western edge of Massachusetts, a few miles from New York State. In the Berkshires, but far from beautiful. Industrial, drab. A Republican stronghold, like most of the state. Hence the president's political interest.

These were impressions, nothing more. I would see what the place was like once I got there, not before. No longer was it too early for a drink.

The call for my train—"New York Central, to Danbury and points north"—came none too soon. I dragged my valise through the waiting room and along the platform. My compartment was in the farthest car. The woodwork was worn, the seat cushions torn. It would do. It would have to.

I found the parlor car, claimed an upholstered chair, ordered a whisky, and opened a volume I had slipped from between unruffled shirts. The cover was lush, the lettering in gold on a regal red.

THE HOUND
OF THE
BASKERVILLES

ARTHUR CONAN DOYLE

The spring's literary sensation. Sherlock Holmes had supposedly died eight years before, fallen to his death at Reichenbach Falls. Everyone knew that. But now he was back for another yarn, which supposedly happened prior to his demise. A "prequel," to coin a word. I had to admire the author's audacity. Or was it cowardice, to yield to the seductions of commerce? Any writer should be so tempted.

To be sure, I still worshiped Vidocq. For one thing, he had been real, the master criminal turned France's master detective, the founding director of the Sûreté nationale. Eugene Vidocq was Victor Hugo's model, in *Les Miserables*, for Jean Valjean *and* for Inspector Javert. Vidocq, however, relied on deception and disguise in solving crimes—hardly my forte, even as a diplomat. While I deified him, I would never wish to emulate his methods.

But Sherlock? No dabbling detective, such as myself, could fail to adore him. I admired his skills at boxing and at the violin and, of course, his brains. He noticed everything, missed nothing, understood the implications, then thought and thought and thought about how the pieces fit, amid clouds of pipe smoke and snorts of cocaine. He was smarter than I could ever be. On the other hand, he wasn't real, which gave me an edge. Though an edge in what, I couldn't say with any assurance.

What, in fact, *was* my advantage? I evaded the question by turning the page and starting to read. The master detective was examining the thick, bulbous-headed walking stick a would-be client had left behind. Inside of four pages, Holmes deduced everything about its owner, his background and position and sense of self. Only then did the owner arrive, in need of a detective to look into Sir Charles Baskerville's recent death on the moor. Holmes was peeved to be described as Europe's second-finest detective, next to Monsieur Bertillon, who had pioneered the use of eleven bodily measurements to identify criminals. Sherlock (if a colleague in detection may assume familiarity) was brilliant, yes, but in need of affirmation, and not beyond pique. Even this fictional detective had his faults. I sighed with pleasure. There was hope for me yet.

CHAPTER FOUR

I woke up and had no idea where I was. Then I remembered. I had arrived in Pittsfield the night before, three hours delayed, due to a cow on the tracks in the wilds of northwestern Connecticut.

If the Hotel Wendell was truly the stateliest lodging that Pittsfield could offer, I dreaded what else I might find here. I sat up. The hotel was new, but the canopy over the four-poster bed was already frayed. The walnut wardrobe was big enough to hold two or three corpses. Heavy beige drapes blocked any risk of daylight.

What time was it? Did I care? Yes, I cared a lot, though God knows if I could have explained why, even to myself.

A line of poetry floated in front of me. I had only to reach for it, which I did.

The boondocks need not be Western.

The last line of . . . something. Something bad, no doubt. I cringed—my most reliable indicator that something wasn't up to snuff. The only poetry I've written that ever sold a lick was those odes to platitudes, in frontier dialect, that took me all of a week to write. Although I have to admit they weren't bad. As for everything else, I was trying too hard. (Story of my life.)

So, what rhymed with *Western? Lectern. Pesterin'. Festerin'.*

I kicked the covers off and hopped to the window and pulled the curtains aside. The sky was a shocking blue. I looked down upon the storefronts across West street and sideways toward a swath of greenery.

I bathed and chose my less wrinkled frock coat. I was, after all, representing the president.

The elevator was slow in coming, and I was starting toward the stairs—five stories!—when it arrived, responsive to competition.

"Lobby, please," I said to the operator. He was an old gent with a rutted face and tufts of gray hair in his ears. I added mildly, "I understand you had an . . . accident here in Pittsfield. Involving the president."

The old fellow closed the cage, swiveled the brass handle to the left, and said, "Best thing e'er happen to this burg. Nuttin' e'er happen here."

"You got your wish, then."

"But warn't no accident."

"What do you mean?"

"No, sir."

"Why do you say that?"

"Ask the boy at the desk." The elevator slid to a stop, rattling like a tubercular clearing his throat. "Go 'head, ask 'im."

The hotel lobby had lush carpets, deep sofas, and fresh daisies in hideous vases. The reception desk was polished to a shine. Behind it, the clerk was skinny and had a shock of carrot-colored hair; the freckles on his pimpled cheeks danced as he nattered with a lodger. He looked fourteen but must have been nineteen at least.

I sidled up to him and said, "I was interested in the, uh, accident on Wednesday involving the presi—"

"You chattin' up Wally there, huh? Well, was nothin' of the sort, mister. I knows it. No accident. Heard 'em talkin' 'bout it."

"Heard who?" I said.

The boy was leaning over the reception desk but jerked his head up at me. "And who do I have the pleasure of addressing, sir?"

"John Hay," I said.

"Hey, ain't you . . . an actor, maybe?"

"A boxer," I said. "Used to be."

"Oh, yeah, musta seen your pitcher in a old magazine. Well anyway, some fellas from New York that was stayin' here, standin' just about where you're standin', and loud, if you don't mind my sayin' so, gab-bing 'bout not gettin' ta the country club in time ta see ol' Teddy. 'Bout slippin' the motorman a fiver ta make sure ta get there first."

"You think they were serious?"

"Well they was drinkin' a little."

"At what time of day was this?"

"Early. 'Fore nine, I'd say."

"Did you see them after that?"

"Say, why you askin' all these questions, anyway?"

"Because I want to know the answers," I said. "I am . . . looking into the . . . circumstances."

"Yeah, but why?"

Sharp fellow. I hadn't figured out yet how much to say and to whom. Less was more, I figured, especially if it was dressed up to look like more. Rather like diplomacy. I took out my wallet instead. "A fiver, you say."

The old five-dollar currency showed Benjamin Harrison's picture on the front—surely a lampoon from the Treasury boys, exalting this icicle of a president. I laid the bill on the counter. The boy's eyes lit up. It was early and his day was looking up.

The four New Yorkers had checked in the night before the collision—this, extricated from the hotel's registry—and checked out two morn-ings later. Their names meant nothing to me. They might mean more to Chief Nicholson. Eight o'clock at police headquarters, per Cortelyou's arrangement.

I pocketed an apple from the dining room, a misdemeanor I had learned from Lincoln, and ventured outside. The air was crisp—a New England fall. The Berkshires weren't the Rockies, but they deserved re-spect as hills. Autumn here settled in early.

The center of Pittsfield was a block away. It felt more substantial than I had expected for a community of barely twenty thousand souls. West and East streets and North and South streets all converged at the green-ery I'd glimpsed. Park Square, it was called—though it was an oval! On every side, formal limestone buildings housed lawyers, bankers, in-surance agents, the city's fathers and kingpins. The marble courthouse,

a block to the east, explained why. As the Berkshire County seat, Pittsfield's sense of importance was not entirely a delusion.

The procession of rigs a-rushing was unending. I watched an old
woman venture into the street at a steady pace, forcing a dray to yield to
her will. I figured it was never too late to learn, and only a single rude
gesture, from a thatch-haired youngster driving a brougham, tainted
my success.

I cut diagonally across the park. Its wide gravel paths were swept;
even the pigeons looked clean. It felt oh so New England, with its
birches, elms, and oaks, its stone benches and quiet self-regard. No
sign of the bandstand where the president had spoken, but its presence
lingered. I could almost hear his squeals of patriotism, of optimism, of
moralism, of righteous anger, all greeted by waves of delight.

School street was a block to the north, exactly where the desk clerk
had told me. The police headquarters occupied a low brick building that
might have passed as a tooth powder factory. Its entrance was unlocked
and unmanned.

I passed the empty reception desk and was halfway along the corridor when a baritone snarled behind me, "Halt!"

I halted. I offered a sheepish smile, hoping to draw the same, but I
had known too many policemen to feel disappointed. He was as expres-
sive as an ice wagon. I introduced myself and said I wished to see Chief
Nicholson. Yes, he was expecting me.

"Wait," he grunted.

He backed me into the entrance hall, which had a slimy tile floor.
I found a metal seat but decided to stand. It wasn't long before the
ice wagon reappeared. He beckoned me back into the forbidden corridor, which was poorly lit and painted vomit green. At the far end we
entered an anteroom, which had two hard-backed chairs and a shiny-
topped desk. I was told again to wait. This time I sat.

Soon the inner door opened. The middle-aged man who emerged
was tall and lean, with a long face and a gloomy demeanor. His heavy-
lidded eyes were dark and deep. His hair, tawny mixed with gray, was
matted and in need of a trim; an untamed beard climbed his cheeks.
He crossed the anteroom and crushed my hand. "John Nicholson," he
said. "You came from Washington to see me?"

"John Hay," I replied. "That I did."

Inside his office, I took the armless chair across the desk. "Thank you for taking the time," I said.

"Did I have a choice?"

I chuckled, but he was not joking. "Of course you did," I said. "I am obliged to you."

Chief Nicholson sat unblinking. It was still my turn to speak.

"I am here at the president's behest," I said, "to inquire about the . . . collision, involving his—"

"What is there to know?" he said.

Bluntness begat bluntness. "Are you certain it was an accident?"

The police chief's stare moved from my face to my right shoulder and beyond. "Why do you ask?" he said.

Another question answered with a question. Why not do the same? "Have you or your men investigated the . . . collision?" I said.

"What is there to investigate?"

Why should I end the streak? "What can you tell me about Euclid Madden, the motorman?"

"What do you want to know?"

Tired of the game, I waited.

Chief Nicholson relented. "He is thirty-nine years old, a family man, a wife, five children, a sixth on the way. Of French Canadian stock, born in Canada, but lived here most of his life. A house out on Alder street, that's north of here—they rent. Has been with the trolley company for about a year. Before that, he worked for one of the mills out on the river. No trouble with the law. Not in this county, anyway."

So the police *had* investigated, at least a little.

"Do you know him at all?"

"One of his girls goes to school with one of ours. If I saw him on the street I would know who he is but probably not say hello."

I wasn't dealing with an undiscerning cop. "You have spoken with him, yes?" I said.

"I have."

"And he was cooperative, would you say?"

"To a point. His lawyer was there and wouldn't let him tell me much of anything. Not until after the inquest, he said. William Turtle is the lawyer's name. Billy. A big man in these parts. Literally and figuratively. A member of the state legislature *and* the lawyer for the streetcar company. As for Mr. Madden, he seemed mild-mannered enough. You never can tell, though."

"Do you know of any reason he might want to harm the president?"

"Do you think he did?"

"That is what I am trying to find out," I said.

No reply. This was a man who said nothing when he had nothing to say.

"There were two arrests?" I said.

"Yes. Mr. Madden and the streetcar's conductor, James Kelly. James T. Kelly."

"On what charges?"

"Manslaughter, in the death of William Craig. Both of them. They were arraigned yesterday and pleaded not guilty."

"So you must have reason to think it was not an accident."

"Not necessarily. Manslaughter means there was no premeditation, no intent. In other words, an accident."

"Why charge the conductor, too? What was he doing?"

"He was out on the running board, making change, so he says. I have no reason not to believe him. The charges are not up to me. The district attorney files them, not the chief of police."

"*Do* you think it was an accident?" I said.

"I have no reason to doubt it. Do you?"

I told him about the New Yorkers in the Hotel Wendell lobby who wanted to get to the country club ahead of the president. I read him the four names.

"I know two of them," he said. "Daniel and Wrenn. New York police officers, Broadway squad, on vacation here. They offered their services for the occasion. Anything to save the taxpayers a few simoleons. They were riding with me."

"With *you*?"

"Oh yes. I was in the carriage just ahead of the president. We had already crossed the tracks."

"Oh! Did you see the, uh, collision?"

"I did not, I'm afraid."

"Or the trolley at all."

"I was in conversation at the time with Lieutenant Wrenn. Benjamin Wrenn, a very fine fellow."

"They just happened to stop into your office and offer their services. For the occasion, you say."

"Yes, and I was glad to have the help. We are pretty well strapped as it is. Then, when the president comes here and I need men to protect him, a gift is a gift, as I see it. I can always use an extra hand."

"Did you have any doubts about these men's credentials?"

"None. Why should I?"

"Did you happen to hear where they were staying?"

"At the Wendell, I believe. Why?"

⊢——⊣

"Right about here." Chief Nicholson pointed to a culvert that funneled a bubbling brook underneath South street. We stood at the bottom of the long, languorous hill, skipping to the side for the occasional buggy. Weather-worn farmhouses stood behind low stone walls. Overhead wires hung along poles, carrying electricity out from Pittsfield to the trolleys. The dirt roadway was wide enough for four carriages abreast, two on either side of the streetcar tracks—until right here, where the tracks squeezed to the right.

"The carriages have to cross here," Chief Nicholson explained with a deliberativeness I was inclined to trust. "Any motorman would know—*should* know. Though Mr. Madden was new to the route, as I understand it."

"Why do the tracks *do* that?" I said.

Chief Nicholson shrugged. "Quickest route to the country club, I wouldn't be surprised. It's up ahead, just over the rise."

"An exposed spot, I would say. I suppose anyone could have shot him. With a gun, not a Kodak."

"Nobody did," Chief Nicholson pointed out.

We were standing by the tracks, facing south, when there was a low rumbling behind us. I turned and saw a trolley bearing down. The motorman stood like a statue behind the triptych of glass across the front. The streetcar was yellow and green and *fast*. Man was not meant to go so fast. Railroads, yes. But they belched and bucked and farted—mechanical monsters. This was more like a puma, quiet and deadly.

I jumped to the roadside. I felt a gust as the trolley whooshed by.

"How fast would you say it was going?" I said.

"Approximately eight miles an hour. It's not supposed to go faster than that."

"Seemed faster to me."

"You were standing close."

Not in front of it, at least. "How fast was the other one traveling, do you know? The one that struck the president's carriage."

"There is a difference of opinion on that."

⊹—═—⊹

The wrecked carriage lay on its side, like a sick dog waiting for a belly rub.

"How did they move it here?" I said. Surely the country club would never have allowed it on its premises, so close to the first tee, for a president who wasn't a registered Republican.

"Oxen righted it," Chief Nicholson said, "and horses dragged it here. And some fool in New York is buying it, for a hundred dollars. To put it on display. The darnedest thing. People would pay to see *this*?"

The carriage was a jumble of smashed woodwork, mangled metal, and wheels with broken spokes. The side toward the sky was staved in. Its twin lanterns were intact, but the high driver's box, where Craig had sat, was gone.

"There is something I need to show you," Chief Nicholson said. I followed him around to the far side of the carriage, closer to the tee. A golfer was taking practice swings, while his companions peered our way. I couldn't blame them. "This," Chief Nicholson said.

The carriage's back wheel, hanging in the air, looked intact except for a snapped spoke. I must have looked puzzled, because he was quick to explain. "The streetcar's fender barely grazed *this* wheel and slammed into the front wheel instead. And the nigh wheel horse. A slanting blow. *That* is what sent Mr. Craig flying under the trolley."

I tried to picture a man flying through the air. Or five men, landing hither and yon, wherever fate and physics decreed. One of them under the sharpened wheels, sliced to death. Virile one moment, dead the next. How capricious. How pointless. How absurd.

Chief Nicholson was still talking. "Suppose the carriage had been traveling a tiny bit faster. Instead of brushing by the back wheel, it would have hit the hub of the wheel head-on, and—who knows?—it might have been the president who was thrown onto the tracks. And maybe the governor and Mr. Cortelyou as well."

My breath caught. "How close?" I managed.

"How close *what*?"

"Between what happened and what . . . might have happened?" Still vaguely phrased. "Between the hub of the back wheel and where the trolley struck. How far apart?"

Chief Nicholson rubbed a rough-skinned thumb over the rutted woodwork and studied the carriage door that would never close again. "Two inches," he said, not looking at me.

I felt myself getting frantic and willed myself to calm down. "The president missed being killed—*might* have missed being killed—by two inches," I said, surprised that my voice sounded steady.

He did not reply. I was not asking a question.

Two inches, I was thinking, and I might now be president. Which I have never, ever—ever—wanted to be. Honest.

+>===<+

"Number twenny-nine, the hoodoo car." The burly black man with a scar on his cheek flashed a shrewd smile.

"The what?" I said.

"Yessuh, the hoodoo car. No end o' trouble with it. Collided, head-on, in Dalton a whiles back. And just last week, a motorman git burnt when the controller overheated."

Chief Nicholson said, "Euclid Madden?"

"No suh, was Mistuh Reese."

"Is he all right?" I said.

"Doctors say he will be."

"Yes, we would like to see it," Chief Nicholson said. "I believe Mr. Dolan has . . ."

"Oh yessuh. Mistuh Dolan ain't here, but he leave word. Come with me, please."

The large man was surprisingly light on his feet as he led us across the trolley repair yard on East street, into a one-story brick building with an aluminum roof.

"You know, I don't believe in hoodoo," Chief Nicholson whispered.

I was tolerably sure I agreed.

On the farthest tracks, number twenty-nine looked forlorn, like a racehorse put out to stud and still awaiting a client. The green and yellow paint could use a fresh coat, and the eight rows of seats looked abandoned; the side panels were gone. The terminus sign above the side door said "Country Club." The three-sided windshield was intact.

"Ready to run, she is," our host said.

"No real damage?" I replied.

"A scratchin' on the fender, a scrape here and there, nothing mo'."

I examined the front of the trolley and noticed nothing beyond the usual wear and tear.

"The brakes?" said Chief Nicholson.

"The old wheel brakes, not the newfangled air brakes. But they work just fine."

Chief Nicholson said, "You check them?"

The streetcar worker raised himself to his full six-foot-four, gazed down upon the police chief, narrowed his eyes, and nodded.

"But otherwise, the trolley is ready to run, is that correct?" Chief Nicholson said. "Nothing wrong with the engine? Not damaged too much?"

"Runnin' fine. A sixty-horsepower Westinghouse engine." The man waltzed around the front of the streetcar, as proud as a new father. "Can run fourteen and a half mile an hour on flat land with all o' the seats, forty-eight of 'em, filled to the gills."

"And on a hill?" I said.

"Depend on the hill, I suppose."

"Mind if I take a look?" I said. Without waiting for an answer, I continued around number twenty-nine and climbed aboard. I raised myself onto the high leather seat and felt like a king on a throne. Through the high windshield I examined the crushed rear of the streetcar just ahead; number seventeen had seen worse than hoodoo. Our escort stood behind me.

"Over here the controller, and here the brake"—handles at the motorman's left and right. A rope hung from a round iron bell near the ceiling.

"And clean," I said. I would have expected grease and grime in the crevices of the floor and below the motorman's seat.

"Yessuh." The man beamed. "Spick-and-span."

I cursed to myself. "Who told you to clean this up?" I said.

"Mistuh Dolan did."

Yes, I would like to talk to him.

I tried to swivel to the right—had the motorman seen the trolley coming?—but the padded seat wouldn't budge. I clutched the front edge and tried again, to no avail. My hand slipped inside, through a gash in the leather, and my fingers touched something that crinkled. Using two fingers as pincers, then my thumb, I pulled out a paper that was folded into fourths. The piece of foolscap, off-white, was unlined and torn along one edge. It was rough in texture; the sharp fold had required a firm thumbnail. I unfolded it once, prying it apart, then a second time. I flattened out the paper across my knees.

A map, in pencil, was crudely drawn. No mistaking, however, what it was. A road, bisected by tracks, with a dotted line across. Near the top of the map, an oblong was marked "PCC."

Pittsfield Country Club.

Where the dotted line crossed the tracks, William Craig had lost his life, and President Roosevelt had nearly joined him.

+——+

"So, what do you think?" I said.

"About what?" Chief Nicholson replied, quite reasonably. The carriage rocked as we returned along North street.

"The map that was stuffed in his seat."

"Do we know it was his? And from that day in particular?"

"Good questions. How about if we pose them to the elusive Mr. Madden."

"Mr. Turtle won't let you anywhere near him. Not 'til after the inquest, and probably not 'til his trial."

"*You* can talk to him. I'll just tag along. Aren't the police in Pitts-field permitted to question a . . . suspect?"

"A suspect in what? Tell me, has a crime been committed?"

"Precisely what I am trying to figure out. Manslaughter is what he's charged with. Isn't that a crime? Possibly something worse."

I was gazing out the window, passing churches and a funeral home and the sprawling houses of the city's industrialists, when another piece of Nicolay's advice came back to me. *Work in from the edges.* Don't start your questioning with the man at the center. Work around him first, and learn whatever you can, before you try to pin him to the wall.

"Kelly!" I exclaimed.

"Who?"

"Kelly, James T. Or is it C.? The streetcar conductor. The other man-slaughter*er*, so alleged."

"T. What about him?"

"Let's talk to him."

"Mr. Turtle will—"

"I am pleased to go alone," I said. "If you would kindly ask your driver to drop me off."

⊢⇒══⇐⊣

It was half past four. The gray wooden siding looked drab, even in the late afternoon sun. The screen door hung awry. To my right, along the unpainted porch, a rocking chair rocked on its own. Because of the wind, I hoped, though I did not feel any.

The gabled dwelling at 36 Hamlin street was a boardinghouse. Two knocks on the front door brought no response. I grasped the knob and turned it. To my surprise, the door opened. I stepped back to let Chief Nicholson enter first. Surely the police chief would have more cachet in Pittsfield than a mere secretary of state. Chief Nicholson smiled—he *was* capable of it—and gestured for me to precede him.

A hausfrau with lumbering breasts waddled toward us. "Yeah?" she barked.

I offered my name and introduced Chief Nicholson. "I am looking for James T. Kelly."

"Expectin' ya?"

"Police business," Chief Nicholson said, flashing his badge.

She looked bored. "T'ird floor. Number seven."

The stairs were steep and creaky. The first landing smelled of camphor, not quite masking the acrid odors of humans in pain. The banister wobbled on the second stairway, which ended at a closed door, marked in chalk with a seven.

My knock set off a scurrying inside, like a squirrel in the attic. I deciphered the grunt as "Wait." The sounds subsided, and I was about to knock again, when a man shouted from inside, "Who is it?"

I turned a pleading look to Chief Nicholson, who sighed and said, "The police, Mr. Kelly. Please let us in." The police chief's right hand rested on his pistol.

A latch turned and the door inched open.

The young man in the doorway wore suspenders over an undershirt that left his bony shoulders bare. He had a thin face and sparse, sandy hair. "I've already talked to the—"

"But you haven't talked to me," Chief Nicholson said. The heel of his hand hit the door, suggestively close to Kelly's temple.

The threat of violence, the thrill of it, hung in the air.

Kelly backed away from the doorway, creating a vacuum that drew us in. The bed was unmade. Kelly swept a pair of trousers and several dust-colored garments from the two chairs and onto the floor. Chief Nicholson and I remained standing.

"Whaddya want?" said Kelly, sinking onto the edge of the bed.

"Just a question or two about the collision," I said.

"My lawyer tells me not to talk to nobody."

"I understand that," I said. "But nothing here is on the record. Nothing you tell us will harm you." I hoped this was true. Chief Nicholson did not correct me. "We know you had nothing to do with the collision."

"Then why in the hell am I bein' charged with manslaughter? Gonna wind up in jail, I am. And I had nothin' to do with it."

I had no response and glanced over at Chief Nicholson, who stared at the floor.

"I cannot help you, I am sorry to say. It's between you and your lawyer and the—"

"*He's* the one who keeps telling me to—" Kelly halted.

I started to prod him, but Chief Nicholson stopped me with a gesture. My detective skills were rusty.

Or maybe not. Kelly had gone catatonic. Chief Nicholson, at last, did some prodding, though equally without effect. Kelly snapped awake but stared blankly at his interrogator.

I tried. "My concern is something different. I am here representing the president . . ." No reaction. "Trying to understand exactly what happened. Not who was at fault." Strictly speaking, this was a lie. "Exactly where were you when the collision occurred?"

"Back with the passengers, collecting their fares, making change."

Hallelujah, the lie worked! "Out on the running board?"

"Yeah, sir."

"Did you see the carriage coming?"

"Nope. Was on the opposite side." Kelly's eyes had crossed, as if he were viewing a moving picture that was perched on his narrow nose. "Was givin' two dimes back to a lady with a 'at that 'ad a bullfinch— can you believe? Then suddenly, *boom*, and everyone went flyin'."

"Out of the trolley?"

"Mebbe some of the folks on the running boards did. Inside, into the bench in front of 'em. Was nobody hurt much."

"Did you notice anything out of the ordinary before the crash?"

"Such as?"

"Such as anything."

"I seen nothin' . . . No, nothin' at all."

He was lying, I just knew it, being practiced at the art myself, as any diplomat was. "Was Mr. Madden behaving oddly at all?" I said.

"N-no, nothin' I seen."

I was getting closer. But to what? "He was driving a little too fast, perhaps?"

No reply. Closer still.

"How fast would you say?" I tried. "Twenty miles an hour? Fifteen?"

Kelly squirmed on the bed. Fast indeed, was my guess. But I had a feeling he was hiding something else. A hunch, I suppose you would call it. Isn't that what detectives had?

Did my hunch extend to *what* he was hiding? Actually, yes!

"Mr. Kelly," I said in my most commanding voice, the one I use with German envoys who consider the kaiser a deity, "that folded-over paper—who handed it to Mr. Madden? Who was it?"

The conductor looked stricken. "I had nothing to do with it," he pleaded.

"I have no reason to think that you did," I said.

"I can't," he rasped.

"And why not?" Chief Nicholson said, in *his* most intimidating voice.

"I just can't. He would kill me."

"Who would?"

"I can't."

"My men will protect you," the police chief said.

"Against . . ." Kelly whined. "Mr. Hull?"

Chief Nicholson looked stunned.

Kelly's whimpers dissolved into tears, thence into uselessness.

⊹═⊰

"The Republican machine is what its enemies call it," Chief Nicholson said. He had shed his jacket and was pouring two whiskies.

"It runs the city, I take it," I said, sipping. Warmth descended my chest.

"County, too. Even the state, right now, though Murray Crane is his own man. Rich as Croesus from the family mills." By federal contract, the Crane mills manufactured the paper used for every rectangle of currency in every American's wallet. "Though you didn't hear it from me."

"What can you tell me about this James Hull?"

"Not a lot to tell. Grew up near Albany, came to Pittsfield as a young man, as an office boy for the national bank. Went over to the insurance company and rose through the ranks on the strength of his penmanship, if you can believe that. He is the company's secretary and now also the treasurer. Good Republican, good family man, a wife, five children, three servants. Not many friends, not many enemies. Not one of these backslappers. Silly-looking fellow, but that's his business. Oh yes, and he's also a director of the street railway company. He helped get it started. One of the civic-minded men of business"—a wry smile— "who manage the affairs of our fair city."

"So any mere motorman would do whatever he . . . suggests."

"Only if he wants to keep his job."

This was a cop I could like.

+⟩═⟨+

The second whisky, in the dimmest corner of the hotel's dining room, brought me to my senses: Clara was the woman for me. She had been, from the moment we met, in her aunt and uncle's parlor on Thirty-seventh street in New York, even if it took a month or two or three for me to see it. I admired her before I loved her, but when I fell, I fell hard. She was calm and reserved, sweet and serene—everything I was not. Even since Del's death. She had been stoic, Lord knows, a boulder in a wild-running stream.

But something had happened between us—I couldn't deny it. It wasn't clear what. There was an uneasiness, a gulf. I couldn't shake the feeling that she blamed me for Del's death. It was an accident! We both knew it. And yet . . . it hung there, suspended, keeping us . . . apart. The very thought set the earth trembling under my feet; at stake was all that I held dear.

The third whisky sent me back to Lizzie. She was any man's dream—or nightmare. Lithe and lovely, beguiling. So far my marriage vows were intact, but not for want of trying. Well, not trying exactly—I hadn't actually *tried*. I had hinted and nudged and winked in the time-honored manner, which gave us both an out, for good reasons or none.

Did I want to take Lizzie to bed? Yes. No. I don't know. Of course I did, in a way. Any man would, wouldn't he? There was nothing sinful about the wanting, even (or especially) at my age. Surely that was the true cause—time-honored as well, I suppose. Age, I mean. A man starts to see the end in sight and he wants whatever he can't have. A cliché, to be sure. But clichés are clichés for a reason. Still, could I imagine actually following through, instead of continuing to let us pretend? I shook my head. I hoped not, although I couldn't be certain. Was I a bad person? I didn't feel like one, although I guess the kaiser didn't, either.

I pulled my calfskin notebook from the side pocket of my frock coat along with the nub of a pencil.

A woman is a woman, every fiber of her self

Nice rhythm, a trifle trite (or worse), with a monosyllabic punch at the end. And timely. *Self*—the center of the new psychology. But what in the hell rhymes with *self*? *Elf. Shelf. Guelph.*

Start again. That never hurt.

No woman is a woman without a sense of self

Better. That actually meant something. About both women.

If she's haughty—No, naughty . . .
If she's haughty—or naughty—let her seem so.

About Lizzie. And veering toward meaninglessness.

Now, to face the problem I had been postponing and dithering over. In diplomacy, ignoring a problem often solved it. Not in poetry. Nor, I feared, in love. I knew I loved Clara, as much as I understood what love was. She gave me a center to my life, a keel. She made me feel complete. But was it Clara that I loved—I knocked back a swig of whisky—or was it me I loved when I was with her? With Lizzie, the question never came up; she appealed to the part of me that carried no obligations.

I was so damn tired of obligations. What a relief it would be to break free of them, to not think, to just do. To be truly selfish for once—twice? thrice?—the mortal's thrill. (Which all of our rules are meant to prevent, and rightly so.)

No woman is a woman without a sense of self
If she's haughty—or naughty—let her seem so.
If she is ugly, or flighty, send her to Guelph . . .

I snapped my notebook shut and stuffed my pencil away. Why did poems have to rhyme, anyway?

CHAPTER FIVE

I pulled the heavy drapes aside. The sunlight surprised me. Shouldn't the heavens be as gloomy as my world was? As this case was? Assuming—*assuming*—it was a case. The threshold question: Had a crime been committed?

Possibly. Manslaughter, the authorities alleged. Or, if Theodore was right, something worse.

I plumped up the pillows and rested my head and considered the mystery of Euclid Madden. The perpetrator, by all available accounts. His name, for one thing—a Greek first name and a . . . what was *Madden*? French Canadian, Chief Nicholson had said. I needed to see the man, and not only to question him. To *see* him. With luck, to see inside of him. As a means of figuring out why.

Yes, why. Why on earth would a streetcar motorman at the edge of Massachusetts want to murder the president?

Because he could. Yes, but as an explanation that hardly sufficed. Just because he could doesn't mean he would. Why *would* he, then? This was harder. Political fervor? Plausible. An anarchist had murdered McKinley. Was Madden an anarchist, or even an agitator? He was mild-mannered, but so was Guiteau. Still waters run deep, and all of that. Far-fetched, I must say, but I couldn't rule it out.

Or money. A motive for murder that was tried-and-true. Five children and a sixth on the way? On a motorman's salary? He could surely put the money to good use. Anyone could. That could be checked, if a bank was involved.

Or maybe it wasn't the president that Madden wanted dead. Theodore hadn't ridden alone. Maybe Madden had wanted to murder . . . William Craig. Ridiculous! Why would anyone want to kill Craig? The Scotsman had never seen Pittsfield before. (Probably.) Or maybe the target was Governor Crane. That made slightly more sense. He was from Dalton, the next town to the east, and was wealthy and powerful enough not to care what anyone thought. Lord knows what kinds of resentments and rivalries simmered hereabouts.

⊹⊨═⊨⊹

"He was scheduled to visit Pittsfield for fifteen minutes at most," May Nicholson was saying. "Nothing fancy, nothing showy. It just grew and grew. You know how these things are. Once the schools shut down and the GAR wanted a parade, next thing you know we had a bandstand and a speech in Park Square. I don't know who all got involved."

"A thousand dollars in decorations," Chief Nicholson chimed in.

His invitation to Sunday dinner had startled me. I could only assume his wife was behind it. The house at 75 Center street was small but well kept—the yard neat, the porch swept, the shutters recently scrubbed. Inside, the furnishings were late 'eighties, plush and wine-colored, lived in, able to take a punch and bounce back. At the dinner table, the gold-flecked tablecloth set off the platters of lamb, sweet potatoes, and summer squash.

"Tell me, Mr. Hay, are you a churchgoing man?" Mrs. Nicholson said in all gaiety and innocence. She, too, was small and well kept—well *kempt*, rather—with a lithe figure, crinkly blond hair, and a cherubic face. I died for her dimples.

"When my wife tells me," I said.

Chief Nicholson restrained a laugh, and both daughters giggled. Mrs. Nicholson bristled. I deduced that the master of this house felt the same.

"What do you think of our fair city, Mr. Hay?" she said, recovering nicely, maybe from practice.

"It is quite . . . *handsome,* I would say. Buildings of considerable dig-nity." *Not including the police headquarters.* "Park Square is such an elegant . . . centerpiece. It reminds me, I must say, of Lafayette Square. That's where I live. Do you know of it?"

She didn't, which I found enchanting.

"And I like the feeling here of being in the mountains, even if you don't always see them," I said. "The air is clean. Far away from the world; comfortably remote."

"I wish we were, Mr. Hay, but I assure you that we are not remote in the slightest from the outside world and its sins. Pittsfield is no Eden, as my husband's work will attest."

"I have never seen an Eden myself," I said. "Have you?"

"Someday I might," she said dreamily.

I felt only envy.

"I fear that people are the same everywhere, good and bad," I said. A platitude, but like most platitudes, generally true.

"Not in my school," Marion, their younger daughter, piped up. She was a pretty girl, with blond curls and a yellow polka-dot dress she had outgrown. Her expression was somber.

"Oh?" I said. "How would you say they are different?"

"They are meaner," she said.

"They are merely training for life, my dear," I replied. "How old are you, Marion?"

"Twelve and a half."

"Not an easy age," I said. "Though what age is?"

The familiar ache.

"And what brings you to Pittsfield?" Mrs. Nicholson said.

I finished chewing a hunk of lamb that had lost its flavor. "The col-lision last Wednesday," I said, swallowing.

"Oh, that," she said. "We could have been Buffalo."

"But we weren't," Chief Nicholson said sharply.

Marion said, "What about the collision?"

"Marion!" Chief Nicholson said, half rising, leaning dangerously over his antique water glass.

"Because it's that Mary Madden who is the meanest to me. She's in my class."

"That's the eighth grade, at Center Intermediate," Mrs. Nicholson explained. Then, to her daughter, "Mean in what way, dear?"

"Calls me names, says she'll hit me and get her friends to help. And I bet she will."

"Why would she want to do that?" Mrs. Nicholson said.

"I don't know. Because she hates me." Marion's voice quaked. "Because they're going to blame her daddy for something that wasn't his fault."

I said, "What does she mean, wasn't his fault?"

"It was something that somebody else did. Or made him do. Something like that. Anyway, it wasn't his fault. But he's the one getting blamed. He might even go to jail. And she acts like it's *my* fault."

"Or mine," Chief Nicholson said. His eyes were aflame. "Except it isn't mine, either."

"Marion, do you have any idea what she meant?" I repeated. Had my detective work come to this—the badgering of a child?

A blank look: I had lost her.

"Do you know the family?" I asked her parents.

"I know the mother a little, from the school," Mrs. Nicholson replied. "She's all right, I guess. It's him that struts around Park Square in a bowler hat, looking like a circus clown."

"Really!" I said. "Since the collision or before?"

"Always," she said.

⊷══⊶

"He will be in his office on a Sunday?" I said.

"Oh yes," Chief Nicholson said. "I told him to."

The Berkshire Life Insurance Company's headquarters stood at the corner of North and West streets. It had a mansard roof and enough pillars and pediments and arched windows to drive an architect giddy. The door was locked; an elderly servant let us in. He pointed us to an office at the end of the deserted hall. Our footsteps echoed between the tiled floor and marble walls.

At the appointed place, a glass panel announced, in a Gothic script, "James W. Hull." The door was ajar.

The man behind the desk had white side-whiskers that reached to his chest. I had never seen them so long, bushier than my old editor Horace Greeley's (and *he* went insane). I wanted to yank his whiskers on both sides, like an udder. I shook his hand instead.

A reliable man, Chief Nicholson had told me. Whatever that meant. I had my doubts.

Introductions were made and the usual insincerities exchanged. Hull pointed at me and snapped, "What is *he* doing here?"

I was wondering the same thing myself. "I am making inquiries on behalf of the president," I said. Each time I explained this, it sounded lamer. "Last Wednesday morning, you were a passenger in the street-car that collided with the president's carriage, were you not?"

"What about it?"

"Can you tell me anything that would shed light on what caused the . . . accident?" I said. Too vague.

"Accidents happen," Hull said. "Why must anyone be at fault?"

I had said nothing about fault. Or about anyone. Chief Nicholson was leaning forward in his seat. Best to circle back.

"The streetcar was full of passengers, correct?" I said.

"Out to the running boards."

"All heading to the country club? Hoping to get there before the president did—is that right?"

A hesitation, then a tentative "Yes." A pause. "Why are you asking me these things? I know terribly little about it, really. Only that I was present at the scene."

"Where were you sitting?" I said.

"The first row, almost directly behind the motorman."

"Did you see anything out of the ordinary?"

"Not until all hell broke loose. The motorman lunged at the brake and started ringing the gong. Only then did I see the carriage."

"Coming across the tracks?"

"Yes, coming from the right. Directly into my line of sight."

"How fast would you say the streetcar was traveling down the hill?"

"I have no way of knowing. Fast. I wanted to get there. That, I admit."

Admit? I had said nothing about guilt.

"Did you say anything about this—about wanting to get to the country club in time—to the motorman?"

"As I say, he was very busy."

"Before that, I mean."

"Not to speak of."

"What does that mean?" I said, casting diplomacy aside.

A pause. Hull's side-whiskers jiggled. "A little," he said at last.

"You said a little to him about wanting to get to the country club in time to see the president?"

"So he would stop there. He said he would. Or somebody said it for him. I am a member of the country club, you know, a director." Chief Nicholson hadn't mentioned this. "So I have seen the man before."

"The president?"

"No, no. The motorman. He's new to the route. Mr.—I didn't know his name until . . . all this happened. Mr. Madding."

"Madden."

"Yes, Madden. See?" One word too many to convince me. "We had a chat, nothing to speak of. About the president, the crowds, the streetcar route, the fine weather—Roosevelt weather, they call it. Nothing of note."

"A long chat," I said. "About the streetcar route?"

"I . . . we . . . wanted him to get moving."

"He wasn't moving fast enough?"

"He wasn't moving at all."

"What do you mean, he wasn't moving at all?"

"I tell you, he wouldn't move. Way before we got to the bottom. The streetcar stood still at the top of the hill for . . . who knows how long."

This was news to me. "How long do you think?"

"Ten minutes? Twelve minutes? Fifteen minutes? It seemed like forever."

"What on earth for?"

"That's what I wanted to know. I kept asking him."

"And what did he say?"

"Something about his schedule. But there was no schedule. This run was a special, for us. You know, they stopped all the streetcars while the president was in town, except for this run." That was another thing Chief Nicholson hadn't told me. "We had to get there before the president did. We *had* to. Otherwise the president wouldn't stop. Or he would leave before we arrived."

"Did you give him something?"

"I . . ." Hull paused. "Give him what?"

"You tell me."

"I don't know what you mean."

"It was folded over."

Hull stared at his file-strewn desk.

"And a map was drawn on it," I pressed. "Does that help?"

He glanced up with a look of relief.

"When did you draw the map?" I said.

"While we were waiting at the top of the hill."

"But why? The man knew the route."

"Not well enough. A new man. Just to show him where the carriage would cross, to get past it, to avoid it."

"Not to hit it."

"Oh my, no. Why would I want to do that?"

My question exactly. "Tell me, was there . . . anything else included with the map? An incentive of some sort?"

"I don't know what you mean."

"You know damn well what I mean." Best to avoid the word *bribe*.

He understood. *"No!"* he shouted.

"But he kept the map," I said.

"I don't know what he did with it."

"He stuffed it into his seat. I found it there. And the money? Did he keep that, too?"

Gold strike.

"No, he didn't." He sounded resentful.

"He gave it back?"

The barest of nods, then an explosion: "A twenty-dollar bill. Can you imagine? Fair recompense, I should say, for getting us to the club in time. I would have given him more. Everyone wanted to see the president. There was nothing wrong with that. But when I handed him the bill—"

"Inside the map."

"No, folded up in my hand. I gave it to him and he handed it back. Wouldn't take it. 'No need,' he had the gall to tell me."

"'No need'? That's an odd thing to say."

"Well, that's what he said."

+≻═≺═≺+

Big Bill Craig's big casket was still at the undertaker's, about to leave for the Pittsfield railroad depot and thence to Chicago, where his mother lived. Chief Nicholson was right to think I would want to tag along. Governor Crane was there, too.

In the carriage, I asked—no, suggested—that Chief Nicholson delve into Euclid Madden's finances, such as they were. After much throat clearing, he agreed, mumbling about 'phoning the banks in the unlikely event that the motorman had an account.

The stumpy brick building at 186 North street housed the George N. Hopkins Funeral Home and Professional Embalmer. Around the corner stood four carriages, one of them a hearse with matching white horses, resembling the four-in-hand that had delivered Mr. Craig to his death.

I climbed down from the carriage and followed Chief Nicholson inside. The casket, in the main chapel, was covered by a wreath of asters. Two overgrown young men hovered shoulder to shoulder along the far side. Craig's brothers, no doubt. An ascetic man was brushing dust from the casket, adjusting the flowers, checking his pocket watch. I had seen him before and had met him more than once—and nearly served with him in the president's cabinet. It was Winthrop Murray Crane, the governor of the Commonwealth of Massachusetts.

He was pushing fifty years old but looked sour enough for seventy. Maybe that was what the voters liked about him; they took his sobriety for substance. Really, how hard is it to succeed in this world when your family has wealth and connections? He was an odd-looking man, with huge flappy ears, a mustache that overwhelmed his thin face, and a bony skull with a hairline like an island besieged by the bay. A veritable Ichabod Crane, gangly neck included. We had last exchanged pleasantries, as spare as a New England Yankee could manage, nine or ten months before. Theodore was pressing him to serve as his Treasury secretary, who was next in line for the presidency after yours truly. (Anything to be rid of that bewhiskered boob Lyman Gage.) Perfect complements, the president and the governor—impulsiveness versus caution, loquaciousness instead of brevity. Each man possessed what the other one lacked.

Chief Nicholson stayed in the shadows as I introduced myself to Craig's brothers and described, with all sincerity, my admiration and sorrow. Governor Crane and I exchanged pleasantries, this time with a side order of condolences, and arrived at the familiar awkward pause. I've always been a pretty good talker, but I do need some cooperation.

"Can we talk?" I whispered.

The briefest of nods.

I glanced down at Craig's casket and said, "Someplace else?"

Chief Nicholson stayed behind as Ichabod led me through a side door into a chapel. Low benches faced a pulpit and a machine-made piece of stained glass. He took a seat in the front pew and looked like he belonged. My choices were to stand behind the lectern or to sit beside him in the pew. I sat, staring at the side of his head. I supposed that was the point—so he could avoid looking at me.

"What are you doing here?" he said. He spoke as if someone was charging him per word. Per syllable, perhaps. He prided himself on never having delivered a political speech, which he had turned into a political plus.

"The president sent me."

"Thoughtful."

"In a way," I said. "Were you hurt—in the collision, I mean?"

"Not to speak of."

I waited for the governor to elaborate but realized he had meant his words literally.

I dragged him through a recounting of the collision, of how Big Bill Craig had leapt to his feet, prompting the governor to swivel toward the onrushing trolley, a hundred feet away or more; of how he had heard the ringing of the gong but assumed the trolley would yield the right-of-way; of how he had flung his arm across the president's breast (rather a heroic pose, I thought); of how he had no memory of being thrown from the carriage, beyond what he had been told; of how his right shoulder still felt stiff but no worse. No, he could not say how fast the trolley was traveling. *Fast.*

The poor man was gasping for breath, exhausted by verbiage.

And yet he summoned the strength to describe the arcs of electric sparks that had welcomed the president to Dalton the night before. And the serenading outside the governor's house. And the president's exultation at the Berkshire sunrise.

By the time I could get a word in, he looked drained. The word I got in—the three words—were "Who sat where?"

His head jerked sideways as if I had slapped him. I suppose I had, in a way, jolting him from his reverie. "I was here," he said, his left hand pressing down, "facing the front. Cortelyou sat across from me, facing the rear. Behind him, high on the driver's box, was Mr. Craig. The president sat to my right, looking at the driver's back."

"Who decided that arrangement, do you know?"

"I do not, sir. I imagine it was Mr. Cortelyou. It is my impression that he had his hand in every such thing. He agreed to my choice of horses and of Mr. Pratt. That's the liveryman, a friend of mine from Dalton—he has driven for me for years. Such a courteous man."

"I saw the carriage," I said quietly.

All the while, Governor Crane had kept his eyes on the stained glass. Now he turned slowly toward me, as if a holy relic had been invoked. His dark gray eyes held mine.

"Do you realize how close you came to . . ." I said.

No reply.

"Two inches," I said.

Was it cruel to tell a man he had cheated death? Or would he find it exhilarating? Governor Crane's expression did not waver. I would just as soon not live that way.

"One last question, Governor, if I could. Is there anyone who might want to do you harm?"

I expected a glare, but his lips curled into what I took to be a smile. "In the last election," he said, "one hundred twenty-one thousand, one

hundred fifty-eight men of Massachusetts voted for my Democratic opponent, not counting the socialists and the prohibitionists."

I waited for him to continue, but he had nothing more to say.

+≻—=≺+

The new House of Mercy stood high on a hill, out along North street,
as imposing and soulless as an axle factory. I was relieved to see it,
exhausted as I was in trying to converse with Governor Crane. Every
conversational foray, even about the beauty of Berkshire County, elic-
ited a yes or no or a grunt or nothing at all. But his offer had been
such a surprise that I leapt at the chance to talk with Mr. Pratt, the
carriage driver. Surely he would be more forthcoming in the presence
of a friend.

All the governor had told me about David Pratt was that he used
him whenever he was home, and that his mother did, too. The liveryman arrived when he said he would; his word was his bond. What else
was there for a New England Yankee to know?

"A broken shoulder, is that what he is . . . suffering from?" I said.

"Dislocated. Sprained ankle. Scrapes. Under the dead horse." For Ichabod, another torrent of words.

Our carriage halted under the hospital's pillared portico. As we passed
through the lobby, Governor Crane muttered, "Higginson room."

"What is the Higginson room?"

"You'll see."

I certainly did. David Pratt's hospital room was bigger than my
boyhood home—and prettier. The floors were maple, the furnishings
mahogany, and the blue in the rug matched the draperies and the embroidered covers on the oak bureau and nightstand. Lying in bed was
a bullet-headed man with a flamboyant white mustache and a prizefighter's flattened nose. A muscular young man sat by the carved head-
board. His wild red beard and long, tangled hair made me think of
Samson.

The patient was awake—and livid: "I don't give a damn what Davy
wants. I don't even care who knows anymore. You can tell whoever you
damn well want. It's up to Arthur. Francis is *his* boy, even if—" He no-

ticed us. He looked startled and not a little embarrassed, and abruptly changed his tone. "Twice in a day, Governor!" the liveryman exclaimed. "You are too good to me."

"Mr. Pratt, you look well," Governor Crane said. Untrue but understandable. "This gentleman here, Mr. Hay, would like a word with you. Let me introduce you to the secretary of state."

"Of which state?" Samson snarled.

"All of them," the governor replied.

"Actually, none of them," I said. "It means that I can take a fast note."

"Mr. Hay, this is Frank Forney," Pratt said, pronouncing it in the French way. "He lives in my household. A servant." Iron in his voice.

I extended my hand across the bed, but Samson—Forney—glared at Pratt and neither stood nor looked my way.

"Seems like you're lucky to be alive, Mr. Pratt. If you're up to it, I would like to hear what happened last Wednesday morning, from your point of view."

Forney snapped, "What about it?"

Pratt sat up in bed. "Frank, he was talking to me. But the question is a fair one, Mr. Hay. What about it, indeed?"

I wished I knew, so I sidestepped the question. "The president wants to know what happened. A man who was dear to him was killed."

"That's what the inquest is for."

"Even so. Tell me, please, if you would, when did you first see the trolley?"

"I heard it first," Pratt growled. Either his voice was sonorous or he was coughing up some phlegm; in either case, he overtalked Samson. "I was most of the way down the hill when I saw it—heard it, I mean—coming from behind me. I was getting ready to cross the tracks at the customary spot; that's when I turned and saw it."

"You didn't hear the gong?"

"I guess I didn't. There was noise everywhere, and the wind was in my ears."

"Did you hear Mr. Craig and Governor Crane shouting?"

"Oh yes, *that* I heard. How could I not hear? That's when I turned to look, but it was . . ." His head sagged onto his chest; Forney grasped his shoulder. "Too late. I pulled back on the reins—I couldn't have pulled harder—but it wasn't . . ." Pratt put his pudgy fingered hands to his face and cried, "Was it *my* fault?"

Forney was glaring at me. I couldn't blame him.

"No, of course not," I rushed to assure him. "I don't know what the law says ordinarily, but with the president in your carriage and all street-car traffic supposedly stopped while he was here, I would think you had the right-of-way. Isn't that correct, Governor?"

"I am no expert in traffic laws," Governor Crane replied.

"After the collision," I said, "what can you recall? Anything?"

Pratt shook his head, and his shoulders rose from the bed. The right one was bandaged. "Not until I was in that house," he said.

"Not even being dragged from under the horse?" I said.

"Holding tight to the reins saved his life," Governor Crane said. "You saw the carriage."

"Could the streetcar have stopped in time, do you think?" I asked.

"I don't know," Pratt replied. "It was coming so fast, I don't see how. The man was trying to run me over."

"Why do you think that?"

"I don't know. He was coming so damn fast, and he knew I was there. Why else would he be ringing the gong?"

"How fast was he going, would you say?"

"As fast as a train, I'd reckon. How fast is that, I don't know. Faster than a horse, is all I can say. What else mattered?"

⊹═══⊹

"So, lilies?" I shouted into the telephone. From my hotel room in Pittsfield, Washington felt very far away.

"No, dandelions," Clara replied.

"Can we afford them?"

"You'll just have to write a little faster, my dear."

Our standing joke. Most of our income came from Clara's father's estate, which I had managed in Cleveland for too many years. An easy chore, which gave me time to write, in league with Nicolay, our ten-volume opus on Lincoln, admired by everyone and read by no one other than Theodore. Also my only novel, about Labor versus Capital (naturally, I took Capital's side). It sold well to the wealthy. Who else bought books?

"Everything else ready to wed?" I said.

Her throaty laugh made *me* laugh. She could still do that.

"A few details here and there," she said. "The color of the napkins. Do you have an opinion on that?"

"If I weren't color-blind, I might. Let me do the *placement*. Knowing who hates whom—*that* is what I'm good at."

"Everyone loves everyone, is that not the case?"

"Not even in Pittsfield, my dearest."

✦

I asked at the hotel desk about restaurants that stayed open late. The carrot-haired clerk giggled and directed me to a tavern instead. I ambled out of the Wendell and along West street, toward Park Square.

The moon was slender in the starry sky. A crispness in the air told of the winter to come. The bulky buildings seemed sad—abandoned, really—in the absence of pedestrians or rigs. The electric streetlamps did little to relieve the gloom. The park beckoned like a haven, protected by the branches overhead.

I was lost in thought, not about lilies—dandelions suited me fine— but about David Pratt. I tried to imagine sitting up on the driver's box, crossing the tracks. One moment, the world is attar of roses; the next moment, chaos and death.

These grand thoughts must have concealed the footsteps behind me, until a hand clamped on my right shoulder. I spun around, fists cocked. Then I saw the gun.

I could not see who held it. His face was concealed by a hood and a scarf, and a long coat hid everything else. He was a half-foot or more taller than I, and broader, even with shoulders slumped.

Using Marquess of Queensberry Rules, I might have prevailed. By street rules, probably not. Certainly not against a gun. This fight wasn't fair. But I felt curiously calm. My wallet held enough cash to keep a small-city thief in Pikesville rye for a year. I hoped he would not notice my grandfather's pocket watch.

"You stay away from this, Hay," he hissed, "or you're a dead man."

Without a warning, he swung his left arm and whacked the barrel of the gun across my cheek. Pain streaked my face. As I felt myself falling, I thrust out my left leg—boxing had taught me about balance—and stayed on my feet. I swiveled my hip and, with all of my might, punched the man in the jaw. I heard the crack of bone, and he toppled backward onto the gravel path.

Only then did I remember his gun. Before I could curse my own foolishness, he jumped up and fled into the darkness.

I was too dazed (and not stupid enough) to give chase. But my mood soared. For one thing, I was alive. For another, somebody must think I was closer to the truth than I had figured I was. And I realized something else: that this truth mattered enough to threaten me with death.

CHAPTER SIX

R ight about here." I had summoned Chief Nicholson to Park Square. "He came at me from . . . about where you're standing. With a gun."

"What kind of gun?" he said.

"I don't know guns. It looked big."

"They always do."

I recounted the rest and finished, "And he knew who I was. That's what worries me."

"He never asked for your wallet."

"I didn't give him a chance. But no, he didn't."

"What did he say, exactly?"

"I'll tell you exactly: *You stay away from this, Hay, or you're a dead man.* That's it. Words I shall never forget. It wasn't my valuables he wanted."

"Had you ever seen this man before?"

"Not that I know of. I hardly saw him this time." I offered the best description I could, which was pitiful. Height, shape, voice, eyes— *taller, wider, gruff, dark.* Describing thousands of men in Pittsfield alone.

"Age?" Chief Nicholson said.

"Can't say. Not too old to run away."

"You punched a man who held a gun on you."

"I didn't mean to," I said. "Honestly, I forgot about the gun." Maybe I had been hit in the head too many times.

"His second week on the route," said Peter C. Dolan, glancing up from the ledger before him.

It was eight fifteen. The office was shabby and smelled faintly of turpentine. The general manager of the Pittsfield Electric Street Railway Company had a round face, suspicious eyes, and two or three chins. My working assumption was that everything he said was a lie. Nothing else made sense. His company was on the hook for nearly killing a president. And here I was, the big man from Washington, popping into his office at an inconvenient time to pose dangerous questions. I understood that the truth posed a risk.

"Why the change?" I said.

Dolan shrugged. "We do it. He asked."

"He asked? Why would he do that?"

Another shrug.

"When, do you know?" I said.

He riffled through the records but found no refuge. The electric lamp glared off the pages. "A few weeks ago, I guess."

Around the time that Roosevelt's schedule had become public.

"On the morning of . . . September third, did you give permission for number twenty-nine to run its route?"

"That is what . . . *he* says." Dolan bent his head toward Chief Nicholson but did not look at him. "I did nothing of the sort. That's the city's job—it wasn't up to me."

I turned to Chief Nicholson and said, "And you didn't, either?"

"I already told you I didn't," he replied.

"Then who did?" I said. No response. "And why put Mr. Madden on the route that morning, if he was so new to it?"

"It was his morning on," Dolan said. "We weren't shut down for that long—only while the president was here. And then the regular schedule resumed."

"Mr. Madden has been with you for about a year, is that right?"

Dolan checked back and forth in the ledger. "Fifteen months. Fifteen and a *half*"—proud of his precision.

"Has he been in an accident before or been cited for any . . . violations?"

"No," Dolan said, a little too quickly.

"You are certain," I said.

"Of course I am."

"A dependable employee, would you say? Diligent?"

With a show of exasperation, Dolan swiveled in his seat and limped across the room to the banks of files. He tried three drawers before he gave a grunt of approval. The manila folder he extracted was thin. He returned to his desk and busied himself in reading.

"A single complaint, from a passenger he yelled at, and not without reason. The ostrich feather on her hat kept brushing his cheek while he was driving the streetcar and she refused to step away. She happened to be the mayor's sister-in-law."

"He has a temper, would you say?"

"Doesn't everyone?"

"People have different thresholds," I said. "Where is his?"

"Couldn't say. Never saw it."

Dolan's jaw was working. I appreciated the spot he was in. Anything that was Madden's fault would reflect poorly on his employer—and on his supervisors—unless it was so reckless that they could not be held responsible. Except that he, as the general manager, would bear responsibility for having hired a reckless man. I felt sure he was holding something back.

"Did he have strong . . . political feelings, do you know?"

Dolan stared at the ceiling; the paint was peeling in strips, curled like pigs' tails. He said, "I will tell you this: the man never stopped whining."

"About what?"

"Wages, hours, rat droppings in the lavatory—the typical complaints."

"Did he ever have a point?"

Dolan sat back in his chair and gave me a hard look. "The man is an agitator, pure and simple," he enunciated, so that even a simpleton from Washington could understand. "He might be a Red, for all I know. Or one of them anarchists."

Chief Nicholson stirred beside me and said mildly, "You really think so?"

"Wouldn't surprise me," the general manager replied.

I said, "Do you have any evidence?"

"Wouldn't surprise me."

+≻━≺+

The inquest into the death of William Craig, on the third of September in the year of Our Lord nineteen oh two, had started before I got to the courthouse. Dr. Lung, the president's physician, was describing the goriest details. I enjoy violence as much as the next fellow, but I wasn't sorry I was late.

The county commissioners' chamber was a miniature version of a committee room on Capitol Hill. It had wood paneling and fluted pillars, a dais higher than the witness table and lower than the paintings of Great Men (county clerks of yore, in place of congressional autocrats). The room was empty but for the judge, a stenographer, a bailiff, a streetcar inspector, and a couple of overdressed gentlemen seated below the high windows. The inquest was private, I had been told, although it was not clear to me why. I had gained admission on Chief Nicholson's coattails; my letter of introduction from the president counted for nothing.

"Thank you, Dr. Lung," the judge said. The president's doctor strode from the chamber. From the pomaded hair to the uniform with its braided epaulets to the shoes that shone like onyx, he looked every inch the navy surgeon. No wonder Theodore liked having him near.

"And now, bailiff, if we could hear from . . ." Special Justice Charles L. Hibbard paged through papers at his desk. He had taken the place of the usual judge, who also served (according to Chief Nicholson, eyebrows cocked) as the trolley company's president. Ah, a trivial conflict of interest. The solution, however, wasn't much cleaner. The special justice's father had been a law partner to one William Turtle, who was representing the streetcar company *and* its employees. My head spun. "From Mr. Eugene . . . no, Mr. Euclid . . ."

Before the judge could finish *Madden,* the portly man by the window unwedged himself from his seat, like a whale struggling for the surface. "I object, Your Honor!" he rumbled.

"Yes, Mr. Turtle. State your objection."

"My clients are not ready to testify, Your Honor."

"'Clients,' plural?"

"Mr. Madden and Mr. Kelly."

"I see. Both men have been arraigned on charges of manslaughter, as I understand it. And they pleaded not guilty. No need to worry. This inquest won't compromise their trial."

"Their pleas were provisional, Your Honor."

"I see," Special Justice Hibbard said.

I didn't. Did this mean they might change their pleas to guilty? I wondered if the accused themselves had any inkling. No way to know: they were nowhere to be seen.

William Turtle, on his spindly legs, turned his bulk and crossed the room and exited. By the time I got out to the corridor, he was gone. Across the hall, the unmarked door was swinging shut. I caught it and went in.

The room was crammed with desks, the walls lined with file cabinets. Two women scrambled out the side door. Turtle stood amid the desks like a colossus, feet planted. His square face and handlebar mustache spoke of a solid disposition, one that had earned the support, if not the trust, of voters and politicians alike. His chest and belly vied for pride of place.

"Who are you?" he said, glowering. His tonnage produced a tenor so sweet a hummingbird would have swooned.

I introduced myself.

"I heard you were here," he growled, "tampering with my client. I don't take kindly to that."

"Tampering? Talking is more like it."

"Asking intrusive questions, without his lawyer present. You consider this ethical behavior? You have no jurisdiction here, Mr. Hay. Or anywhere, from what I gather."

"I am here representing the president of the United States." I omitted *of America* as showy.

"Yes, so? Does this give you the right to enter a private citizen's home and conduct an inquisition?"

I had to admit (though not out loud) that he had a point. "That is rather an extreme interpretation, Mr. Turtle." He tilted his head, as if to say, *This what I get paid for.* "And I was not alone in speaking with your client. The chief of police was with me, Mr. Nicholson, and he had every right to be there."

"Without notifying a lawyer?"

"Your client had every opportunity to do that." Only a slight exaggeration. "In any event, it is another of your clients I am interested in now."

"Mr. Madden."

"The same. May I speak with him?"

"I can't see why I should allow it."

"Why wouldn't you?"

"Tell me, how could this possibly benefit my client?"

"Which client?"

"Mr. Madden, of course."

"Not the streetcar company? Speaking of ethics, how can you represent both the company and the motorman? And Mr. Kelly as well?"

"I see no conflict here, Mr. Hay. Nor do any of my clients. And frankly, this is none of your concern."

I had him in a corner and kept punching. "Does Mr. Madden know that he will be pleading guilty to manslaughter? Have you told him yet?"

"He will do whatever is in his best interest. Mr. Kelly will, too."

"And not in the company's best interest?"

"Mr. Hay, there is no conflict."

"Why not let me talk with Mr. Madden, assuming he has nothing to hide?"

"Everyone, Mr. Hay, has something to hide."

⊬━━⊬

"The world shall remain all quiet, no doubt, until my return," I shouted into the 'phone. "And we need to be discreet here." I had to assume the hotel desk clerk was listening in.

Margaret Hanna repeated my sarcasm, and Alvey Adee chuckled. "Yes, your reverence, all is calm," he said. "A bit of fuss in Europe, some in Venezuela and Colombia and always in Nicaragua and, yes, trifles in Asia, east *and* south. Canada has quieted down, except for that tariff business—isn't that right, Margaret? Otherwise, all is silent as the grave. Not a squeak out of Australia or Antarctica. And how is Pittsfield?"

"Just ducky. I've seen only one gun so far. Pointed at me." That was for the desk clerk's benefit, in case he had tipped off the gunman.

"What?"

"Long story—well, fairly short, actually—but a happy ending. I will tell you when I get back. Which I hope is soon. Very soon. Homesick for Washington—who'd have thought? Is there anything I need to know urgently? And again, be—"

"Nothing that can't wait."

"Deposited in cash?" I said.

"The bank is making sure," Chief Nicholson replied. "If it was a check, we can trace it. A new account. And an odd amount. Three thousand one hundred and eleven dollars and seventy-nine cents."

"That isn't pigeon feed."

"Enough to buy a house in Pittsfield," Chief Nicholson said.

"A mansion, I would guess."

"No mansions out this way."

As the police carriage hustled along North street, the storefronts gave way to houses of substance and then to mill homes half the size. Alder street was at the edge of the original village, Chief Nicholson explained, and now was home to janitors, clerks, liverymen—"plain folks."

The house at 117 Alder street was no mansion. The warped siding might have been yellow once; now it was the beige of too many rough winters without paint. Where on earth would an eighth person sleep?

"You are prompt, gentlemen." William Turtle filled most of the porch.

"I try to be," I said.

Turtle's change of mind had caught me unawares, and I didn't understand it, which made me nervous. Was he playing a game by rules I hadn't learned? Or might Euclid Madden, indeed, have nothing to hide?

"Shall we go in?" Turtle said.

The porch creaked under his weight. I followed him with trepidation.

If it could hold his bulk, it could hold mine, but not necessarily both. Chief Nicholson was wise to wait.

Turtle turned the doorknob without bothering to knock, and we followed him in. "Wait in here," he said, gesturing toward what I supposed was the parlor.

The bookcases were filled with classics—Shakespeare, the Brontës, even Aeschylus and Homer. I surmised that the ancient Greeks would appeal to a French Canadian named Euclid. What on earth had his parents been thinking? He had done the same in naming a son of his own—his second son, meaning he'd had time to think it through.

A stunted man appeared in the doorway, and Turtle materialized behind him, like a mountain looming over a shrub. Euclid Madden was short and square, with a hairline retreating like the tide. His face had pleasant, unmemorable features—watery brown eyes, a limp mustache, a receding chin. Hardly the face of a murderer. Not that I've seen all that many. Looks don't usually deceive, but they can, and sometimes they do. Remember, I saw Guiteau once, and he looked as meek as a chipmunk. This time, I thought I saw something sinister in this would-be assassin's face. Its very blandness concealed . . . God knows what. An inner cunning, perhaps. Or a deep-running hate. Or merely a stratum of evil, such as all of us possess.

Unless, of course, I was imagining it all. Never trust a novelist—that's what Henry says, and he should know. His anonymously written novel outsold mine.

"Chief Nicholson wants to ask you a few questions," Turtle said, nudging the motorman into the parlor. "And Mr. Hay. You need not answer any question you don't like."

Either Turtle had coached his client diligently or he did not care if Madden messed up. Or he was convinced of his client's innocence—or he wanted me to think so.

Madden chose an oversize armchair that swallowed him. Turtle lowered himself onto a settee, facing his client, within arm's length. Chief Nicholson took a slat-backed chair, driving his knees into his chin, and nodded at me to begin. I preferred to stand. Rarely did I have the advantage of height.

"Thank you for seeing us," I said. Madden's eyes looked up at mine and flitted away. "I would like to ask you some questions about the . . . events of Wednesday last." I sounded like a lawyer. "We would like to hear what happened, from your point of view. Nothing you say will be used against you in court." I hoped this was true. No peep from Turtle.

The motorman told the tale of coasting down the hill with all due care, assuming—no, *knowing*—he had the right-of-way. Yes, he had seen the carriage, and yes, he knew it was the president's. But what difference did that make? Was the president above the law? When he realized the carriage was not about to stop, he tried everything he could. He shut off the controller and tightened the hand brake, ratcheting it tighter, as hard as any man could. Then he deployed the sander and pulled on the rope that rang the gong. How many hands did one man have?

"And you were unable to stop," I said.

"I tried."

"I understand that your streetcar sat for a good while at the top of the hill."

"For nineteen minutes. What of it?"

"Why?"

"I was ahead of schedule." His voice was high and tight. He did not like being contradicted.

"There was no schedule."

"Of course there was. There is always a schedule. By my watch," he said, lifting one from his vest pocket, "I was nineteen minutes ahead. It was a regular southbound car and I was keeping to the schedule. If I didn't, the company would . . ." His face was turning red. "There's no telling what they would do. They pay a man next to nothing and they get you for anything they can."

"Then how fast were you . . . coasting, would you say?"

No faster than eight miles an hour—on that point the motorman did not budge. He felt bad about the collision, but it was an accident for which he was not to blame.

"Then why are you pleading guilty to manslaughter?" I said.

"I am?" Madden glanced wildly around for his lawyer, who was sitting at his knee.

"We will talk about that later," Turtle said.

The motorman's eyes widened, and he seemed to retreat into himself, like a daguerreotype that was starting to fade.

I glanced back at Chief Nicholson and pointed. He said, "You have a savings account at Berkshire Loan and Trust, do you not?"

No response.

Chief Nicholson went on. "Can you explain why you recently deposited three thousand dollars? Three thousand one hundred and eleven dollars and seventy-nine cents, to be exact?"

Madden looked dazed. William Turtle leaned forward in the settee and began the arduous task of rising to his feet. To end the session, no doubt.

His dallying gave me time to hurry another question. "Did Mr. James W. Hull offer you anything?" I said.

The motorman blinked and seemed to wake up. "Tried to."

"But?"

"Didn't want it. I give it back."

"Didn't want what?"

"Twenty."

"Oh yes, the money," I said. "How about this? I found this underneath your seat."

I drew the map out of my side pocket and unfolded it on top of a thin piece of cardboard I had brought with me. I held it from below and handed it to Madden, who took it with his fingers and thumb. He stared at it and trembled. The map slipped off his fingertips. I saved it before it reached the floor.

"Never seen this before," Madden mumbled, as Turtle nudged us out. "Never did, never, never."

That was three too many *nevers* to sound like the truth.

┼══╾══╾┼

What a Sherlock I was! I couldn't help but boast to Chief Nicholson.

"Where did you learn about fingerprints?" he said.

"Life as a dilettante had its pleasures," I replied. "I don't know a lot about anything, but I know a little bit about everything. Now that I have his fingerprints on the bottom, we can see if he ever unfolded the map. Especially his thumbprints. That's how he would hold it, right?"

"And what if he did?" Chief Nicholson said.

"He would know the exact spot where the carriage would be crossing the tracks."

"He would know anyway," Chief Nicholson pointed out. "It's his route."

"I defer to you on that," I said. "But I want to know if he opened the map to look at it. Maybe he wanted to make sure of something. And I want to know if he just lied to us. If he lied about that, he might lie about anything."

"Maybe he plucked the twenty-dollar bill out and gave it back."

"Maybe," I said. "But why not give back the whole packet. Instead, he gave back the twenty dollars—he and Hull agree on that. He didn't *need* it, that's what he told Hull. No wonder. Three thousand dollars just dropped into his lap. But then he stuffed the map into his seat. Why would he bother?"

"Maybe not to trash up the floor? Maybe as proof of bribery, should the need arise?"

Maybe, maybe, maybe. Something, I felt, wasn't right. If only I could figure out what. Sherlock Holmes could.

<hr />

"This came for you, sir."

The carrot-haired desk clerk handed me a sealed telegram along with the iron room key. I was morally certain who had sent it. Who else fired off telegrams wherever I happened to be?

I carried it to the corner of the lobby of this new hotel. The faux marble pillars annoyed me. The sofa was stiffer than it looked. Damn this modern furniture, built for appearances. I gave up on finding an arse-comfortable spot and tore open the envelope.

I looked at the signature first. No surprise.

"THEODORE."

Then at the text of the wire: "COME BACK. CORTELYOU HAS AN IDEA."

Oh, crap. That's all I needed, Mr. Know-It-All's *idea* for my investigation. But it was also what I wanted: to come back. To go home. To see Clara.

The next train to New York left at seven forty-five. I had already checked. I was rushing toward the elevator, to pack my valise upstairs, when the desk clerk called, "This came for you, sir."

"Just now?"

"A little while ago, while I . . . stepped away. It was left on the counter here."

The envelope was smudged, and the cursive across the back resembled a child's.

John Hay.

I returned to the unwelcoming sofa and started to rip open the sealed envelope, until a feeling of . . . caution came over me. I had to be careful with this. It might be evidence—of what?

My request for a letter opener brought a snicker from the carrot-haired clerk. I carried the weapon back to my seat and needled its nose under the flap and pried it apart. Inside was a rough sheet of lined white paper, torn at one end. Pasted on were scraps of newspaper copy, from headlines and advertisements.

DEAR PRESIDENT Hay,
Who DIES *next*? YOU?
AN *admirer*

⊹══•══⊹

"I was having a hard time," the carrot-haired clerk explained with a smirk. "If you know what I mean."

Suddenly, I did. Oh, Lord. This was an alibi I was not inclined to try to disprove, which I supposed was the purpose.

We were jousting in the manager's office when Chief Nicholson rushed in. His face looked more drawn than usual. I showed him the note.

"I see," he said.

I wished I did.

If the note was meant to drive me from Pittsfield, it succeeded. Or so I kept commiserating with myself as the train rumbled out of the depot. *Coward, coward, coward,* in the quickening rhythm of the wheels. Was I? Nah, I was no coward. I had proved that to myself in the ring. Besides, I had every good reason to leave. For one thing, the Secret Service needed to see this note, slathered with fingerprints as it probably was. For another . . . Well, first and foremost, the president had ordered me to. So here I was, occupying an otherwise empty seat in the almost empty club car, with a scotch over a chunk of chipped ice that tickled my nose.

This left unanswered who sent the note—and why. The first question I delegated to Chief Nicholson and his men. The question of why, that was mine.

As for the answer, I had no damn idea.

Yet.

What *did* I know? I knew the scotch felt warm going down. I knew there had been a collision. I knew a man had been killed. I had known the man. I knew that another two inches and somebody—or somebodies—else might have shared Craig's fate. Two inches! And I might have been president. Did God have a hand in close calls?

A longer sip.

What else did I know? I knew that someone in Pittsfield knew who I was and why I was there. And wanted me gone. (And I'd left!) Someone had attacked me and then sent me a note. Why would he—I was assuming it was a *he,* and that it was the same *he*—send me a note? To scare me? He hadn't, though he might be thinking he had. Could Euclid Madden have sent it? I had just left his house; he would have been hard-pressed for time. But possible. Or he might have sent an accomplice—a child, perhaps.

What did I know about Madden? That he was a mild-mannered man who nursed grievances. (Didn't we all?) That a hunk of money had found its way into his bank account, details to come. That his streetcar had stopped at the top of Howard's Hill for nineteen minutes, to follow a schedule he had no need to keep. That he had rejected a bribe—or *incentive,* to be nice—but had stuffed a hand-drawn map under his seat. That his lawyer was bullying him to plead guilty to manslaughter, plausibly at the company's behest. That the men who controlled the streetcar company seemed to control everything worth controlling in Pittsfield, including the judiciary and possibly the police. Maybe that's who was behind this—all of it. A political machine protecting itself. Hardly unheard of. But why target the president—or the governor, for that matter? And why would they rely on a marsh-mallow like Euclid Madden?

To that last question, I proposed an answer: Because he was in a posi-tion to do what they wanted without being traced. They had only to pay him.

Implausible, I had to admit. But impossible? No. Some of the most astonishing events in history had been implausible until they occurred. Ask Jules Verne. One day, all of his tales will come true.

But what else did I *know*? Not much more. Enough with the sup-positions and the slipshod connections. I took a heartwarming sip of scotch and reached into my valise. The red and gold cover offered a tac-tile pleasure. So did the story of the detective who always knew, or who knew when he didn't know and knew how to figure it out. I was never too old to learn—one of my few saving graces.

I found my place in the story and read of Sherlock accompanying Dr. Watson to the station to send him out to Baskerville Hall alone. Watson's assignment was to report the facts as fully as he could, any-thing that might bear on the case, even indirectly. Then he would let Sherlock piece the facts into a theory.

I sighed. This was my job, too—Watson's and Sherlock's, both. Col-lect the facts first, then fashion a theory. The logical order of business. Ha! If only life were logical.

Conan Doyle's tale was rooted in an illogic, a horror, the Baskerville family curse. Hugo Baskerville, the evil seventeenth-century forebear, had ravished and murdered a maiden, until a huge and hellish black hound with dripping jaws tore his throat out. The mystery unspools with a note spelled out in letters scissored from the *Times* of London: "As you value your life or your reason keep away from the moor."

A note! A chill ascended the nape of my neck.

Still, I had to admire Conan Doyle's skill at creating a mood, and the easy-to-swallow implausibility of a plot that made even less sense than this mystery of mine. I marveled even more at Sherlock Holmes and his formidable powers of observation, the subtlety of his logic, the fierceness of his brain. These were not my strengths. I could be staring at a tub of lard and (as Clara enjoyed pointing out) see everything except the lard. I was reasonably confident that two plus two equals four and even that twenty-five squared was . . . I had to think . . . six hundred and a little more. But I could never match Sherlock in sheer brainpower. Nor did I share Vidocq's flair for disguises or his talent for infiltrating the forces of villainy.

So what in the hell *was* I good at? I don't mean as a husband or as a father or even as a secretary of state. My deficiencies in each of those roles are no secret, at least to me. Nor is the pain that they cause, the clench in my stomach when I make mistakes. Of which I have made more than my share. I'd like to think that comes from reaching so high, trying so hard, but I'm probably just excusing my shortcomings. Am I a perfectionist? Don't make me laugh. At times I stand astonished at how imperfect I am. Let me count the ways. (Oh no, allow me.) As the chief diplomat for a self-consciously virile nation, I've been clever but not as blustery—my stick isn't as big—as Theodore would like. As a husband . . . My faults—of the heart, not of the flesh—grind like wet, cold sand.

As a father . . . My throat clutched. It's so easy, being a father of girls. You tell them how pretty they are, which is even easier if you don't have to pretend, and you keep their heads from swelling unduly; you find them husbands, or they find husbands for themselves, and your duty is done. With a son, however, your job is to turn him from a boy into a man. This requires molding and the sort of interventions that any red-blooded boy would resist. Only later would he see the benefit, and surely Del did. He seemed to be happy at the end—he *seemed* to be— and Lord knows I hoped he was. Until then, I had never felt old.

But this was all beside the point, for the moment. I struggled to resume thinking of the matter at hand—this time, with a spurt of success. As a detective, what was my advantage? Surely I had one or two. My record of success was respectable. Granted, the denominator was small—Willie Lincoln and a smattering of other weird deaths over the decades—but the numerator was no smaller. I had solved them all.

I tried to focus on the mystery—mysteries—before me. Why on earth would Euclid Madden want to kill a president—or a governor? And had he actually tried? How could I read another man's mind? But that's exactly what I needed to do. And I was good at it, not incidentally.

Oh yes, *that* was my advantage. I was skilled at hearing what people *didn't* say and at understanding the minds and motivations of men— why they do things, why they don't. (Women were another story.) From time to time, I even understood myself.

CHAPTER SEVEN

A glorious morning, in my own bed, with my own dear wife in my own caressing arms, the muscle memory of lovemaking. Streams of sunlight and strong hot coffee in my favorite mug. I tried to imagine lying in bed next to Lizzie Cameron. She would talk too damn much, and in too arch a tone. Clara was quiet, unless she had something to say. That counted. In a world of deceit and turmoil, Clara Stone Hay was a haven. But havens can get taken for granted or, worse, feel constricting, even (or especially) after a child dies. Besides, was I seeking a haven or an adventure?

Both.

Haven't I learned by now that you can't have everything you want?

Apparently not.

I had always admired Lizzie from afar. How could I not? She was . . . magnetic. The Camerons had lived for years on Lafayette Square, and I could hardly avoid her as she ambled with a parasol or fed the squirrels in the park. But she was Henry's dream, not mine, and he was my friend—*is* my friend. Eventually Henry's dream dissolved, as dreams do, and still I kept her at a distance, for years. Her marriage of convenience to a dissolute politician (who owed his career to his tyrannical father's success) became her barricade of choice against her many suitors. Only a year ago or so did I begin to . . . compete. Halfheartedly, I must add. By which I mean wholeheartedly at some moments and noheartedly at others. She was prone to do the same, which left us both unbalanced. I suspected that neither of us wanted to succeed—or, perhaps, to stop.

Over breakfast, Clara explained why the lilies had prevailed over roses—a matter of informality, not of cost. I had been agnostic on the floral question but had rather enjoyed the Talmudic disputation and was sorry to see it end. Now, all that remained was the wedding itself.

"Do you think Henry will give Alice another small Rodin?" I said over the chipped beef and poached eggs. That had been his wedding gift to Helen last winter.

"How many could there be?" Clara said.

"As many as Henry can sculpt."

Clara laughed. "Do you think Theodore will come?"

"To New Hampshire? On a Tuesday? I doubt it. We'll have to invite him. He does love weddings."

"Funerals, too," Clara said. "Such is envy."

I had told her about my doings in Pittsfield—about the wrecked landau and the impervious streetcar, about the stoic carriage driver and the defiant motorman, about the map stuffed under the seat and the trolley's nineteen-minute delay atop Howard's Hill. I hadn't decided whether to mention the assault in Park Square. I saw no compelling reason to scare her. This was the question at hand: Was I her protector or her confidant—her intimate?

I decided incorrectly.

Clara's face went white. "You are too old for this, John."

"The hell I am!" My vehemence surprised me, though it shouldn't have. I didn't like being sixty-three, nor did I believe it, although my arithmetical skills were generally sound. Truth be told, sixty-three didn't feel all that different from fifty-three, or even from forty-three. Nor, I liked to believe, in the face I showed to the world. I was surprised, when I looked in the mirror, to see the fissures in my forehead. But I also saw the same young—well, youngish—countenance, the wry mouth, the mischievous hazel eyes. I counted on my snowy beard and lush mustache to hide everything else. That face in the looking glass was still mine.

⊹⊱━⊰⊹

Cortelyou leaned forward to shake my hand. "A pleasure, a pleasure," he said, as if we had never met.

I was tempted to introduce myself. Instead, I summarized for the president and his private secretary what I had learned in Pittsfield. "Two inches!" I held my thumb and forefinger apart. "Mr. President, that was your margin between life and death."

"Bully!" he exclaimed, his eyes alive. He seemed transported. To San Juan Hill? Or to his bodyguard under the trolley?

A window on the first-floor parlor of the temporary White House was open to the breezes from Lafayette Square. Surely the Secret Service men realized that a tall passerby could shoot a shotgun into the room.

When I recounted my encounter in Park Square, punching the man who had pulled a pistol, I left no detail untold. Theodore lit up again.

"I am proud of you, my boy!"

I blanched, not because I was older than him but because the last thing I would ever want to be was his son. He taught his children to swim by making them jump from a dock into the deep water.

I turned toward Cortelyou and said, "I understand you have an idea . . . for me."

"I do, I do," he replied.

Roosevelt beamed like a proud papa and clicked his teeth. I kept my grimace to myself. "I'm all ears," I said.

"The president was good enough to tell me of your theory that the collision in Pittsfield was not an accident."

"*My* theory?" I said.

"That the wretched motorman was . . . presumably behind this. The question, then, is who was behind the motorman."

"That had crossed my mind, yes. And you have a theory about that, I imagine."

"In fact, I do. Who would you say has the most to gain from the president's . . . premature departure from the presidency?"

"Besides myself, you mean," I said.

Roosevelt cackled. Cortelyou's face remained sober. It was an open secret in Washington that, once Congress got around to creating a Department of Commerce and Labor, Roosevelt would name Cortelyou as its first secretary. This would place him eighth—and last—in the line of presidential succession. "Yes, besides yourself," he said.

"The list is long, I would guess," I replied. 'You can measure a man's greatness by the enemies he makes." No one could have imposed a nobler gloss on Theodore's predilection for picking fights.

"I love mine enemies," Roosevelt said. "I glory in them. They bring me pride."

"I have a list," Cortelyou said. He plucked a paper from his breast pocket and flicked it with his finger. "At the top is Northern Securities."

In spite of myself, I saw the sense. The Northern Securities Trust Company was a proposed railroad monopoly from the Upper Midwest to the Pacific Northwest, to be formed by merging the railroads currently competing along parallel tracks. One of them was controlled by J. P. Morgan and James J. Hill, the other by E. H. Harriman and the Rockefellers—robber barons all. Industrial trusts had become the rage throughout the economy, investing the immense profits spewed by the war against Spain. The beef trust, the sugar trust, the steel trust, the wire trust, the lead trust, the borax trust, the leather trust, the flour trust, the Standard Oil trust, the cracker trust—the very word *trust* was a perversion of its plain meaning. In baseball, the upstart American League was swiping ballplayers from the hoary National League, and there was talk the two circuits might combine. Why couldn't railroads? Who would stand in their way?

Theodore would. He had ordered the attorney general to block the merger; the lawsuit was heading toward court.

"Is that the sort of thing they do?" I said. "Assassination?" After all these years, was I still naive?

"If it's necessary to get their way," Roosevelt replied, his face flushed with pleasure.

"By murdering *you*? And getting . . ."

The throaty cough in the doorway coiled the hair on my arms.

"Well, hello, Sister," the president said. "How long have you been listening?"

"Long enough," she replied. An ivory-colored silk gown with rose buttons to her neck covered Alice Roosevelt's lithe, languorous form.

"Long enough for what?" her father said.

"To tell you what to do."

"And that is?"

"Senator Hanna," Alice said.

"What about him?" Roosevelt said.

"For one thing, I should hope he ranks second—or possibly third, Mr. Hay, after yourself?—on Mr. Cortelyou's list of who would stand to benefit from Father's . . . departure. The good senator desires nothing more in this world than to be president. He lusts for it. You can smell it on his cheap frock coats. Ask *him*," Alice added, "about Northern Securities."

"Ask him what?" the president said.

"Why does he own stock?"

"In what?"

"In Northern Securities."

"How in God's creation do you know that?" Roosevelt said.

"It is something I happen to know," she replied, with a coy smile and a toss of her head. "Father, you are not the only member of this family who knows it all."

I, for one, did not doubt it.

+⟩═⟨═⟨+

The Treasury Department building, on the opposite side of the White House from the State, War, and Navy Building, was grandiose, but in a different way. *Stolid* was the best you could say of its imposing, pillared, Greek-aspiring bulk. More accurate was *boring*. Which, arguably, a treasury department ought to be.

I used the entrance that faced the White House. This was the direct route, so I would run into fewer people who might want a minute of my time. I climbed the semicircular staircase. I liked this building. Other than the electric chandeliers and the elevators stuffed into the stairwells, nothing had changed inside since Lincoln's day. The corridors went on forever, and the tiles in black and white diamond could give you double vision. But I found it comforting—familiar, anyway. I liked things that didn't change. I knew what they were.

John Wilkie's office was on the third floor. It was a small, cocoonish,

cantilevered room with low windows on three sides and a marble fireplace in the angled corner. Behind the desk sat the forty-two-year-old
Secret Service chief, the youngest in history. He leaned back in his
revolving chair and put a fresh match to his meerschaum pipe. Clouds
of smoke sparkled in the sunlight.

I took his coatless informality as a compliment. His pince-nez, his
center-parted hair, his mustache curled to points, and his dandyish dress
did not distinguish him from young men in every barbershop across
America. But two things did. One was the depth of his gaze—not
piercing, in the manner of a policeman on the prowl, but penetrating in
a leisurely way, like a wide-eyed child's. The other distinction was his
demeanor—patient, controlled, almost serene, like neither the newspaperman he had been nor the sleuth he was now. I had known his daddy,
a Civil War correspondent for *The New York Times*. The younger Wilkie
had been a crime reporter and then the city editor of the *Chicago Daily
Tribune* before he became the unconventional choice of the very conventional Treasury secretary, a fellow Chicagoan, Lyman Gage.

But the match of man to job had succeeded. And why not? Both a
newspaperman and a detective tried to get to the bottom of things, to
ferret out the truth, to add two and two together and conjure up four, or
maybe four and a half. Wilkie had been brilliant in rounding up counterfeiters, the Secret Service's main chore (and also in making sure the
public learned of his triumphs). Since the tragedy in Buffalo, the agency
had taken on the responsibility of protecting a gregarious president who
resisted having a nanny. It had just lost an agent while doing so.

In a fog of a sweet-smelling smoke, Wilkie finished telling me about
Agent Craig's funeral in Chicago, which he had attended in Theodore's
place. "The president sent flowers," Wilkie said. "Purple and white asters, hydrangeas, and I don't know what all."

I could think of nothing to say, so I sipped my coffee.

"It was a year to the day since President McKinley was shot," Wilkie
said. "One of the pallbearers was the agent who tackled Czolgosz after
he fired."

Again, I kept silent. Losing a president was as sad as losing your father.
How many could you stand to lose in a lifetime?

"Do you have it with you?" Wilkie said.

I had wired ahead. "I don't go anywhere without it," I replied.

Wilkie's laugh was easy and warm. He leaned across his spotless desk, his sinewy forearms flexed in anticipation.

I had wrapped a folio beneath the cardboard that held the map. I explained that the motorman had denied looking inside at the map, and I asked how certain a match of fingerprints might be.

"Better than Bertillon, that I can tell you. You can make a mistake with calipers but not—if you're careful enough—with the loops and arches and whorls. And our men are careful."

"No one is careful all the time," I said.

"They'd better be." Which did not mean they were. "And, frankly, it takes less skill to read a fingerprint correctly."

"Are they good enough to use in court?"

"Soon enough." In other words, no. "I will send this to the lab."

"And this." I handed him the note fashioned from newspaper scraps.

He read it and said, "Congratulations, Mr. Secretary. A genuine death threat. Your first?"

"Yes, thank you. And frightfully overdue, I must say. A measure, perhaps, of my lack of—what?—provocation."

"Ah, I lost my virginity a few years ago, from a gang of counterfeiters we caught in Wichita. Beady-eyed promises they made. None of them, as you can see, kept." He added, before I could, "Yet."

Wilkie examined the note, which he balanced on his delicate fingertips like a waiter's at Delmonico's. "We should be able to identify the fonts," he said.

"I've matched a couple of them, from *The Berkshire Eagle*." I had brought copies of the local newspapers with me. "Though I'm not sure what that tells us, except that whoever sent it lives in Pittsfield or nearby. Which narrows it down to twenty-some thousand people."

"Only the ones who can read," Wilkie said.

<hr>

"It's a derringer." I pulled the silver-plated, rosewood-handled pistol from my waistcoat pocket and showed Alvey Adee. "A twenty-two caliber, American Arms Company double-barreled derringer, to be precise. Wilkie forced it on me."

"Cute," Adee chuckled. "I fear for the fawns. Bullets, too?"

"Oh yes, he trusted me that far. I must warn you, Adee, don't get me mad. You can never tell what's in the heart of a man." I was at least half joking.

"And a holster?"

"No sir, a cowboy I shall be. Like the president." Except that I *was* a westerner (an Illinoisan, anyway), born and bred at the edge of the frontier. "So, what's on the boil here?"

Adee was carrying his folders of he-must-sees and if-there's-times. "The usual annoyances," he said. "Yet another ultimatum from the kaiser about the Venezuelan debt—the man doesn't know when to quit. An angry letter from Colombia's senate president about the canal."

"That damn canal." Dickering with Colombians for rights to dig across the Panama isthmus, which they owned—America wasn't the hemisphere's only imperialist power—was like grappling with a squid.

"A request from Morocco for the use of a warship. That's Abdelaziz, our favorite sultan."

"Why isn't he asking Root?" As the war secretary, Elihu Root dispatched the warships.

"He doesn't like Root."

"So? Nobody does."

"It's you the sultan loves."

"I am blessed. I will need to talk with Root and the president. What does he want it for, and for how long?"

"To scare the pirates, as I understand it. The saber of big, bad imperial America. His letter and my typewritten transcriptions—well, Margaret's, with my annotations—I'll leave them with you."

"I can't thank you enough. Anything else?"

"The Mormon missionaries ousted from Prussia."

"Can't say I blame Prussia."

"Even so."

"Yes, even so. Draft a letter to the foreign minister. Freedom of religion. American citizens. Et cetera, et cetera."

"And Italy's new restrictions on importing American bacon and lard."

I covered my face with my hands. "Another letter."

"And here's another draft of the letter on Roumanian Jews. I . . ." Adee paused and peered at the ceiling.

"If you have something to say, say it."

"This is none of our business, you know. We had nothing to do with that treaty." The Berlin treaty of 1878, ending the Russo-Turkish War and creating the Balkan states, was the European powers' handiwork. "There is a bloody good argument for staying out of it."

"I understand that. I do. But we shall make it our business. We are the big chaps on the block now, Adee. I'm not sure I like it, but reality is not to be trifled with. And what is the good of being a world power if you can't have a little fun from time to time? What is the point of power other than to use it? I must say, there is something satisfying, if a little quaint, about doing what's right."

I listened to my own last words and quivered inside. I tried to block Lizzie out of my mind, with my usual lack of success.

⊹

"No shortage of suspects, I should think," Henry Adams said. He looked shriveled, like a gnome; his energy was cerebral. "Everyone loathes our dear president."

"I don't," I said.

"You just won't admit it, old boy."

"You're incorrigible, Henry."

"One of my finer traits."

Ladies twirled their parasols in the late afternoon sun, while their servants trailed a step behind, juggling packages. Barouches clattered past. Connecticut avenue was the closest that Washington came to Paris—not quite a near miss, but a respectable attempt. The wide boulevard was newly paved with asphalt, sticky in the summer, slippery when wet, dusty when dry. It boasted the city's smartest shops, the chic restaurants, the fashionable apartment houses. I was planning to build one of the latter myself, right where we were standing, on the southeastern corner of Connecticut and L.

"Those," I said, pointing to the low row houses along L street. "They'll be gone. We're going eight stories high, two hundred feet along L, a hundred sixty-four along Connecticut, almost to K. One of the biggest in the city. Curved cornices, balconies, the finest limestone, first-rate construction."

That I felt the need to boast was telling. It came from embarrassment—I understood myself enough to know *that*. No reason for it, I guess. Getting rich quickly and undeservedly, wasn't that the American dream? The Klondike Gold Rush and all of that.

We strolled north along Connecticut avenue. Buildings were going up everywhere. Merely looking at the construction felt exhausting. Henry had stopped paying attention. He was saying, "Too many people would want him . . . out of the way."

"Want who out of the way?" I said.

"*Him.* The list of possible suspects, I would imagine, is endless. Besides you and his great rival Hanna and the anarchists and the socialists and a few million Filipinos. Any self-respecting southerner, for example, should hate him for dining at the White House with Booker T. Not even Lincoln broke bread with Frederick Douglass—or did he?"

"I wish he had. McClellan might have defeated him in 'sixty-four and he'd have lived."

"And the southerners are just the beginning. The generals aren't so fond of him, either. He's certain he knows more than they do about war—and maybe he does. Nor does his own party adore him. The Wall street Republicans and the chamber of commerce patriots are stuck with a man who frightens them, and for good reason. Not to mention the anti-imperialists and the railroads and the coal owners. Oh yes, and the consumers of anthracite, too. Everyone has a reason to hate this man. Not to mention the people who actually know him."

"Henry, Henry, last time you said that whatever happened was his fault. Now it's everyone else's."

"And the trusts—God knows *they* hate him, though he claims not to hate them. These are the men his beloved daddy begged for donations to the charities he took credit for."

"Henry, now you're just being vicious."

"Another of my virtues. What is vicious is pulling a gun on my dearest friend." (*How news spreads!* I thought.) "My point is, how many sworn enemies can a president earn in less than a year? Our beloved

Theodore outpaces even your beloved Lincoln. There's no end of possible suspects. Assuming that anyone was to blame in the first place."

"Which I still *don't* assume. As dear departed Nicolay used to—"

"Yes, I know. Never assume."

Henry had a certain scorn for anyone else's epigrams. As a scholar, however—as a judge of information—he was rigorous and fearless and obsessively fair.

This gave me an idea.

<hr/>

"Did you ever consider becoming a lawyer?" I said, pouring the tea, spilling a little from too showy a height.

"Did *you?*" Henry replied.

I had to laugh. "The requirement of moral character is what stood in my way. Politics has no such barrier."

"Nor does Harvard." Where Henry had taught.

Clara listened with a faint air of amusement, as if she were watching a vaudeville skit with timeworn jokes.

"But did you?" I persisted. "Ever want to be a lawyer, I mean? Because now is your opportunity."

"For a moment or two, once. The majesty of the law has too much structure for my tastes. I wouldn't say you've taken to it yourself, dear boy."

"For a moment or two, once. Then Lincoln came calling—well, Nicolay. And for me, that was the end of the law. So I went into politics and then diplomacy and then journalism and then business and a bit of writing and then back to diplomacy and, voilà, here I be. Which is probably just as well. The law is built on logic. Diplomacy is built on illogic—like people are, or nations. More in line with my talents, such as they are. The reason I ask about the law is that I think *you* would be good at it."

"Is that a compliment?" Henry said.

"Actually, more of a tactic." I enjoyed his puzzlement. "Of persuasion. To get you to do what I want."

"Don't I always, old boy?"

"Often enough. I am hoping to snatch you away from your beloved twelfth century to spend a day or two or three in the twentieth. Could you withstand the shock?"

"I don't know," he said gravely. I could not tell for sure if he was kidding, but I suspected he wasn't. "All right," he said at last. "I am listening."

I had drilled down to the seriousness beneath Henry's cynical pose. I explained, in confidence, about Cortelyou's hunch that Northern Securities wanted Roosevelt *gone*—such a nicer word than *dead* or *murdered*—and that a run-on sentence or a crumpled letter in the boxfuls of documents amassed for trial might betray the trust's intentions. I needed an inquisitive—and, dare I say, lawyerly—mind to pore through it all. The trial was to take place in Saint Louis, but in the meantime the evidence was stored in the bowels of the Justice Department, on Pennsylvania avenue at Seventeenth street.

Henry's head tilted back, until his hairline disappeared. He was interested. "First thing in the morning," he said.

I consulted my watch. It was twelve minutes before five. "Gulp down your tea," I replied.

━━━◆━━━

A machine behind the seats hiccupped and growled and a shaky image shimmered across the screen. It was thrilling to watch the coronation ceremony of King Edward VII, in all of its pomp and glory. Naturally, it wasn't the actual event (no monarch would allow a cumbersome motion picture camera to intrude) but a reenactment, in what looked like Westminster Abbey. Who needed color or sound? Even so, it was amazing. A theater devoted entirely to moving pictures had opened recently in Los Angeles, the nation's thirty-sixth most populous city. Washington, two and a half times as big, had its Halls of the Ancients.

This palace of entertainment, on New York avenue between Thirteenth and Fourteenth streets, had just reopened under new management. The Armat Motion Picture Company had kept the "halls" of reproduced antiquities—the columns of Karnak, the Assyrian throne room, the Theban gate. But now, past the Roman atrium and before the Moorish palace, a new lecture hall had thirteen rows of seats for a cinematograph exhibition that ran five times a day.

For the eight thirty show, Clara and I sat in the front row, where no ostrich-plumed hat could block the screen.

"Look, look," Clara burbled, as the archbishop of Canterbury, or someone in his garb, tottered toward the throne. She had relished my sixteen months as ambassador to the Court of Saint James's, with all of the wigs-and-ermine silliness. "He's going to trip," she said.

"We'd have heard," I whispered back.

Queen Victoria's forever-patient eldest son (or his doppelgänger) was on bended knee on August 9, while the archbishop tapped with a sword and lowered the crown. Thus the age of Victoria ended and the new century truly began.

This took four minutes, tops, before the screen went black.

We stirred in our seats. "These moving pictures, or whatever you call them, might catch on," I suggested—rather boldly, I thought.

I turned and surveyed our fellow adventurers into the future. Women favored gowns of taffeta or velvet, often with evening cloaks of brocaded satin. Their hats were laden with lace, ribbons, flowers, fruit, and deceased birds. (I swore I saw a robin's egg nestled in straw.) The men wore black. Everyone was dressed as for a ballet, not that Washington had any such ornament.

"Mr. Secretary!"

My breath caught, just hearing the seductive alto I knew too well. It issued from the sixth or seventh row, near the center.

"Mrs. Cameron," I called back, as nonchalantly as I could, across the too-attentive crowd.

"Wait!" she said. It was more than a request.

Lizzie pushed past the overfed doyennes entrapped by the plump-is-pretty ideals of the past. Lizzie was not plump and, strictly speaking, she was not pretty; her chin was thin, her nose too long, her mouth too squat, her face top-heavy. But she was stunning. In part it was because of her figure—a corseted hourglass, a sensation of the new Gibson Girl style. But more than that, it was because of her bearing. *Regal* was trite. But what else do you call a woman whose lustrous brown hair was piled high like a temple of an Eastern religion, whose neck was long and elegant, whose sparkle captured your attention, whose slate-blue eyes grabbed yours and let them go if and when they wished. Lizzie *was* beautiful—and, oh Lord, did she know it. She accepted the attentions of men as natural and inexhaustible—her due—and useful besides. Who was to say she was wrong?

To-night she was sublime in a lime-shaded dress that sheathed her slender figure without mercy. I dreaded the conversation to come.

"Hello, Mrs. Hay," Lizzie said sweetly, once she had bullied her way to the aisle. "It is always a pleasure to see you."

"And for me as well, Mrs. Cameron," Clara said. Did I mistake it, or had Clara stressed the *Mrs.*? "We miss you on the Square."

"I miss living there, I must say. There is no place lovelier in the spring, or the autumn."

"Where are you now?" Clara said.

My question exactly.

"At the Willard, for most of the month. My husband is at his . . . our farm, up near Harrisburg." Donald Cameron, the former senator from Pennsylvania, was a quarter century her elder, and a lush. "Can you imagine me milking a cow?"

"You must stop by and see us," Clara said.

"Yes, you must," I echoed.

"Nothing would please me more," Lizzie said.

I could think of nothing that would please me less.

CHAPTER EIGHT

O*ld* is a state of mind."

"That's hogwash, and you know it," I replied, although my noun was stronger.

The masseur laughed. "I know nothing of the kind," he said. Ewell Lindgren, big and blond, was a Norwegian who lived a block to the east, along H street. On most mornings he jostled my muscles and tendons awake; the constrictions of Pittsfield needed some kneading. "And with all due respect, Mr. Hay, I know more older people, more . . . intimately, than you do. Your body is not old. Nor is your mind."

"My mind is a mess, and why do I ache all the time?" If your masseur can't command your honesty, who can? "You are . . . what . . . thirty-four?"

"Thirty-five."

"You know nothing." The heel of a palm pressed into my hamstring and I grunted.

"Say that again," he panted, and I did. He pressed harder into my leg, until I squawked.

"Be careful," I managed. "I feel a poem coming on."

The edges of his hands chopped at my unresisting back, further breaching the boundary between relaxation and pain.

+≡+

"So why *do* you do these things?" Clara liked to get to the point. (Diplomats prefer to digress.) I swallowed another spoonful of blueberries and cream. We sat in a sunny spot in the kitchen.

"I don't know," I said. "Each time, I've been drafted. First by Lincoln, in Willie's death. Now by Theodore. By all of them. You tell *me* why."

"Because you seem to figure it out in the end." Clara smiled over her teacup.

"So far," I said. "This time, I'm still not sure there's an *it* to figure out."

"Oh?"

"Theodore certainly thinks so. And this motorman does have some . . . peculiarities, shall we say."

"Such as?" Clara said, always interested in human foibles she can find a way to excuse. She saw the best in people, even in me.

I sighed. "He is an odd mammal. A timid man, but they can be the nastiest. A bit of an agitator, says his boss. About hours and wages—the usual."

"Not unreasonable."

"Agreed." I told her of the motorman's three thousand-plus unexplained dollars and the unresolved question of the trolley's speed. "Beside that map that one of the streetcar company's directors . . ." I exhaled. "Never mind. I'm tired of this. Tell me what is happening here."

"Nothing."

"With the wedding?"

"Happily, nothing. Alice is sunny as always. The RSVPs—a lot of noes. The distance, you know."

"Perfect," I said.

I couldn't help but think about who wouldn't be there. He had fallen three stories to his death. In New Haven for his Yale reunion, Del was lounging in the window of his hotel room at two thirty in the morning. A half-smoked cigarette was found on the sill. There was no question of ill intent, by himself or by anyone else. It wasn't his fault. And it wasn't mine. That much I knew—really I did. But it made no difference in how I felt.

"Is Theodore coming, do you know?" Clara mercifully broke in. "People might change their minds if he does."

"I doubt it. That limp of his isn't getting any better. He'll probably decide the day before."

"It's always such a circus when he's around."

"But entertaining, you've got to admit. He's always interesting, even when he won't shut up. He's made entertaining the voters a legitimate function of democratic government. Why do you think he invites the reporters in at one o'clock every afternoon to watch him get shaved? His personality is bigger than he is; you can't avert your eyes. A new kind of president for a new century."

"But I want an old-fashioned wedding," Clara said. "Let him do whatever he likes with *his* Alice, whenever the poor groom is trapped and bound. But not with our Alice, thank you very much."

I couldn't disagree. (Nor would I dare.)

⊢━━⊣

How convenient life in Washington could be, if you were lucky enough to live a block from your office and around the corner from your morning rounds. Lafayette Park was quiet but for the scampering of squirrels. (An animal fancier from Virginia had recently let loose nearly a hundred of them.) My footsteps scraped in the gravel. The magnolias' succulent leaves, which I so admired, were edged in brown. The air was brisk.

Congress was out of session, so the republic was safe. It also meant Mark Hanna would be at home, lingering over breakfast, such as he had shared with McKinley when 21 Madison place was known as the Little White House. The door knocker was shaped like a lion's rump— landlady Lizzie's sense of humor, no doubt—and I allowed it a certain respect. It fell heavily. The door opened right away, as if someone was waiting.

That someone was Elmer Dover. I had met him too many times. He was a large and obnoxiously cheerful young man, not quite thirty years old, with broad shoulders and a clean-shaven, jowly, blandly handsome face. There was never a cloud in his liquid brown eyes or an unkind word on his lips. Elmer Dover accomplished his evils without a grimace and behind your back (and behind mine, in 'ninety-six, when one of my donations to McKinley's presidential campaign went . . . astray). Officially, he was the clerk of the Senate's Relations with Canada Committee, which Hanna had served until recently as chairman. In practice, he was Hanna's private secretary, his henchman, the man who heard the senator's wishes and fulfilled them, who made the senator's political problems go away, without always explaining how.

"It is such a pleasure to see you at this pleasant time of the morning," Dover said.

"The same," I replied. "Is the master here?"

"At breakfast," Dover said, "if you would care to—"

I accepted.

The breakfast room, on the first floor, faced a walled garden that was overwhelmed by the six-story hulk of the opera house. It was a woman's room, with flowered curtains and late-season daisies in delicate vases of a vaguely Oriental design. The junior (by a single day) senator from Ohio sat at the table, struggling with a soft-boiled egg. The puckered brow on his porcine face suggested that the egg was winning. Hanna's huge, dark eyes look sadder than usual. His black silk bathrobe, loosely tied, showed a trapezoid of hairy belly. I suspected the Chinese letters embroidered in gold spelled out, depending on inflection, "Almighty Dollar" or "Besotted Plutocrat." Thomas Nast would have adored the man.

I didn't. Nor did I despise him, as Roosevelt did. But then, I didn't have as much cause. He hadn't called *me* a damn cowboy and a madman one life away from the presidency (though, under present circumstances, I was arguably the latter). We had a lot of history, Hanna and I, not all of it unpleasant, and more in common than I cared to admit. One was our debt to the dear departed McKinley. Another was the industrial city of Cleveland. It was Hanna's hometown and also Clara's. Hanna had co-owned, with Clara's father, the *Cleveland Daily Herald*, until it failed. Besides his coal and iron ore mines, his steel-hulled ships and streetcar lines, Hanna owned the Euclid Avenue Opera House, on the street where Clara and I had lived for a half decade while I was managing my father-in-law's business interests.

"You are looking well, Senator," I said. In Washington, flattery never hurt, and usually helped—the wilder, the more beloved.

"You are as blind as a hog in a tornado, Hay."

"On my better days, Senator."

I sat across the small table, so as not to see his midsection. Elmer Dover pulled up a chair at the end. I had hoped to keep him away.

"And what can I do for you, Mr. Secretary?" Hanna said. "Breakfast?"

I glanced at the massacred egg and the corned beef hash. "No, thank you," I said. What I wanted was information, but not the sort that was simple to collect, especially because I didn't know what it was (often a drawback). Asking directly about the collision seemed like a stupid idea. I was interested in Northern Securities, on the slim chance the railroad monopoly wanted Theodore dead. Not slim that they *wanted* him dead, but that they would try to make it happen. The more I thought about it—and yes, it was a little late—the more I regretted taking Alice Roosevelt's tidbit seriously. At the tender (*ha!*) age of eighteen, she was already an accomplished poseur. If she hadn't made up this provocative fact, she had no idea what it meant.

Nor did I. Which was why I was here.

"I am interested in Northern Securities," I said.

"We all are," Hanna replied. "What about 'em?"

"Do you think they will succeed?"

"If your damn president . . ." Hanna ripped a cinnamon roll in half and shoved a hunk of it into his mouth, so I guessed he finished by saying, "Will let 'em."

"How far do you suppose they would go in making sure of it?"

This gave him time to swallow, raisins and all. "I don't know what you mean," he said at last.

"Yes you do." An outrageous accusation seemed my best play.

His melancholy brown eyes narrowed, and they slithered toward Dover, who shook his head.

"I'm sorry, I don't," Hanna said. "It has been a privilege to see you this morning, Mr. Secretary."

"The pleasure is mine," I said. "Before I leave this good company, may I ask if you happen to own stock in Northern Securities?"

Hanna stiffened, and his jowls seemed to swell. "And what business is it of yours, may I ask? Or of the president's?"

I had no good answer for that. Only that the railroad scandals of President Grant's day had shown the dangers of mixing politics—or politicians—with business, especially the business of railroads, and that the public had a right to know it. An argument that would cause him to scoff. He was Wall street's man in the Senate; he recognized no boundary between business's interests and the government's. An alternative was to ask him to trust me—and be laughed *at*. Or . . . I figured Hanna might respond to bluntness. "The president thinks that Northern Securities might want him dead. It's . . . possible they've already tried."

"Of course they didn't," Hanna said. He stabbed at the hash with his fork. His long, slender fingers did not belong to his burly physique.

"You know that for sure?" I said. "It makes sense that they might. In their shoes, *I* might."

This gave him pause, as I'd hoped. "I have no reason to think that they do," Hanna said. He glanced over to Elmer Dover, as if to say, *Do they?*

Another imperceptible shake of the head.

"And what if they did?" Hanna said.

That gave *me* pause. "It would be . . ." I wanted to say *criminal* but feared that would end the conversation, such as it was. "Worrisome," I said.

Elmer Dover started to say something but thought better of it, lowering his coffee cup to the table so violently I thought it might shatter. I knew better than to open my mouth. At last, Dover said, "You say they've already tried?"

"A possibility," I said. "I'm not authorized to say anything more, I'm afraid."

Hanna said, "I wish I . . . we could help you."

"Maybe you could," I replied. "Who takes care of their business in the capital, do you know?"

Hanna shrugged. Elmer Dover sat still.

I had mishandled that one.

I diverted the conversation onto a safer topic, Canada's tariffs on iron ore, a matter close to Hanna's heart (assuming he had one). The Ohio magnate buttered his rolls and rattled on about the greedy Canadians who deserved nothing less than annexation. "It would be good for them, and for us as well." The issue had been simmering for decades, driven by American farmers and industrialists in search of fresh markets. I was careful not to nod to such nonsense—I was still the secretary of state—but listened with a pretense of respect. Why give him any more reason to fight Theodore for the nomination, two years hence?

Hanna's joy in discussing dollars and cents faded and he lit a Havana, probably not his first of the day. My stomach roiled from hunger; the cigar smoke did not help.

I rose unsteadily to my feet, then tried one last time. "So please tell me, Senator, do you own stock in Northern Securities?"

Hanna glared. "I don't need to answer that."

"No, you don't," I said. "But you just did."

Elmer Dover saw me to the door—to make sure I left, no doubt. "You look tired," he said. I hate when people tell me that; it makes me feel tired. "When did you get back?"

"Late last night," I said. "I'll catch up."

I don't trust cheerful people. I figure they're hiding something, probably from themselves.

+≡≡+

The tone in Adee's latest handwritten draft on Roumanian Jews seemed right at last—factual more than sentimental, ingratiating without being obsequious;.

The United States welcomes now, as it has welcomed from the foundation of its government, the voluntary immigration of all aliens coming hither under conditions fitting them to become merged in the body politic of this land . . .

It described the plight of Roumanian Jews, treated as aliens in the place they were born, forbidden to own land in the countryside or to work on farms, banned from the learned professions and from many trades, excluded from secondary schools, delivered into beggary, forced to flee the only home they had known—not only to European countries, whose governments had created Roumania, but to America. This gave Washington the standing to intrude on another nation's affairs.

The argument was a little tenuous, I admit, but it wasn't stupid. Would it convince the European powers that had created that mess of a country in the first place? I knew the odds were long. But first I had to convince Theodore.

Soon, however, I found I was reading the same sentences three or four times while thinking about the blob of treachery who called himself Mark Hanna. Didn't Theodore, that damned cowboy, stand in the way of Hanna's route to the White House? Nobody had a stronger motive to murder President Roosevelt—other than myself, of course. But I was satisfied that *I* was innocent.

A knock at the door brought Margaret Hanna, bearing a message. Her smile suggested she knew something I didn't. I tried to smile the same smile back, with less success. I considered asking her if her unrelated namesake might be capable of murder, but thought better of it.

The note was a summons from John Wilkie. I left at once.

I passed the White House, unoccupied for months now. From the outside, no scaffolding was visible; all the chaos was inside. Beyond the stone foundations for a new East Wing, I entered the Treasury Building and climbed the semicircular steps to the third floor. A prim-looking man in a worn frock coat scurried across my path, hugging folders of documents he would guard with his life. The Secret Service chief waved me in. He, too, smiled as if he knew something I did not. Unlike Margaret, however, he intended to tell me.

Through the haze of pipe smoke, Wilkie's eyes were alert, like a bird's. His desktop shone. "How's the derringer?" he said.

I had almost forgotten it. I patted my waistcoat pocket. "Unfired," I replied.

"May you keep it that way." Wilkie gestured at the scrawled map of Howard's Hill in Pittsfield that lay open at the center of his desk. "My men worked through the night," he said with pride.

"And?"

"They found your fingerprints, which you thoughtfully provided on your coffee cup yesterday."

A little unnerving.

"On the outside *and* the inside of the map," Wilkie went on. "And Madden's, too. You did a nice job, incidentally, of capturing his fingerprints on the cardboard. They were clear. No question they matched."

"On the inside, too—on the map itself? He told me he never opened it."

"Oh, they were there, all right. Not *they*, exactly. One fingerprint, but a clear one, of his right index finger. In an interesting spot." Wilkie raised his own right index finger like a man of the cloth citing the Prophets. Then it arced toward hell. "Directly over the site of the collision."

The motorman *had* lied. "And nowhere else on the inside?"

"Only there. And only one set of prints on the outside—his thumb on one side and his fingers on the other. He was holding it like a book."

"Consistent with pulling out a twenty-dollar bill and handing it back?"

Wilkie thought a moment. "I would say so."

"And consistent with stuffing it into his seat?"

Wilkie took in a mouthful of smoke and loosed it upon the world. I realized the slowdown was the point of a pipe. "Possibly," he said.

"Or possibly not?"

Another puff. "Or possibly not."

Wilkie's men had found other fingerprints, too. He presumed that one set belonged to James Hull, the company director who had sketched the map and had offered the twenty-dollar bribe (no other word fit).

"And another set," Wilkie said, "which took us a while to match. But we did. Around six o'clock this morning, one of my smartest men had a hunch and tested the letter you gave us that authorized us to take possession."

"You mean *my* fingerprints."

"No. Someone else's."

I was puzzled for a moment about what he meant. Then I remembered.

"Chief Nicholson!" I said. "Inside the map?"

"Inside and out."

+━━+

Odd.

The White House was in a haze. Pennsylvania avenue and its traffic and its pedestrians had faded from view. I kept walking to my office as I contemplated the oddity: Chief Nicholson had never handled the map, not while it was in my keeping. I had made sure of that, in order to leave the motorman's fingerprints unsmudged. But when else might he have touched it? The explanation must be simple—I just wasn't seeing it. Had I forgotten?

I probably insulted a civil servant or two by brushing past as I scuttled up the marble stairs to my office.

The telephone operator connected me to Pittsfield immediately. Chief Nicholson was at his desk. My lucky day.

"What?" the police chief shouted. I was grateful for the scratchy line; it gave me a chance to rephrase my question.

"The fingerprints—*your* fingerprints," I shouted back. I held the tubular receiver aloft, cradling it like a pipeline to God. "Why are they on that map?"

"They are?" he said.

"Yes."

Silence but for the crackle of invention. I waited. I doubted he was calculating how much this telephone call was costing . . . *me*. Then he growled, "I know they are."

Why was I not surprised? Of course he knew. "Oh?" I said.

"Because I put it there—put it back there."

"What do you mean, 'put it *back* there'?"

"I found the map under the seat and examined it and put it back there." A pause. "For you to find."

"*What?*"

"You heard me."

"I couldn't have. Why would you want to do that?"

"Not to disturb a crime scene. So you could see it as it was."

"But you disturbed it."

"I had every right to. May I remind you that I am the police chief here. And besides, I restored the crime scene. What difference does it make?"

Must I explain the sanctity of evidence to a police chief? And did I believe his far-fetched story? I trusted the man, but what did I really know about him? Only what he wanted me to know. He had seemed candid enough, strikingly so, willing to tell a stranger (me) about the

THE ATTEMPTED MURDER OF TEDDY ROOSEVELT 125

flaws of a political machine to which he was beholden. Maybe he was merely a truth teller, guileless—a guileless police chief?—and therefore unlikely to succeed. Or maybe he was too clever by half, and therefore unlikely to succeed. I'd thought I understood him, at least a little, but maybe it was just that I liked him. A risky confusion for a diplomat. For a detective, too.

I was barely listening as Chief Nicholson reported on his interview with the motorman's previous employer, Taconic Mills, which had fired him for distributing leaflets extolling the dignity of labor. Was that illegal? Suspicious, perhaps. Also understandable (though please don't tell anyone I uttered such a heresy; I'm a good Republican, among the best). He had also quizzed the two New York cops overheard in the Hotel Wendell lobby. They had been "just gabbing."

My attention revived as Chief Nicholson described what he had learned at Madden's bank. The three thousand–odd dollars looked legitimate, a windfall from the estate of a recently deceased, childless uncle in Pennsylvania, produced by selling anthracite coal stocks, divvied up five ways. Anthracite! Surely a coincidence. In any event, was that a motive to murder a president?

"You've never searched Madden's house?" I said.

"We tried, but Mr. Turtle blocked it in court. By way of the regular judge."

The streetcar company's president, that is. "So what do *you* think?" I said.

"About what?"

"About Mr. Madden's . . . role in this." Why not just say it? "About his guilt."

Chief Nicholson's sigh overtook the static. "I wish I knew the answer to that. But I will tell you what I testified at the inquest this morning. From everything I've been told and my men have learned, I think . . . I do think . . . the trolley could have stopped."

"But was it on purpose, do you think?"

A longish pause. "I cannot see inside a man's mind," Chief Nicholson said.

That was my job, I guess. "Then they will plead guilty, I take it—Mr. Madden *and* Mr. Kelly."

"That is my current understanding. The court date has been put off for another two weeks, at the defendants' request. You may get a chance to make inquiries before I do."

"How's that?"

"Their esteemed lawyer is on his way to your fair city, even as we speak. Scheduled to arrive to-night, a little past eleven."

I imagined the great and grand Mr. Turtle waddling into Washington. "For what purpose, would you happen to know?"

"No, Mr. Secretary," Chief Nicholson said. "Why don't you ask him?"

✦

"Just what this blessed nation needs, old boy!" Henry Adams exclaimed. "A few million more Israel Cohens!"

"Henry!" How much of what Henry said he actually meant and how much was for show or for shock I could never decide for sure. (I am not sure he could, either.) I had mentioned, mainly for the sake of conversation—and yes, to draw a reaction—the missive to European capitals on the Roumanian Jews. "Anyway, more would be staying in Europe than coming here."

"Have you *been* to the Lower East Side?" Henry said.

"Yes. Have you?"

"I've seen pictures."

I reminded him of my foray into the squalid Jewish ghetto in Vienna as a chargé d'affaires decades ago, and the empathy I'd felt ever since. It only deepened his scorn.

"Henry, do you have any feeling for anyone besides yourself?"

"Of course I do. For you, dear heart."

"Allow me to decline the honor," I said.

"As everyone does, my nieces excepted."

This conversation was making me sad. This afternoon's stroll had taken us south along Seventeenth street to the Potomac banks, into the past. I could pretend that B street was still a canal and an open sewer, as when I'd first arrived, forty-one short years ago. The Washington Monument was then a third of its present height and its grounds a swamp, not terra firma. The river was still untamed—the whitecapped moat that had kept the Confederacy (mostly) at bay. I was pretty sure I smelled sewage, although it might have been my memory playing tricks. The ground was spongy; the marshy shoreline sucked at my boots. Henry refused to risk his shoeshine, so we turned back.

"Find anything?" I said, as casually as I could, reluctant to ask a scholar for his conclusions after a single day of perusing a railroad trust's effluence of paper.

"No end of *forthwith*s and *pursuant*s and *parties of the first part*s. Legal gibberish. It is a crime that people are paid to write such things."

"Probably more than you earn. Or me."

"I appreciate your pointing that out."

The walk home took us past the ironworks, the Tea Cup Inn, and an ice-cream shop, then the Corcoran art gallery and the War Department offices. At the corner of Seventeenth and G, a bareheaded black woman watched as we ambled past. I tipped my top hat and said, "Good afternoon, ma'am."

She nodded gravely, willing to treat me as an equal.

Henry was babbling on about the need for all right-thinking men to protect the canon of Western culture. Naturally, I agreed—how could I not?—but my heart wasn't in it. What use was Homer or Kipling at a time like this? I worried instead about the . . . I went blank. Alice's wedding, I guess. What could matter more?

⊢══⊣

The New Willard, in truth, was nothing like the old. The former, plain-named Willard, where president-elect Lincoln had stayed, was an attractive but unornamented building, five stories high, rounded at the corner of Fourteenth street and Pennsylvania avenue. Its recent replacement was an explosion of Beaux Arts style, with a pillared entrance and twelve stories of eye-catching gray, capped by a mansard roof of lavish cornices and a cupola. All was meant to dazzle, and it did.

The lobby was a feast of mottled marble pillars and sensuous chandeliers. I zigzagged past the clusters of guests and early drinkers. The farthest of the three elevators was waiting, operated by a coffee-colored man with a shock of white hair and a dignified bearing. He was willing to deliver me to the fifth floor.

My watch said five thirty-five. I knocked on Lizzie's door with trepidation. I had been drawn here, almost unthinkingly, but I couldn't say why (not that I had asked). I heard footsteps and an unlatching—but nothing like *Who is it?* Did she think she knew already? Did she assume it was somebody else?

The door swished open, and there she stood, radiant. It would probably be physiologically inaccurate to say that my heart skipped a beat, but metaphorically it counts as true. She had what Clara lacked—a sinuous body, a coy manner, an easy and seductive laugh. And a cruel streak, like Kate Chase's, back when I was young and she was the Treasury secretary's daughter and the capital's belle. (She had married for money but died a pauper three years ago.) Lizzie Cameron was trouble—this, I knew. But somehow this was part of her allure. Why, I'm not sure I could tell you, even assuming I wanted to know.

She was taller than Clara, and dressed more stylishly, even in the boudoir, in a green satin robe with navy blue trim and a fetching paisley scarf. As usual, she scared the hell out of me but, also as usual, I rose to the occasion.

"Lizzie," I said, with barely a tremble. "May I come in?"

An instant's hesitation. "Of course, Johnny," she said, and stood aside.

"Your husband, is he here?"

"You know he isn't."

"I suspected it, I must confess." I placed my silk hat on the Queen Anne armchair. "And I came despite that."

"You must be very brave," Lizzie replied, with a mirthless laugh.

"Determined, anyway."

I draped my overcoat across the top of the chair.

"Please have a seat, Johnny," she said. "I wish I had something to offer." My chuckle brought an amendment. "Besides bourbon, I mean. A bottle that Don left behind—inadvertently."

Nothing I could say would advance my cause.

What *was* my cause, exactly? I wished to hell I knew. I stepped toward her, and she stepped back.

"Would you join me," I said. "In a drink, I mean?" I meant no more than that. I swore that was so, with an air of desperation that I didn't trust.

What *was* her pull on me? No puzzle, really. It was that I wanted her, pure and simple. I knew I shouldn't, but I did. That was a fact. An inconvenient one, to be sure, one I ought to resist, and I did—and I would. But facts, by their nature, are hard to deny. Isn't it best to confront them? Denied, they have an ugly habit of sticking around.

"I suppose I would," she said.

"Allow me."

My drink was deeper—I figured I needed it more—but hers went down in a gulp. "Another?" I said.

"Oh no, this will work."

She had seated herself on the beige divan, on the far end from my chair. "You seem to have something in mind," she said.

It wasn't my mind on my mind. I sighed. I was, uncharacteristically, tongue-tied. "You are a difficult woman to please," I said at last.

"Not always."

"Thank you. I feel even worse."

She laughed. This time she meant it.

+⊨≡⊨+

I was heading home before eight o'clock, none the worse for wear. Why had I had gone to see Lizzie at all? I knew why: If I hoped to master my own emotions, I needed to feel them first, and *then* walk away. I had to see her to know if I could resist her. And I could. I did. Granted, with her help, saving me from myself. In any event, I counted the visit as a success.

The sky was clear and moonlit. The gravel in Lafayette Square scrunched under my feet. The park was crossed with shadows and the archway over my front door resembled a cavern roof. The entrance was unlocked. Nobody came to greet me, which was just as well.

On the silver tray in the foyer, an official-looking envelope had my name on it, written in a familiar hand. I considered ignoring it, but only for a moment. I slit open the envelope with my thumb and unfolded the paper, then placed it under the flickering bulb. Embossed across the top: SECRET SERVICE.

Then a scribble:

> *Hay,*
>
> *Reptile staying at the Willard.*
>
> *Wilkie*

First thing to-morrow.

CHAPTER NINE

Daybreak brought a liveliness to Washington that I had grown to detest. Had I become an easterner at heart? The city wasn't sleepy like it used to be, nor was it quite as Southern. (Nor, happily, was it New York.) I didn't mind an early hour, but it was better to let the world simmer a spell, if it would, which too often these days it wouldn't. I'd found that, unlike mysteries of the heart, traffic quandaries had a way of resolving themselves if you left them alone for a while. That included the jam on Pennsylvania avenue east of Fifteenth street. The barouches and landaus and drays—eventually, all of them would reach their destination. The rumble of a streetcar scattered the pedestrians like a fox disperses hens. I imagined the chaos if and when automobiles became a regular part of the daily free-for-all rather than a passing nuisance.

I was up and out early this morning—I regretted rushing off without even an apple in hand—to assure myself the advantage of surprise. At the stroke of seven o'clock, I rapped on the door of the Ulysses S. Grant suite, up the twisting staircase beyond the reception desk at the New Willard Hotel.

No response.

I banged again and heard a padding of footsteps, which stopped just short of the door.

"Room service?" A sweet tenor.

I grunted.

The door opened. William Turtle, with all of his flab and folds, over-flowed his tartan dressing gown. "You again!" he squealed.

"The pleasure is mine," I said. "May I take a moment of your time?"

"You already have."

He started to shut the door in my face, but I put my foot in the way—mundane but effective. I wondered if Sherlock had tried it.

"A moment more, then, if you would," I said.

Turtle considered his choices—I could sense the machinations in the willful blankness on his face—and stepped aside.

The eight-sided, high-ceilinged sitting room was sumptuous—mahogany furniture, gilded mirrors, a painting of the eighteenth president above the marble fireplace.

"There," Turtle said, pointing to a divan perpendicular to the windows. "Give me a minute or two."

Turtle shambled into the hallway that led to the rest of the suite. What remained of his hair lay in strips across his scalp. I thought I heard a woman's voice, back in what I presumed to be the bedroom. A few syllables, nothing more.

I passed up the appointed divan, with its gold-braided upholstery and frilly pillows, and stepped to the window. From above, the traffic along the avenue reminded me of an intricate Black Forest toy crushed by an ogre. Across the roadway, the widest in Washington, the Grand Army Hall stood like a redbrick sentry.

I rehearsed my opening question. *What brings you to our fair city, Mr. Turtle?* Ah, such a punch to the gut, sure to provoke anyone to spill all secrets. Or, say, *Tell me, Mr. Turtle, did your client or clients attempt to murder the president?* Sherlock would drool with envy.

Ten minutes must have passed before Turtle returned. He wore a white shirt but no cravat, baggy brown slacks held high by yellow suspenders, and a soiled frock coat. He lowered himself into an over-stuffed armchair opposite the divan, where I now sat. His jowls sagged, pulling his cheeks down, which lent him a look of perpetual sadness.

"Welcome to Washington, Mr. Turtle," I began. "If I may ask, what brings you to our fair—"

A knock at the door.

"My breakfast, if you will excuse me," Turtle said. He raised himself onto his feet, wobbled a moment, and crossed the room. He opened the door and exclaimed, "You!"

The gun went off.

The sound was the loudest I had ever heard. I froze, disbelieving. I could not hear myself moan. I could not hear anything. It took me a second or two—or twenty—to accept what I was seeing, as Turtle crumpled ever so slowly to the floor. I jumped from my seat, sprinted to the doorway, and leaned out.

Smoke filled the corridor; the sharp smell of gunpowder nearly knocked me flat. I thought I saw a pair of narrow heels rushing away and I screamed, "Stop!"

I was straddling Turtle, grazing his shoulder with my foot. I looked down at him. He lay on his back, an arm flung over his head, a leg pinned beneath him at a sickening angle. His dark eyes were open. A small, precise hole, edged in black, pierced his forehead. He lay still, an astonished look on his face.

The telephone was on a marble-topped table by the divan. I ran for it, to summon a doctor—unnecessarily, I was certain—and the police. Only then did I search the dead man's pockets.

I had never been in manacles before, and I wouldn't recommend them, especially if your nose has a tendency to run, as mine does. It was damn annoying, and embarrassing besides.

The police were their usual unfriendly selves. Their only concession to my high-blown status had been to spirit me out the Willard's back door, to prevent the newspapers from witnessing the spectacle of the secretary of state being detained in a murder.

The city's police headquarters was a bunker at C and Fifth streets northwest. The holding cell stank of urine. None of it was mine, although I imagined that might change. I sat on the edge of the lower bunk, grateful to be alone, listening to the chatter of fellow prisoners in the neighboring cell. How on earth had I ended up here? It was true: you never knew what would happen when you woke up in the morning.

I could understand, albeit dimly, the grounds for suspicion. My presence in Turtle's hotel room, for one thing. My smell, for another. I reeked of cordite—even I could tell. And my derringer. What choice did I have but patience? Never my strong suit.

As it happened, I didn't need much of it.

My rescuer was a portly guard with a rust-colored mustache and a gap between his front teeth.

"You!" he snarled. I flinched. "This way."

The guard pulled a key from his belt and unlocked the cell door. I followed him along corridors fragrant with a century of evil men. Three turns later, I was ushered into an office that smelled as fresh as an oasis after a rain, although the furniture must have dated to the war, and not the Spanish one.

"Have a seat, Mr. Secretary." The booming voice belonged to the superintendent of the Metropolitan Police—one Major Richard Sylvester, according to the nameplate on the gleaming desk. He was a sturdy fellow, with a wrestler's shoulders and twinkly blue eyes that invited confidences but promised none in return. "We have a few questions to ask you. This is Detective Flather."

Only now did I notice the sour-looking man seated in the corner, by the flagpole. He had a thin face and a scar on his cheek. For his vitality, he might have been in rigor mortis.

"A pleasure," I said, distorting the truth. "Do I need a lawyer?"

"No need for that, I shouldn't think," Major Sylvester said, flashing a smile that put me on edge.

He led me through the morning's event. I was surprised at how little I remembered. Everything was a blur, other than the sight—which I knew I would never forget—of the astonished look on Turtle's fat face.

I told him whatever I knew. That the killer was someone Turtle had recognized at the door. But I didn't mention the woman's voice in Turtle's bedroom. I kept that to myself for now, although I wasn't sure why.

Actually, I did know why. Out of a wild fear that I knew who she was. This, I needed to think about later. And to make inquiries—*an inquiry*—on my own.

Toward the end of my recital of ignorance, while trying to describe my dip into deafness, Detective Flather awakened. "And your pistol, Mr. Hay," he whined.

"What about it?" I said.

"Exactly. What about it? Did it remain in your pocket all that time?"

"All *what* time? We're talking a few seconds here. And yes, it did."

"Why, then, has a shot been fired?"

"What do you mean, from *my* gun? That little derringer?"

"You heard me." Detective Flather had stood and was looming over me. Tall and gawky, he cast a shadow. I wanted to punch his receding chin, but knew this was not a wise idea. I had outgrown that stuff anyway. (Hadn't I?)

"I have no idea what you're talking about," I said. My neck ached as I kept looking up. "The Secret Service must have fired it before they gave it to me." Surely Wilkie would explain this to the police and clear up this idiocy, assuming I could reach him from my jail cell (my sense of humor was still intact).

"You stank of gunpowder," Flather said. "You still do."

"The smoke was everywhere. I ran out into the hallway." A slight exaggeration.

Detective Flather looked at me as if he knew I was lying. "Once we hear from the coroner, we can determine whether the bullet fired from your chamber matches the bullet fired into Mr. Turtle's forehead."

"I assure you that . . ."

I had lost my audience. Detective Flather resumed his seat and his previous quiescence. Major Sylvester had been listening with amused indifference.

"You are going to hold me, then," I said. I shivered at the thought of returning to that cell.

"You haven't been charged with anything," Major Sylvester said.

"And I won't be?"

"I didn't say that."

⊹═╾═┥╀

I must admit I was shocked—and relieved, more than anything—when my possessions were returned intact. Those included the pocket diary I had filched from Turtle's inside jacket pocket. I had told the sergeant it was mine, and no one bothered to check the handwriting against my own. As Henry said about playing whist, you can usually count on your opponents' ineptitude to hand you a trick and a half.

I spirited the pocket diary home, along with my wallet (all forty-three dollars accounted for), my keys, and my grandfather's pocket watch. Major Sylvester had summoned a hansom cab to get me home swiftly and was kind enough to pay the fare in advance.

I was never so happy to sit in my library, in my maroon leather armchair. I considered a scotch but thought I might need to see Theodore; he wouldn't approve. Nor would I, in the abstract. But life was not lived in the abstract. I had had one hell of a morning. I had never seen a man die before.

I had never seen a man die before.

I had seen men dead. At Bull Run, as a spectator. On two other battlefields, as Lincoln's emissary. Besides a cousin who had died (too young) in bed. But to watch as a man *lost* his life, was alive one moment and dead the next, was impossible to fathom, except that I had seen it for myself. The miracle of childbirth, in reverse. The impossibility did not end there. The death I had witnessed was not merely a death; it was a murder.

I cradled the dead man's pocket diary in my lap. The thin leatherbound volume was slightly larger than a postcard. The cover was gilded, "1902."

The pages were crinkled, as if victim to a sudden squall. The early months needed prying apart. I leafed through and saw nothing of note. A scrap of newspaper marked the page I cared about: September 11. Today.

The page had two entries. At eleven a.m., Cortelyou. At six p.m., Hanna. Everything else was blank.

Cortelyou, the gateway to the president. Mark Hanna, still the party's chairman and, if he had his way, the twenty-seventh president of the United States. (Assuming, God forbid, it wasn't me.) Why on earth would Turtle want to talk to them—and why would they be willing? I needed to find out. Turtle might be impervious to questioning, but Cortelyou and Hanna were not.

I turned the page. Friday, September 12, had a single entry, at ten a.m. My mouth went dry when I read it.

Hay.

"You ran *toward* him!" the president exclaimed. "Bully for you!"

That was not the reaction I had expected, but I should have, knowing Theodore. He detested cowardice. I had been tested under enemy fire and found worthy, as simple as that. (As if there had been any place to flee to.) I said nothing about the derringer that had stayed in my pocket.

The back room at the temporary White House had become Roosevelt's sanctum. He used the front parlor for the senators and diplomats he was unable to escape and reserved the rear for intimates, or Theodore's version of them. The furniture was seedy and the room had the sharp scent of pine. Theodore sat nestled in a thin-cushioned chair of brown corduroy, his injured leg propped on a mismatched hassock. He looked tired.

"I felt for his pulse, but there was nothing to be done. Nothing that—" I began to choke up and Roosevelt reached across and patted my cheek, which calmed me. (This couldn't be about Turtle.) I told him of 'phoning for a doctor and then for the police. "Who arrested me!"

Theodore clapped his hands in glee. "For what?"

"As a material witness, it seems, not for the crime. Yet. Apparently I am a suspect. There's a detective who thinks *I* killed him."

A belly laugh that became a cackle. "And did you?"

"I hope I don't need to answer that."

"Bully for you, my boy. Bully for you."

This was the asthmatic boy who, with unrelenting effort, had made himself into a manly man and assumed—yes, assumed—that anyone else of mettle could do the same. (Have I mentioned how I would have hated to be his son?)

"Well, thank you," I said, "but it leaves me with a problem. Two problems. I was a witness to this . . . murder, so I am now involved. And if . . . something *had* happened to you, I would have stood to . . . gain, at least in some people's eyes. I have terrible conflicts of interest here. I am enough of a lawyer to know *that*. So how can I continue to investigate all this?"

"Are you saying these . . . incidents are related?" Theodore's eyes narrowed. "This Mr. Turtle's . . . murder, as you say, and what happened to me?"

"I have to think so," I said. This had not occurred to me explicitly, but he had to be right. The lawyer for the motorman accused of manslaughter in the death of the president's bodyguard—and by extension, in the attempted murder of the president—was himself murdered, and before my eyes. A coincidence? Conceivably, but unlikely. "Which makes it even more imperative that you find someone else to investigate."

"Nonsense, Hay. Your involvement makes you all the more . . . qualified to ferret out the truth. You have every incentive, I must say. That is the only thing I care about, John—the truth. Not about the rules or the niceties of *procedure*." He spat the word. "Only about the truth and about right and wrong. Nothing else matters." I imagined a scribe behind the curtain—or rather, imagined that Theodore was imagining a scribe behind the curtain—scribbling down every word for history. But when Theodore wanted something, who could say no?

I waited until his oration was finished and then told him I needed to ask Cortelyou about his scheduled eleven o'clock appointment—fated to be unconsummated—with the late William Turtle. Theodore could shed no light on the possible subject but had no objection to my inquiry.

"Tell me, John, how did you learn of this appointment, given that Mr. Turtle was, through his misfortune, unable to confide in you?"

An astute question, and I gambled on the truth. I told him of finding the pocket diary and claiming it as my own. This onetime police commissioner was entertained rather than horrified at my deceiving the constituted authorities.

"I will need to confess my sins to Wilkie," I said. "He won't be pleased."

"I shall fix things with Wilkie," the president replied. "He works for me."

"You think he does, and as your protector he does. But as an investigator he works for himself—or, as you like to say, for the truth. Any investigator does, if they're any good."

"Including yourself, I take it."

"I do this at your pleasure, my dear Theodore. I also do it in pursuit of the truth. I will take this wherever it goes; you know that. I must assume you would want nothing less."

That was my speech, and I hoped the scribe got it right. Without waiting for Theodore to counter-orate, I left. The Roumanian Jews would have to wait.

+——+

I hated to confess my sins, though Lord knows I'd had plenty of practice.

"It didn't *fall* out, exactly," I said, handing Turtle's pocket diary to John Wilkie.

"I gathered that." The Secret Service chief leaned back in his seat and drew on his pipe. The smoke swirled toward the ceiling, slightly smellier than the day before. "This was tampering with evidence, you understand."

"Technically, perhaps," I allowed.

"The world lives on technicalities. My world does."

"In diplomacy, the vaguer the better. Harder to get trapped that way. Anyway, I didn't tamper with anything. I just took it. And here it is." I plunked it on the table. "Besides, you're the one who sent me there."

"You sent yourself," Wilkie said. "And I never suggested that you tamper with evidence. Oh, forgive me"—before I could open my mouth—"that you *steal* it."

The swirls of his pipe smoke had grown less turbulent. I deduced that his misgivings about the pocket diary had passed.

One more confession, then, the first one having gone so well. "I am under suspicion, for Turtle's murder."

Wilkie did not laugh. "Says who?"

I told him of the DC detective's questions about the bullet evidently fired from the derringer I was carrying (*had* been carrying, for the police still had it) at Wilkie's behest.

"I fired it," Wilkie said. I felt a wash of relief. "On our rifle range, down in the basement. To make sure it was accurate."

"And it was?"

"Accurate enough."

"And you didn't reload it?"

"I told . . . someone else to. The man who runs the range."

That should be good enough to clear me of suspicion. Especially if the caliber was different from . . .

"Tell me, is my derringer a twenty-two or a thirty-two?" I felt stupid having to ask; it was like inquiring whether your horse was really a mare. But I had to. Suppose the range manager, out of self-protection, insisted he *had* replaced the bullet. That would leave me with a bullet to explain.

"Twenty-two," Wilkie said, trying hard not to smile. He didn't succeed. "What was Turtle shot with, do they know yet?"

I shook my head. "This afternoon."

Wilkie leaned back in his swivel chair, propped his feet on his desk, and blew an elephant-shaped cloud of smoke into the murky air. "There is someone you should meet," he said at last. "She is looking for . . . not a job, but a . . . project. A cause, even. She might be able to help."

✦

I knew her by name, of course. Everyone had heard of Nellie Bly, although a half dozen years had passed since *The New York World* had last bragged of her byline. Wilkie ushered me through the lobby of the Ebbitt House, across Fourteenth street from the Willard, and into the "red parlor," the gentleman's lounge. There she was, at the farthest table, seated in a high-backed leather chair. Her presence drew stares from all over the red-and-gold-draped room, but the cutaway-clad waiters were evidently too gentlemanly to evict her. She sparkled.

She half stood and I realized how tiny she was, slim and dainty. Her delicate features suggested a deference that her fierce hazel eyes dispelled. She offered her hand coquettishly, but her handshake was strong. This was the daredevil who had feigned lunacy and spent ten days in a madhouse. Who had encircled the world in seventy-two days, without a Sancho Panza to smooth her way. Who had made herself the center of every story. Who had married a man four decades older, after a two-week courtship, and stood to inherit his wealth. Who was nearing forty with flawless skin and self-possession. The eighteen-nineties' vaunted New Woman, personified. And dressed like one, in a sensible white shirtwaist, practical and confident—for my benefit, I had to assume.

Wilkie introduced her as Mrs. Elizabeth Seaman. "May I say, she came into my office this morning, unannounced, and offered her services. I thought of you."

"You may call me Nellie," she said. That was her pen name, after a racehorse in a Stephen Foster ditty.

I doubted she meant this as a compliment. "You may call me . . ." I was tempted to say *Mr. Hay,* but that was a rude way to begin. I surprised myself—and Wilkie—when I said, "John."

Wilkie excused himself.

"What are you drinking?" I said.

"Bourbon," she replied. "Care to join me?"

I did. The waiter did not cast Nellie a glance.

"And what brings you here . . . Nellie?" I said.

"Boredom, I suppose."

An honest answer. "With?"

"Milk cans, John."

I laughed.

"No, really," she said. "And garbage cans and kitchen sinks and hot water heaters and galvanized this and that. Everything the Iron Clad Manufacturing Company manufactures."

She had been running her husband's factory in Brooklyn since 'ninety-nine. He was nearly eighty and just about blind. I surmised that Mr. Seaman was part of her boredom.

"I am a married man, you know," I said. I was shocked at myself—how *un*diplomatic.

She burst into laughter. It was a carefree sound that lit up her face. "And I am a married woman," she replied, and again she extended her hand and shook mine heartily. "The pleasure is mine."

"How else, then, can I relieve your boredom?"

"What have you got?"

Oh Lordy, what a pistol she was—more than a derringer!

I suddenly got serious. I'd decided to trust her. I *needed* to trust her—I needed the help. "I'll tell you what I've got," I said, and proceeded to tell her about the collision in Pittsfield and the president's suspicions, then about the murder of William Turtle. "Before my very eyes," I added, still amazed and, yes, a little shaken by what I had seen.

Something happened in her face. It softened—grew innocent, vulnerable, enticing. I knew this was her reportorial persona (I had been enough of a journalist to recognize technique), but I didn't care, and she knew I wouldn't.

"So tell me, what can I do?" she said.

I suggested that she venture to the Willard Hotel—"Excuse me. The *New* Willard Hotel"—and question the desk clerk and the doorman and anyone else who might have caught sight of a murderer in flight.

"Who shall I say I am?"

"Tell them who you are—Mrs. Elizabeth Seaman, yes?—and that you are . . ." How best to phrase this? "Working with the Secret Service."

"And if they ask for proof?"

"I'm sure you'll think of something," I said.

That melodious laugh again. "Tell me," she said, "does the local constabulary have any suspects in mind?"

"Oh, yes," I replied. "Me."

Elmer Dover filled the doorway with a phony grin and announced, "Mr. Hanna ain't here."

"When might he be back?" I said. I was standing a step below him, on the doorstep. It was hard not to contemplate an uppercut, but I did my best.

"And why is this any business of yours, Mr. Hay?"

I flashed my most ingratiating smile, just to annoy him. "I have a question to ask the senator."

"Maybe I can answer it."

"Maybe you can." I glanced up and down Madison place, as if to say, *Here?* Not entirely obtuse, he invited me in.

But not beyond the foyer. The stylish entryway, the black-and-white-tiled floor, the tall mirror with the throne-like seat, these were obviously Lizzie Cameron's (that is, the landlady's) taste. Not Hanna's, and decidedly not Elmer Dover's.

"So, what is your question?" said Dover, standing uncomfortably close. I recognized this as *his* technique, bordering on brutish intimidation, to which I happened to be generally immune. (Another benefit of boxing.)

I told him that Senator Hanna's scheduled meeting at six o'clock this evening with the late William Turtle would need to be canceled.

Dover's eyes grew wide.

I told him briefly what I had witnessed and added, "Would you happen to know what he wanted?"

Dover shook his head.

"Would Senator Hanna know?"

"Couldn't say."

Because he didn't want to, I wondered, or didn't know?

"Then let me ask you again." I pressed closer to the big man and looked him levelly—well, up at an angle—in the eye. "When will the senator return? Or is there another place I might find him? At the Capitol, perhaps."

"You can look for the senator if you like, sir, but he won't be able to help you. I can assure you of that, Mr. Hay."

But I had a sneaking suspicion that Elmer Dover could help, though only if he wished.

+≻═≺+

"The strenuous life, the strenuous life—I'm sick of hearing it," Henry said. "It's enough to wear a fellow out."

"Our friend Cortelyou is just as strenuous," I said. "A swimmer, an oarsman, a horseman—a boxer, for God's sake."

"An Adonis," Henry said. "But tell me, old boy, have you ever heard our Mr. Cortelyou laugh?"

That made *me* laugh, because the answer was no. I said, as casually as I could, "So tell me, Henry, do you suppose he's capable of murder?"

"Of course he is. Aren't we all? All we need is a reason."

"Speak for yourself, Henry."

"I am. And climb down from your high horse, my dear boy. Are you claiming, on the honor of your forefathers, that you are incapable of taking another man's life?"

"Leave my forefathers out of it. You may talk about yours all you like, but mine were a questionable lot."

"My forefathers are all that I've got, dear boy. Oh, to have an influence on the world beyond words! Or any at all. But you're not answering my question. Could you take another man's—another person's—life?"

"A serious question?"

"Always."

I pondered it for a minute or two. Could I hate anyone that much? Probably, although no one came to mind. At last I replied, "Not coldly."

Our stroll had begun none too soon, given the horrors of the day. I had stopped by my office and found no solace there. A setback in the negotiations with Nicaragua over the alternative route for the canal. If only Theodore could calm his obsessions—this time, over "man versus mountains," in Henry's formulation—our negotiators might have more leverage to apply. Worse, the German warship that intervened in the uprising in Haiti had set Theodore to fantasizing about annexing that unhappy place. That's all we need, another country we insist on straightening out but refuse to understand. The white man's burden was a . . . burden.

We walked east along Pennsylvania avenue. The Capitol dome loomed in the distance. When I had first arrived in Washington, at president-elect Lincoln's side, the dome was under construction (replacing the low-slung affair that had looked insipid between the new congressional wings). So much had changed in the four decades since, along the fifteen blocks from here to the Capitol. Mathew Brady's studio was gone, of course, and so were the organ-grinders and six or eight hotels. In their stead stood the flamboyant New Willard and the post office's new clock tower, almost as tall as the Capitol, concealing the squalor and slums to the south. Center Market had survived—half of it, anyway. (The rest had become a National Guard armory.) The city's center of commerce had shifted to F street, a couple of blocks to the north, while the avenue had grown a little shabby.

Henry and I exhausted the topic of Nicaragua, given the constraints on what I could say, when Henry exclaimed, "What *about* Cortelyou? Did he murder someone?"

I had to laugh. "You're too eager, Henry."

"Now you've *got* to tell me. Did he?"

"Not that I am aware of. Not that he isn't capable of it . . ." I bowed

Henry's way. "Even more, perhaps, than either of us." I told him of Cortelyou's eleven o'clock appointment with the man who had been murdered in front of me four hours earlier.

"So what did our Mr. Cortelyou say?"

"Haven't seen him. Nobody has, all afternoon. He isn't at Jackson Place—"

"Unless Theodore stashed him upstairs."

"And as far as I know he isn't at home."

"You checked? And didn't take me along?"

I told him about Nellie Bly's volunteer legwork while I tried to carve out an hour here and there to run the world. Her involvement seemed to perturb him, which I took as charming evidence of . . . jealousy?

"You find anything to-day?" I said. I meant in the Northern Securities papers.

"Why use three words when ten words will do? Are lawyers paid by the word, like Dickens?"

Ah, the source of Henry's distress: he hadn't found anything yet worth the search. Maybe there was nothing to find. That was the likeliest explanation, and no cause for shame.

+⇒⇐+

At home with Clara, a second evening straight.

So rare.

So relaxing.

So . . . dull. Deliciously so.

We sat by the hearth in the parlor. A fire blazed. As delicately as I could—there was no good way—I described what I had witnessed that morning. (Our 'phone call after the police let me go had been brief.) I was surprised at how I had distanced myself from the horror. Then I noticed that Clara was shaking. I crossed to her chair and cradled her head in my belly as she cried. The tears were not for William Turtle. How could they be? She had never met the man. They were for Del, then. Unless they were for me, for what I had seen.

Once they passed, Clara buried her face in the latest issue of *Harper's Bazaar*. The cover was a dreamy portrait of three generations of American womanhood cozying under a tree.

I took up *The Hound of the Baskervilles,* trying to recall where I'd left off. Dr. Watson had arrived at Baskerville Hall, out in Devonshire, charged by Sherlock Holmes (still on a case back in London) to record all facts that might touch on the mysterious death of Sir Charles Baskerville at the edge of the moor. There was talk of a convicted murderer who had escaped onto the moor. In the dead of night, Dr. Watson heard a woman's sob of despair, and his suspicions turned to Mrs. Barrymore, the servant.

The next day, Dr. Watson was walking on the moor when a stranger called his name. It was Stapleton, the eccentric neighbor and naturalist, butterfly net in tow. Near the treacherous Grimpen Mire, where a single misstep promised death, "a long, low moan, indescribably sad, swept over the moor." The murmur became a roar, then again a murmur. Stapleton recalled that he had heard the sound once or twice before, but never so loud. The peasants, he explained, believed it was the hound of the Baskervilles, shrieking for its prey.

It was a story, nothing more, but I shuddered.

"John, where are you?" Clara said. She was staring at me—for how long, I had no notion. "Any place . . . interesting?"

"Not especially. The moors. The Willard."

Clara looked pained. Was it because she knew Lizzie was staying there, too? I was spent. I had been awake for too many hours, and I had started out the day seeing what no one should see.

The Willard. That terrible room, the smoke-filled corridor—all a blur. First I tried to ignore it, and then to bring it back to mind.

Black, black smoke and the thunder in my ears

Yes. Now I needed a verb.

Wreaked . . .

No, thunder doesn't wreak.

Crashed like a wave on the shore.

A cliché.

Black, black smoke and the thunder in my ears
Wrapped around my soul like a shroud,

Passable.

And a man at my feet, unmoving, unbowed

Actually, he was plenty bowed. Try rhyming with *ears.*

in tears.

Turtle wasn't crying; he was dead. For God's sake, dead! Who gave a damn about rhyme?

CHAPTER TEN

Mark Hanna had skipped town (to Cleveland, I was told), and Cortelyou sent a messenger to say he was far too busy to see me until three thirty at the earliest. So I stopped in to see the Secret Service chief, to learn my fate.

"The caliber matches, sorry to say." John Wilkie could deliver bad news with an affecting nonchalance. "A twenty-two."

"That doesn't prove anything," Nellie Bly chimed in. I had asked her to come, so we could continue on to the Willard. She sat in a hard-backed chair, her feet barely reaching the floor.

"It doesn't disprove anything, either," I pointed out. "Did you ask your man if he put a bullet back in the chamber?"

"He says he did," Wilkie replied, "but between you and me, I'm not sure I believe him."

"Why on earth not?"

"It's a mistake no rifleman would want to admit."

"So I'm not off the hook?" I said.

"To me, you were never on it. But I can't speak for the DC coppers."

"Your opinion might count with them," I said.

"Ha! You live in your world; I am stuck with mine."

So far, the newspapers had printed nary a word about Turtle's murder, though how long this blessedness would last was anyone's guess. Should the yellow sheets learn that the secretary of state was a witness, much less a suspect, in a cold-blooded murder, the furor would make "Remember the Maine!" look like an afterthought.

"Anything else in the autopsy I ought to know?" I said.

"Nothing useful. The bullet went into the brain stem, angled down, which suggests that his assailant was tall."

"Or shot from up here," I said, raising my arm.

"Could be. In any event, death was instantaneous."

That, I knew. "Then Miss Bly and I—sorry, Mrs. Seaman and I—should be . . ."

"What do you know about this man Turtle?" Wilkie said.

"Not a lot," I replied. "I met him in Pittsfield. Not a pleasant experience. He's a big man up there. Rather a slithery fellow, for his size, but civil enough. He did let me talk to his client. Hard to figure out whose side he's on, other than his own."

"You think he recognized the killer at the door?"

"Oh, yes. He said, 'You!' It was someone he knew. I am sure of it."

"That should narrow it down, at least a little," Wilkie said. "Are there people who would want to kill him?"

"I would wager my last Garfield fiver on it. His funeral may draw a big crowd, but I can't say he'll be mourned much."

+=━=+

"Garbage cans, huh?" I said.

"And milk cans—what of it?" Nellie said. We were rounding the corner of the Treasury Building, waiting to cross Fifteenth street. An automobile horn blared, causing a nag to rear, tying up traffic. "Somebody has to make them. There's money in it."

"I'm sure there is."

"Tell me, John, have you always been wealthy?"

"How do you know I am?" I guided her elbow behind the rig, whose horse had returned to earth.

"I make it my business to know," she shouted.

"Then you should also know that the answer to your question"—we reached the opposite sidewalk, by the tailor's—"is no. I got rich the old-fashioned way—I married well. And you?"

I braced for a slap and got a guffaw.

"Funny thing is," I went on, "I wasn't even thinking about money when I married her. I really did fall in love." I was surprised at my own candor, especially on the street.

The morning traffic had eased, but the sidewalks were full. The sun was bright in the sky. Women ambled along in slender overcoats and wide-brimmed hats, spinning parasols; the men hustled by, the derbies outnumbering the top hats. A street piano man playing ragtime teamed up with a black boy, whose whistling kept harmony—so much sweeter than an organ-grinder's screech. I dropped a dime into their cup.

"What do you hope to find out?" I said, pointing to our destination.

Nellie shrugged. "It depends on what we see."

The hacks jostled for attention in front of the Willard's entrance. Everyone entering or leaving the hotel looked important—rather, self-important—including me, no doubt, and certainly Nellie Bly. The grand lobby fostered the conceit; the marble Corinthian pillars and the high ceiling dwarfed the people below but, paradoxically, made them feel big.

Nellie was already at the hotel desk, in pursuit of the clerk who had been on duty the morning before. The same one as to-day, a young Irishman named O'Brien. He was seated on a low stool, so she could look down at him, which she did. He was a fair-haired fellow with freckles and an unlined face. His pale eyes were agog. He would tell her anything, truth be damned.

"You heard the gunshot?" she was saying.

"Oh yes, ma'am."

"Where were you at the time?"

"Over here, ma'am. I mean, over there." He pointed to the far end of the cherrywood counter, closest to the entrance.

"After you heard the gunshot, did you see anyone leave through the lobby?"

"Oh yes, ma'am."

I bellied up to the hotel desk and listened. First, gain their trust. Pay attention to what they say—and don't say. Then go for the jugular, by way of a capillary. Something like that.

"All right, who?" Nellie said at last.

"Four or five of 'em," the young man sneered.

"Four or five of what?" Nellie said.

"Them ladies . . . You know what I mean."

"How did *you* know?" I said.

He looked at me for the first time. "Oh, you can tell," he said. "You see 'em ever' mornin' comin' through. Not all at once, though. Takes a gunshot to clear 'em out! They was a-rushing out o' here like goats chased by a coyote. In case the cops were gonna show up, which they darn well did."

"Where were they coming from?" I said.

"The cops?"

"The . . . ladies."

"How should I know?" the young man chortled.

I said, "Did they come from the elevator or down the stairs?"

That made him think. He closed his eyes and his hands shimmied; he was trying to picture the scene. "From the elevator, I guess," he said.

"All of them?" I said.

"Seems so." He squirmed in his seat. There was something he wasn't saying.

"Anyone else?" Nellie said.

The right question. The desk clerk shut his eyes again and watched. "Just a man," he said. "In a cloak. Dark plaid."

Nellie said, "Did you see his face?"

He shook his head. "He was wearing a slouch hat of some sort, pulled down over his forehead. Not lookin' this way or that."

"Short or tall?" I said.

"A little tall. Prob'ly taller than you."

"Hurrying?" I said.

"Not really. The . . . ladies, they was. But he was . . . a pretty good pace, passing through. But not . . . runnin' or nothin'."

That suggested someone with aplomb. The kind of man who could open a door, shoot a man in the forehead, and make his getaway, all without exciting suspicion.

Other than mine.

I left Nellie to question the doorman and the hack drivers at the curb, to find out if a mysterious man in a cloak had sought a ride. I had a rendezvous upstairs. The subject of the rendezvous was unaware of this.

The elevator operator was as scrawny as a pterodactyl bone and almost as old. I asked if he had been on duty the morning before. He had.

"Do you know Mrs. Cameron?" I said.

His grin revealed several teeth.

I was nervous about asking the next question, but I saw no choice.

No, he hadn't seen her yesterday morning.

"Thank you," I said. I meant it.

I knocked on the door of her corner suite. Lizzie Cameron was wearing a thin robe of crocheted white cotton that covered slightly more than it revealed.

"Hello," I said, choosing the conventional.

"Hello, Johnny," she replied. Her long neck was uncoiled, like an asp's. "Would you care to come in?"

A silly question. Why else was I here? "I would, thank you," I said. "Your husband is here, I hope."

"I'm afraid he isn't. Would you still care to come in?"

"I suppose I would, thank you."

We settled into opposite loveseats in the octagonal sitting room. She apologized for having nothing to offer beyond cold coffee (which I declined) and said, "And what brings you here, Mr. Hay?"

"Business," I said.

"A pleasant change of pace."

"If you say so. The untimely death yesterday morning of William Turtle."

A crooked nod, meant to ingratiate. "What does this have to do with me, pray tell?"

"It happened three floors below you, precisely." I pointed between my feet, at the Oriental rug. "Did you happen to hear anything? A gunshot?"

"What time was this?"

"Seven fifteen or thereabouts."

"I heard nothing, Johnny. I was sound asleep, I assure you. Do I need to prove it?"

A curious response. I had said nothing about any suspicions. "Of course not. How could I not believe every word you utter?"

A hearty laugh. "As I do you, Mr. Hay. As I do you."

I punished her with my most diplomatic smile.

"And what is *your* interest in this, if I may ask?" she said.

"I was there."

A sharp intake of breath. "Where?"

"There. In the room. Directly below this one. I was sitting . . . just about . . . here . . . and he was shot . . . there." I pointed to the door.

Lizzie leaned back in her seat.

"And you heard nothing?" I said.

"No, no." Her phlegm-tinged voice went up an octave. "I was asleep, I tell you."

I would have believed her but for those last three words. "Alone, I take it," I said, and regretted it immediately.

"Is there anything else, Mr. Hay?"

There was plenty, but most of it was nonprofessional, even unprofessional, and I left.

+━━━+

As the elevator descended, I ignored the operator's nattering and considered the questions Lizzie *hadn't* asked. For one thing, who was William Turtle? And why had I been in his suite? Maybe she already knew the answers, although her surprise at my presence had seemed real. Or maybe she didn't care enough, either about Turtle or about me. That seemed likelier. Or maybe it just hadn't occurred to her—she wasn't always as sharp as I was inclined to assume. I had another question for myself: Why would she *want* to kill Turtle? Why would anyone? Except that somebody did.

The elevator dumped me into the wondrous lobby. I was crossing it when I heard my name. A woman's voice, one I recognized.

Nellie Bly had planted herself near the entrance, oblivious to the streams of passersby. "Hay," she said—or did she mean *hey?*—"come with me."

Disobedience did not cross my mind. I turned and trotted behind her, back past the registration desk to the winding staircase that led to

Turtle's unlucky suite. A few steps below the last landing, she grasped my elbow and stopped. "Here," she said.

"Here what?"

"Look," she commanded. "At the carpet."

I was grateful for the hint. The carpet was beige and brown, of thickly woven wool, as deep as a baby's bath, but otherwise of no particular interest. "I'm looking," I said.

"At the indentations."

I squinted and saw what she meant. At just the right angle, I spied an indentation, or what had once been an indentation but had mostly, though not entirely, sprung back up. Then I saw another one, a few inches behind, and yet another to the right, two of them.

"High heels," she said. "*High* high heels."

"Maybe it happened to-day," I said.

"Maybe. But the police weren't letting anyone through until this morning."

"You should make sure that the carpet hasn't been cleaned. You never know what these—"

"I checked." She grinned. "That ain't all. Look at *this*."

I followed her up to the landing. This time I saw what she meant, the line of shallow indentations that stretched to the tile floor. I stooped when she did and examined the nearest indentations. Each had a shape, faint as it was. Not the usual trapezoid or rectangle or semicircle of a high heel but—I counted the sides—a hexagon. Six sides. Parallel lines in the front and the back, pointed at both sides. A kind of heel that Nellie said she had never seen before.

I thought of telling her about the woman's voice back in the bedroom. I hesitated. Who might I be implicating? Yet, if Lizzie was lying or concealing something—more than her usual—I had to know. Did I want her or not? Could I trust her or not? I swallowed hard and asked Nellie to check Mrs. Cameron's rooms for hexagonal heels, using a tone of voice that invited no questions.

+=====+

One thing I understood about Cortelyou was that, in his Prussian psyche, status and symbols mattered. That was why I had left a note at 22 Jackson Place asking him to come see me at three thirty, sharp. I wanted him at maximum discomfort.

Margaret ushered him in at three twenty-nine. Again, I was astonished at his physical resemblance to Theodore—the pince-nez, the mustache, the center-parted hair, the set of his jaw. I half expected him to squeal, *Dee-lighted.* I remained engrossed in a stack of forgettable correspondence for approximately a minute—childish, I know, but a wolf's urine spray in Washington dominance.

"Glad you could come see me, Bruce," I said at last, using his Christian name as a cudgel.

"Anytime, John," he replied.

"Have a seat, please."

The plush chair was a little too low, especially for a man of Cortelyou's athletic build.

"Entirely recovered?" I said.

A pause. "Oh, from the collision, you mean. Pretty much. A bruise here and there, mostly faded. Nothing to speak of. I appreciate your interest." A gimlet-eyed stare.

"And the president?"

"Improving. Every day."

I knew for a fact that Theodore's leg was getting worse. "Relieved to hear that," I said.

"Did you ask me here for my medical judgment?" No attempt at an insincere smile.

"Only in part. I need to ask you about William Turtle. Did you know him?"

"I can't say that I did. I do know what happened to him, but nothing more."

"May I ask how you learned?"

No reply. This meant the president had told him.

"And did he . . . did you learn that your name turned up in Mr. Turtle's pocket diary?"

"I . . . I . . . No." Cortelyou licked his upper lip; his mustache quivered. He started to say something but thought better of it.

"It seems you had a meeting scheduled with him for eleven o'clock yesterday."

"With this unfortunate fellow Turtle? I don't know the man, I tell you."

Not quite a denial. "And you had nothing scheduled with him?" I said.

"I did not."

I would have preferred if he had consulted his own pocket diary.

"Our unfortunate Mr. Turtle presumably wanted to see you in order to see the president."

"That is the customary procedure." Cortelyou's coal-black eyes never left mine.

"Would you have any idea about the subject?" I said.

"I told you, I've never met the—"

"That's not what I'm asking!" I rounded the desk and stood over him.

"What are you accusing me of?" he growled, as he leapt from his chair.

I stepped back, but not quite far enough. He was taller than I, and compactly muscled, and when his head grazed my chin, my instincts took over (so often the trouble with humans). My fists clenched and I pressed them against his chest and pushed him back into the chair. Mine weren't the only instincts, however. Cortelyou rose out of the chair like a pop fly. This time, I stepped far enough away that we were left glaring at each other across a foot of floor. His dark eyes had gone flat.

"I am accusing you of nothing," I whispered, in what I hoped was an ominous tone. "I am looking for information, at the president's—the *president's*—direction. Please answer my question. This is important. Do you have any idea why Turtle wanted to see you?"

"I told you I don't."

"So he *was* going to see you."

A long pause. "We had nothing scheduled," Cortelyou said. "He telephoned on . . . Monday, it was, and asked to see me. He said he had information about the collision. This was the lawyer representing the motorman who killed Craig and almost killed the president. And almost killed *me*. Of course I was willing to see him. I was in that carriage, too, John. But what he wanted to tell me, I haven't a clue. Do you?"

—✦—

"You?"

That's just what Turtle had said. This time it was Chief Nicholson, and I was grateful for his incredulity.

"Yes, me," I replied. "Maybe he was the detective who 'phoned you. Flather is his name. I asked them to, before I realized that I was a suspect."

"Have they cleared you?"

"Not that they've told me. They still have my derringer. They must be testing the bullet and the gun—or whatever they do."

"They're just trying to unnerve you," Chief Nicholson said.

"Well, they're succeeding." I realized I was telling the truth. I didn't enjoy being accused of murder, even as a ploy. *Especially* as a ploy—but for what? So I'd tell them what I knew? I had already told them . . . most of it. "Whatever information Turtle was peddling—and nobody here seems to know what it was—it was enough to get him killed."

No sound but static.

"Is there anyone in Pittsfield you can ask?" I said. "His law partner? The motorman? Maybe Mrs. Turtle—is there one?"

More static on the line. "A current and maybe a former," Chief Nicholson said. "I'll let you know if I learn anything. Mr. Turtle was known for playing things close to the vest. Very close. Big vest."

—✦—

"May I ask you something bluntly?"

"Any day," Theodore said. "Any hour."

"About Cortelyou."

"My fellow Dutchman." Roosevelt leaned back in the swivel chair and smiled broadly; his teeth reflected the chandelier's light. "I heard."

"About our . . . ?" No one else had been present, and I hadn't told a soul.

Why would Cortelyou divulge such a thing, except to bolster himself or to undermine me? I shouldn't have been surprised; to Cortelyou, life was a struggle to rise. As it happened, Theodore was amused, not

angry. He saw conflict, even violence, as essential to the human condition and therefore to be cherished.

Theodore said, "What is your blunt question?"

It seemed too silly to ask. *Was Cortelyou to be trusted?* Of course Theodore's answer would be yes. How could he say otherwise, no matter
how he felt? And in at least one way, Cortelyou *could* be trusted: to not
kill himself. That was the fatal error, so to speak, in raising any suspicion about Cortelyou's involvement in the collision. He had been in
Roosevelt's carriage. Any threat to the president was a threat to Cortelyou, who was the furthest thing from suicidal. Nor would he have
reason to kill the abettor of his ambitions, the president who planned
to elevate him into the cabinet. I couldn't say I liked the man, but I
certainly didn't think he was a killer.

Instead, I said, "Why is he so"—I remembered Theodore's aversion
to swearing—"resistant to telling me anything at all? It's like pulling
teeth."

"*That* is his value to me," Theodore said. "Part of it."

Good point. "He isn't entirely honest, you know. Only under duress."

Theodore's eyes twinkled.

Maybe being a chameleon wasn't necessarily a sin, I decided, if it
meant molding yourself to be useful to your boss.

When I started to raise the problem of the Roumanian Jews, Theodore told me someone was waiting. "You have a soft heart, Hay," he said.

I didn't take it as a compliment.

＋═∷═╪

Washington at night has its thrills, licit and otherwise. An estimated 139
bordellos persisted south of Pennsylvania avenue, between Tenth and
Fifteenth streets. You can find an opium den on Four-and-a-half street.
A box of cigars for a hotel clerk, a hansom cab driver, a saloonkeeper, an
older messenger boy—or many a policeman on the beat—can procure
information about pursuing pleasures that are not in accord with the
law.

Kernan's Lyceum Theater, at Thirteenth and Pennsylvania, stayed
within legal bounds. It advertised its bill of fare as "polite" vaudeville.
The occasional bouts with lady boxers were cast as entertainment, skirt-

ing the ban on prizefighting inside the city limits. Even so, it was rare that Clara accompanied me to Kernan's. The female impersonators repelled her, and to-night's climactic act was even less of a draw: a wrestling match between Washington's welterweight champion and New York City's. Clara detested combat in every guise, not excluding my boxing, which she was kind enough not to point out.

Nor did she like this late hour. But to-night she had come, without complaint, at the president's request. Theodore was unaccountably nervous about how the crowd would receive him, which Clara found charming. He was entirely too aware that he hadn't been elected in his own right; it scared him, if anything did.

We arrived early, presumably to instigate cheers if none broke out unprompted. Cigar smoke and the odors of lager and excitable men suffused even the dollar seats. My cushion was thin. The place was packed. The workingmen and ruffians, the Negroes and newsboys upstairs, drowned out the Spanish violinist and the dancing pantomime and even the minstrels. Clara pasted on a smile.

The singing sisters from Ecuador finished their set and the wrestlers came on stage. "Josie! Josie!" came shouts from the gallery, for Joe Grant, the local champ. That was when I heard a different shout. From the rear of the hall, a manly chant—*"Ted-dy! Ted-dy!"*—was surging my way.

CHAPTER ELEVEN

I savored the smell of moldy straw in the stable behind my house as I caressed Single Malt. What a mare! She was my favorite horse since Hasheesh. (Their respective names tell you everything you need to know about my past forty years.) I fed her half an apple and she nuzzled against my shoulder. It was the simplicity of the transaction that was so appealing, a thoughtful gift in exchange for heartfelt, albeit conditional, love. If only people—or nations—made such sense. I produced the other half of the apple and Single Malt offered more of her temporary devotion. If you want a friend in Washington, get a horse.

I had decided to ride rather than walk the seven blocks. Sixteenth street was still what it had always been, a dwelling here and there beneath a canopy of elms. I detected scents of the countryside, or could pretend to. (Just think, if Jefferson had gotten his way, Sixteenth street would have served as the planet's prime meridian, instead of Greenwich.) An old man's pleasure—a trot into the past.

I remained lost in another time until my thoughts played ahead to my destination. Henry Cabot Lodge was as frosty a man as any I had ever known. Seeing him was Theodore's idea, and not a bad one. Other than Edith, he probably counted as Theodore's truest friend—and a greater mismatch in personality I could hardly imagine. As a senator from Massachusetts and a pharisee, he was as likely as anyone in the capital to have learned of any wayward behavior by one William Turtle, late of the Bay State, and he would not hesitate to speak ill of the dead. Cortelyou (of course) had 'phoned ahead on my behalf.

I slowed Single Malt to an amble, past the Cuban embassy, the wood and coal yard, and the shabby Gordon Hotel, just reopened after its summer hiatus. Dwellings clustered like teeth in a boxer's mouth. I guided the mare past the scowling statue of Daniel Webster and west onto Massachusetts avenue. Thus we entered a different world, hushed and cloistered, one that must have reminded Cabot Lodge, the Boston Brahmin *plus ultra,* of Beacon Hill. The adjoining brick houses were imposing, all of them holier-than-thou. Lodge's was the holiest, the grandest, three stories high and two houses wide, as spacious as Henry Adams's and mine combined. Its stately Georgian style, the arches and peaks and bow walls, reminded me of Harvard. Surely no accident.

Inside, I talked my way past the butler and entered what my friend Clemens called the Gilded Age. And what an opulent age it was— cosseted with wine-colored fringed furniture, protected by carved bookshelves, dazzled by rococo chandeliers, swaddled in Persian rugs. I was requested to wait behind the closed double doors, which I did, for the most part patiently, for nine minutes (but who was counting?). On the bookshelves I found hundreds of histories, from ancient Greece to modern America, including my ten volumes on Lincoln and all nine volumes of Henry Adams's epic on the Jefferson and Madison admin- istrations. The spines of my books were intact; several of Henry's were cracked. Then again, Henry had taught Lodge at Harvard while the future senator was burrowing into the past for his PhD.

I heard footsteps, and the doors swung open. Senator Lodge was tall and thin, every inch the ascetic Yankee, with a sharp chin and a gray- ing goatee that made him look longer still. His muted cravat, below the high collar, was perfectly tied. His skin, an alabaster white, looked sickly. Were I to press his cheek, I wondered if it would bulge back. He deigned to shake my hand and then quickly withdrew his.

"You wished to see me, I understand," he said in an aristocratic whine.

"At the president's suggestion, Senator." I had known him for more than a decade, but we were still on formal terms. "I apologize for in- truding on a Saturday. It is about a state legislator from Pittsfield named William Turtle. Did you know him?"

"You employ the past tense. I heard something about that."

Not from the newspapers. "I was there," I said.

"Really?" His marble face was capable of showing surprise. "Why?"

"To question *him*."

"For what purpose?" Lodge said.

Who was supposed to pose the questions here? "Has Theodore discussed this with you?" I said.

"Discussed what?"

"The collision in Pittsfield."

"Oh yes. He says he wants to sue the motorman who killed poor Mr. Craig."

My turn to say, "Really?" Theodore hadn't said that to me. Maybe with Lodge he had been letting off steam. Or maybe he meant it. With our impetuous young president, you could never tell for sure. Nor, I suspected, could he.

"Well, Mr. Turtle was the motorman's lawyer. And the conductor's *and* the streetcar company's. I am guessing this had something to do with his . . . death. His murder. I want to learn anything I can about him. As I say, he was a legislator, so I hope you might have known him."

A look of disbelief crossed Lodge's face, presumably at the notion that a man of his breeding and position might know anything at all about a mere member of the Great and General Court. "A little, I suppose," he said.

"What was your impression of him, then?"

We sat in deep leather armchairs, cups of bitter tea at our elbows, before a blazing fire that was making me perspire.

Lodge tilted his head back and literally looked down his nose. His high brow and his hooded eyes looked formidable. "Not a favorable one, my dear Hay. Rather uncouth, wouldn't you say? And a rather . . . *large* man. And crass, I must say, in how he went about things."

"Any particulars?"

Lodge waved his hand at the flames—he was a man of conclusions, not of details—and waited for a worthier question.

"Ethical in his dealings?" I tried.

"I would have no way of knowing," Lodge said. "I have every good reason to doubt it."

"Namely?"

"You only had to look at the man to know he lacked honor."

I couldn't disagree. "I do need specifics," I said.

"Why? Once you know a man, you know him. The rest is just fill. What do you want to know about him, specifically?"

He had me there. I decided to be frank. (Dangerous, I know, for a diplomat.) "I want to know if the late Mr. Turtle was, in your considered judgment, capable of trying to kill a man. A president." I surprised myself at the question, but I knew Theodore wouldn't mind.

"Of course he was. Anyone is."

Just what Henry had said. "Not all of us act on it," I pointed out. "Almost nobody does. The question is, did he?"

"You seriously think that this wretched man Turtle had something to do with Roosevelt's . . ." Cabot Lodge was speechless, for once in his life.

"He had *some*thing to do with it. Look at his clients. He represented everyone involved. Well, not everyone, but on the streetcar company's side of things. He came to Washington to . . . I don't know what. I am trying to figure that out. To see me, among others, but I have no idea why. This is why I am asking you, can you shed any light on this man?"

"Not in the way that you want. You should ask Governor Crane— he is arriving here to-morrow. He is a man of specifics. As you point out, I have only a general impression of the man. Your Mr. Turtle, as I understand things, is—was—at the center of the Republican . . . organization . . . out in Berkshire County." I gathered that the senator, as a Cabot *and* a Lodge, had never needed to rely on anything as vulgar as a political machine. "Your Mr. Turtle knew how to make deals. He knew men. And how to cheat them. How to make them do what he wanted, whatever was required. *Whatever* was required. That is what he was good at. A valuable skill in politics. Maybe the most valuable. But rather a disagreeable quality in a man."

You should know, I thought uncharitably. I had rarely heard the acerbic Yankee so passionate about anything. I pressed my luck. "A plausible mastermind, do you suppose, of a plot to, say, assassinate"—I luxuriated in every syllable—"the president?"

"Absolutely," Lodge replied. He squinted and knocked over his tea. "Or a victim of it."

I left and learned that Single Malt had bitten the bark from an elm.

⇥⇤

I repeated Lodge's three words to Nellie Bly. *Or a victim.* We sat in my library on opposite settees, sipping coffee that Clara had brought us. A generous gesture, I thought, given the press of our evening's plans. But I understood why she bothered: to catch a glimpse of the famous woman I had mentioned a little too often. The two women seemed to like each other, to my relief.

"Why would somebody want to kill *him*?" Nellie said.

"Good question. But let's start with the fact that somebody did."

"As you can testify."

"Which I may have to. Possibly as the defendant." Was I bragging?

"Maybe a better question is this: Why would somebody want to kill Turtle *then*? As soon as he arrived here. Just before he was going to see—"

"Yes," I pounced, "to prevent him from talking to . . ." I told Nellie of the pocket diary. "Cortelyou, Mark Hanna, and . . . me."

"Talk about what?"

I smiled and extended my palms in supplication. "I wish I knew."

"Any hint at all? You were with him."

"For hardly a minute. We hadn't really started to talk. He went to get dressed and had already called for breakfast."

"Did anyone know you were there?"

"Only Clara. And . . ." I decided to come clean about the woman I'd heard back in the bedroom. "But she wouldn't have known who I was."

"Unless he told her."

"True," I conceded. "But she was almost certainly a . . . a prostitute." Unless she wasn't. "Did you find anything in Lizzie's . . . Lizzie Cameron's"—a knowing look from Nellie—"rooms?"

"Nothing," Nellie said.

"Nothing?"

"Nothing to speak of. Quite a lot, actually. Mrs. Cameron does not travel lightly."

"She does nothing lightly."

That knowing look again, deserved.

"A dozen pairs of shoes," Nellie said. "None of them with hexagonal heels."

I exhaled, for the first time in a while. Then a contrary thought. "Unless she was wearing them when you checked."

"Why don't *you* check the next time you see her?" Nellie said, with a level stare.

I chuckled to myself, loudly enough that she could hear. "I just might do that," I replied, "and I will be sure to tell you everything I learn." I stared back. "*And* my wife."

"Naturally," Nellie said.

I didn't enjoy being ribbed about something I was agonizing over myself. I was stupid as hell; I knew that. Otherwise, why would I jeopardize everything I held dear—my wife, my daughters, my surviving son—in pursuit of a woman who would bring me nothing but grief? I *knew* all of that. Any yet . . . And yet what? Yes, Lizzie was beautiful to look at. Enthralling, really. All true. But so what? Was I truly that shallow? That *callow*? I used to be, I know, and at times I am embarrassed by my former self. By my current self, too, I'll admit. Had I learned nothing over the years?

"How did you get in, by the way?" I said. "Merely as a matter of craft, if you would."

"It was easy." A prideful smile lit up her face like a lantern in a belfry. "I, uh, borrowed the key from the front desk while the clerk was . . . away. And I . . . just in case . . . dressed like a chambermaid."

I was impressed. "Where on earth did you find a uniform?" I wasn't sure I wanted to know.

"Easy again," she said. "I stole it."

Thus confirming my fears. Should the newspapers ever get wind of my role in a murder—innocent, inadvertent—I was a goner.

+═══+

I was perusing the *Evening Star*, trying not to doze off in my favorite leather chair. Pershing was making headway in the Philippines. Transpacific mail left daily for China. (How the world was shrinking!) Typhoid fever had slammed other cities worse than Washington. Prince Henry of Prussia, the kaiser's brother, had taken out the first-ever insurance policy on an assassination—his own. Croquet was reviving. An item in the neighboring column caught my eye:

The Penalty of Progress

From Life.

Is it anybody's business to keep count of the number of persons who are killed by accidents from day to day in this country? The number must be enormous, and most of the victims die of modern improvements of one kind or another. Fatal trolley car accidents are more common and comprehensive this year than ever before; railroads kill and maim about as usual; automobiles do their share . . .

All right, all right. I was fundamentally a nineteenth-century man, still a believer in polite dealings, deliberate thought, gentlemanly restraint—in transport and in life. So sue me. I wasn't proud of these fetishes, like Henry Adams was, but I was honest enough not to deny them. As if anyone gave a damn besides myself. The age of invention had its wonders *and* its perils, but the age of the gentleman was dying if not dead. My advantage over Henry was that I was adaptable to modern ways—educable, even into my sixties. In the boxing ring I had learned to escape corners.

The past is a land in which I was born

Not bad.

And where I've spent my days.

Redundant. Worse, boring.

> *The past is a land in which I was born*
> *And where my life . . .*

I was rescued by a scraping in the room and discovered that my eyes were closed. I opened them and there Henry stood, in front of me. His beard looked less devilish than usual. An angelic smile wreathed his face.

"This is a dream, right?" I said.

"If you like," he replied. He was waving a paper at the edge of my vision.

"Take a seat, Henry," I said.

He was too excited to sit. That excited me, too. Henry came at the world with the scholar's perspective of centuries. There was little that was new under the sun. But occasionally there was.

"I found something," he said unnecessarily.

"Tell me."

"It was deep in one of the boxes. It's a letter. Quite a tedious one, actually. Written by the lawyers, surely—they *must* get paid by the word— and signed by the principals. From Morgan, J. Pierpont himself, to James J. Hill, *him*self. Almost impenetrable, the letter, about the Sherman Antitrust Act and whether it might be applied by an unsympathetic administration."

"The Sherman act. Lizzie's uncle. Ha! And might it?"

"Precisely what you would expect from Northern Securities lawyers who want to remain employed as Northern Securities lawyers. A railroad monopoly is a boon to heaven and to all of mankind, a veritable fulfillment of the Founding Fathers' rosiest vision." Those Fathers included Henry's great-grandpappy, John, and *his* cousin, Sam. "But what their lawyers think isn't what's interesting." Henry stopped, as if to gather himself, and shoved two pages of typewritten, single-spaced, impenetrable prose under my nose.

> My dear Mr. Hill:
> If we intend to succeed in our endeavor . . .

Those were the last words in English, before an onslaught of "whereas" and "foregoing" and "thereunder" and "conspiracy in restraint of trade" and, turning the page, "political animus." Well, those two words I understood, along with the four that followed: "of the current administration." By the current president, it meant. Lawyerly language for *loathing*.

"There!" Henry pointed, once I got to that phrase.

"I see it. Seems reasonably polite, given that the administration is taking them to court to break them up."

"You're not seeing it, old boy. On the side."

I had missed it because it was handwritten with a hard, sharp pencil along the right margin. I shifted the page to find the light.

Hay > TR!

I cursed to myself.

Apparently the pencil point had broken on the exclamation point, because the words underneath were ragged and thick: *'Phone me.*

'Phone me about what? I must have spoken that aloud, because Henry said, "My question precisely."

"It could mean anything, I guess."

"It could."

"Are you certain this is Morgan's handwriting? That's what you're suggesting, correct?"

"You are quick to catch on, old boy. I am no . . . graphologist, I believe they are called, but if you will examine the capital *P* in *'Phone* and the capital *P* in his signature"—JPM—"to my eye they look similar. More than similar. Identical."

I glanced back and forth three, four times, and I had to agree. "I'll ask Wilkie to have his men take a look. So, what do you suppose it means?"

"What it says."

"It doesn't mean they *did* anything about it."

"It means he wanted to—*wants* to. One thing you can say about J. Pierpont Morgan, he gets what he wants, *if* he wants. Has he ever said anything about this to you?"

"That he'd rather that I . . . Of course not—I hardly know the man.

Why on earth would he . . ." I had broken into a sweat. "When was this written?"

I was fumbling with the pages when Henry replied, "August third, this year. In the defendants' latest filings."

Henry was talking like a lawyer. "One month before the collision," I said.

"To the day."

CHAPTER TWELVE

Matters of church and God I left in Clara's hands—the earthly decisions were daunting enough. Besides, Saint John's suited me. The Episcopal church was certainly convenient, directly across Sixteenth street, and historical as hell. Every president since Madison has prayed there, with varying degrees of success. And the place was pleasing to the eye. The modest stucco church, pale yellow, made even the godless feel at ease. Not that I am godless (I lack the moral courage to follow the preponderance of evidence to its conclusion), but I have always been inclined to hedge my bets. Personally, I doubt that an hour's presence on Sunday morning matters very much to my destiny, eternal or shorter term. But as my sainted mother used to say, it can't hurt. Besides, it made Clara happy, which counted.

Inside, the church's simplicity suited me, too—the easy curves of balconies, the arched ceiling, the understated warmth. Clara's concession was to take seats in the last row, on the right, in case I needed an escape. My excuse was that it had been Lincoln's pew (probably for the same reason) whenever he worshiped here. I also liked the vantage point, the detached view of the proceedings and of the man in the pulpit, the Reverend Alexander Mackay-Smith.

On this particular morning, such a detachment was to be prized. The Reverend Mackay-Smith was a handsome young man with a barrel chest, a mustache as lush as Grover Cleveland's, and a magnetic presence. He delivered a perfunctory tribute to President McKinley, dead exactly one year now—the sermon's supposed topic—before he turned his oratorical attentions to the parishioner in the front row.

"Who can read history and believe that the course of events happens by chance?" the good reverend cried out. "It was by no accident that Judas betrayed the great Nazarene to be crucified. But who can tell why Mr. McKinley was so suddenly taken from the earth in the hour apparently of his greatest usefulness? Who could fill his place?

"Fortunately, a David was vice president. How came he to be vice president? Was it by accident?"

I imagined the David I knew to be turning red.

"How the love of him is filling the hearts of the people!" The Reverend Mackay-Smith leaned over the pulpit toward his subject. "His honesty, his bravery, his positive convictions, his resolute purpose, his frankness, his impartiality, his independence, his ability and willingness to look at every side of a question, his kindness of heart, and his democratic simplicity command the respect of every rank."

How Theodore hated being praised to his face. I half expected him to stomp out. His discipline awed me, and scared me a little.

+====+

There was a peremptory knock at the door. I answered it myself, as a mark of respect for the office but also for the man. For nigh on a year now, Theodore had stopped by my house most Sundays after church. For a dozen years before that, since he became a civil service commissioner for the forgettable Benjamin Harrison, I had hosted him for the occasional meal or salon.

It wasn't Theodore at the door but Princess Alice, dressed in white. Her broad-brimmed hat had more flowers than we had ordered for *my* Alice's wedding.

"Mr. Secretary," she said, bowing low, in mocking deference. "My good sir, may we enter?" Her father stepped from behind her.

"Anytime," I replied.

Alice helped her father limp up the steps to my doorway. He looked pale, his eyes unfocused. He was trembling.

We went into the parlor, though it could barely contain them. Both of the Roosevelts seemed caged. Theodore squirmed in his seat and Alice refused to take one, pacing along the walls, prowling the bookshelves, brushing her fingers across the marble and onyx in the mantel. Clara poured the tea, but I was the only taker. Maybe they feared spilling it, or perhaps they meant to leave soon. I needed to talk with Theodore first.

"What did you think of the sermon?" Clara said, either from obliviousness or—my guess—from a desire to cut to the core.

Theodore's fist pounded the table; the tea tray jumped.

"I have something I need to discuss," I said, glancing over at Alice in the corner. She was examining a Japanese vase with a covetous air.

"What is it?" Theodore said.

This would have to be in Alice's hearing. "Henry found something," I said.

My tone must have given me away, for the president's face snapped to attention.

"What?" he said.

I told him about the note in the margin, and not without apprehension. *Hay > TR!* was not the message I hoped to convey. Especially the exclamation point.

"Who wrote it?" Theodore said, as gruffly as his high pitch would allow.

"Morgan himself, best we can tell. Though it takes a handwriting expert to confirm it."

"Get one," he said.

I nodded.

"And Morgan, too," Theodore said.

"What about him?" I said.

"Ask him."

"Ask him what—does he want you dead?"

"Exactly. As soon as you can. I'll have Cortelyou arrange it."

Alice's head jerked up. "Father, who wants you dead?"

Roosevelt chortled. "Everyone," he said. "Don't *you*, Sister?"

"Oh, Father, don't joke like that."

How sweet, for Alice.

"And you, Hay?"

I assumed a falsetto and said, "Oh, Father, don't joke like that."

No laugh. His eyes had become watchful, like a predator's in the bush. I realized his question was serious. So I offered a serious reply: "No, you are much more fun alive."

"Sometimes," Alice said.

Theodore's face lit up. He probably got more joy out of life in a day than I did in a month.

⊬══⊣

John Wilkie rocked on his side porch, sucking on his pipe, waiting— for me, I had to assume. But how could he know I was coming? I hadn't told a soul. Oh. Theodore had, after I left. Probably 'phoned Wilkie himself.

The Secret Service chief lived at the edge of the city—beyond it, by my figuring—a mile north of Florida avenue (originally Boundary street, between Washington City and Washington County). Single Malt enjoyed the ride as much as she could with a man on her back. The occasional rabbit required a pull of her reins. Out here, Thirteenth street was a dirt roadway, lined by clusters of houses and by tangles of bushes and trees. Morgan avenue, a short, slender street just west of New Hampshire avenue, was succumbing to settlement. Wilkie's house was the farthest north, a three-story duplex with a side yard and a roofed porch that wrapped around from the front.

"A pleasure as always, Mr. Hay," Wilkie said, gesturing me into the adjacent chair. "Mr. Cortelyou said you were coming."

"And Mr. Cortelyou is always right," I said.

Wilkie snorted. "He would agree."

I knew I liked this man. "Did he say what I wanted?"

"I thought I would let you do that."

Clickety-clack. Clickety-clack. The sound came from the side window. Wilkie listened alertly, then shook his head. "The telegraph," he explained. "I had them put one in here. For days like this."

"Are all days like this?"

"Most of them."

A girl of twelve or thirteen popped her blond head through the door. "Later, dearie," Wilkie said. The smiling face withdrew.

"How many do you have?" I said.

"One of each."

"You are a busy man, I can see."

A quick, professional smile. I noticed furrows beginning to form near the corners of his mouth. "And what can I do for you, Mr. Hay?"

My request for a handwriting expert to confirm J. P. Morgan's signature got his attention.

"May I ask why?" he said.

I produced the two pages Henry had found and pointed out the capital *P*s.

"I can help," Wilkie said. "How quickly?"

"Yesterday?"

"Let me see what I can do."

I told him I was leaving shortly for New York and expected to speak with Morgan in the morning. "Mr. Cortelyou is making the arrangements."

"Can you leave these with me?" Wilkie balanced the pages on his fingertips and rested them on the metal table between us. He added, "There is something I need to tell you."

"Oh?"

"That bullet? The one the doctors extracted from Mr. Turtle's cranium? It looks consistent with the bullet missing from your derringer, judging by the one that wasn't fired. They fired a test bullet and it's consistent with that, too."

"What in the hell does that mean—'consistent'?"

"Just what it says. Maybe it came from your derringer. Maybe it didn't. They can't say any better than that. This is my lab men, and they're the best in the business."

"So I'm still under suspicion, you're saying."

"Let's say you're not entirely free of it."

"This is ridiculous!" I sputtered.

"Agreed. I am with you on this. All the same, you might want to check in with the local folks before you leave the city."

"Before I *what*?"

"Just as a courtesy."

"I'm going to New York overnight, at the president's—"

"You might want to say something to . . . what was that detective's name?"

"That big gawky fellow? Flather?"

"That's the one. Just to let him know. In case he's looking for you."

"To ask permission, you mean?"

"No, no, just to let him know."

Wilkie scuttled inside and I stayed on the porch for a spell.

"Anything new?" I said, trying to sound disarming.

"Nothing to speak of," Detective Flather replied.

That was ominous.

I was sitting by his desk at police headquarters. The place was almost deserted on a Sunday, but not deserted enough. I had figured to leave Flather a note. Imagine my surprise when the sergeant led me back to a detectives' room that, despite the afternoon sunlight streaming in, looked dank and generally downbeat about the human experience. Flather had glanced up and glared at me. I hoped he did that to everyone.

Once I had borrowed his attention from the worn manila folders, I told him I was traveling to New York overnight. "Just in case you wanted to know."

That brought a grunt of indeterminate meaning. I studied the detective's face and saw only lumpy features and gauzy eyes. "Why?" he growled.

How much did I trust him? Not much. "On the president's business," I said. How do I tell a real detective that I was playing at his game? Except it wasn't a game. People got killed, as I could attest. I made up my mind. "It isn't clear that the president's collision in Pittsfield was an accident," I said. Flather's sleepy eyes snapped to alertness. "I am . . . looking into it."

"And you think the two are connected," he said. "That and . . . this." Flather waved his hand across his desk. He was not as dumb as he looked.

"It is possible," I said with care.

"I agree." Flather's face had relaxed; his dark eyes focused. He knew what he was doing. "We found something," he said.

That *something* was a letter of introduction in Turtle's valise. The handwritten note was unexceptional—"This is to introduce . . ."—other than the identities involved. The letter, undated, was addressed to "My dear Mr. President" and signed "Murray Crane." That was Winthrop Murray Crane, the honorable governor of Massachusetts.

⊢━•━⊣

"I think he trusts *me,*" I said. "He showed me the letter."

Nellie Bly flashed a look of pathos she might reserve for a fifty-year-old who hasn't learned how babies are made. "Maybe he does," she said, "and maybe he doesn't. I doubt your personal detective trusts any-one very much. I would hate to be his wife."

"Have you met him?"

"No, but I know the type."

I would hate to get on *her* bad side. "So you think I'm still consid-ered a suspect," I said.

"How can I know?" Nellie said. "But, in this country, you are guilty until proven innocent." Emma Goldman couldn't have put it better.

The Willard's bar was closed on a Sunday, of course, so we sat in the lobby, behind a marble pillar, as far as possible from anyone else. The hotel was not only the scene of the crime but also where Governor Crane was staying. Ichabod was prickly to question; a woman's salve might help.

"Which room?" I said.

"This, you're not going to believe." Nellie had made inquiries of a desk clerk she had befriended. "The same as Turtle's."

"You're kidding."

"He asked for it. The police said they were finished."

"Why on earth would he . . ."

"One way to find out," Nellie said.

We passed the registration desk—the clerk's gaze followed Nellie like a hunter's in a blind—and climbed the staircase. I could have found the room with my eyes closed. I asked Nellie to knock on the door.

"Who is it?" came a parched voice from inside.

I gave my name.

The latch was unhooked and the door opened.

Neither Governor Crane nor the late William Turtle stood in the doorway, but rather a giant with an unkempt red beard. I had seen him before but couldn't remember where. He seemed startled to see me.

"Who are you?" I rasped.

"Forney," he said.

Oh yes: Samson. David Pratt's man. From Dalton, Massachusetts. As Governor Crane was.

"Is the governor here?"

"He expecting you?"

"Not unless he's clairvoyant."

Samson grimaced. "Yer name?" he said.

I reminded him.

With nary a glance at Nellie, he closed the door and left us waiting outside.

"Who is *he*?" Nellie said.

I explained, best I could, that Frank Forney was an angry French Canadian who lived as a servant of some sort in David Pratt's—the carriage driver's—household.

Two or three minutes passed and then the door opened again. Governor Crane, his cravat half tied, looked unaccountably harried. "Come in," he said. "What can I do for you? And for . . . ?"

I introduced the awkward governor to the pert and poised Mrs. Seaman. No hands were shaken. We crossed the octagonal sitting room, a place I remembered all too well—the gaudy furnishings, Grant's portrait, a gunshot in the doorway, louder than any noise I'd ever known. I stared at the windows, their curtains closed, to avoid looking at the door. Nellie and Governor Crane shared a divan. I remained standing.

"I have been in this room before," I said.

"With Lincoln?" Governor Crane said.

"That would be the old Willard," I replied. "No, with Turtle, three mornings ago."

I had thought his spare Yankee face incapable of additional longitude, but his mouth dropped into an O. I told him briefly what I had seen. "In his effects," I said, "the police found a letter from you."

I waited for a look of surprise.

"Do you know which letter I mean?" I said. A slight nod, which for a man like Ichabod Crane connoted high emotion. "Do you happen to know why he wanted to see the president?"

I was glad he sighed, because it meant he was breathing.

"How well *did* you know Mr. Turtle?" Nellie purred.

Governor Crane seemed startled by her presence. He gathered himself and croaked, "Well enough."

"Well enough to what?" I said.

"To write."

"Do you often write the president with letters of intro—"

Nellie raised a palm. "Was he a good man, do you think?"

An eloquent shrug.

"When did you write this letter?" I said.

Governor Crane looked puzzled for a moment, as if I had spoken a language he had learned as a child. "Last week," he said.

After the collision.

"It was good of you to do that, Governor," Nellie said. "What inspired you to this kindness?"

I worried she was overdoing it, but no, the crusty Yankee lapped it up. "He asked me, and I was happy to oblige."

"Where was this?" she said.

"In the corridor of the statehouse. Later he came to my office to pick it up."

"Why did he want it? Did you ask him?"

"In so many words."

"And what did he say?"

A pause. A noise back in the bedroom alarmed me. "He had something he needed to tell the president—that's all."

"About what, did he say?"

He shook his head.

"No idea at all?" I said.

Nellie said, "You were in the carriage, too. He must have told *you*."

"All he said is that the collision wasn't an accident and that he could prove it. But it was something he could only tell the president."

"So you gave him the letter of introduction," Nellie soothed.

"I had already written it for him," Governor Crane explained. "I would not waste good stationery."

⊹╼━╾⊹

As busy as an anthill was the Pennsylvania Railroad Station on Sunday evening. I sidestepped the star marking Garfield's shooting and weaved my way unrecognized through the passengers scurrying past. I took a seat in the least crowded car and held *The Washington Post* in front of my face. Two trains collide in Colorado. Milliners in Chicago form a labor union. The president will hunt for ducks in Virginia. Nebraska's governor threatens a lawsuit if packinghouses merge. The price of anthracite coal soars to twenty-five dollars a ton, in the eighteenth week of the strike; in hopes of arranging a settlement, Pennsylvania's governor and the capitalists are traveling to New York to call on J. Pierpont Morgan, like paying homage to the Buddha.

As was I.

J. Pierpont Morgan—the august name conveyed an image either of utter rectitude or of utter greed—was more powerful than any president or potentate. The Wall street financier had his hand in everything across the economy and, inevitably, in politics, too. The banks, the railroads, the steel mills, the steamships, the coal mines—during the past quarter century's surge of an industrial economy, his word ruled everywhere that mattered. Since the Spanish war he had reigned as monarch of the trusts, the financial genius behind the creation of U.S. Steel—the world had never known a more valuable company—and the Northern Securities railroad cartel. I had dined with him once, at the White House, back in 'ninety-eight, and found him . . . shy.

"Wait, aren't you . . ."

Damn, I had let my newspaper slip.

A round-faced man with a belly was peering at me. "Aren't you Mr. . . . You know, that secretary of . . ." I hated that the newspapers were publishing photographs. "You know . . . What's the name? Root. Yep, that's the name. The war fellow, E-*li*-hu Root."

"I get mistaken for him all the time," I said. Root had a stern face and no beard.

I cast the newspaper aside and returned to my traveling companion and mentor—ha!—Sherlock Holmes. My bookmark was a ticket to a recent prizefight, out in Maryland. I took up where I'd left off, trying to let the fictional mystery distract me from the menace of the real-world murders I faced.

CHAPTER THIRTEEN

I awoke at ten past seven and felt like a caboose had sideswiped my fore-head. Not from an excess of scotch the night before, although that might have contributed. Or from the quality of the scotch. Or from the lateness of the night. Or from the pillows, as cuddly as mica. Or from the mattress . . . the room . . . the hotel . . .

I was staying at the Astor House—for old times' sake, certainly not for the facilities. The hotel was already old-fashioned when I lived there in the 'seventies, and it hadn't done much to spiff itself up. The marble floor in the lobby had taken on a brownish tint and the porcelain spit-toons had webs of cracks in the sides. The rooms lacked telephones, which in a way was a plus. If the world was collapsing, Adee could leave word at the desk.

Moving my head from side to side brought a spectrum of pain. Ol' Pierpont wouldn't see me until ten o'clock. Maybe the headache pow-der would work by then.

Only when I had forced down a breakfast (of porridge and tea) and exited the Astor, onto Broadway, did I realize the source of my distress: Manhattan. My aching head was a sensible reaction to all the noise and congestion. After decades in the East, in Providence and Washington and New York—and London—I was gratified to learn I was still a boy from Warsaw, Illinois. Too much was going on. *Too much!* That was the ugly variable—the multiplier, if you will. The men were monochro-matic in their derbies and frock coats, unlike the ladies in their flowered bonnets and long, sweeping skirts. Pedestrians clogged the sidewalks, crossing Broadway at every angle, dodging the horse carts, minding the trolleys, ignoring the policemen in their round bobby hats. A chaos of choreography. It was a marvel that every moment did not bring a collision. I felt trapped and exhilarated, both at once.

Crossing Broadway would lead to the *Tribune*'s offices, my old haunt. Instead, I turned south, past Saint Paul's.

Let me stipulate here that I hate crowds. Anyone who believes in the dignity of man (and woman!) should. Think of the hajj, in Mecca; you might be trampled at any instant, at a sudden sound. Crowds steal your sense of self and mock the illusion of control over one's fate. So, without a further thought, I plunged in.

I felt surrounded and smothered and breathed on, and I craned my neck and twisted it—and saw him. He was reflected in the slanted glass of a florist's window. I am not sure why I noticed him at all. He was unexceptional looking—egregiously so. Maybe that was why: he looked so damn ordinary, of medium height and complexion, with regular features and the ubiquitous derby, as if he was trying too hard to blend in. Something about the angle of his gaze. He wasn't looking straight ahead, as any pedestrian would. He was staring at me. And for an instant, by way of the florist's window, I stared back. Our eyes met.

I sped up, and he did too. I was south of Maiden lane when I glanced back and nearly collided with a matronly woman—"Oh, sorry," I muttered—and the man was still behind me. Instead of panicking, I considered my options. The most obvious was to start running, which I rejected for fear of the attention this would bring, even in Manhattan. Besides, he could probably outrun me. Or I could stop and confront him. I had my fists and my derringer—Wilkie had loaned me another—in addition to my vaunted way with words. (I am known as the literary secretary of state, if you must know.) This dangled a certain emotional satisfaction but seemed less than reliable as a route to success. Or I could . . . lose him. Outthink him. As Sherlock would do.

I darted into the street, just in front of a trolley, without pondering how stupid this was. Once the trolley passed, I looked back across Broadway and did not see my pursuer in the crowd. I leapt onto the curb—and there he was, a half block behind me, on my side of the street. Damn!

I ducked through the last doorway before Liberty street, which happened to belong to a grocery. I must have looked a mess, because the redheaded young woman behind the boxes of apples and pears gave me the kind of glance my mother favored when I picked a fistfight with my older brother out of boredom.

"May I help you, sir?" she said.

"A back door?" I said. I considered waving the derringer but decided it would not bolster my case.

"Certainly, sir," she said. "May I *help* you?"

"An apple, please." The politeness was also my mother's doing.

I tossed a penny on the counter. I figured the apple could always serve as a weapon, and the purchase gave me standing as a customer to state again, "Back door!"

The disapproving look recurred, but she pointed past the displays of cheeses and beef at the rear.

"Thank you," I said.

I skedaddled past the woven curtain and through the storeroom with boxes piled high. There was a door at the end, on the right. I worried that it might be locked and that, by the time I returned to the front, the store would swarm with policemen. Possibly to my advantage, but I would rather arrive at Pierpont Morgan's premises alone, preferably without manacles. I pulled on the sturdy metal door—and it creaked open.

I darted out into the daylight, onto Liberty street. I glanced back toward Broadway and saw no one I wished not to see. I fled in the opposite direction, at a New Yorker's fleet but unexceptional pace. At the corner, I turned right onto Nassau street, heading south. I was entering the realm of money, no subtlety about it. The names carved over the doorway betrayed their temporal concerns. Bank of Commerce, the Equitable Building, the Western National Bank. Now I crossed Pine street. Hanover National Bank. Buildings needn't be nineteen stories to exceed human scale. *That* was New York: the loss of human scale. The slabs of marble or steel or limestone made me feel small, as they were meant to.

I kept glancing behind me as I hurried along. My pursuer was gone. I took a bite of the apple. It was crunchy and sweet.

I reached Wall street. The buildings were slathered with enough Greek pillars for a heathen temple. On the far corner, straight ahead, the New York Stock Exchange embodied solemnity and self-regard—deserved, no doubt, now that Wall street rivaled the City of London in financing the world. Facing the stock exchange stood 23 Wall street, the marble fortress of J. P. Morgan & Company. Well, almost facing—from its catty-cornered entrance, more like a sideways glance. An apt metaphor for how this brusque and willful genius had leveraged his millions to gain control of any industry that needed a hand.

No corporate name decorated the exterior; none was needed. I pushed on the heavy brass door, which swung ajar with no help from me. I stepped through, into the cool of a mausoleum.

"Good morning, Mr. Hay." I jumped back and felt for my derringer; my apple dropped to the floor.

It was the man who had chased me.

"I hoped to catch you on the street," he was saying, "but I must have lost you in the crowd. Mr. Morgan has been delayed. He should not be much longer. If you would be kind enough to wait."

My erstwhile pursuer was horrified when I asked for a *New York World* instead of the highbrow *Sun* or the stodgier *Times*. I chose it because of Nellie Bly—the *World* was still as lively as she was. A drawing of the locomotive whose boiler exploded in Pennsylvania. The millionaire's son who posed as a tramp. Mrs. William Rockefeller overruling her husband to let baseball nines play on their Greenwich, Connecticut, estate. Digging the city's subway tunnels, three-fifths completed, had cost twenty-four lives so far. Christy Mathewson won't deny rumors he might jump from the National League's Giants to the fledgling American League. A letter to the editor championed pineapple juice as a medicine for indigestion—"the pure juice . . . only, never swallow the pulp."

The absence of serious news was giving me a bellyache, and then I was summoned from my uncomfortable chair in the lobby. I will remember the ancient elevator until my dying day. It felt like a coffin, lacking silk frills but fashioned of finely carved walnut, the brass fittings as polished as an admiral's buttons, as stately as the Union League's hearths. A casket for three, counting the white-haired operator and my nursemaid.

We emerged on the top floor and I was startled to see the great man himself, behind a glass wall, in his wood-paneled office. He sat in a swivel chair behind his rolltop desk, dictating to a fast-scribbling young man who was as handsome as Morgan was ugly. Any of his subordinates lucky enough to work up here could see him—and he could see them.

I was left standing with my nose to the glass, and I studied the man I had come to question. He *was* ugly. The famous nose, of course, misshapen like an Asian fruit. (Most of the photographs touched it up, taming its size and bulbousness.) But it wasn't his nose so much as the shape of his head. It was bottom-heavy, as if the formidable brow had sunk over the decades, compressing his face and puffing his jowls. Beneath the aggressive mustache, his thick lips snarled.

When the letter was finished and the young man had left, I was audacious enough to step inside. Morgan ignored me while he read, reread, and signed a letter on his desk, all the while chewing on a fat black cigar. He wore a stiff collar and a frock coat. He looked up, half stood, held out a pugilist's thick hand that enveloped mine. His gray eyes latched onto my own and would not let go. He nodded me into the abandoned seat and said, "Well?"

This would not be easy.

I saw no point in small talk. I opened my valise and slid out the thin cardboard, folded over. Inside was Morgan's letter to Hill, the one Henry had found and Wilkie had returned with admirable dispatch. I asked him to be careful not to touch the letter itself. I made sure he pressed his fingers into the cardboard.

"Did you write this?" I said.

Morgan glanced over it and replied in a foghorn voice, "What if I did?"

"If you would kindly read the note in the margin."

Morgan's eyes blazed. "I did," he said.

"You wrote it?"

"So?"

How could I answer without explaining too much? "Is it true, then, that you would prefer . . . someone else as president?"

"Just about anyone," Morgan said, his gray eyes narrowing into points. "Except that jackass Bryan."

"Including me?" I said.

"Anyone."

"So your note in the margin here . . ."

"Is a statement of fact. How did you get this?"

Now what? Do I accuse the most powerful man in America of trying to murder the president, without a shred of evidence beyond wanting him gone? Not a winning tactic. The Morgans and the Roosevelts went way back. Their fathers were friends, and Theodore (after some urging) had named Morgan's son as a special attaché to King Edward VII's coronation.

"Did Jack enjoy London?" I said.

"Yes."

Thus ended my attack at his flank. Morgan was not a bush I could beat around, and I needed to be careful. "This preference of yours," I said. "Would you"—the subjunctive to the rescue—"ever take action to make it come to pass?"

Morgan's brow expanded and his mighty mustache bristled. He half rose—he was a big man—and leaned over me.

"How much?"

"How much what?"

"Money."

"What? I'm not asking for . . . Money for what? You think I'm trying to bribe you?"

"Is that what you call it? Hanna called it a donation to make America greater."

It dawned on me what Morgan meant, and I burst out laughing. Morgan looked offended. He did not like to be laughed at. (Who did?)

"I am not running for anything," I assured him. "I don't even want the job." Each time I said this, I was a smidgen less sure it was true.

"What *do* you want?" Morgan said. "And how did you get *this*?"

Two good questions. I wanted to know if he had had a hand in trying to murder President Roosevelt or if he knew anyone who did. But on its face, the question somehow seemed silly—more precisely, far-fetched. I could ask him and search his face for a glimmer of . . . what?

The second question was easier, and I mentioned the materials that Northern Securities had filed with the court. Then I tackled the first question. "The accident in Pittsfield," I said. "We are not certain it *was* an accident."

No reply except a blank look, possibly one he had mastered.

"It might have been an attempt on the president's life," I said.

A pause. "So?"

I nodded toward the letter on his desk.

Morgan sat upright. Then he laughed. A high-pitched cackle. I had never heard it before, nor imagined it. A horrible sound. Once it ended I would not have sworn it had happened.

"Ask the man who sent you," Morgan said, then turned his attention to the stack of correspondence on his desk. I sat for a moment. Before I felt my dignity begin to erode, I retrieved the letter and the cardboard and took my leave. No nursemaid was in sight.

+➤══➤+

Ask the man who sent you.

What in the hell did that mean? Theodore had sent me. Ask Theodore about an attempt on his life? He would be the last to know. Wouldn't he?

The train was rumbling past the truck farms of New Jersey. In the late afternoon sunlight, bales of hay dotted the honey-colored fields. I watched with a scotch in hand, as I sank into the plush vermillion chair. The evening papers sat unread on the elaborately carved ebony table.

Ask the man who sent you. Maybe Morgan had meant nothing at all, merely a cryptic comment to mark my dismissal. Unlikely. Morgan's words were few, and never extraneous. All right. I'll ask Roosevelt. But ask him what?

Or Hanna. Hadn't he hounded Morgan for money to make himself president, and hadn't Turtle planned to meet with him, too? I needed to question him again. Or Cortelyou. Yes! This whole endeavor had been his idea. Maybe that's what Morgan meant. But how on earth would Morgan know? Maybe he hoped to smear him before Cortelyou became the inaugural secretary of commerce and labor. But in that case, why not be blunt? Because he had no evidence to offer? Still, I needed to chat with Cortelyou, preferably in a way that kept my purpose masked. Not easy; the man was shrewd.

Then I thought of a way.

I sat back and bolstered my scotch and pulled *The Hound of the Baskervilles* from my valise. The cover, a red threaded in gold, nearly matched the color of my seat.

I had left Dr. Watson puzzling about the strange silhouette on the moor, and meanwhile a clue turned up regarding Sir Charles Baskerville's mysterious death. Dr. Watson learned of a partially burned letter, signed "L. L.," inviting Sir Charles to meet at ten p.m. by the gate to the moor. Laura Lyons, for that was her name, claimed she never kept the appointment. Her story rang true, and Dr. Watson's questions couldn't shake it, so he had to figure she was telling the truth.

Oh Lord, I knew how he felt. If Pierpont Morgan was telling the truth . . . And I had to figure he was. Because of *who* he was, in part. And because of something he had misunderstood—that I was seeking a campaign donation, not a bribe. There was something else, too, and I had known it all along: If Pierpontifex Maximus wanted someone killed, would he rely on a trolley motorman in Pittsfield to do the deed? The very notion was absurd.

But where, exactly, did this leave me? Approximately where I had started, that's where. What did I *know*? That Big Billy Craig, the president's bodyguard, was dead. That the president might have been killed but wasn't. That someone had murdered William Turtle at the Willard Hotel—and it wasn't me, no matter what the police wanted to think. That Turtle knew something about the collision in Pittsfield— proof that it wasn't an accident! He apparently planned to tell Theodore, Mark Hanna, and me, the latter two having the most to gain from the president's demise.

What else did I know? Not a lot. A damn muddle, it was. The trolley might or might not have been hurtling down Howard's Hill and might or might not have stopped in time. The motorman, who might or might not have harbored anarchistic feelings, had come into a three-thousand-dollar windfall of dubious provenance. Despising the president did not necessarily mean wanting to murder him, although it helped. If Pierpont Morgan tried to kill a president, he would do it in a way no one would ever detect. But by way of a trolley collision in Pittsfield?

All right, I *knew* next to nothing. What did I suspect? That Cortelyou should not be trusted but was most unlikely to put himself—or Theodore, his patron saint, his golden goose—in danger. That Euclid Madden, the motorman, needed money for his family and presumably would do whatever he must.

Or maybe it *was* an accident, and nothing more. This is what I wanted to believe. Collisions occurred every day, didn't they? Two facts, however, stood in the way. Fact one: a man had attacked me in the center of Pittsfield and knew my name. Not to mention fact two: William Turtle had been murdered before my eyes.

I stared out the window into the darkness and then napped through Delaware.

+=—=+

The naphtha lamps around Lafayette Square barely dented the darkness. I returned the glare of the Secret Service man—he was a new one—with a genial smile. It didn't fool him. He had no intention of letting me in or, certainly, of awakening the president.

"But he is awake," I protested. "His light is on." I pointed to the third floor, although I had no idea whether Theodore slept in the front or the back.

"Wait," he ordered, and went inside. A lock clicked.

I stood on the sidewalk, cooling my heels—literally. My pocket watch said twenty minutes past ten. The night had a chill; leaves rustled in the park. I felt autumn in the air.

The lock clicked open and the bodyguard stepped outside. He looked too young for the incipient fissures from his nostrils to the corners of his grim mouth. He withheld the courtesy of words as he invited me inside.

Theodore was waiting for me in his bedroom, at the back of the house. His study, at the front, was also lit.

"I was thinking of a book," he said, pacing by the fireplace in his blue-and-white-striped dressing gown. "Writing one, I mean."

"About what?"

"Wilderness. The one out there"—he swept his arm in the general direction of the continent—"and the one inside our souls. And the connection between the two." With an intent look, he examined my face for a reaction.

I had none, other than amazement. How could any one man find the time? I had little doubt he could accomplish it. He had written a baker's dozen books already—and effortlessly, best I could tell—which, as an occasional author myself, drove me wild with envy. Still, this wasn't the same as studying law while vice president. Didn't he have a country to run? And a family? Alice alone was more than a part-time job.

"Sounds fascinating," I said, which it did.

"Thank you," he said. "I was writing."

"I will be quick, then. Mr. Morgan had nothing to do with the . . . collision. I am convinced of it."

"He told you this?"

"He didn't have to. He just laughed."

Theodore sat on the edge of the bed and nodded. He understood.

I also told him that Mark Hanna had been to Wall street, begging for donations to a presidential campaign.

No look of surprise or concern. "Anything else?" he said.

I thought about mentioning Morgan's assumption that I was doing the same, but I decided that no president—no politician—would be amused.

"No," I replied, and bid him a productive evening. A day had only twenty-four hours, and I appreciated a few minutes of his.

The bodyguard was gone from the porch—even the soberest of men had physical needs—when I took my departure. The air felt fresh, but I was tired and more than ready to get home. To Clara. Waiting up for me, I hoped. I had told no one but Clara and Alvey Adee when I'd be home.

I crossed Jackson Place and ambled along the edge of the park. Branches reached over the sidewalk like eaves; shrubbery intruded. The valise felt heavy on my shoulder. The lamps crackled, or was that the crickets? I thought I heard voices behind the trees.

Maybe I should have left Theodore alone until morning. The little I had learned could have waited. Though he had seemed not to mind. *Wilderness?* Well, no accounting for taste. Give me civilization—vaudeville, the Edison cylinder, a smooth scotch, a moving picture—any day of the week.

I was nearing H street, watching the lights in Henry's windows, when I heard the scrape of footsteps behind me. Suddenly, the crook of a left arm wrapped around my neck, and a blade, sharp and hard, touched the right side of my throat. A body taller than mine squeezed from behind. The hot breath in my ear smelled of cheap rye.

"Tol' ya, Hay, drop it, ya fuck"—a nasal, nasty voice—"or Lovey gets hurt."

I started to say something—I wasn't sure what, but it was bound to be clever—when I felt a scratch on my throat and then a push from behind. I went sprawling. The herringbone brick sidewalk stopped me. It struck my hands, not my face, I am relieved to report, or I might not be telling you this tale.

Footsteps scampered away, although in my mind I imagined them to be loping. All I could feel was a chill and a craving to sleep.

⊹⊱━⊰⊹

"Nothing was stolen," I insisted. "Why on earth should I bother the police?"

"You were the victim of a crime," Clara said. She was propped up in our four-poster bed. The room was decorated in Clara's taste, in pastels and flutters of fabric, but I had stopped noticing it years before. "You were stabbed. With a knife."

"Not stabbed. Sliced."

"Forgive me—sliced. You are a man of words. Is it still warm?"

I was lying beside her as she pointed to the gauze at my throat. The compress had grown chilly, but it hurt to shake my head. I didn't need to. She pulled the pinkish compress away and wetted another one. "See a doctor, at least," she said.

"It's nothing," I said. "We'll talk about it to-morrow." I reached under the fringed silk shade and switched off the electric lamp.

Clara fell asleep, but I lay awake, listening over and over. *Or Lovey gets hurt.* The voice was gruff, exaggeratedly so. *Or Lovey gets hurt.*

Only one person had I ever called Lovey, and no one else knew it— or so I had thought. Only Lizzie Cameron and me.

CHAPTER FOURTEEN

E well Lindgren pressed the heel of his huge hand into the small of my back, and I nearly dived off the table.

"Yes, a little bit tense," he said. His Scandinavian lilt undermined his certitude.

"Getting knifed will do that," I replied, with a trifle too much pride.

He had noticed my throat right away and was stunned I hadn't consulted a doctor. In the light of day, so was I.

<hr />

So was Theodore. I had to tell him, of course. It was not much of a wound, but it was hard to keep secret from anyone who was observant, a category that often—but not always—excluded my current host.

"Ah, a scratch," Roosevelt said when I pointed it out. "But I shall call Dr. Lung."

"Not necessary."

"Yes, it is." Sometimes there was no arguing with him. Most of the time, actually. "Does it hurt?" he said.

"Only when I talk," I said. Both of us laughed. "Or laugh."

"Then don't," he said. "But you need protection."

"No. If he had wanted to kill me, he would have. And I don't want somebody following me around." For reasons Theodore could well understand, and for one that he couldn't. "Shouldn't you have more than you do—than you did?"

"I have plenty," he growled. "Now, tell me again what the blackguard said."

"He told me to drop it, using . . . rather colorful language. And he knew my name. Like in Pittsfield."

"Same man?"

"Don't know. I don't think so."

"Same method?"

Theodore should be the detective. "No," I said. "This one had a knife, not a gun."

"You have told the police, of course."

"Not yet."

The former police commissioner's eyes narrowed. It gave him a studious look. "Do so," he said. "Forthwith."

"Let me tell Wilkie first," I replied. I also had another stop in mind.

Theodore asked if I wished to withdraw from the investigation, but I declined. For reasons beyond the altruism of aiding the president or the satisfaction of solving a mystery. This was personal. Theodore was famous for his point-to-point walks in Rock Creek Park, leading sons, senators, foreign ambassadors, and other unfortunates on hikes in a straight line from one chosen point to another, over or under all obstacles, never around. So far, I had managed to avoid thesè hikes. I simply hadn't wanted to be graded, not by him. But now I had lost to him in the boxing ring, so skillfully he never saw I meant to. This, then, counted as Theodore's latest test of my manhood. I did not intend to fail.

+>====<+

With a grave manner, Dr. Lung informed me I had a shallow cut across my throat and applied a flesh-colored bandage. I thanked him for the excellence of his professional judgment. He missed the sarcasm, as I figured he would, or I probably would have refrained.

I left the temporary White House and crossed Jackson Place, into Lafayette Park. I froze, then whipped around, looking for . . . what? For *whom*? I might have broken into a run, had the park been empty of witnesses. I passed the Treasury Building, glancing over my shoulder, and saw no one I recognized. Which meant nothing. I weaved through

clumps of . . . Who *were* all these people? Tourists or malingering man-
darins, no one was in a hurry but me. Crossing Pennsylvania avenue,
I dodged the rigs and managed to sidestep a pyramid of manure. My
gait felt unsynchronized.

The Willard lobby hummed with men who had money (or pretended
they did) and wanted more of it. I asked at the desk whether Mrs. Cameron was in. The clerk—I had not seen him before—checked the
pigeonhole and found her room key.

My shoulders relaxed. "May I leave a note?" I said.

> *Lizzie,*
>
> > *I need to see you. Soonest.*
> > *When and where?*
>
> > > > *Yr. obedient servant,*
> > > > *J.H.*

I folded it, sealed the envelope, wrote "Mrs. Cameron" on the opposite side, and felt lucky to make my escape.

⊹═◄⊹

John Wilkie's head was shrouded in smoke, and his feet were propped
up on his desk.

"Halloo, Hay! We were just talking about you."

Nellie Bly was seated on the leather divan by the wall, beside the
marble-topped table. Hardly the usual furnishings for a government
office.

"Nothing pleasant, I hope," I replied.

"It was about the world being in such a mess and wondering what
you were doing about— What the hell?" He had noticed my bandage.
"Oh, forgive me, Miss Bly."

"Mrs. Seaman," she said. "What in the hell *did* happen, Mr. Hay?"

I took the straight-backed chair by Wilkie's desk. I kept my recounting brief, hoping to elicit fewer questions. Wrong audience for that.

"What did he say *exactly*?" Wilkie said.

The question I had feared. I saw no way out but . . . omission. "Best

I can remember," I said, to give myself a bit of latitude, "he said, 'Drop it, Hay, you—'" I looked over at Nellie; her eyes were bright. "'Hay, you fuck.' Actually, the first thing he said was something like 'Told you.'"

"'Told you' like 'Told you before'?" Nellie said.

"Maybe. Or 'Told you so.'"

"Either way," she said, "doesn't that prove it's the same man?"

"Or they're working together," I said. "He didn't say *I*; he didn't say *we*."

We both turned toward Wilkie, who was staring at the ceiling, lost in thought. "Tell me again," he said, not looking our way.

"All right, best I can remember: 'Told you, Hay, drop it, you—'"

"That's not what you said last time," Wilkie said.

"Yes, it is."

"No, you told me a different order. Where your name was."

"Well, *best* I can remember, 'Told you, Hay'—you're right—'Told you, Hay, drop it, you . . . you fuck.'"

I stopped. Wilkie's head popped out of the swirling smoke. "Yes?" he said.

"Yes *what*?" I said.

"That's all?"

I felt a knot in my chest. "Just about," I said.

"Oh? It sounds like he should finish by saying, 'Or else . . .'"

I turned toward Nellie. The eight or ten seconds seemed much longer, until the message registered. A shadow crossed her pretty face and then, without a word, she left the room, shutting the door firmly but gently.

"Or else *what*?" Wilkie said.

"Or else Lovey gets hurt."

Wilkie was all business. "Who is Lovey?"

"Do I have to answer?"

Wilkie's laugh was one of genuine amusement.

I sighed. "Mrs. Cameron," I replied. "I call her that. Sometimes."

"I see."

I could not gauge his expression through the haze.

He said, "Does she know that your . . . assailant . . ."

"Not yet," I said.

"She needs to. And she needs our— *Are* you going to drop it, your investigation?"

I pursed my lips and shook my head. Wilkie waited for an explanation, but I had none I wanted to give.

"So she will need our protection," he said. "And you will, too."

"Oh, no. No."

"I am sorry, this is not up to you, Mr. . . . . Secretary."

"We are back to that, are we?"

"Oh yes. We are sworn officials of the United States government, long may it live."

"The answer is still no," I said. "For me, at least. And I will get the president to back me up on this. He of all people will understand. As for Mrs. Cameron, I'll ask her. Is there a way to protect her without anyone knowing . . . the exact reason why? Other than herself, I mean."

"I'll try," Wilkie said. "No promises, I'm afraid."

"This is important, you understand."

"I do, Hay."

We were unofficial again, and I was tempted to trust him. He was an honest man, or tried to be, which in Washington was the best you could hope for. And really, what choice did I have?

+≒═≒+

"What in the hell happened to you?" Alvey Adee was staring at the bandage on my throat.

"Accident shaving," I said.

"You have a beard."

"You are observant."

"Which is what they pay me for," Adee said. "That, and my facility with falsehoods."

I laughed. *This* was Adee's value: his levity (and efficiency) in a world as confused and unpredictable as a Ouija board. He sat across my desk and recited a litany of overnight events, none of them urgent. The attorney general's early departure from Paris without any agreement over a canal route through Panama. The Russians' latest attempt to outflank the Germans in Mesopotamia by using their influence in Persia. (Good luck with that!) The third assistant secretary of state's report of progress, such as it was, in the Russian seal arbitration at The Hague. The president's compulsion to shift our European ambassadors around like chessmen.

"What he worries about, as I understand it," Adee said, "is that Vienna won't want a Catholic and that Meyer will be thought of as a Jew in Berlin and won't have the social recognition an ambassador needs."

It sounded to me as if one of the Henrys (Adams or Cabot Lodge) had gotten to Theodore, although maybe the objection was apt. I said, "I don't think Meyer *is* a Jew."

"Does that matter?"

"It ought to. Anything else?"

"Nothing you need to bother your pretty little head about," Adee said.

Margaret knocked at the doorframe and entered. "A wire for you," she said.

It came from Pittsfield: "MADDEN IN MY OFFICE AT 2. NICHOLSON."

The grandfather clock in my office said one forty-five.

"When did this come?" I said.

"Just now."

I shooed them out and shut the door. Madden held the secret to the entire affair. How could I worm anything out of him—and over the telephone, for God's sake—after Nicholson and his men had failed in person? How could I dislodge the motorman from the story he had told time and again and—true or not—had probably come to believe?

I arranged with the department's operator for two o'clock sharp. On the first ring, Chief Nicholson answered.

"Is Madden there?" I said.

"Oh yes. Not a happy man."

"Has he told you much?"

"Not a thing worth knowing. Your turn, if you like."

"Oh, thank you," I said.

"My pleasure," he replied.

A fumbling of the receiver sounded like the staccato of a gasoline-fueled automobile.

"H-h-helloo." Euclid Madden's voice was frailer than I remembered.

Maybe it was the connection. It was astonishing I could hear him at all from nearly four hundred miles away.

"Mr. Madden," I said.

"Y-yes. Yes, sir."

"How are you?" Another of my vices was politeness, whether called for or not.

A pause. "Gettin' along, I s'pose."

"Glad to hear that," I said. "Did you hear what happened to Mr. Turtle?"

No response.

I had decided on shock as a strategy, from a flank. "That he was murdered? Here in Washington. I saw it."

Static on the line.

I said, "Do you know anything about it?"

No reply.

"I think it had something to do with your case," I pressed. "Did you know he was coming to Washington?"

"No!" Madden wailed. "Why are you blaming me?"

"I'm not blaming you," I said. "Your lawyer did. Apparently he said that it wasn't an accident, that he has proof of it. *Had* proof of it. And he wanted you to plead guilty to manslaughter."

"But I'm not guilty!"

"Your lawyer says—said—you are."

"But I'm not."

"So you wanted him gone, is that right?"

"What are you accusing me *of*?"

A fair question. Of murder, I suppose. But I never had a chance to say. I heard a click and then Chief Nicholson yelped, "Gosh almighty! Pick that up!" Then a smothered "G'bye."

Another click, and another, and the connection went dead.

⊹⇒━⊰⊹

I arrived ten minutes early. The Corcoran's new edifice stood a block and a half from my office and was almost as French. Not in the exuberant ornamentation of the State, War, and Navy Building, but more austerely, in a stolid Beaux Arts style, with a rounded prow that reminded me of a beached whale. The entrance was near one of the fins. I sidled in, as if to a secret rendezvous, which in fact this was.

The sly-looking guard gave me barely a nod. Adultery-minded men must show up here all the time. This did not describe me—not to-day, anyway. To-day I was a detective pursuing a case involving a possible attempt to assassinate the president. I had every right to be here. I was *working*, for God's sake. Even if my work required a rendezvous with a woman who wasn't my wife.

Entering the gallery was a joy. The atrium was two stories high and blindingly white. It was surrounded by balustrades and peopled by statues in varying states of undress. Glass panels in the ceiling opened to the sky. I was wading into Greece on a sun-filled day, when the future looked eternal.

We were meeting in our customary spot. *Night* was on the second floor, in the north gallery. It was considered Rebouet's finest, which is to say, his most risqué. The room was empty, other than Lizzie seated on a slatted bench. A daffodil-yellow frock clung to her shoulders and her hair was braided in the back. Her head was cocked, as if entranced by the painting she was facing. I knew better. *Night* was a black-and-white portrait of a nearly naked witch riding the back of an owl. Advertising cards used the image in cigar stores all over the city, but here it was Art. I found it arousing. Lizzie found it a tease.

I wanted to touch the nape of her neck, and she wanted me to, but I didn't, not to-day. I called to her instead, in a stage whisper.

"Mrs. Cameron." This was official.

She turned with a coquettish smile and raised her face to be kissed. Instead, I said, "Hello, Lovey."

"Hello yourself." She studied my face, which was unlike her. Not everything she saw satisfied her. "Is anything wrong?"

"Uh-huh."

"Sit," she said.

I obeyed. Our knees touched, and I pulled back.

"This looks serious," she said. No one would accuse Lizzie Cameron of missing the subtleties.

"It *is* serious. I was attacked last night by a man with a knife"—Lizzie gasped—"in the park, Lafayette Park, just across from my house.

I was walking from the . . . where the president is staying. Somebody jumped out and held a knife to my throat."

"Oh my dear, were you hurt?" Her eyes widened like spring pools. She grasped my forearm.

I was touched by her concern, though not fooled by it. "A small cut, nothing worse. It *could* have been worse. He wasn't trying to rob me— he didn't—or kill me. He had something else in mind. To stop me from . . . *This* is what he said to me." I wanted to avoid her eyes but dared not pull away. "'Drop it, Hay'—I omitted the vulgarity—"'or Lovey gets hurt.'"

Another gasp. Lizzie's head drooped to her chest. "Who *was* it?" she moaned.

"Precisely what I'd like to know. Lovey. Does anyone else call you that?" I was being mean, but I intended to be.

A miserable shake of her head.

"Who else knows that *I* do?"

A shrug.

"Who?" I wanted to shake her.

"Nobody," she muttered.

"Not a single soul?"

She shook her head but would not look up at me.

"I know *I* never told anyone. Could someone have overheard us?"

Another shrug.

"Well, somebody knows," I said. "Multiple somebodies, if the gentleman who pressed a blade to my throat wasn't the same somebody who learned this lovely tidbit of our lives. Could one of those somebodies be your devoted husband?"

"That's absurd, and you know it. Besides, Don wouldn't remember it even if he happened to hear it."

"This, he would. Any man would. To his dying day, he would remember it. The question is, would he tell anyone if he had? Such as you. Or would a cuckold be too embarrassed?"

"Cuckold?" she said. Her head popped up, and her face came within spitting distance of mine. "May I remind you, Mr. Hay, that you and I have done nothing that would merit such a . . . rudeness?"

I remembered the instant our relationship had taken a turn toward the . . . intimate. Albeit never as intimate as I had pictured. We were at a reception at the British embassy and her husband had imbibed one (two? three?) too many. I took his other arm in easing him into a gold-covered divan, and our fingertips touched at his waist. Electricity jolted from Lizzie to me, and also—of this I felt sure—in the opposite direction.

"No reminder is necessary," I said. This meeting was no longer official. "I apologize for my . . . imprecision. But my question remains. Might he have overheard us and told someone else? Or opened your mail, perhaps?"

"Or someone might someone have overheard *you*. By your telephone stand. Or on another extension."

"Have I ever said—"

"Several times."

"I don't think I—"

Lizzie cocked her head in a way that thrilled me. The glistening below her eyes might or might not have come from the electric lights.

What was she hiding? "Not to repeat myself," I said, "but somebody knows. *That* is a fact. Maybe I could ask him."

"Don? Don't you dare!"

"Then you'll need protection." I told her that Wilkie had insisted.

"The hell I will. How would I ever explain *that*?"

A reasonable question. I had an alternative idea, and Lizzie went for it. Nellie Bly was an explainable guest, and she was someone you would want on your side in a brawl.

+≡≡+

I mentioned nothing to Henry Adams about Lizzie. I was careful about his feelings. His infatuation had been worse than my own—longer lasting, anyway. I had certainly heard enough about it at the time. That far-off look would enter his eyes, the tremor in his voice, whenever he spoke of "Mrs. Cameron"—it was always "Mrs. Cameron," with a catch in his throat. That was long ago, but I understood that Henry's feelings were painful still. Mine were. Henry had been a widower, but

I assuredly was not. I hated doing what I was doing—more precisely, what I thought about doing—to Clara, even if she didn't have a clue. I knew that I shouldn't—couldn't—do it anymore. I *knew* it.

Henry and I passed the blacksmith's and the machine shop, heading south on Thirteen-and-a-half street, before turning east on D. More visible in the daylight than the whorehouses were the ironworks and the brass works and the lumberyard and the Potomac Electric Power smokestacks belching soot. We kept sight of our feet, to keep them from stepping into— Best not to think about that.

Meanwhile, I filled Henry in on my genuflection before Pierpont Morgan and on my lack of any temporal benefit. "A statement of fact, he says, nothing more. He would prefer me as president. Period."

"I shouldn't doubt it," Henry said. "So would I."

"But doing something about it . . . That's a step I very much doubt he took. I have to wonder if this was the kind of crime—assuming there was a crime—that a man like Pierpont Morgan would commit."

"I never said it was," Henry said.

An exaggeration, to be sure. He had showed me the scrawl in the margin and pointed the way to a suspicion. But he had let me—and Theodore, of course—jump to a conclusion.

┼═══┼

"Donald Cameron couldn't kill a polecat," I told Nellie Bly, "much less a president. He'd have been a bum without his pa." Simon Cameron, Lincoln's venal war secretary, became a Pennsylvania senator who bequeathed his seat and his political machine to his son, who had squandered both. "It's not Don I'm worried about. If he *had* known about Lovey, would he have told anyone? I wouldn't have."

"Then who *are* you worried about?" Nellie said. "Mrs. Cameron?"

I hoped she was kidding, but I doubted it. "I don't know. Maybe she was overheard. Or she had told somebody who told somebody else."

Nellie agreed to the plan right away, and we were meeting in the Willard lobby, behind the marble pillar farthest from the door, before I delivered her to Lizzie's suite. She was dressed like an industrial magnate's wife, in a gray, high-necked street gown with a cameo at her throat. She also had a pistol in her purse. My long-winded explanation of what she needed to know had, by necessity, included more of a confessional nature than I was accustomed to sharing. But duty called. She was kind enough not to giggle at *Lovey*. Or to inquire further.

"Lizzie—Mrs. Cameron—is hiding something," I said. "I know she is. She almost admitted telling someone, by what she wouldn't say."

"Any idea who?"

"That's your job."

Nellie's small smile grew.

The old elevator operator nodded gravely, noticing Nellie's leather Gladstone bag, and without a stop or spasm delivered us to the fifth floor. The corridor was empty. Before we reached Lizzie's door, we heard shouting from inside. A man's voice.

I rapped on the door, and the shouting continued. I rapped harder, and it ceased. I kept knocking until heavy footsteps approached.

"Who is it?" A growl.

"Senator Cameron, this is Secretary Hay," I said. Best to make this official. "I have somebody here you should meet."

A pause. "Who?"

Got 'im! "Nellie Bly," I said.

"Nellie . . . Oh, her. . . . Why would I want to . . ."

"Because your wife wants to meet her." I hoped he would not ask how I knew.

Another pause. "All right." The latch grated and the doorknob creaked. In the doorway stood the shell of a man once known as Donald Cameron. His cheeks were red and his droopy mustache twitched. I could smell the bourbon from where I stood. "What do you want?" he said. "And who is this?"

"Nellie Bly," I replied.

"So you said."

"May we come in?"

"Why?"

"Miss Bly will be staying here to-night. Your wife was kind enough to invite her." I stepped through the doorway and he edged back.

"She di'n't tell me."

"Ask her," I said.

"You telling me what to do?"

"No, of course not, Senator." Once a senator, always a senator.

"With my wife, damn it?"

"No, no."

"'Cause you, of all people . . ."

I didn't see his fist sweep from above and to my left, beyond my peripheral vision. It was outside of all expectation, which is my only excuse for not trying to duck.

Only after I departed, leaving Nellie behind, did the pain set in.

+══+

"Why would he want to do that?" Clara said.

Not an unreasonable question. I was lying in bed, and she was bringing me another warm compress. This one was scalding. Her compassion was wearing thin.

"Ask *him*," I said. "I gather he doesn't like me."

"I thought maybe he gave you a hint about why. Like the fellow did last night, the one who cut your throat."

"He didn't quite cut it."

"Oh yes, he did. Literally."

"Well, not deeply."

"That is why you are here and not in the morgue."

"I get your point."

"Do you? So when are you giving this up?"

I hoped she meant the investigation.

I lay awake for hours, listening to Clara's breathing. It pulsed like the waves in a lake—lazy, contented, unending. I wondered what she knew and what she thought she knew. And what there was to know.

What I did know was this: when I was with Clara, I was calmer than when I wasn't. Is that love? I think so. It's part of what love is, anyway. The part of love I must be true to. Beyond the sparkle. Enduring love, I mean—a deeper love, an unflashy love, arguably the only kind worth having.

Arguably.

CHAPTER FIFTEEN

———

Y*es*, it hurts!" I said.
    I figured your masseur was like your lawyer or your pastor—
whatever you said was a secret and would not count against you in
court or, with luck, on Judgment Day. There, I would need all the help
I could get.

I had told Lindgren about the punch I had not seen coming, and
confessed that the perpetrator was a drunken fool. My defense, as it were.

"A drunk is like a child," he replied, pressing into my clavicles. "You
don't know what they'll do next—because they don't."

He suggested a salve for my bruise. "I have some with me," he said.

+======+

"On my right side." I managed a laugh. "And how was yours? Restful?"

"Restful enough," Nellie Bly said. "And productive."

I had guessed this, for she had shown up unannounced at my house
in time for breakfast, looking marvelous in an arctic-white gown. As
she ladled marmalade onto her toast, Nellie glanced over at Clara. I
prayed that she would leave *Lovey* unmentioned.

"Any signs of danger?" I said.

"Only from the man of the house," Nellie said.

Clara snorted—at Don Cameron or at me, I wasn't sure.

"Any more violence?" I said.

"Not after you left. A lot of shouting. A visit from the night manager, but only once."

"And for you," I said. "How late did it go?"

"You mean, how early did it start again."

"How early *did* it start again?"

Nellie checked the diamond-flecked watch she wore around her neck. "Early," she said.

"See how lucky you are," I said to Clara.

"Oh yes, things could always be worse," Clara replied, I hoped in jest.

Nellie carried her coffee to the library. I closed the door and said, "'Productive' how?"

"She did tell someone about Lovey," Nellie said. "Her sister Mary."

I should have guessed. Lizzie and her oldest sister were close. "How did you get her to tell you?" I said.

"Easy. She wanted to tell me—was bursting to. Happens all the time. You'd be surprised. People love to be asked about themselves. They're flattered. They *want* to tell you things, even intimate things, if you're interested enough to listen. As a memento of their time here on earth, I suppose." Nellie's smile was angelic. "It also helps to be a woman."

I understood why Lizzie did not want to tell me, although I must say I felt a little insulted. "If Mary knows, then her husband must know," I said. Mary was married to Nelson A. Miles, the commanding general of the U.S. Army since 'ninety-five. "Right?"

"Maybe," Nellie said. The corners of her mouth curled into a smile. "Is the reverse true?"

That stung, as I felt pretty sure it was meant to. "General Miles," I said. "He hates the president. For good reason, I must say. The president humiliated him, and not in private."

I told her the tale of the Civil War hero, whom Roosevelt had scorned as a "brave peacock" during the war against Spain. The pompous old gent saw himself as a plausible president—as a Democrat, perhaps. When he told an interviewer something he shouldn't have, thereby interfering in a military court, he hurried to the White House to explain. At an open reception, the president had bawled him out.

"She didn't say a word about that," Nellie reported.

"She must have figured everyone knows what happened, given the dozens of gossipy witnesses. It wouldn't have surprised me if the good general had gone home that day and done what the Japanese consider the honorable thing. But he didn't. He isn't that brave—or that honorable."

"Is that reason enough to kill a man?"

"How much of a reason do you need?" I said. "His ambitions? His humiliation? His dishonor? Or all of them combined?"

⊹══⊹

The trim brick town house at 1746 N street, between Seventeenth and Connecticut, was four stories tall and wider than any other on the block. This was an elegant but unostentatious neighborhood, not far from the Lodges. Here, the door met the sidewalk.

I knocked. It was half past ten.

No answer.

I engaged the door pull and produced the chimes of Big Ben, for my enjoyment alone. (I had sent Nellie back to protect the Camerons.) I knocked harder and heard light footsteps.

A uniformed chambermaid, no older than sixteen or seventeen, opened the door. Behind her, the spacious hallway ended in a sweeping staircase. I gave her my card and asked whether Mrs. Miles might receive a visitor.

"Is she expecting you, mistuh?"

"I'm afraid not."

The girl was flustered for a moment, but she ushered me into the parlor, on the left, and abandoned me there. The room was distressingly formal, with sober armchairs, heavy drapes, and time-darkened paintings of military men. Glass cases on the wall each contained a sword and a brass label noting the wars against the Confederacy, Crazy Horse, or Sitting Bull. Over the mantel, in a gilded frame, hung the congressional Medal of Honor, awarded for the young Miles's derring-do in the Union's defeat at Chancellorsville. I was examining the attitude of the eagle perched on the golden star—vengeful, I decided—when a sultry voice behind me said, "And to what do I owe this pleasure, Mr. Hay?"

"The pleasure is mine," I said.

We stood for a moment. Mrs. Miles hunched forward, head cocked, intelligent eyes alert. She was reputed to be the Sherman family beauty, although her mouth was pouty and her pile of chestnut-brown hair looked like a mop. She offered me a seat but not a beverage. I would not be staying long.

"This is a delicate matter," I began. I had been unable to decide on a strategy and hoped that coming face-to-face with her would help. It did not. "It involves the security of . . . the nation," I tried. This had the advantage of being true, or true enough, and usually it worked. "It involves your sister, Mrs. Cameron."

"What about her?" Her voice was low and throaty, protective—menacing.

I decided to get straight to the point. The wife of a general, even this general, might appreciate that. (Or might not.) "Have you ever heard about someone calling her . . . Lovey?"

A lift of her eyelids suppressed a look of surprise. She *knew.* "Don, you mean," she said.

"No, somebody else."

"Did Mrs. Cameron suggest that you speak with me?"

"No."

"Did you ask *her* this question?"

"I did."

"And what did she say?"

"Well, here I am," I said, hoping the deflection would succeed.

Mrs. Miles sat back in the oversize armchair and said, "Only once." *Yes!* "By someone"—she stared at me in astonishment—"she used to care for."

So Lizzie had mentioned *me.*

"Let me explain why I ask." I told her of my attacker's threat against Lovey. "So I need to ask you, did you tell anyone else?"

Her eyes widened and her head shook as if she were ill.

"Your husband, perhaps," I added.

She snapped out of her torpor and declared, "How dare you ask me that! What business is this of yours, Mr. Hay?"

Mrs. Miles was no milksop. "It is very much my business, if your husband had a hand in . . . in what happened to me the other night."

I told her of the knife at my throat and the whispered warning about Lovey.

"Why would my husband want to do something like that?" she said.

So she *had* told him. "I am making inquiries on behalf of the president. I imagine your husband doesn't hold him in the highest regard."

I expected fire or ice but got neither. "He is the commander in chief," she replied. A verifiable fact.

⊱━━⊰

I was only half aware of the *clip-clop, clip-clop* of the rigs along Connecticut avenue or the unpredictable screech of the trolley. I dodged pedestrians without looking or thinking.

Would General Miles wish to murder a president who had humiliated him? Anyone might. Would he actually try? Conceivably, if—a big if—he still had the courage he had shown at Chancellorsville. But would he try it by using a trolley car as his weapon, in the hands of an unknown motorman? Is that how a military man would react? Unlikely. Or he might have mentioned *Lovey* to someone else, as his contribution-in-kind to an assassination plot. Was this plausible? Not especially. But not impossible.

The commander of the United States Army occupied an office two floors below mine. It was fancier—more colorful, anyway. I chalked that up to the Stars and Stripes along the walls, the Cuban flag over a bookcase, and the ribbons across General Miles's chest. I could tell he was expecting me, by the fresh smell of cologne. Obviously his wife had 'phoned. I'd have been disappointed had she not.

"I am at your service, Mr. Secretary." General Miles rose from behind his desk—I feared he was going to salute. Obsequiousness was his habit, no doubt, granted to anyone above him and expected from everyone below. (His abrasiveness had deterred at least one promotion.) He looked like what he thought an old general should look like, with a broom of a mustache on a square-cut face, a broad chest, and a broader belly. His uniform was starched and looked uncomfortable; its epaulets must have worried the nation's supply of golden tassels. His handsome face—the Sherman girls insisted on manly beauty—was devoid of expression.

The only available chair had a hard wooden back and a cushionless seat. This was not a self-confident man.

"I am conducting an investigation for the president," I said.

"Yes, sir." A military man understood authority, even if he hated the source.

"So there is only so much I can tell you. But let me ask you this. Your brother-in-law, Senator Cameron, have you been in touch with him of late?"

"No. I believe he is up at his farm, in Pennsylvania."

"Actually, he is back. He, uh, punched me last night."

General Miles looked puzzled, unsure if I was kidding. "Why would he want to do that?" Clara's words exactly. "Let me amend that," he said. "Why *did* he do that? I can definitely understand the desire."

Maybe the man was not as dim as I had thought. "Well, thank you," I said—not stiffly, I hoped. "You would have to ask him why. Though I wonder if *he* knows. Or remembers."

For the first time, Miles looked me in the eye. He understood what I meant.

"Let me ask you this, then," I said. "Did he—or anyone else— mention anything to you about . . . Lovey?"

"Pardon?"

"Lovey. A pet name, as it were. For your sister-in-law."

General Miles's face drained of color, which left it as bleached as a barnacle. "Why are you asking me this?" he said.

"It is a matter of . . . our nation's security . . . and the president's." To the commander of the army, surely a winning argument.

"I see," he said. I hoped he didn't. "I have heard this . . . word . . . this gossip. Though not from Don, I don't think." He stopped, having remembered who told him. "From someone," he said. He remembered something else. "It was *you*—what *you* call her. Why are you asking *me* about—"

"Because I was attacked last night, and the man who attacked me threatened Lovey. I want to know who attacked me, and I want to pre- vent any danger to . . . Mrs. Cameron."

"Are you accusing *me* of—"

"No." This was at least partially true. "Did you happen to tell any-one else?"

"Tell them what? This piece of gossip? Why would I want to do that? Besides, who would possibly care?"

That, indeed, was the question at hand. And it had an answer, one I hadn't found yet.

I tried once more, with a jab to the chin. "You have reason, do you not, to think ill of the president?"

General Miles's face went rigid, and his eyes stared unfocused at a distant point. He sat stock-still, not even fidgeting. I let the silence build. At last, he said, "He is the commander in chief."

His wife had said the same, word for word. A verifiable fact.

⊢—══—⊣

"General Miles is too stupid to invent a plot like that," Theodore said. The back room on Jackson Place had taken on his personality, with a maelstrom of papers on his desk, piles of books and magazines, and a zebra-skin rug. He loved the temporary White House because he could avoid his usual morning routine of chitchatting with lawmakers and ag-grieved citizens. "It takes imagination, creativity—a mind."

"So why is this unimaginative, uncreative man still commanding the army?" I said.

"He doesn't. I do. I don't want a man with imagination. That's my job. I am the commander in chief."

On that last point, everyone agreed. I recalled that, as the assistant navy secretary after the *Maine* exploded, in 'ninety-eight, Theodore had taken advantage of his boss's absence one Friday (to see a podiatrist about his corns) and ordered the Pacific fleet to rearrange some ships and to stock up on ammunition and coal—all useful, it turned out, when Dewey defeated the Spanish Navy in Manila Bay that spring. A commander in chief in the making.

"Why would you think he had anything to do with this? Any evi-dence?"

I had to be careful what I told Theodore, straitlaced as he was. A men-tion of *Lovey* was out of the question, regarding a woman who was not my wife. "He has a motive," I said, "and a pretty good one, I would say. The memory of physical pain isn't painful, but the memory of humiliation *is* painful, and keeps being painful, every time you remember it."

"You think he *did* have something to do with it?" he said.

"Wouldn't say that, either," I replied. "He might have a motive, but I haven't seen any evidence he did anything about it. Besides, it doesn't strike me as the way a commanding general—an unimaginative general—would act. Too roundabout; too hit-or-miss. And, in fact, it missed."

"I am inclined to think that Miles would be nasty indeed if the opportunity arose. Is he a killer? I should hope so. Any soldier needs to be—even a general. Is he a fool? Without doubt. But is he an assassin?"

Before leaving, I asked Theodore whether he had read my proposed letter to our envoys in the European capitals, challenging the treatment of Roumanian Jews. He had.

Could I go ahead?

"If it amuses you," Theodore decreed. "It always benefits a nation to act like a gentleman."

+══════+

"Any love notes to-day?" I said.

"Mercifully few," Adee said. "Do you want to be loved or do you want to be feared?"

"Either would do. We may soon be adding to our death threats." I told him of the president's consent to the Roumanian letter and suggested we send it by Atlantic cable to our embassies in the seven affected capitals. "To-night, in case he has second thoughts."

"Comes to his senses, you mean."

I chuckled. "As you like."

Adee went looking for Margaret to arrange for the cables, while I read through the final version, on my desk.

The political disabilities of the Jews in Roumania, their exclusion from the public service and the learned professions, the limitations of their civil rights and the imposition upon them of exceptional taxes, involving, as they do, wrongs repugnant to the moral sense of liberal modern peoples . . .

I thought it struck just the right tone. That, and the cadence reminded me—not to be overly grand—of the Declaration of Independence, the boring part, beyond the rhetorical flourishes, the lawyerlike list of grievances against a distant king.

I was admiring America's rare lapse from hypocrisy when Margaret came rushing in. "For you," she told me. "Chief Nicholson. On the 'phone."

"Tell Elsie to put it through."

I lifted the receiver from the side of the telephone box. Amid the familiar squawk of the connection came scraps of sounds that merged into words.

"Delayed until January."

"What was?"

"Their trial, on the manslaughter charges."

"I thought they were pleading guilty."

"They haven't yet. They still might. But now their lawyer is . . . gone. As you are all too aware."

"Surely they have another."

"Yes and no. Long story, for another day."

"Has Madden said anything more? If he doesn't have a lawyer, he doesn't have a watchdog."

"I will try him again."

I suspected that Chief Nicholson was dragging his feet. Plausibly for the unexceptional reason that he had matters more urgent to pursue.

"One more thing," Chief Nicholson said. "Mr. Pratt, the carriage driver, he is ill. Very ill." In a whisper: "The cancer, they say."

"Oh my. He didn't look *that* bad. Does he know?"

"Probably not. But I couldn't say for sure."

"How long does he have?"

I imagined a shrug but heard only static.

+≡≡+

"Oh, Henry, where in the hell am I?"

"At the corner of Connecticut and L, dear heart, where your handsome apartment house will mark the capital for a hundred years or more."

"That's where *we* are," I said. "But where am *I*?"

"Ah, a harder question. If I knew, I wouldn't dare tell you, because you wouldn't believe me. Anything in particular troubling you to-day, old boy?"

I kicked a stone out of the way, into L street. Just ahead was the Gothic edifice of the Visitation convent and school.

"Not really," I said, "except that everything is a muddle."

"Everything in the world? In your life? In your . . . ?"

"In my so-called investigation. I keep running into dead ends. Take Pierpont Morgan, for instance."

"Thank you, but no," Henry said.

"And General Miles. And Cortelyou. And Governor Crane. And"—I bowed toward Henry—"Theodore himself. All of them highly unlikely." I left the Camerons unmentioned. "That leaves Mark Hanna, I suppose. I'm told he's coming back from Cleveland to-night. Certainly he has the most to gain from Theodore's untimely departure—besides yours truly, of course—and he is far more than willing than I am to do whatever he must to get what he wants. Though using a trolley in Pittsfield as his weapon of choice seems a little . . . roundabout, I must say, for a man of his blunt tastes."

"And don't forget that poor Mr. Turtle was planning to see him."

"True," I said. "But remember, he was planning to see me as well. And *I* didn't try to kill him. I am reasonably confident of that."

Along Connecticut, we passed the fancy dress shops and the Turkish baths and the furniture store. In the next block, the crowds on the wide sidewalk thinned. Here, the handsome four-story brownstones with the bay walls and pointed roofs were still homes; one of them was the domicile of Alexander Graham Bell.

"You find anything else of note in those mounds of documents?"

"Nothing to speak of," Henry said. "Only hundreds—nay, thousands—of reasons I feel fortunate to not be a lawyer. And how was our good friend General Miles?"

"Dull," I replied. "Too stupid, to quote Theodore, to plot anything like this."

"Too subtle for a military mind. To a soldier, every problem calls for a rifle or a cannon, not a trolley."

"He does have every good reason, though. Or reasons."

"He can stand in line for that. Anyone else on your list of prime suspects?"

"The Republican machine of Berkshire County. Rather extreme for Massachusetts, I'd think, but Governor Crane has enemies, too."

"Who would go so far as to try and kill him?"

"No reason to think so," I said. "Besides, there are easier ways. Same for Mr. Craig, who *was* killed. Who would want to murder him? Envy him to death, maybe, but murder him? These are all dead ends, Henry. Frankly, I don't know a damn thing more than I did when I started. Except that I'm pretty sure it wasn't an accident."

"Really!" Henry exclaimed. "You sure of that?"

"I wasn't at first. But twice I've been attacked and ordered to drop what I'm doing. So what I'm doing is bothering somebody, or somebodies, quite a lot. I have to think I'm on the right track, if they're going to such trouble to stop me."

"Unless that's what they want you to think."

"That's one twist of logic too many, even for you, Henry." To my surprise, he put up no argument. "And then there's our unfortunate Mr. Turtle. I know *he* was murdered. Was it related to whatever happened in Pittsfield? I can't prove it, but I've got to figure it was. That's why he came *here,* to talk to . . . well, me included. And none of us has a clue about what he wanted to say. Except that it wasn't an accident. But why else would you murder the lawyer involved, unless he knew things you didn't want told?"

Henry stumbled on a bump I could not see. "Maybe something went wrong," he said.

"I would say so."

I needed to hit something, preferably something hard, and something that wouldn't hit back. Sometimes, nothing else worked.

I headed for the boxing gymnasium in Swampoodle. This was the Irish neighborhood just north of the Capitol, a lawless and malarial place beyond the swamps. Single Malt quickened her pace as she realized where we were going. She relished the crowded neighborhood—goats and chickens in the yards, garbage in the gutters, a kaleidoscope of delightful stinks.

When I could persuade her to move, Single Malt kicked up dust from the roadway. Just ahead, four or five urchins were kicking a battered ball around the street, and a boy in a plaid slouch cap aimed it at my head. He missed, because I ducked, but Single Malt shimmied and started to rear, to her tormentors' cawing. I calmed her with soothing words and, with a glance of disdain, she trotted past them.

The gymnasium was in a rickety building just off north Capitol street, next to a blacksmith and across from a livery. I left Single Malt at the stable—she seemed not to mind—and grabbed my knapsack with battered gloves and a change of clothes. The entrance was on H street northwest. The narrow concrete steps were pockmarked and the pipe railing was gone. I pulled on the metal front door. From inside, I heard the refreshing *thwack thwack thwack* of fists pounding inanimate—and, from the sound of it, animate—objects.

"Hello, sir," the young fellow said. He had tattoos on his neck and a smile on his clean-shaven face. "Welcome back."

No matter how long I had been away, I was remembered here. And why not? I had sparred with a few of the young Irish toughs and lost more rounds than I won. But I had never been knocked down (indeed, I had decked one of them on a fluke) and had always held my own. I also knew when to tap gloves and step out of the ring. They would ask me how old I was and I would tell them and they would laugh. I didn't care a fig for the kaiser's or the tsar's—or the president's—opinion of me, compared to the respect I had earned here.

My young friend pointed me to a lumpy boxing bag in the far corner. Single Malt could have the street's smells; I loved the ones here. Of sweat and hard effort and doing what you never thought possible. I could forget myself in the gymnasium and come out cleansed.

My hand wraps, however, reeked. I twisted them like phylacteries around each wrist and hand, between my fingers, and around the base of each thumb. A ritual, meant to ward off the pain. The ten-ounce gloves, originally shiny and black, were still black. I pulled on the left one with ease but needed the young fellow's help to push the right one on and to tie them tight.

Then I went to work.

I circled the boxing bag like a jaguar stalking a mountain goat—eyes intent, forearms relaxed, until I pounced with a jab. I snapped it and stepped back. Another jab, then a right cross. How I loved my right cross! It ascended from my leg through my hip, hurtled down the reach of my arm and into my fist, and slammed into . . . the boxing bag, with a thud. Again. And again and again and again. A drumbeat. Pound that thing. I put a face on the bag, of the stolid, stupid, square-jawed General Miles. I unleashed a hook into his temple, and a hard right cross, and then another, into his teeth. The face became Pierpont Morgan's and his gimlet-eyed disdain—*wham!* An uppercut and then a right cross, two of them, and two more, into that histrionic nose. How satisfying! My arm felt deliciously tired. I stepped back and sucked in the fetid air. As pure as the Alps, to me.

Cortelyou's slicked-back face was coalescing on the bag when somebody called, "Hey, mister, want some?"

I stepped back toward the bag and took my orthodox stance and raised my fists to my temples.

"You! Want some?"

He *was* talking to me. He looked familiar—big-boned, heavy-jowled, dark-haired, glaring. I must have seen him here before. "Want what?" I said.

"This," he replied, raising his right glove.

"Anytime." I withheld the epithet.

"How about now, old man?"

"Who are you?" I said.

"Does it matter?"

Almost everyone I have met in a boxing gymnasium has been a . . . well, not a gentleman, so much—if it takes three generations to make a gentleman, some of these fellows are mired in the first—but a decent human being. They accept the discipline of physical training and the humility of recognizing that, unless they were James J. Jeffries, the heavyweight champ, someone in the world could beat them up. Not so this bristling young man.

The boxing ring was empty, and we leapt up onto the apron and climbed through the ropes.

What in the hell am I getting into? And why is he bothering me?

The boxing ring was worn, its floor uneven. Some of it felt springy; certain spots seemed ready to give way. Boxers drifted over from around the gymnasium and gathered to watch. I hardly noticed. I did notice that just the two of us were in the ring. No referee. Oh my.

I was nervous as hell. I willed myself to ignore it, and once we touched gloves, I pretty much could. I had never learned to think in the ring (about more than one thing at a time, anyway), but I knew how to concentrate, and I did. Facing a flurry of fists was a mighty motivation. Not wanting to embarrass myself in front of my chums was another.

I raised my gloves and peered into my opponent's eyes. He was a boy, for God's sake, not more than nineteen or twenty, his whiskers as sparse as the wings on a hog. He was sneering at me—did he hate his father, or what? How I longed to punch him in the face.

I got my chance and I took it. Maybe he forgot to defend himself, or maybe he was so busy casting his curse that he neglected the temporal threat of my fists. I delivered a stiff jab followed by a quick, fierce right to the jaw. His look of surprise surprised me. And surprised me again, when I saw the gape of open defiance behind the childish, slack-jawed grin. Then I knew who he resembled.

Del.

It wasn't that I hadn't tried with Del. To the contrary, I had probably tried too hard. That might not have been true for Clarence, our younger son, an easygoing boy who got lost in this large family's shuffle—a blessing for him, no doubt. But the elder son and all, I wanted him to be like me, and he simply wasn't. Physically he took after Clara, with a full face and torso. A big boy—as a fourteen-year-old he was taller than I was—but . . . *too* big. Once, he had come home in tears from the football field and I forced him to return, to confront his aversion to blocking. There was the time I upbraided him—in private, let me plead in my defense—for his vulgar comment to the Brazilian ambassador's daughter. I kept telling him to work harder, that his fate was in his own hands. I admit to it—was that so wrong? The boy's wit wasn't quick; he was, shall we say, thoughtful. Other boys would jump; Del would watch first. I was hard on him, I know, but only because he had such potential, such promise. And he did! He turned out beautifully . . . Well, didn't he?

I was doubling over even before the younger, stronger pugilist punched me in the gut, and I was out of breath before he struck my chin. I knew I could never hit him again. I had already hurt him enough. Lying on the canvas, such as it was, was a relief. I could not decide whether it was my lunch or my tears bubbling up, before everything went mercifully black.

⊹══⊹

"You are tougher than you look, old man." Theodore, far too cheerful, was hovering over my bed. At least it was *my* bed.

"Is that a compliment, Theodore?"

His teeth clacked. I took that as a yes.

It was nice that he stopped by, but he was an exhausting visitor. He asked about the bout, punch by punch. I had no choice but to tell him I had stopped fighting—and why. He was wrapped up with his own children, and best I could detect from the look of horror on his face (though who could tell anything for sure about this emotional yet impenetrable man?), he did understand. He even empathized.

After a while I feigned sleep, and he clasped the back of my hand and made his departure.

The next time I opened my eyes, it was dark outside. A small bulb was lit by my side of the bed. Clara was rocking in the wine-colored chair.

"Morning, dearest," she said.

"Morning?" I started to scramble out of bed.

"No, no," she said with a laugh. "Just morning for you. It's a little past ten. At night."

"I'm hungry," I said.

In the kitchen, I watched Clara standing at the cast-iron stove. The sizzling of the eggs and the toasty smell flooded my heart with grief. For Del, of course. He was a part of our lives—our plans, our pride, our affection. Throughout, my one source of comfort has been Clara—her sanity, her courage. She has character enough for both of us.

The moment passed, but my eyelids felt sticky.

Otherwise, I was none the worse for wear, or so I preferred to believe. Just a little hazy. Not sure how I got home, but Single Malt was back in her stall. I had never been knocked cold before, and I didn't like it. But I felt lucky, tell you the truth. I had nothing left to prove, not even to Theodore—or to myself.

I relished the fried eggs and the thick-sliced, buttered bread. Clara sat across from me at the small, square table that the servants and the children used,

"You are an idiot to do this, you know," she said. But she wasn't angry.

Nor was I. "I know," I said.

To change the subject—and also to put it in grander perspective—I told Clara about the carriage driver's cancer. She looked stricken.

"How old is he?" she said.

"Sixty-two."

A year younger than I was.

"How long does he . . . have, do they say?"

I shrugged. Nor could I say if he knew. Funny, those were the two questions everyone asked, the answers unknowable and nosy, respectively.

"They shouldn't tell him," she said, with uncharacteristic vehemence. "What would he have left to live for? I meant that literally, not rhetorically. A man who is dying has nothing to lose."

There was a lot I loved about Clara. Her understanding of the human condition, for one, as well as her understanding of each human's condition, including mine. Including the carriage driver's, though she had never met him. I admired this in her, and I loved her for it, too.

Her sentence kept me awake. *A man who is dying has nothing to lose.* A man who knew he was dying might feel released from all earthly restrictions.

I bolted up in bed.

A man who knew he was dying might be willing to die sooner if the cause—or the money—was right.

Suppose the collision in Pittsfield hadn't been an accident, and suppose Euclid Madden, the trolley's motorman, *was* telling the truth—that he was an innocent man. If both of those were true, or so I deduced, the universe of possible culprits dwindled to one. The carriage driver, David Pratt, had nothing to lose.

CHAPTER SIXTEEN

Chief Nicholson, I'm glad I caught you at home. I need something, if you could." The static on the 'phone line seemed worse in the morning. "A couple of things," I said.

"I'm listening."

Yes, he would have his men call the local banks to learn whether David Pratt held an account that showed any recent deposits. And yes, he would ask the carriage driver's doctors whether the patient had been told he was dying.

"Glad to oblige." That's what Chief Nicholson said, although his tone was less than convincing. He was doing his duty. I had no right to expect more.

"A third thing, actually," I said, pushing my luck. "Life insurance. And whatever else you can learn."

The exhalation was audible across the hundreds of miles. "I will try," Chief Nicholson replied.

"Thank you," I said. "Thank you."

⊹⊱━━⊰⊹

"It was too goddam hot," Mark Hanna belched, in his sun-drenched kitchen.

It was my fault, I suppose, for interrupting the senator's breakfast (again). This morning, at least, Hanna was dressed, if you count a plaid smoking jacket and a polka-dot cravat (which I did). He chattered with

his mouth full, about the mercurial weather in Cleveland and about the
shenanigans of the city's radical mayor.

"I need to ask you about something unpleasant," I interrupted.

Hanna scowled.

"Do you know a man named William Turtle?"

A look of Neanderthal puzzlement crossed Hanna's face, and then a
ray of comprehension. "Wasn't he shot?" he said.

"Yes. How did you know that?"

Hanna gulped and shrugged, as if he had said too much already.

"The evening of the day he was shot," I said, "he was planning to
come see you."

I waited for a look of astonishment, but I was disappointed. Elmer
Dover must have said something, because Hanna waved his hand like
a monarch dismissing his courtiers and guided a forkful of sausage into
his maw.

⊹━━⊹

I like talking things out with a deaf man. I can think aloud and not
worry overmuch about how it sounds. And Adee often has wisdom to
dispense; maybe hearing only part of things improves one's perspective.
This morning I interrupted his daily recital of the world's overnight
woes to ask him, slowly, as he trained his sharp eyes on my lips, how to
plumb a dying carriage driver's mind.

Leonardo da Vinci should have observed the muscles pulsate in
Adee's temples. At last he said, "He would want what he wanted, for
loved ones first."

So saith the childless bachelor; it made my heart ache. I kept hoping that, someday, Adee and Margaret Hanna might bicycle into the
twilight.

"Clara's view is that he has nothing to lose," I said.

"That could make a man dangerous."

We let that sink in.

"Who could tell me about this man?" I said. "Governor Crane, I suppose. This fellow Pratt was his liveryman, as I understand it, whenever
the governor was home in Dalton. He is back in Boston now, I would
guess."

"You could telephone him there."

"I don't . . ." I shook my head. "That man is difficult enough to converse with in person. And what am I supposed to ask him: Did the liveryman he personally recommended for the president turn out to be an assassin instead?"

+‡=‡+

"To get away from those brats. Why else?" Cortelyou said. We were striding across the carriageway toward the western wing, still under construction. "That's what Princess Alice says, and she ought to know." I was pleased to hear his disrespect.

I suspected that Cortelyou's own four children behaved more like civilized beings than the president's half dozen did. Not to mention my four—excuse me, three. (That was a hard thing, when people asked you how many.) Helen, the poetess, had married last winter, and sunny Alice's nuptials were days away. Clarence, our overlooked seventeen-year-old, had escaped to Harvard. Plus Del. *Minus* Del.

"And not enough bedrooms," I replied, for something to say.

Cortelyou had been surprised at my sudden interest in touring the White House renovations. He had shown me first around the White House proper, still crowded with workmen and scaffolding. The main staircase was nothing more than wooden planks. The Corinthian pillars in the main vestibule looked lonely, even vulnerable, with the floor and walls ripped away. Beneath the East Room floor, I'd glimpsed the new iron beams that shored up the rotten timbers. It seemed ludicrous to think the Roosevelts could move back in by Thanksgiving, as Edith wished. For one thing, the White House painters had just gone out on strike, and the plasterers threatened to join them.

"This used to be the conservatory—the greenhouse," Cortelyou was saying, as we reached the new wing. "Also the rose house, the grapery, and the fern house. But you knew all that already."

"That, I did," I said. *Since before you were born.*

The high-ceilinged lobby of the new West Wing was aswirl with dust. Workmen darted hither and yon, their ladders clattering.

"The tin roof is corniced," Cortelyou continued, as my docent, "and the balustrades are up and painted—finished, thank God, before the strike. And we extended the coal vault in front, for additional storage."

I passed through the lobby to the spacious room at the rear, its curved windows facing south. I said, "The president's office, I gather."

"No, the secretary's office."

Ah, Cortelyou's. "And where is the president's office?" I said.

"This way." Cortelyou led me through his office-to-be and across an anteroom into a square corner chamber that was less centrally located and slightly smaller than the secretary's. The walls needed plastering, and the beams were exposed in the ceiling. Electrical cords hung like nooses at the center of the room.

"Very nice," I said.

"I'm glad you like it," he replied.

"I hope *he* does, too."

"He will."

Which was different, I reflected, from *He does*. I wondered if Theodore had noticed the disparity. Probably. Did he care? Evidently not, for he could have altered the design if he liked.

"But to meet with visitors," Cortelyou went on, "the president will still use his old office, in the original building, upstairs. And over here"—he guided me back through his office and beyond the telegraph room—"is the staff room." It was more than twice the size of the president's office. Men were laying the wooden floor. "How big was the staff in your day?"

"Two. Nicolay and me. And part of a third."

"We have forty now, counting the eleven clerks and six messengers on loan from the departments. They need to be organized, like in a business, and now we will have the space for it."

"I marvel at your capacity for detail," I said. *And fear it.*

Cortelyou's capacity for work was legendary. Had the man ever made a mistake? I had heard a rumor once that, as President Cleveland's stenographer, he had nearly touched off a war when he heard *would* instead of *wouldn't* in transcribing a diplomatic note to the tsar. But I doubted it.

"Thank you," he said.

"I must tell you, by the way, that the driver of the president's carriage in Pittsfield—"

"And mine."

"Yes. He is still in the hospital. The doctors say he has . . . cancer."

A sigh. "What is his name?"

"David Pratt," I replied. "Senior; there is also a junior. Did you know him?"

"In the carriage, certainly. We must have shaken hands."

"Before that? Did you not approve all of the president's logistics?"

Cortelyou rested his elbows on a sawhorse, then stood straight and dusted off his wrists, which were already clean. Beneath the spotless frock coat he wore a stiff white vest and high collar; his brilliantined hair, salted in gray, was brushed back.

"I had that honor," he said.

"Did you meet Mr. Pratt then?"

"Who had the time? How would I know a livery driver in Pittsfield?"

"Dalton."

"Dalton—see? I left those arrangements to Governor Crane. I understood that this man Pratt sought the job. A personal acquaintance, I gather."

"How, do you know?"

"I imagine everyone in Dalton knows everyone else. Certainly the governor does. His hometown. Whatever he wanted was fine with . . . us."

That rang true.

"I'll tell you this about the man," Cortelyou said. "He was as nice a fellow as could be. He suggested the president could get a better view if he switched sides with the governor."

"And did he?"

"No. He liked it where he was, behind the driver. Mr. Pratt wanted him to sit on the left side of the carriage, directly behind the bodyguard, Mr. Craig."

⊹╾━╼⊹

Directly behind Mr. Craig. Why else would David Pratt have wanted the president to move other than to . . . to kill him?

And himself. I should not forget that.

I stumbled across the White House grounds, weaving among the piles of lumber, to the State Department building next door. I kept thinking about the carriage driver. What would impel a man of seemingly sound mind to drive his carriage in front of a hurtling trolley, on purpose? Knowing that anyone or everyone aboard might die. Including the president. Including himself. Who on earth would do that?

This was who: A man who was dying and had nothing to lose. Who maybe had something to gain. Financial or otherwise.

I thought I heard the guard at the door say, "Good afternoon, Mr. Secretary," but I couldn't be sure. I was too impatient for the elevator and climbed the marble steps two at a time.

It was the question Cortelyou hadn't asked that was troubling me. *Why* was I interested in David Pratt? Did Cortelyou know the answer already? He made it his business to know. Everything. In his ruthless quest for efficiency, he understood that information is power. Information gushed in; a trickle came out. Cortelyou was opaque because he tried to be. If he was the ideal of Twentieth-Century Man, I trembled for my country.

I found a note on my desk: Chief Nicholson had 'phoned. Main got him on the line immediately. (Elsie was at lunch.)

"I asked for this an hour ago!" he was shouting. A throat clearing and a sip of something. "Is that you, Mr. Hay?"

I assured him it was.

The man from the bank had been helpful. David J. Pratt Sr. had opened an account not quite two weeks before the collision, at Agricultural National Bank of Pittsfield. "They have a branch in Dalton. He opened it with a cashier's check. Five thousand dollars, exactly. It was drawn on . . ." A rustle of papers. "On Riggs National Bank of Washington, DC. Do you know it?"

"Do I know it?" I said. "It's a block away from my house." Clara and I had a couple of accounts there. So did everyone I knew.

"And you asked about life insurance. Another five thousand. Also purchased last month. On the fifteenth."

About the time the president's schedule became— No, not known yet to the public. But decided upon and known to . . . a few. A week before his New England tour got under way.

"And the cancer?"

"Well, let me finish with the life insurance, because I doubt they're ever going to pay up. Because yes, he does know his diagnosis, and he has known it for a while."

"For how long?" I said.

"The doctors couldn't remember, and his son isn't to be found. Three or four weeks at least. Maybe since before he bought the policy. Happily, it's not my job to figure that out."

"Before the collision."

"Oh yes. And even now he *seems* pretty healthy. Double vision, some awful headaches. Nothing anyone else would necessarily notice."

"Double vision?"

"Occasionally. Not until after the collision, he says."

Having been found unconscious but groaning, beneath the nigh wheel horse's carcass, could have caused all sorts of symptoms. Not cancer, however.

"How do they know he *has* cancer?"

"They say they know. Who am I to say otherwise?"

I was about to replace the receiver when Chief Nicholson spoke up. "One other thing, by the way—probably irrelevant. The president of the Agricultural Bank is a celebrity hereabouts: Governor Crane."

<hr />

"My dear Mr. Secretary, to what do we owe this honor?"

Ah, the royal *we*. I wish people would quit invoking honor when they meant merely to flatter.

Charles Glover, the president of Riggs, was a banker's banker, a pillar of the community, a giver to all civic causes—a man made of marble, by my lights. His face had no sharp edges. His cheeks were smooth, as was his forehead, and his demeanor. Not a gray hair was out of place. Only the bristly, clipped mustache betrayed the aggressiveness I presumed lay underneath. Also his eyes, which narrowed and never left mine. He happened to be a neighbor on Lafayette Square, catty-corner from my house, a vacant lot away from the temporary White House. Neighborliness did not always breed affection.

"It is a question of the highest security," I said, indulging in flattery myself. "Information that may affect the president's physical safety. That is all I am permitted to say." I paused to gauge the effect. There was none. I described what I knew about the cashier's check deposited into David Pratt's account. "Someone had to come into the bank here in order to send the cashier's check in the first place. Is that right?"

"I will check and let you know," Glover said.

He meant that as a dismissal, but I stayed in my uncomfortable seat on the uncivilized side of the vast, gleaming desk. "I'll wait," I said.

"As you wish," Glover said, lifting the telephone receiver from its cradle. "You will be more comfortable, however, out in the lobby."

The new Riggs building, at Fifteenth and Pennsylvania, was made of granite and felt just as cold, inside and out. The exterior was meant to remind you—and it did—of the Treasury Building directly across the avenue, but the interior had none of Treasury's stolid charm. Its marble and vaulted ceiling, all in golden hues, was meant to persuade people to part with their money, but it left *me* worried about how the money was spent. I chose a high-backed chair with a clear view of his door.

> *Marble, marble, money, and garble,*
> *Make us rich or make us horrible.*

Hmm. Maybe the *or* should be *and*? Funnier, and probably truer—which, in poetry, I suppose is the point. And rhyming, I had to admit, still had its pleasures.

The door to Glover's office opened and an august forefinger beckoned me back in.

"He is coming," Glover said.

I was expecting a Zeus, but a meek-looking man with thin, sandy hair and a pallid complexion sidled in. His cravat was askew and a thin folder was in his hand. He glanced around as if he had never been here. I wondered if he had met the bank's president before, much less a secretary of state. He was introduced as W. J. Flather, an assistant cashier.

"I just met another Flather," I said, "down at police headquarters."

"My little brother."

His little brother was bigger. This one's eyes grazed mine, and he raised the folder to his face like a shield. Inside of it was a single sheet of paper. "The account belongs to a company called Intrepid Americans Incorporated," he said. "It was opened on the twentieth of August."

Two days before the president set off on his New England tour. "Opened by whom?" I said.

Flather examined the paper and passed it to me. It was a scrawl. The first name might have started with an *I* or a *J* and the second name definitely with an *H*. The address was also indecipherable, although it was probably Thirteenth, Sixteenth, or Eighteenth street, definitely northwest. From his vest pocket Flather produced a magnifying glass. I handed the paper back, and a look of the most intense seriousness overtook him. His narrow face seemed to expand.

"Sixteenth," he announced. "That's the street. And there's a number in front. Three digits—they all look alike. Zero zero zero—couldn't be. Six zero . . . No, eight zero zero. That's it: eight hundred Sixteenth street northwest."

That was my house.

+>━━<+

Lafayette Park was alive with the scampering of squirrels, the warbling of birds, the long looks of lovers. I saw none of it. The one thing I knew for certain was that I had not opened that Riggs account. Why would someone say that I had? A practical joke?

I felt a chill up my spine.

Then I got scared. The twentieth of August was two weeks *before* the attempt on Roosevelt's life, if that is what it was. Meaning it happened before Theodore even asked me to investigate. Someone was out to get *me*. Or tease me. Or hold this in reserve against me. Who? And for what unearthly purpose?

I shook my head fiercely and uttered a one-syllable word that caused a lady in a saucy hat to clench her parasol.

I was heading home, although I was needed at the office. Instead of either, I knocked on Henry's door. He was in, and at work (on whatever it was), but was pleased to be disturbed, if I would kindly wait a minute or two, which I did. Henry's foyer was simple and spartan but as fascinating as most men's craniums, and more exotic, what with its teak umbrella stand from Siam and the carved wooden mask with its nose pointed like a stalactite. On the wall was a black-framed photograph of Chartres. I assumed it was Clover's—she had been accomplished at the art—but I had never dared ask.

I was marveling at the splendor of the steeples when the familiar breathy voice said, "Phallic, yes?"

I doubled over in laughter. Other than a lady's ankles, I had never heard Henry refer openly to anything below the waist. The man was sixty-four; it was time.

"Not exactly," I said. "Pointy, and two steeples. I can see you're having a difficult day."

"Sometimes the words won't flow."

"What words are those?" I pried.

"Words. Flimsy things."

Instead of taking a stroll, I looked for an empty bench in the park. I found one by the new statue of General de Rochambeau, in the corner nearest the White House West Wing. Henry had a quizzical look, as if he expected a flogging for someone else's crime.

A woman ambled by, leashed to a poodle that stopped at every shrub to sniff. I had perfected the practice of speaking under my breath, so that only one person could hear. If that person wasn't hard of hearing, which Henry was.

"My epiphany!" I said. I told him about David Pratt and the likelihood of his guilt. By a process of elimination, bolstered by a cashier's check and life insurance. "He *wanted* the job—that's what Cortelyou says."

"For more than one reason, perhaps."

"Including money, apparently."

"Often suspected as a motivator of men," Henry drawled.

"In this case, a total of ten thousand dollars. For a man who is dying."

Henry rocked back on the bench and said, "In . . . what . . . sense . . . dying?"

"In the usual sense." I lowered my voice and named the dreaded disease.

"I see," Henry said.

"There is more," I said. I described the bank account at Riggs on which the cashier's check had been drawn, opened with a bogus name and address. "Mine! This was *before* the collision. Before I ever got involved in this. What on earth do you make of that?"

Henry stared into his lap, lost in thought. At last he looked up and shook his head. "I wish I could help you," he said.

───✦───

Clara and I were halfway through the pheasant when James tiptoed in and told me that someone was waiting. I wasn't expecting anyone. Or wanting to see anyone.

"A Mr. Flather," James said.

Damn! Was I about to be arrested? I had assumed—*assumed!*—that peril had passed.

"Excuse me, dear," I said, wondering when I would see her again. My stomach heaved.

I followed James to the front hall and was relieved to find the timid bank clerk. "Oh, Mr. Flather, what can I do for you?" I gushed. "Please come with me. We can join my wife. Would you like some coffee?"

"Er, no," he said. "I mean, no thank you, Mr. Hay . . . Mr. Secre— I don't want to . . . Please forgive me . . . sir. I waited 'til dark." He glanced back at the door.

"Let's try the library," I said. "Coffee?"

"Oh no, sir. I can't stay long."

I nodded at James and said, "Please tell Mrs. Hay."

The electric lamp beside my chair made the cranes look alive and ready to swoop. My preferred Mr. Flather squirmed in the red plush chair. If he had rehearsed what he wanted to say, it was lost to him now.

"Take your time," I said. "Why did you wait until dark?"

"Not to see Mr.— So he wouldn't see . . ."

"Mr. Glover," I said. My neighbor; his boss.

Flather's head bobbed, and kept bobbing, as he struggled to say something that was building inside him. It rose out of his scrawny chest and exploded into the stuffy air: "It was me!"

"*What* was you?"

"*I* handled it. Opened the account. With the . . . wrong . . . false . . . name and address. I know I . . ."

Now I understood why he didn't want Glover to know.

"Did you check on his identity?" I said.

His eyes went wide, like a guilty child asserting his innocence. "I took his word for it."

"I can understand," I said, almost truthfully. "Can you describe . . . *him*?" I exhaled with what I hoped was unnoticed relief.

"Yes, him . . . I can't rightly recall. It was weeks ago, and I see dozens of people a day. I half remember a funny little man—not handsome, not ugly, well, a little bit ugly—who insisted on using his own pen. A smooth little number it was."

"Whiskers?"

He squinted, trying to recall. "I guess so. Yes. A full beard, rather like yours."

"Hair color?"

A puzzled look. "He kept his hat on. I'd forgotten. I thought it was odd at the time."

"How did he pay? Do you remember that? Five thousand dollars is a lot of greenbacks."

"That I do remember. It was cash, all of it cash. Fifty-dollar bills, the new ones, with Sherman." That was John Sherman, Lizzie's uncle, the former secretary of state. "I remember because I counted them out."

He seemed out of breath and rose to leave. "You know, you're not the only person to be asking about this," he said.

"Oh?"

"That's really why I came here." Flather had ceased being timid. "Last week sometime, we received a wire from a man who was interested in this particular transaction. He said he would come by, but he never showed up. He had an unusual name. A rodent of some kind."

"Turtle?"

"Yes, that's it. Not a . . . but, yes. I wouldn't have told him much anyway, it being none of his business, you know. But as I say, he never showed up."

Theodore had his nose in a book, literally, when I entered his sanctum. His legs were propped up on a hassock, the inevitable cup of coffee at his side.

I knew he was aware of my presence because he raised a forefinger as he finished a page. He was reading *The Virginian*, the year's best seller. "Listen to this," he exclaimed, leafing back to the opening page. "*For the first time I noticed a man who sat on the high gate of the corral looking on.* The cowboys, you understand, were trying to break a wild pony. *For he now climbed down with the undulations*"—every syllable drawn out—"*of a tiger, smooth and easy, as if his muscles flowed beneath his skin.* Beautiful, yes? This is life in the West as it was."

This was rank sentiment, of course. Everyone knew that cowboys were lowlifes who worked on a whim and spent too much time in saloons. They weren't the novel's silent, stoic, heroic figures that Theodore adored. No surprise that he did, considering that he had been one of those cowboys, despite his Tiffany's bowie knife, gaining his brethren's respect by knocking down a bully in a bar who had called him Four Eyes. Besides the fact that the novel's author, Owen Wister, was his Harvard chum. Theodore was as skilled as any politician in rearranging history to his liking. Maybe more so, being a historian himself.

"You must read it," he said.

"I've started it," I said. In truth, I had not made it past the dedication—*To Theodore Roosevelt*—with the (arse-kissing) "author's changeless admiration."

"I need to ask you something," I said.

My tone must have betrayed me, because he laid the book in his lap and gave me his undivided attention. I felt privileged, as he no doubt intended.

"The carriage driver in Pittsfield—David Pratt was his name. Do you remember him?"

"Oh yes. Rather a tall fellow, a little on the ungainly side, I thought. Pleasant enough. Governor Crane's man."

"Did he ask you to switch seats with the governor?"

"I suppose he did. I didn't think anything of it. I was fine where I was. Why do you ask?"

"That would have put you right behind Mr. Craig."

"It would have." He understood instantly what I meant. "But Murray Crane wasn't hurt."

"True, true. But he might have been."

"Why don't you ask the governor? He is still in the city, working with me on the coal strike. I have never known a more honorable man."

An impressive endorsement, given Theodore's strict standards. "He is the one who told me," I said. "There is also this." I described the five thousand dollars sent to Pratt from a newly opened account at Riggs.

"Whose account, do we know?" Theodore said.

I appreciated the *we*. "The short answer is no."

"The longer answer?"

"There's a name on the account, but it isn't the correct one," I said. "It's . . . mine."

Theodore burst out laughing. "You keep edging your way into this case, my dear Hay. One might almost think you had a vested interest."

"I keep telling you I shouldn't be doing this. Even I can see the conflict of interest here."

"So you say. Except when you tell me you want to *keep* doing this."

"Well, I'm just trying to keep you—and me—out of trouble, physical or political. Or ethical," I made sure to add. To Theodore, life was a morality play—his father's gift (and burden). Anything that involved right and wrong was sure to entice him.

⊢══⊣

"Where is your . . . servant?" I said. I meant Frank Forney, the red-bearded Samson.

"Back home," Governor Crane replied. "Had to go."

Ichabod had answered his own door, even at twenty minutes past ten. His octagonal sitting room at the Willard was dimly lit, courtesy of the lamps along the avenue outside. He was still dressed for dinner. So was I.

"I have a couple of additional questions," I said.

His stone face was probably the one he used in facing all of life's annoyances.

"One of them has to do with the Agricultural National Bank of Pittsfield," I went on. "You are the president, are you not?"

No reply.

"Five thousand dollars was deposited into Mr. Pratt's account at the bank—a new account. Deposited in cash. Would you know anything about this?"

Governor Crane rocked back in the Queen Anne chair and, miraculously, moved his mouth. "I am the governor," he affirmed. "That occupies all of my time."

I waited for him to tell me something I didn't already know. In vain. My turn again.

"My second question," I said, "is about Mr. Pratt. How well do you know him?"

"Years."

"What do know about him?"

A quizzical look, as if to say, *How much does anyone know about anyone?*

"Is he a good man, would you say?" Another vapid question. What *did* I want to know? It was this: Would he murder a president? Oh yes, that was a question sure to bring a candid response.

I was flailing for what to ask next when Governor Crane snapped out of his trance and stated, in no uncertain terms, "Yes, he is a good man. A Christian man; a family man. He would do anything for his family. Anything."

"Including . . . ? Actually, I have a third question. Do you know of anyone who would want to kill *you*? Maybe the president wasn't the intended target."

Crane laughed. I am not sure I had ever seen that before. "I should hope so," he said, "or I wouldn't be much of a governor. But there are easier ways to kill me, if someone is so inclined. He needs merely to come to my office and make an appointment."

+‒·‒+

Clara was asleep, and I awakened her to say good night. She didn't seem to mind. She even managed a smile before her eyes closed again.

I promised myself I would never give Lizzie Cameron another thought. I recognized I had promised this before. But this time I meant it. Clara was dear to me in a way that no one else has ever matched, or ever could. That I *knew*. If I knew anything at all—and I had learned a thing or two in my time—I knew that your good fortune must not be assumed. I was a lucky man to be worthy of her love. By Lincoln's deathbed, I had learned that nothing was certain in life. But Clara's devotion to me, and mine to her, came pretty damn close.

CHAPTER SEVENTEEN

The note arrived at eight fourteen—I noticed because my pocket watch was dangling from the stool. Lindgren was venting his own marital frustrations on my hamstrings, which were as tight as piano wire. It was unlike James to interrupt me, unless he thought it was important. How he could tell, I never understood, but he could. The old butler had a preternatural sense of these things.

I sat up at the edge of the table, unsure why I was trembling. The envelope was small—dainty, really. It was ivory colored with faint blue lines meandering through. The flap was unsealed, and I pulled out a page, folded over. The paper was cheap and rough, with wide lines, ragged along one edge, as if it had been ripped from a schoolchild's pad.

Six words. I read them twice and let the note flutter onto the floor.

"Lovey is ours. Wait for word."

I vaulted off the table and grabbed my clothes. Without a word to Lindgren (or to anyone), I rushed from the house. Had I gotten Lizzie involved in this, or had she involved herself?

I crossed diagonally through Lafayette Park and rushed east along Pennsylvania avenue to Fifteenth street, then turned back onto the avenue. I had walked this way thousands of times, no doubt, and the view never grew old. In the distance, the Capitol dome hovered over the street and below the clouds. I must have drawn stares—I had left without my hat, for the first time in memory—but I didn't take the time to notice.

I dashed across Fifteenth in front of a trolley whooshing by, armed with my irrational faith that all would be well.

The Willard's lobby was busy with railroad men and off-duty generals. The elevator stopped at nearly every floor. On the fifth floor, I rapped on the door to Lizzie's suite. Light footsteps approached and the door swung open to reveal Nellie Bly.

"Good morning, Mr. Hay," she said with a lilt.

"Where is Liz . . . Mrs. Cameron?" I said.

"She went out, before I was up. She left a note, saying she'd be back. Would you care to come in?"

"I got one, too," I said, "but not from her."

I told her about mine, and we rushed out. The elevator operator had not seen her leave, nor had the desk clerk. I dispatched Nellie to ask the doorman. She needed no more than a minute before she fairly skipped back through the lobby and found me by the newspaper stand. "Two people killed in a train wreck," I said. "Forty-two injured. In Ohio."

"Around back," she replied. "The Willard livery. The driver's name is Demetrios."

The livery stable fronted on F street, directly behind the hotel. The telephone was ringing, and men in black leather aprons were hitching horses to buggies of all kinds. It smelled of horseflesh and hay.

Demetrios stood in the back, chomping on a hard roll. He was a strapping young man with an open face, a shock of dark hair, and a hearty manner. I introduced Nellie and myself.

"Whatcha want?" he said. He was speaking to me but gazing at Nellie.

"About a passenger you just had. A lady."

"What's it to you?"

I slipped my wallet from my breast pocket and removed a dollar.

"A lady and a gent," Demetrios said, eyeing my wallet. Another dollar. What had happened to my bargaining skills?

"Just one gent?"

"Yeh, yeh. I done nottin' wrong."

"I'm not saying you did. Can you describe him?"

"A stupid-looking fella, le' me tell ya. Not that he don't got the brains.

But that he's the bloke you'd pick on, back o' the pack, were you the sort. Which I'm not, le' me tell ya. But he the type."

I said, "Tall? Short? Fat? Thin?"

"Toward the tall; short to me. And slow. I could take 'im wit' one hand."

A stab of pain—a memory of Del as a boy, failing to slip my playful punch, which glanced off his unblinking eye. "Whiskers?" I said.

"Not a hair. Mebbe he couldn't. A fat fuckin' face." He noticed Nellie again. "Pardon my French, ma'am."

"And the lady?" Nellie said, her head cocked, eyes steady.

"She be quite a lady. The neck of a f— Of a giraffe. And the way she sashayed. She were mine, I'd knock her down a few. After . . . well . . . She some lady."

I couldn't disagree. "Did she seem . . . unwilling to go with the gent?" I said.

"Not so's I could see. And I seen plenty of that. All seemed . . . how you say . . . hunky-dory."

I said, "Did they seem . . . close?"

That made him think, which entailed a glance at the hayloft and a raggedy cough. "Wouldn't say so," he said. "I can tell that too."

I wasn't proud of my sense of relief. "Where did you take them?" I said.

Demetrios started to say something, then caught himself. He looked at my breast pocket and said, "Five."

"Five?"

He knew when he had a fish on the hook, and he knew that I knew. I paid him.

"Up to Georgetown. Thirty-second street wharf."

"What were they doing there?"

"They don't say. I don't ask. They tell me where, that's where I take 'em. The pay ain't great, but that's what I do, mister. What'd you say your name was again?"

"You busy?" I said.

⊢✕⊣

"Dropped 'em off jes' 'bout here." Demetrios smirked. "They go out to the end of the dock, like they figgered a boat was waitin'."

Between K street and the river, in Georgetown, was the industrial part of town, and it stank. The morning gusts brought signs of the coal yard, the soap factory, the fertilizer warehouses, more of sewage than the sea. Typhoid germs loved the Potomac, and the river loved them back.

"She still seemed willing?" I said.

"Didn't see 'em all the way out, but what I see, yeah."

"How long did you watch them?"

"A minute, no more. The gent pay the bill. No tip, though."

"I could fix that," I said, "if you could wait."

Georgetown College's boathouse blocked the foot of the wharf. It was a squat wooden structure with opaque windows and in need of fresh paint. The Columbia Athletic Club, the driver had told us, used it, too. Nellie and I stepped around the shack and plunked onto the dock.

Small boats bobbed along both sides. The clouds had darkened and scudded across the sky. The river showed occasional whitecaps between here and the wooded Virginia shoreline.

"What then?" I said to no one in particular.

"What then *what*?" Nellie replied.

"What in the hell did they do next? Oh, pardon my—"

"Oh hell, forget it," Nellie said.

"The hell I will," a man whooped from the last boat on the right, at the end of the pier. With its dark trim and clean lines, the rowboat looked sleeker than the rest—more so, certainly, than the two men seated cross-legged, sharing a flask. One was fat, one was thin; neither had an honest beard or could accurately be considered clean-shaven.

"Top of the morning," I said.

"Just gettin' started," the fat man replied, saluting with the flask.

"I'm looking for a tall, pretty woman"—another whoop—"and a man. They were here maybe an hour ago."

"We git a few of 'em each and ev'ry hour, as you can rightly see, generous sir."

"I would need to know where they went."

"Coulda gone anywheres. You can git to Bal'more from here. Or to London or the coast of Brazil. Can't rightly say."

For five dollars, he could. For another fiver, he agreed to take us.

"There," he said, pointing south. "Mason's Island."

That is what old-timers in Washington (such as myself, in this city of transients) called Analostan Island. Plopped in the river between Washington and Virginia, it invoked the name of George Mason's son, an early owner.

"You saw them go *there*?" I said, gesturing toward the island's northern shore.

"Naw, not the old ferry landing. *There!*" The boatman pointed to the bulge in the island's eastern shore. "Past that bend. Nowhere's else they coulda been goin'."

"London," I said.

That drew an affable smile, showing rotten teeth.

The boatman was not as drunk as I'd feared—or as he would be by noon. I paid off the liveryman, beyond dutiful with my tip, and put my life—Nellie's, too—in the boatman's hands. Boat*men*'s. The skinny fellow was coming along.

He sat in the bow while the fat man—Eduardo—manned the oars. With considerable strength and skill, I must say. Nellie and I shared the bench at the back. I felt my jacket pocket and caressed the derringer for comfort.

The wind was whipping up; the whitecaps danced like droplets on a drumhead. Eduardo smiled without stop, which worried me. The little man stared forward, transfixed by something I was unable to see. Just as well, no doubt.

The island's coastline was a jumble of shady groves and scraggly shrubs. The fat man steered the boat around toward the southern shore and eased it onto a mud bank sheltered by low-lying branches. Another boat was tucked beneath overhanging branches a few feet ahead and to the right.

"After you," the fat man growled.

I stepped out of the boat with a minimum of agility. My boots sank into the marshy sand, up to and above my trouser cuffs. I lent Nellie a hand—unnecessarily, for she leapt like a ballerina onto the beach. The instant she touched the ground, the little man jumped out and pushed the boat backward into the water and hopped back in. This was why he had come. I thought of shooting at the boat, to put a hole in it. But what would that accomplish? Besides, they might shoot back. The wind swallowed the fat man's maniacal laughter.

We were stranded. It seemed we were impossibly far from the city, although it was in sight. We could swim if we must. And I remembered the other boat. I hoped it had paddles. I had to assume it belonged to Lizzie and her . . . Who was the gent? A kidnapper? A lover? A cousin or a brother—or a brother-in-law—who sought to . . . Lord knows what he had told her . . . and what he might want.

Whoever he was, where were they?

I motioned Nellie to halt, and we listened, but we heard nothing but the wind. I took three deep breaths and forced myself to calm down— for Nellie's sake, I told myself. Really, for my own.

Lovey is ours.

"This way," I said, pointing uphill, feeling a confidence unencumbered by evidence.

I had been on the island twice before. The first time was back during the war—the *real* war—when it was a training camp for Union troops, who trampled the gardens and orchards beyond repair. I was here again last fall—with Theodore, in fact, to the athletic fields at the northern end, to watch trapshooting and a few innings of baseball. The island's southern tip—that's where we were—still showed the traces of terraced landscaping from antebellum days, but years of neglect had delivered an isle of civilization back into wilderness. I knew vaguely the location of Mason's old mansion and outbuildings, up the hill from this beach. The old avenue, still lined with locust trees, was now a briar patch of weeds. Tangles of underbrush concealed the fields along both sides.

I felt raindrops and looked over at Nellie, who pointed up at the trees. Branches swayed, and the leaves flashed their dull undersides. Nellie ran ahead, her cheeks red—with excitement, best I could tell. She had come to Washington in pursuit of an adventure like this. She leaned into the slope, and I followed. Gravel crunched under my boots.

"The house is up ahead," I said, "or was. It's the only shelter on the

island, as far as I know. I bet that's where they are, if they're here. I do
have a gun, by the way."

"So do I," she said.

"Well, let's hope neither of us needs to use it."

No reply. I wasn't sure she agreed.

I thought I heard a scrape on stone, and I stopped and listened hard,
but the only sound was the wind through the trees. I inched ahead,
at full alert. Nellie walked a step behind me. A blockade of hedges
proved to be the ruins of a decorative circle. The drizzle was giving way
to spatterings of rain. And me without my hat. Nellie had a parasol,
which was almost wide enough for two. She offered to share. I found
it wiser to get wet.

High on the ridge I spied the remains of a stately mansion. Crum-
bling walls were haphazardly spaced; vacant doorways showed nothing
behind them but spindly trees. As we tiptoed nearer, I noticed the orna-
mental brickwork, smothered by heavy branches like roots in a grave-
yard. We slogged through clustered leaves and skirted the nearest
corner of the building. The interior stood as empty as the Parthenon.
Grass jutted up through the vestiges of a herringbone floor. Most of the
roof was gone.

Just ahead was a forlorn stone structure with its roof intact. An old
storage shed, perhaps, or an icehouse or a kitchen. We scooted toward
it, picking a meandering route through the brush. The door was short
and round at the top, as in a nasty fairy tale.

I stopped and mouthed to Nellie beside me, *Ready?*

Was she ever!

I steadied the derringer in my hand, which wasn't as difficult as I had
expected. The door was ajar, and I kicked it open. The hinges screeched.

I heard a scream behind me.

"Lizzie," I shouted.

An explosion ripped through the air. It was a sound I knew all too
well. I crooked my arm around Nellie's neck, dived for the ground, and
crawled inside. The gunshot had hit just above the doorway, intended
not merely to frighten but to kill.

I could taste the wet, loamy earth of the shack's floor. The smell was
rancid and rich, with a surge of cordite.

"You all right?" I whispered fiercely.

"Couldn't be better," Nellie said. Her eyes were aglow.

A second scream—the same screamer—sounded farther away. It was heading toward the boat.

"Let's go," I said. I picked myself off the ground, shifted the derringer to my left hand, and offered Nellie my muddy right.

By the time we got down to the flats, the boat was gone from beneath the boughs. It was nowhere to be seen; it must have turned back north, toward Georgetown, out of sight. We had no choice but to swim.

Actually, Nellie jumped in without a word. Soon she had hired a boy with a rowboat to come fetch me. I was willing to be rescued.

+≍≍+

Tired and broken, the bath felt soothing. I was pondering an emergency call to my masseur when a knock at the bathroom door produced James.

"Miss Bly 'phoned, sir," he said. "She said Mrs. Cameron is back. That you would understand."

I leapt out of the porcelain tub. James handed me a towel, and within minutes I had dressed and left.

Lafayette Park looked revived after the rains. The magnolia leaves shimmered. People hurried to an early week-end. I weaved through them like a college fullback and noticed nothing until I reached the Willard. If I caused an accident along the way or made a matron drop her wrapped-and-bowed package from Palais Royal, I beg forgiveness.

The hotel lobby was buzzing. I cut through that, too. The elevators were engaged, so I took the stairs beyond the reception desk two at a time. I felt the walls of the stairwell closing in.

The fifth-floor corridor was empty. I rushed to Lizzie's door, but as I readied my knuckles to knock, I stopped. Suppose the kidnapper, or whoever he was, was here. Suppose he had forced Nellie to 'phone.

But she would have refused.

I made ready to knock, and nearly fell forward when the door opened before my knuckles struck the wood. It was Nellie. Her face looked tight. "She's here."

"Is she decent?" I said.

"Is she ever?"

Lizzie Cameron was sprawled on a divan. I had never seen her so lovely. Her regal neck extended from a sweeping robe of royal blue with gold piping. She had covered all her blemishes with creams. Nellie returned to the edge of a high-backed chair. I stood between the windows overlooking the avenue.

"It is marvelous what a bath can do, Johnny," she said.

"You've had quite an adventure."

"I have, at that," she said. "And it's your blessed fault."

"My *what*?"

"You heard me."

"I did, but I didn't understand you. My fault? For coming after you?"

"No, no, no." Her torso rose from the divan. "Your note last night."

"What note? I never sent you a note. What did it say?"

"It promised a rendezvous this morning that would please and surprise me."

"A rendezvous with whom?"

"You didn't say."

"I didn't say anything. I tell you, I never sent you a note. Where is it?"

"I burned it, per instructions—your instructions." She nodded toward the ashes in the fireplace grate. Nothing left for Wilkie's lab.

"Did it say anything else?"

"To show up at the livery stable behind the Willard at half past six."

"Did you?"

"Yes, I was punctual."

Now she starts doing what I ask? When I hadn't?

At the livery stable she was met by a clean-shaven young man with broad shoulders, polite manners, and a round chin. Was this the fat-faced, stupid-looking bloke that Demetrios had described?

"What was his name?" I said.

Lizzie shook her head; her bell-shaped coiffure was fraying.

"Did you ask?" I said.

"Of course. I can converse with a fireplug."

"But not with him."

"Not a word."

"Had you seen him before?" Nellie said.

A pause. "I don't think so," Lizzie said.

I knew she was lying. "Did he say where you were going?"

"Not until we got to Georgetown, down to the wharf."

"But the driver knew. Demetrios, I believe."

Lizzie looked startled. "I couldn't say."

"When did you suspect that something wasn't . . . right?"

"When we got to the wharf. You don't like boats. Or the water. I asked the man where we were going, and he wouldn't say. He kept his hand in his jacket pocket in a way that was worrying me."

"So you got out and followed him."

"Oh no. He was following me. To the end of the pier. A boat was waiting."

"And you got in."

"Of course I got in. Now it was two against one."

"Oh?"

"Oh yes. The man with the oars. A big, bruising fellow with a wild red beard."

"Samson!" I exclaimed. He hadn't left town.

"Pardon?"

"Forney. Frank Forney. Was that his name?"

"I don't . . . Actually, I do remember the other fellow calling him Frank. With a tone of contempt, I must say."

"Was he the one who started shooting?"

"Oh yes. And I knew who he was shooting *at*. They knew it was you. That's why I screamed."

"Yes, I heard you. *We* heard you. How did they know it was me?"

"They didn't exactly bare their souls, Johnny. But they knew." She was sitting up. "And they knew about us!"

"What do you mean, *us*?"

"Oh, they knew, and I didn't tell them. 'Tell your boyfriend,' this is what the man with the red beard said, right after shooting at you. 'Tell him that, next time, somebody dies.'"

My bowels twitched. Sure, death threats were a badge of honor, but the reality felt less romantic.

I had never seen John Wilkie angry. "You could have been killed—both of you. *Should* have been."

"Much obliged," I said.

"Fools!" His pipe sent off plumes of purplish smoke. He pointed at me. "And you in particular."

"I couldn't disagree. Are you done yet?"

"Not quite. You didn't need to come to *me*—though you could have—but why in the name of hell didn't you go to the police?"

"I told you, I got this note before seven o'clock, and you weren't here, and we had no idea where we were going until we went there." This was mostly true; what it omitted was that I had wanted to pursue this myself. "As for the police, where do you find one when you need one?"

"That's why God invented telephones." Wilkie was starting to calm down. I figured he needed a fight or two each day to work up an appetite for dinner.

"If they wanted to kill me, they would have already. That, and their bad aim."

"You *are* a fool. They didn't pass up the chance at William Turtle. You willing to risk this for Mrs. Cameron? Or for Miss Bly?"

"Mrs. Seaman," Nellie said.

"Whatever you call yourself to-day." Wilkie was mad again. "I am lending her to you for safekeeping, Mr. Secretary."

"Nobody lends me," Nellie said, half rising from her hard seat. "I lend myself."

"And believe me," I said, "she doesn't need safekeeping. Besides, *you* take risks."

The Secret Service chief swiveled in his seat and said quietly, "Mr. Secretary, I am paid to."

⊢━━⊣

"*Lovey?* What in the hell does that mean?"

This was a conversation I had dreaded, and Theodore was in full falsetto mode. He was a purist about such things, as he should be. (Of course, he had abandoned infant Alice for a couple of years after his first wife died, and he later abandoned Edith—gravely ill—to gallivant into Cuba, but those are stories for another day.) It was not, strictly speaking, my neighbor's wife that I was coveting—*had* coveted. The Camerons had moved away from Lafayette Square years before. Still, the merest hint of adultery, even the acknowledgment of any desire, was bound to upset Theodore. I respected that—admired it, even.

On my better days, I even shared it.

I forced myself to meet his glare. I would not have wanted to be a Spanish soldier on San Juan Hill. "Kind of a pet name," I said. A lame answer, although the truth.

He looked away, muttering, "John, John, John."

"Nothing has come of it," I said. I hated defending myself—or having to. "It is a pet name, nothing more. I have known her—and, yes, liked her—for years. But somebody knew about it and kidnapped her, to stop me from investigating what happened to *you*. Or what almost happened. What *did* happen, certainly, to Mr. Craig."

Theodore looked angry—at me or at the gods or at whoever was responsible for his bodyguard's death, I couldn't tell. Nor could I blame him.

"Does Mrs. Hay know?" he said.

I did not answer, which was an answer in itself.

⊹╼━╾⊹

I couldn't tell her. There was nothing to tell. But I had to say something about *Lovey*. Otherwise, the story of Lizzie's kidnapping and my pursuit onto Mason's Island made no sense.

I will confess that I was a tiny bit untruthful, suggesting it had been Henry's pet name during his known period of infatuation. This raised no suspicions, as far as Clara let on. And I felt the webs of guilt and shame wrap themselves around my spirit as I told the half-truth.

CHAPTER EIGHTEEN

The rasping of the telephone was a sound I had grown to despise. The apparatus had its uses, to be sure. But I missed the quiet of the past, when the noise came mainly from animals (human and otherwise). Nowadays, machinery would intrude at any moment of the day or night—invariably, when I least wanted to hear it. My pocket watch on the side table said a quarter past six.

The 'phone quieted at last, and soon a shuffling of footsteps approached the bedroom door. Clara was up and gone, of course, at the market or a friend's. Two discreet knocks.

"Come in, James," I said.

Chief Nicholson was on the horn. It was urgent.

I put on my dressing gown and rushed downstairs. I had barely said hello when Chief Nicholson said, "Pratt is dead."

"Damn," I said. "The cancer?"

"No. His throat was slashed."

I gasped.

"During the night," Chief Nicholson said. "The morning nurse found him."

I was grateful to have a chair underneath me. "Murder?" I said.

"Looks like suicide," Chief Nicholson replied. "He left a note."

"What did it say?"

"The usual. That he couldn't take it anymore. They never tell you what 'it' is." I had never considered the literary merits of suicide notes.

"The cancer, I suppose. Though the doctors here say he wasn't in terrible pain. Nor despondent, though I suppose that comes and goes."

"'It' could be guilt," I said. "He cut his own throat? Is that even possible?"

"I've heard of it happening. A couple of weeks ago, in North Carolina, I think it was. Here, we found a long-handled razor on the floor next to his bed. And the blood splatter was . . . well . . . the coroner is taking a look, even as we speak. I should know more later."

"And you'll let me know?" I said.

Chief Nicholson hung up without replying.

⊦═══⊣

"What did he have against me?" Theodore said.

"I wouldn't take it personally," I said. "The man killed himself."

"After trying to kill *me*, so you're saying. If you try to kill a man, it's personal. Especially to the intended victim." Theodore grinned at the thought.

I conceded the point. "Seems he had nothing against you, other than ten thousand dollars."

"Is that what a human life is worth nowadays? Does everything have a price?"

"Not to be cynical," I said, "but everything has always had a price."

"I don't!" he sputtered.

I believed him.

"And now," he said, "we'll never know for certain why this fellow Pratt did what he did, *if* he did. You saying Chief Nicholson never got a confession out of the man? Did he even try?"

"Says he tried. I wasn't there."

"You need to be. Go back to Pittsfield."

"I don't see what I can do that Chief Nicholson and his men can't. I am more useful here, I should think. We still don't know who took . . . Mrs. Cameron to Mason's Island. And Mr. Turtle's murderer is still at large."

"What I don't understand about you, John, is your roundabout ways. When you see a problem, the best thing to do is to go straight at it." This explained San Juan Hill and so much else in his life. If something went wrong—asthma, Spain, trusts—he would change it. As always, I envied his certitude. "There is no other way a problem of state—or a problem of the heart—ever gets solved."

I couldn't have disagreed more, but I saw no point in saying so.

┼━═◄┼

For once I was hoping that Lizzie Cameron would not come to the door—or Don, for that matter—and for once I got my wish.

"Good morning," said Nellie Bly. Her lips formed a girlish smile.

"I need to talk," I said.

"Let me talk first," she replied. "I haven't finished my coffee, and they brought a big pot."

Her words poured out along with the coffee. She had located the desk clerk downstairs who had accepted the kidnapper's note for Lizzie—from a street urchin, he said, any of a hundred.

"All in a morning's work," I said.

"Last night, mostly."

"Where is Mrs. Cameron now?" I said.

"Sleeping." Nellie pointed at the bedroom door. "The doctors gave her some laudanum."

"Good," I said. "Put her out of her misery for a few hours. Better that than . . . Let me tell you the latest."

Nellie was as puzzled as I was about David Pratt's suicide. She hypothesized guilt instead of cancer as the reason.

"Or five thousand dollars in life insurance," I said.

"Not if it's suicide," Nellie pointed out.

"So where in the hell does that leave us?" I said. "Another blind alley? Every lead fizzles out. Nothing leads to anything else, unless I'm not seeing it. All this investigating keeps coming back to the same place—nowhere!"

"All right, what do you *know*?" Nellie said.

I'd played this game before. "I know that David Pratt is dead, or so I'm told, apparently a suicide. I know that William Turtle was murdered—I *saw* that—and by someone he recognized. This narrows the list of potential suspects, of which I was—and maybe still am—one. Do I have everything correct so far?"

"You do," Nellie said, an amused look on her face. "And do you know that the late Mr. Pratt was truly at fault?"

"No, I don't know that. But five thousand unexplained dollars in a new bank account suggests . . . I don't know what it suggests. But something."

"And we know that it was sent from Riggs, do we not?"

"Oh yes, although we don't know who sent it. A phony name and address. Mine."

"And do we *know* that the trolley motorman is truly innocent?"

"We don't know that, either. We have no strong evidence that he was guilty, other than a hand-drawn map stuffed into his seat and his mysterious nineteen-minute delay at the top of the hill."

"I'm no lawyer," Nellie said, "but that sounds like evidence to me. Do we know that a crime actually happened—that it wasn't an accident, I mean?"

"I'm pretty confident on that. A knife to my throat persuaded me, if the gun in Pittsfield didn't. That's something else that I know. I was attacked twice, by someone or someones who know who I am and what I am doing and want me to stop. But neither time was I harmed"—I rubbed my throat—"very much."

"Compared to Mr. Craig or Mr. Turtle," Nellie said.

"Or our Sleeping Beauty here. My second attacker threatened her, and she was in fact . . . *kidnapped* I suppose is the most accurate term, and then returned unharmed. *After* you and I were shot at."

"Yes, I would accept *that* as a fact."

"And let's not forget what Turtle told Governor Crane: that it wasn't an accident."

"According to Governor Crane."

"Fair point," I said. "Ol' Ichabod. We keep coming back to him, don't we? He chose the carriage and driver, and our friend Samson answered his door three floors below us. Though I can't imagine that *he* was behind this. He was in the carriage, and he's far too . . . flinty, shall we say, to risk killing himself. I'm been making the same points again and again. I'm not *getting* anywhere."

"Then let's go at it that way. Who else can we eliminate?"

"The president, for one."

"I'll give you that," Nellie said.

"And by the same token, Cortelyou."

"Well, by the same token you should eliminate the carriage driver, and we seem to have decided otherwise."

"True, true," I said. "But Cortelyou has more to live for."

"Let's go back to the motorman," Nellie said. "Maybe he *is* guilty. Maybe he was lying in wait at the top of the hill for the president's carriage."

"He'd have to time it exactly right."

"Which he could, if he knows the route and has the right sorts of brakes."

"Perhaps. But *why*? Why would he do something like that?" I jumped from my seat in despair. "I hate this case. Everything about it circles back. We can't get anywhere and we can't eliminate anything or anyone. It's the anarchists, it's the trusts, it's the beloved senator from Ohio, or our favorite commanding general, our—" I stopped and glanced toward the bedroom door. "Everyone has a motive to want this president . . . gone. Most of all, me. Which is the other thing I know for sure: I didn't do it."

"But you're not so sure about me, is that right?" Nellie said.

"Pretty sure," I replied.

"Let's look at it this way, then: How many different people were involved, total, in all of these . . . stunts? Minimum and maximum, how many did it take?"

"Smart question," I said. "Somebody killed William Turtle, and somebody opened a bank account at Riggs—possibly the same person. There were two attacks on me—by different people, I'm pretty sure. One of them knew about *Lovey*. And two men took Lovey . . . Lizzie . . . Mrs. Cameron . . . to Mason's Island. One of them sounds like our friend Samson—yes, that's another connection to Governor Crane. Anyway, how many people is that?"

"By my arithmetic, a minimum of two, a maximum of . . . say, six. Not including the carriage driver *or* the motorman—probably not both."

"In other words, a conspiracy," I said. "Blithering blazes! A conspiracy to kill the president." The words hung in the air.

When I heard a door handle jiggle, I jumped up and made my escape.

⊹⊱────⊰⊹

Three floors down, Governor Ichabod (oops, Murray) Crane had an impenetrable expression as he blocked the doorway. "What do you want?" he said.

"May I come in?"

"What do you want?"

"Do you know that David Pratt is dead?"

"I know."

"Any idea why?"

"What do you want?"

"I want to know what *you* know about Frank Forney."

"Nothing."

"He answered your door the other day."

"So?"

"And he was David Pratt's servant. And it seems he briefly kidnapped Mrs. Cameron—Elizabeth Cameron—and shot at me."

"What?" Patches of color tinted his face. "I can't help you now," he said.

Before I could make my case of why he should, he slammed the door in my face. I hadn't thought to put my foot in the way.

⊹⊱────⊰⊹

"Go home," I told Adee.

"Same to you," he replied.

The second assistant secretary's head bounced up from the pile of papers on his desk, a beatific smile on his face. He liked being here on a Saturday afternoon. He mattered here. It was where he felt at home.

"Some catching up to do," I said. He was watching my lips, which wasn't always easy, with my beard. "Any good news?"

"A little. We're almost ready to receive the crown prince of Siam—he arrives on Friday. And somebody out there loves you."

"Oh, pray tell, what misguided soul?"

"Your favorites, from the Court of Saint James's. Actually, from their pet newspapers, which is much the same thing. Good show, they say. The *St. James's Gazette* calls you 'an American Hamlet.'"

"Is that a compliment?"

Adee waved a page. "An American Hamlet who says, 'Look on this picture and consider whether old Mother Europe should not be ashamed of herself.'"

"If this is the best I can do," I said, "I shall accept it with pride."

⊰━━⊱

John Wilkie was in his office. Despite a wife and decently behaved children at home, he was as married to the job as Adee was. The telephone receiver was at his ear while he puffed on his unlit meerschaum pipe.

The Secret Service chief replaced the receiver and scribbled some notes on a legal-size pad. "A counterfeiting case in Minnesota," he said. "The new McKinleys, this time. The ten-dollar notes. Not a bad job of them, either."

"They don't waste time, do they?"

"No, and these fellows have talent, I must admit."

"Every profession has its elite," I said. "How did you catch them?"

"We haven't." Wilkie grinned like he had scored the winning run for the Senators. "But we will. And I've been looking for you."

"I haven't gone far."

"It's about the ink," Wilkie said.

"What ink?"

"From Riggs, on the form that opened the account."

"The one with my name on it."

"Yes, that was clever, wasn't it?"

"Not to me."

"Well, my chemists put the ink under a microscope and did . . ." He whirled his hand in the air, conjuring the mysteries of modern science. "Chemical tests. The results, as it happens, were interesting. Not your ordinary American ink. Ink, as you may or may not know, needs what the chemists call a stabilizer to keep it from clotting. Can be a plant resin or an egg white. Best our folks can tell, this ink uses the resin of a holly bush that isn't found in this country. Only in Scotland, a few other places in northern Europe, and the South Island of New Zealand. Parts of Canada, too."

"Sold here?"

"In New York, probably, at the better stationery stores. Not sure about Washington. My men are checking."

"It was his pen, you know. Whoever opened the account."

"Riggs doesn't pay for fancy ink," Wilkie said. He wiggled in his seat and placed both elbows on the desk. "Another fact about this ink. Just to satisfy my curiosity, we tested the note you got yesterday morning, the one that told you about, uh, Mrs. Cameron."

"Yes?"

"The same ink."

<hr>

My Antoinette was not, I'm honor-bound to report, destined for Broadway. I had never heard boos before at the National Theatre—pardon me, the *New* National Theatre. (Did every institution in this city need to boast of its departure from the past?) Such a stately place, facing the avenue, with its handsome twinned towers and its lush crimson decor. The play was risqué, I had to admit. To me, that saved it from mediocrity, or worse. Not to Clara. She found some of the lyrics downright nasty and thought the kissing went on for too long.

Her mood had lightened (wasn't the point of entertainment to be entertained?) by the time our carriage reached home. I was trying to hum the ragtime-ish tune "Life Is Such a Bore," the best of the forgettable music, when I saw James's message by the door: "'Phone Chief Nicholson at home, no matter the hour."

It was nearly eleven o'clock and I was tired and a little out of sorts. No need for the 'phone number—I knew it by heart. The operator put the call right through.

Chief Nicholson answered on the first ring. Poor devil, on the job on a Saturday night.

"Hay here," I said.

"Pratt was murdered."

"*What?* I thought there was a suicide note."

"There was. But he didn't write it. Our handwriting expert says it was close but not quite a match. It was pabulum, somebody's idea of a suicide note."

"Whose handwriting, do you know?"

"Not yet."

"Try Frank Forney, if you can find him."

I told Chief Nicholson about the red-bearded giant who had taken Elizabeth Cameron to Mason's Island and then disappeared. David Pratt's servant, apparently, if not his master.

"But that was yesterday, in Washington," Chief Nicholson said. "Could he have gotten back here in time?"

"I'll . . . check." Actually, I'd have Nellie check. "Why are you so sure he was murdered?"

"The autopsy report. This is what the pathologists found—and the pathologists, you know, have the last word. Try to follow me here. The gash across his throat went from right to left, from just below his right ear, but not quite all the way across. Pratt was left-handed—that's what his widow says—and that's the direction he presumably would have cut if he was slashing his own throat. Except for this. If it were a suicide, the gash would have been deeper at the beginning and shallower at the end, as the victim loses strength and maybe even resolve. But this gash was deeper at the end. So what they conclude is that Pratt didn't do this himself. Somebody else did. Somebody strong."

It took me a while to exhale. "Do you suppose he was taken by surprise?"

"He might have been sleeping, for all we know. And it seems he was taken from behind, judging by the blood splatter. It was uninterrupted. The killer wasn't standing in front. From behind, the killer wouldn't have blood all over him, and if he was careful enough, he wouldn't leave bloody footprints. So he could get away without being noticed."

"That's what happened here, you think."

"That's all my men know at the moment. Though it gives us one useful clue."

"What is that?" I said.

"If he was standing behind Pratt, cutting the victim's throat from right to left, the killer was left-handed."

CHAPTER NINETEEN

S o tell me," I said, "is there a God?"
Whom better to ask than one's masseur? If your body is a temple, isn't he the high priest?

Lindgren pressed the heels of his hands into my shoulder blades. I yelped. "Of course there is," he said.

"How do you know?"

"Everyone says so, and my daddy told me when I was a tot."

I couldn't argue with the latter. "Well, if there is, I've got a few questions to put to him," I said. A sweet pain filled the small of my back. "Maybe it's time to pay the good Lord a visit."

"If he's home," Lindgren said.

An hour at Saint John's did not resolve my query, or queries, although I can't say the time passed unpleasantly. The church itself was calming, and this week's sermon—on the perils of evil and the ubiquity of sin—roused no rabble and required no thought.

My expectations after church were lower still. I answered the peremptory knock with trepidation.

Alice Roosevelt stood tall in the doorway. "Father will be along," she said. "He is giving the pastor a well-deserved piece of his mind." Delight gave her ivory face a rosy hue. Her smile seemed cruel.

"Please come in, then," I said. I almost added "princess."

We had five minutes of uncomfortable small talk (it was disheart-
ening how little I knew about polo) before a confident knocking produced the president. Theodore's scowl darkened the entrance hall. What
I had to tell him would not help.

The news of Pratt's murder stopped him in the shadow of Botticelli's
Madonna and Child.

"So it *was* Pratt," Theodore said, showing a preternatural calm. "These
villains are serious."

"'Villains,' plural?" I said.

"How could one man do all of this damage?"

I thought I detected some respect.

As we entered the library, Alice sprang up from her overstuffed chair
and pressed her father for every detail of his confrontation with the Almighty's nearest envoy. Theodore smiled as he recounted his triumph
in making clear the previous Sunday's embarrassment from listening
to a eulogy for himself.

Alice clapped her hands. "And what did he say to that, Father?"

"What could he say, Sister, but that he was distressed to have caused
me distress, that it was the furthest thing from his mind? So what choice
did I have but to shake the man's hand? He is a fine man, and I would say
we had a meeting of the minds." Theodore's vanity had a dollop of humility. Then he turned to me and said, "You need to go up there again, John."

"Where?" I said, although I knew. "What can I find out that they
can't?"

"Somebody knows what this fellow Pratt knew. His wife, perhaps.
You can find out things they can't. I have every confidence in you."

More than I had.

+>———=<+

I wandered by without expectations. But in Washington, in this speedy
new world of ours, even Sunday was becoming a workday, whether you
were in the office or out.

John Wilkie was in. His coat was off, shirtsleeves rolled up, cravat
pulled loose, and he was puffing away on his pipe. Behind him, the
windows overlooked a green courtyard and the east end of the White
House. Excavations for the new wing resembled an archeological site—

was it an agora or a gladiator's arena rising out of the marsh? Wilkie was reading a document and smiling to himself. I cleared my throat.

"Morning, Hay," he said. "Or is it afternoon?"

"No such luck," I replied.

"What can I do for you?"

"Ink."

"Ah, yeah." He pulled a paper from the top of a stack. "The only store in Washington that sells that particular ink is Brentano's, down the avenue, almost to Tenth. They keep a list of regular buyers, the ones who carry an account. Would you care to see it?"

With a glimmer in his eye, like a pope's to a crippled child, Wilkie handed me the typewritten page. On Brentano's flowery stationery, the list was more than a dozen names long, in alphabetical order. The first one sickened me.

Adee, Alvey.

I forced myself to keep reading.

Brautigan, Daniel
Brooks, Isaiah
Court, Mrs. Franklin
Galston, Mrs. James
Ingle, Dr. Jonathan
King, Llewellyn
McCaughey, John
Miles, Mrs. Nelson

This time I winced.

"Which one?" Wilkie said.

"Mrs. Nelson Miles," I replied. "She happens to be Elizabeth Cameron's beloved older sister."

"Beloved. Are you certain?"

"I was. It's her husband I wonder about."

+>—·—<+

I was praying that Adee would not be in. No such luck. He was at his rolltop desk, his black fountain pen racing over a legal-size paper. I watched him for a while. The pages piled up. His eyes were sharp and his brow remained unfurrowed. He enjoyed what he did, and I enjoyed watching him.

"Adee," I said, and again, louder.

He looked up, smiling, his eyebrows raised in an unspoken question: *What in the hell are* you *doing here?*

"I love your pen," I said.

"Thank you, Hay. I do as well, I must say. I bought it in a village near Lyon." Adee spent weeks every summer bicycling through southern France, alone or with friends. "It fits perfectly into my hand and writes so smoothly. A diamond point." He rolled the pen, as slender and smooth as an ivory hairpin, between his thumb and forefinger. "I could do an advertisement."

"And the ink is awfully nice."

"What a pleasing luster, don't you agree?"

"Where do you buy it, if I might ask?"

"I could get it by the wagonload in France, but, given my usual luck, it would explode in my luggage. So I get it here. Brentano's—you know it? They import it from Paris. You can tell the difference, don't you think?"

"Oh yes, oh yes," I babbled, relieved beyond description at his candor. Would he boast about the ink he used for a kidnapping note? "What are you writing?" I said, to change the subject.

"It is for you, actually. I am drafting responses to the rather impolite notes we've received overnight from Berlin and Moscow regarding the plight of your Roumanian Jews. I fear you are no longer the most popular man in Europe."

"I never was," I said. "Why aim low?"

—⊷—⊶—

The last person I wanted to see came to the door. By early afternoon on the Lord's day, Don Cameron was soused. I had no particular desire to punch him (back)—to my credit, I thought.

"You!" he said.

I had heard this before. "Yes, me," I replied, my wit in short supply. "Senator, is the lady of the house in, please?" I try to remember my manners, especially with drunks.

"Lad*ies*, you mean."

"As you say. Either or both. May I come in?"

He seemed to consider the question before stepping aside. Then he thought better of it. "What's this about?" he said.

"Ink," I replied.

If he thought I was mocking him, he was right. He let me in anyway.

Nellie Bly emerged from the back corridor, looking radiant, like she had just discovered publishable proof of a king's infidelity. For good reason. She had found a railroad clerk at the Sixth street depot who remembered selling a ticket to Pittsfield, Massachusetts, to a large, red-bearded man, around noon the previous day. That would have allowed Samson to arrive at David Pratt's bedside in time to kill him. When I told Nellie that Pratt had been murdered, she eagerly accepted the assignment I had in mind for her: to swoop in on Lizzie's sister, the peacock general's wife, and to wheedle her innermost thoughts on the subject of ink. And yes, Nellie should feel free to ask General Miles the same, if he happened to spend Sundays at home. I gave her the N street address, and she hustled off.

I sat for a minute or three before I went to the window and watched the snarls on the avenue below—the horse carts trotting along, the pedestrians crisscrossing, an electric streetcar sweeping down the center—the irresistible force.

I waited. Lizzie treated herself like a queen of the stage who considered it her due, if not her duty, to make men wait. I was pondering an escape—this was not a conversation I wanted—when she made her entrance. And what an entrance it was. She wore a taffeta gown that folded over itself, showing her underwhelming breasts to best advantage. The skirt rustled as she walked.

She assumed her customary recline on the divan and said, "What brings you here, Johnny?"

"Your sister," I said.

"Mary? What has she done now?"

"Now? What has she done before?"

"Oh, the usual things." Lizzie affected boredom. "This and that."

"What usual things?"

"Why are you interested?" Now *she* was interested.

I debated telling her the truth and calculated I had more to gain—her cooperation, maybe even an insight—than to lose. "Apparently she uses a particular kind of ink, manufactured in Europe, that was also used in the note I received on Friday morning about your, uh, where-abouts." I saw no reason to mention the Riggs account.

Lizzie seemed neither surprised nor distressed. "I can't imagine why you find this interesting," she said.

"I find everything interesting," I replied. This was true, though in-complete. "This in particular."

"I'm sure there are many people who use this ink."

"There are. And your sister is one of them. Can you think of any reason why she might . . . want to . . . to cause you harm?"

Lizzie physically recoiled on the divan. Was she repulsed at me or at Mary? I waited, this time with a purpose—which, after no more than a minute, was achieved.

"No," she said weakly, which I figured might well mean yes.

⊢━━⊣

"The august Mrs. Nelson A. Miles gave me ten minutes and then she ushered me out." Nellie's mouth was scrunched to the point of a daf-fodil's cup. "Politely, of course. You know how these society matrons are. All flutter and light on the surface, and mean as a madhouse guard underneath."

Oh, I knew. "So, what did she say?"

I had run into Nellie, almost literally, in the Willard's lobby, and we had found our quiet spot behind the farthest pillar.

"Not a lot. That she buys her ink from Brentano's, a standing order. That she loves her sister to pieces—her exact words. That she knew nothing of her sister's . . . sojourn on Mason's Island until it was over."

"Did you believe her?"

"That's a good question. I'd say, mostly. She may love her sister to pieces, but she may hate her, too. It happens. And another factor. Just for the shock value, I asked her point-blank if she would like to see her husband, the overdecorated general, as president. 'Who wouldn't?' she said. She's honest, I'll say that for her. That's when she remembered a previous appointment."

Nellie laughed. It wasn't a ladylike titter or a circus guffaw but an up-from-the-belly explosion of merriment, of a sort I hadn't felt in the fourteen months and twenty-nine days since Del died.

⊢⊷⊶⊣

The railcar rattled along through New Jersey, the rhythm of the wheels unrelenting. The finest accommodations that money could buy brought me mild discomfort. My nightshirt itched. I stretched out in my compartment, as it rocked from side to side, and tried to pretend I was sailing to Europe. Ha! This journey to Pittsfield had no prospect of pleasure.

Wait, who cared about pleasure anyway? (I did.)

> *I'm too damn old.*
> *To ever be told*
> *That life is a scold*
> *Except when it's not . . .*

Hmm. Not terrible. Rhyme had its charms. A second verse wouldn't hurt, but I felt too damn tired to think.

> *And I'm too damn tired*
> *Feeling mucked up and mired*

Energetic, at least.

> *In a rut and expired*
> *Ready to . . .*

Ready to . . . what? Oh, never mind.

I closed my eyes and saw Del. He was standing in our entrance, on Sixteenth street, leaning against the doorframe, smiling. Everyone loved him. I ached with loving him. I never told him that I—

My eyes snapped open.

Life was short—another cliché that was true. So what was worth doing in the meantime? In the scheme of things, no other question counted. Be a father, be a husband, be a friend, be a secretary of state. Yes, all of those mattered. And figure out who tried to kill the president—that, too, was time well spent. Though only if I succeeded.

CHAPTER TWENTY

MONDAY, SEPTEMBER 22, 1902

T he carrot-haired desk clerk at the Hotel Wendell greeted me like a
    fraternity brother, and I was duty-bound to do the same. Which I
did, sans the secret handshake.

Salutations completed, he handed me a message from Chief Nicholson: "Come see me."

The morning felt brisk. The maples in Park Square were turning a
startling shade of red. Leaves swirled in eddies. Men in derbies rushed
to work. An old lady was pushing a bag of groceries in a perambulator.

I arrived at the Pittsfield police department's low brick bunker on
School street and was escorted back to Chief Nicholson's office. He was
speaking in staccato on the telephone and waved me into a metal chair.
His face looked even longer and sadder than I recalled. Had I forgotten, or could two weeks have taken a toll? Probably both.

Chief Nicholson rested the receiver in its cradle and offered a perfunctory hello, as if we had shared a pitcher of lager the night before. "I
learned something about our Mr. Pratt," he said. "A conversation he had
the day before he died. With Davy, his son. Davy sneaked his father
out of the hospital—at his father's request, he insists—and drove him
back out to South street, where the collision took place. That's when he
started to bawl."

"The senior Pratt?"

"Yes. Bubbling that it was all his fault. Crying over Mr. Craig, according to Davy."

"So you're thinking again it was suicide?" I said.

"Mr. Hay, I don't know what to think. The lab boys are pretty sure it wasn't. Though not a hundred percent. They are never a hundred percent about anything—you know, in case they're wrong. I was hoping, in fact, that you could tell me."

"I appreciate your faith." I wished I shared it. "Where is Davy Pratt now, do you know?"

"That's why I wanted you. He's here."

"Here?"

"In a holding cell, in this building. As a material witness."

"Do you suspect him of his father's . . . murder?"

"I suspect everyone of everything," Chief Nicholson said.

He led me through two locked gates—he carried an oversize ring of keys—and we entered a concrete corridor painted gray. Cells lined both sides, all of them vacant except for the two at the end. A guard sat in the corridor, between them.

"This one," Chief Nicholson said. He unlocked the door to the right.

Inside the cell, in the far corner, a pudgy young man was cowering on a cot. His eyes were open but glassy; he seemed not to notice us.

"Mr. Pratt!" I said loudly. I introduced myself. "How old are you?"

"Seventeen. How old are *you*?"

"Sixty-three. Though I still think of myself as sixty-two." The joke fell flat. "How old was your father?"

"Sixty-two."

"What happened to him, Davy?"

"How the fuck should I know?" He sank back onto the cot, rattling the chains that anchored it to the wall. "I wasn't there."

"Who was, do you know?" No reply except a stare. "When was the last time you saw him?"

"What is this?" Davy sat upright. A threadbare blanket collected on his lap. His shirt, frayed at the collar, ballooned at his shoulders. "I've already answered everyone's questions."

"Not mine."

"Well, who the fuck are you?"

Not an unreasonable question. I told him my name again and said I was representing the president.

"Yeah? So?" he said.

Also reasonable. "Let me ask the questions," I replied.

"Well, fuck you."

"Hmm," I said. "We seem to be at loggerheads. Let me try again, then. When was the last time you saw your father? Alive, I mean."

"It's none of your fucking business."

"Actually, it is. If he was murdered, and the police think he was, I need to ask you this."

I studied Davy's face. It was round and unlined, like an egg; his profanities seemed absurdities from a choirboy's lips. By now he had stopped listening; his eyes drifted shut. I needed to get his attention. I asked Chief Nicholson to leave.

"Be careful," he said. He shut the cell door behind him and had a quiet word with the guard.

"Davy," I said.

No response.

I shouted his name again, and his eyes sprang open.

"You took your father to the place of the . . . collision . . . out South street."

Silence.

I wanted to grab his shoulders and push him against the wall. I sat. "Didn't you?" I said.

"Yes, yes, yes," Davy whined. "He made me."

"Why on earth . . . ?"

"He . . . just needed to see it."

"Did he tell you why?"

"Not exactly. But he kept asking me if it was his fault. 'Was it my fault? Was it my fault?' He wouldn't fucking shut up about it."

"In what way was it his fault?"

"How the fuck should I know? I wasn't there. All I know is he kept jabbering about seeing two men in the trolley with shotguns, pointed at him."

"*What?*"

"That's what he said."

"That's preposterous. He never told anyone that before. Nor did anyone in the trolley. Two men with shotguns?"

A satisfied smile spread across Davy's featureless face. "Just telling you what he said. Isn't that what you fucking want to know?"

"Is that when you wrote the suicide note?"

"I did not." Less outrage than I had expected.

"Who did, then?"

"What the fuck makes you think—"

"Somebody did. He didn't write it himself, because he didn't kill himself. You know that. Don't tell me you don't."

"That's a pile of crap."

"Did you tell anyone what your father said, that the collision was his fault?"

"Go to fucking hell."

"Nobody?"

"No. Only Frank."

"Forney?"

"Yeah, Frank."

Samson, again. Frank Forney was everywhere. In Governor Crane's suite at the Willard. On Mason's Island, kidnapping Lizzie and shooting at *me*. In Pittsfield, in David Pratt's room at the House of Mercy. I had seen him there. Did somebody see him there again on Friday night?

I can't explain where my next question came from, but I nearly shouted it: "What did Frank Forney have on your father?"

Davy moaned and turned pale.

Suddenly, things made sense. Why on earth would a man of wide respect cause a collision that might have killed the president, the governor—himself? Was five thousand dollars enough? Ten thousand? Money made no sense to me as a motive. *This* was the reason: He had to. He had no choice. Because Frank Forney had something on him; he knew something that David Pratt Sr. didn't want known.

"What did he . . ." I started to repeat myself, before I noticed that Davy's chin had fallen to his chest. His eyes were shut and his torso tipped back down on the cot.

I had lost him, before I could ask whether Frank Forney was left-handed.

At the livery stable behind the Hotel Wendell, I found a buggy that would take me to Dalton. The driver was a bulky young Irishman with a crooked nose. I recognized the facial topography.

"A prizefighter?" I said.

"Was." A proud and wicked smile, a front tooth missing.

On the way out of Pittsfield, we traded tales from the ring. His were more poetic than mine. His snout took its current complicated shape when a muscled African with a shaved head slammed uppercuts into his face while three thousand people watched in silence.

The houses and storefronts of Tyler street gave way to the meadows and orchards and farmland along Dalton road. *Clop, clop, clop*—the only sound, other than our voices. I learned a little about Dublin and too much about Boston and less than I wanted to know about Dalton. Yes, he had known David Pratt. Not a bad fellow. As a horseman, among the best in the Berkshires. A skilled driver, best he knew. One of the governor's favorites, which counted for something. The governor didn't suffer fools, gladly or otherwise.

"You like that about him," I said.

"I do, sir. None of the typical . . ." The driver glanced back at my silk hat—and forgave me for it. "Bullshit. You know these petunias in Boston—in Washington, too."

"I do indeed," I said.

The buggy sliced through dark woodlands and up a slight incline into the town of Dalton. Crane's mills lined both sides of the road. The village had its attractions, if you liked mills—paper mills, sawmills, woolen mills, the gristmill, all powered by the east branch of the Housatonic River. Old stone houses, too—from the century past, but with evidences of the new one as well. When Theodore had arrived in Dalton, the night before the collision, festoons of lights had greeted him—strings of electricity, Chinese lanterns, Roman candles. He had planted an elm on the governor's lawn and spent the night in his home.

David Pratt had lived across the tracks, in a two-story frame house attached to his livery stable. It had rough-hewn gray shingles and a rickety porch in need of paint. The door was ajar. When I pushed it open, it creaked. The foyer was empty but for an elderly armoire and two umbrellas propped next to the door. I heard children squabbling in the backyard. An argument was under way upstairs between a man's rough voice—I knew that voice!—and a woman's sobs. At the thud of flesh against flesh, I took the steps two at a time. There was no railing.

The combatants were in the master bedroom, such as it was. The wallpaper was peeling and the bed was unmade. The gray-haired woman—Mrs. Pratt, I assumed—sat hunched on the bed, her forehead resting on her forearms, weeping quietly now. Standing over her, quivering with rage, spittle at his lips, his right arm raised, ready to strike, was a big, red-bearded man. Frank Forney himself. Samson.

I threw myself at his head, and his arm changed trajectory. His fist caught me under my chin and rammed into my throat. I went down, onto my back, striking the bedpost, gasping for breath. I saw his heel driving toward me and I rolled to my right and felt the breeze of his leg whoosh by. He delivered a gratuitous kick to the groin and hissed, "I told you to stay out of this, Hay!"

I scrunched up in pain. But something had registered: *that* was the voice, the one that had threatened me in Park Square.

Samson rushed from the bedroom and down the stairs. The front door banged.

The silence was stunning. Mrs. Pratt's crying had ceased. My back was wedged into the bed at an awkward angle. My groin was on fire, although my nausea was beginning to ebb.

I must have passed out, at least briefly, and blessedly, because the next thing I remember was opening my eyes and finding myself on a bed. Mrs. Pratt was staring down at my face. Her cheeks looked parched, a schoolmarm's pucker; the bags under her eyes were black.

"I'm fine," I said, the sort of overstatement I would make after a punishing round in the ring. I ached everywhere, especially below the belt. I glanced down to make sure I still had a belt. I did. Trousers, too, although my cravat and my collar were awry. "Are you all right?"

The slightest nod.

"I need to talk to you," I said. "You are Mrs. Pratt, are you not?"

Her worry had changed to trepidation. "What do you want with us?" she said. "Haven't we suffered enough?"

"I have no doubt of that," I said. When I tried to sit up, every movement hurt, but I did it anyway. "But I want to understand what happened to your husband—and what just happened here. Don't you want that, too?"

"Who *are* you?" she said.

I explained as best I could—representing the president, my usual gibberish—but she didn't seem convinced. I couldn't blame her.

"It . . . wasn't . . . his . . . fault," she said. Her husband's words, negated. No coincidence, surely. She had heard his complaints, his fears. His confession?

"*What* wasn't his fault?" I said.

"The collision—it wasn't his fault. You can't blame *him*!"

"Then, who should we blame?" I said.

She moaned; her gray eyes glanced at the doorway.

"What did *he* want?" I said.

No reply.

"Did he strike you?" I said.

Her head shook like an aspen in a gale.

"How many times?" I pressed.

Her lips tightened.

"Why?" I implored. "I know it wasn't your husband's fault." A defensible lie, under the circumstances. "What did Mr. Forney have on him?"

Mrs. Pratt burst into tears. She swiveled her head side to side, unable even to raise her hands to her face. I let her cry, as if I had any choice. It probably lasted no more than a minute, although it seemed like ten.

A gentler approach. "Please, Mrs. Pratt, who *is* Frank Forney?"

She tried to gather herself. "Nothing but trouble," she whimpered. "I never wanted him in this house."

"Then why is he here?"

"My husband insisted. Knew his father, he did—knew him well. Frank Senior was a blacksmith here in Dalton, down from Québec." She pronounced it in the French manner. "We took on his son as a favor. So first he gets in trouble as . . . worse than an anarchist. Canada this, Canada that—his homeland, so he says, though I haven't seen him moving back there. Then look at what . . . he . . ." A sob escaped. "Does . . . to . . . us."

"What did he do to you?" I said. No point in subtlety. "Tell me, what hold did he have over your husband?"

Her eyes closed, as if she were looking at something she wouldn't let me see. I willed myself to patience. When her eyes reopened, they were showing signs of life. She had decided something.

"Have you seen our grandson?" Mrs. Pratt said. "Arthur's younger boy, Francis. *Francis!* He has red hair, too."

+>==+

Back in Pittsfield, I had one more stop to make. The prosperous neighborhood near the House of Mercy was a mix of mill-style houses and gabled Victorians. The livery driver stopped the rig at 65 Burbank. I gawked at the turrets, the stone balustrades, the Gothic windows.

"Should I wait?" the livery driver said.

"You think it's safe?" I said.

"I can take care of myself, sir."

"For me, I mean."

The Crusader-arched door opened before I knocked.

"Mr. Hay," said a young woman with a light-brown complexion and a saucy manner. "Mrs. Turtle is waiting."

She ushered me through the stone foyer and along a marble corridor into a room as spacious and cold as a Bavarian castle. A fire was burning in a man-size hearth, dwarfing the silhouette of Katherine Turtle. She was a small, delicate woman with a defiant posture and huge brown eyes. Her plain black dress reached to the floor and did nothing to conceal the blond ringlets or the rosiness in her cheeks. In spite of her husband's death, I wondered, or because of it? She reached forward in long black gloves and shook my hand. Her grip was strong.

Mrs. Turtle insisted on serving me tea, which I was none too proud to accept. I was famished. The scones were crumbly and sweet.

I said, "Chief Nicholson told you I was coming, I take it."

"No. It was a Mr. Cort . . . Corta . . . an odd name."

"Cortelyou?"

"That's the one. Got a wire yesterday saying you were coming to-day."

Theodore must have told him.

"I came to pay my respects." I gathered up my courage. "I was there."

It took her a moment to realize what I meant. Her eyes bulged and went blank; tears welled. She felt her way toward the nearest seat, a high-backed wing chair that enveloped her. "Tell me," she whispered.

"There's not much to tell," I said. "I was across the room and he opened the door, thinking it was room service, and he seemed to know the—" I stopped. "What do you want to know?"

"I don't know. What happened. What he said."

"The last thing he said was 'You?' Somebody from Washington, I would guess." I said nothing about the woman's voice in the bedroom. "Any idea who your husband knew there?"

Mrs. Turtle shrugged. "He knew hundreds of people—thousands. How could I possibly keep track?"

"In Washington?"

"Everywhere."

I asked why he had gone.

"On business," she said. "I don't know much more."

"He said nothing about the president's collision?"

"Oh, about that, he said a lot. He said he knew who was at fault and that he knew the right people to tell. His information was going to blow the case wide open."

"What did he know?"

"I don't know. He didn't share those things with me."

"He said nothing else about it? Please. This is important."

"I already told everything I know to Chief Nicholson, and it wasn't very much. He was going to meet with some people and, well . . . just what I said. Somebody would be taking the blame. A woman."

"What?"

"Oh yes, I forgot. A woman was involved. Somebody famous, was my impression."

I felt sick.

"He said it would tear Washington apart," Mrs. Turtle said. "He took a particular pleasure in that."

Chief Nicholson looked as if his favorite aunt had died. Come to think of it, he usually did. The bearer of bad news—that described his job, and he was a natural.

"Forney's heading north, toward Canada," Chief Nicholson said. "I got word not ten minutes ago from the chief in Bennington—that's in southern Vermont. One of his men saw his carriage; it's from Pratt's livery stable. They'll catch up with him soon enough."

"That's the man who attacked me in Park Square, I'm almost positive. I recognized his voice right away."

"That's not enough to hold him," Chief Nicholson said.

"Well, he didn't hurt me, either. How about for first-degree murder, in the death of one David Pratt?"

"That would be dandy. We'll have to see if there's enough evidence."

"Or for the kidnapping of Elizabeth Cameron?"

"Elizabeth who?"

+==+

The Connecticut countryside was out there somewhere, in the dark. I watched my reflection in the window. I swore I didn't look much different than I did decades ago. Didn't the beard cover up the changes? Yes, this was my strategy for growing old with a modicum of grace: self-delusion. That, and disbelief.

A scotch in hand, I considered yet again the mystery of Elizabeth Sherman Cameron. A famous woman. What kind of woman was she? What *kinds* of woman, because one thing she was was complicated. And exactly how evil was she? Yet tantalizing, to be sure. A siren, in the mythological sense. Damn hard to resist, especially since—

No, I wouldn't think about Del. I needed to think about Lizzie. Was she seriously willing to assassinate a president? I'm not entirely sure I would put it past her. She was that headstrong. But was she capable of actually arranging it? About that, I had my doubts. Yes, she could charm almost anyone—any man, anyway—to do almost anything she asked. And she was bright as hell, though probably too bright for her own good—or for anyone else's. Worse, she was disorganized and impulsive and didn't work well with others. Or play well, for that matter. Certainly not with me.

But if Lizzie was involved, why had she been kidnapped? *Had* she been kidnapped? She had gone willingly, it seems, until . . . until the red-bearded Samson appeared. That was when she got frightened. Or so she says.

Only now did I notice the rain pelting the club car's window. My scotch had been reduced to melted ice. I ordered another and sipped it with care. I was indifferent to the taste; it was the heat I sought. Raindrops splashed off the window ledge, into the night. I thought again about Del. About Del, about Lizzie. About Del, about—

I sat up with a jolt. Del. Lizzie. Del *and* Lizzie. The timing was indisputable—irrefutable. It had been staring me in the face from the first. I had been loving her, or thinking I did, for a year now. Del had died just a few months earlier.

Del's death was the itch. Lizzie was the scratch. It was so *obvious*. Why hadn't I seen this before? Maybe I had, at the periphery of my understanding, just past recognition. Maybe I hadn't wanted to know.

Now I did. I took a full, deep breath and exhaled slowly through my nose. I felt as if a hundred-pound weight had fallen from my neck. Naming the problem—understanding it—removed the urgency. Shouldn't it? I could hope so, anyway. Maybe I *could* break loose.

I drained the second scotch, decided against a third, and eased *The Hound of the Baskervilles* from my valise. I tried to read about Stapleton wandering the moor, carrying his butterfly net, shocked at the corpse Sherlock had found there. I kept seeing Del splayed across the ground, his limbs at unnatural angles.

I can't remember what happened next, but I must have fallen asleep in my seat, because my eyes snapped open and my head was on my chest. Drool hung from my lips. The screeching of the brakes had awakened me; the railroad car halted in fits and starts. I looked around. I was alone. I was frightened. Of what? A primal, childhood fright, behind the navel, above the bowels. I shook my head fiercely and returned to myself.

Welcome to New York. I passed through Manhattan—the night was a blur—and ferried across the Hudson. Even near midnight, the wide walkway was noisy and smelled of pork. Did Jersey City never sleep? I did. I was sleepwalking, placing one foot in front of the other, heading for the train home. *Home!* Clara, under the sheets! Our sheets.

I emerged into the half-moon's light. Thirty or forty feet ahead of me, the silhouette of a man looked familiar. A big man—broad back, heavy shoulders, straggly mane.

I stopped in my tracks. I knew all too well who it was. Literally the last man I expected—or wanted—to see.

It was Frank Forney. Samson.

CHAPTER TWENTY-ONE

I couldn't sleep. The bed in the Pullman was small and lumpy, and the railroad bumped and swayed, but that wasn't why. What was *he* doing here? He was heading for Canada, wasn't he? What was he doing on his way to Washington? More to the point, who was he going to kill next?

I had an awful feeling I knew the answer to that last question: the president.

This provoked the next question: How could I stop him? He was bigger than I, and surely he was armed; my derringer wouldn't even up the odds. He was somewhere on this train. There was nothing I could do about it now except catch some shut-eye.

Ha!

The night was long, it was long, never ending.

A cadence like the wheels of the train.

Once it started, the dawn never came.

Not bad.

Suppose it never came, never came, never came, never came.
Suppose the world was round.

Stuck. But wait. End it there! The verse, if not the poem. Why not? Forget the rhyme. To hell with the rhyme. Let the cadence, the sounds—and hey, the ambiguities of meaning, in all their glory—prevail.

I stopped writing and fell asleep instead. Then I woke up abruptly, in thrall to a dream of my legs pumping uncontrollably, like a dog's when you scratch the right spot. I blinked my way back to reality, only this time I was the predator instead of the prey. The stalker, not the stalked. The stalked was on the train someplace—that much I knew. I made myself invisible, which meant staying in my compartment, venturing out only for nature's call.

Eventually, she called, and I had to reply.

That was how I came to glimpse the back of Frank Forney's head, rising above the seatback halfway down on the left, in the next car, a second-class car. I knew the head was his; it was *large*. And at my mercy—the prey unaware of the predator. I could steal up behind him (as he had done to Pratt?) and . . . what? I felt in my waistcoat pocket for the comfort of my derringer. Could I use it with other passengers in the car? Knowing how loud it would be? Not a chance. Anyway, what was I thinking about—vigilantism?

The train rocked while I did my business in the lavatory with particular care. As I turned back toward my compartment, I glanced over my shoulder. The conductor was striding toward me when Forney's huge hand stuck into the aisle, crossing his body, a ticket between his thick fingers and a thumb. The conductor took the ticket, examined it, and returned it into Forney's hand.

His left hand.

I hurried back to my compartment and sat at the edge of my bunk.

A left-hander had killed David Pratt from behind. It was Forney. This wasn't proof, but I knew beyond a doubt that it was true. A left-handed gunman had attacked me, as well, albeit with a gun instead of a knife, and he hadn't killed me, as he had killed Pratt. Had chosen not to kill me. I was alive because of his . . . beneficence? Unlikely. Probably he was following instructions.

That made sense. All right, then, whose instructions? Every conspiracy has a brain, and it wasn't Samson's. The only way to find out was to confront him. Better yet, to follow him and keep him in my sights.

Should I sleep? Could I? Might he leave the train in Philadelphia or Wilmington or Baltimore? No. I was sure of that. His destination was the same as mine: Washington. Lafayette Square. In his case, the president's house. A stone's throw from mine.

My heart was beating so hard I heard the thumping in my chest. I tried to think of anything else, which ensured that I wouldn't. My back ached—nerves, for certain—no matter which way I twisted. What passed for a bed was like the battlefield at Bull Run or a gingko's gnarled roots, something I had seen but never fought or slept on.

I lay in the dark, trembling, and I knew why: a killer was in the next car. A real-to-life hound, a fiery beast, a Satan of nature.

Why would he want to kill David Pratt anyway? That was easy: to cover up a conspiracy to assassinate the president by murdering the man who tried. And he might have hated David Pratt, as David Pratt must have hated him, for cuckolding his son-in-law and fathering his grandson. Maybe other reasons, too. The indignities between master and servant no outsider could guess. But why would Samson want to hurt or frighten little ol' me? Also easy: to halt my investigation. I was flattered, I must say. As a detective, it meant I was effective enough to threaten but not enough to kill. At least so far, I am pleased to report.

The wheels rumbled beneath my bed. I tried to pretend they were Lindgren's hands. No luck. Or Clara's. That worked better. I felt warm inside. I dozed but woke up in a sweat. The wheels screeched like a toddler with a flute.

"Baltimore!" the conductor cried.

As I tried to slip back into sleep, I wondered if I would be waking from a dream into a new nightmare.

+>—:—<+

The train shuddered to a stop and I awoke in a fog. My darkened dream vanished, like the floating dust.

"Sixth street station!" the conductor called.

I was home. But not alone.

It was the middle of the night and felt like it. I was muddled and disengaged, as if reality were a foreign country and I was stuck at the border, playing rummy, looking in. Sleeping in my clothes was grittier than I liked. Trying to shake myself awake didn't work. Caffeine might help, or a punch in the face, but neither was immediately available. I was on my own. That would have to suffice.

I sprang from the . . . I hesitate to call it a bed . . . from the cot. My legs functioned as well as before. Still reasonably fast, adjusted for age. Samson's were sure to be faster.

I carried the valise on my shoulder, paused at the end of the corridor, and peered into the next car. No sight of him. I panicked. Had I lost him already, by my reluctance to rise? Sherlock would have wreathed himself in tobacco and stayed awake. Maybe I was too damn lazy to be a detective. I needed my sleep.

My pocket watch showed thirteen minutes before five. I eased down the steps and landed lightly on the platform—and froze. Samson was standing a dozen feet ahead, his back to me, hunched over. I held back, eyes alert, muscles poised, pursuing my prey. After a moment, he reached down for his cardboard-sided suitcase and exhaled a plume of smoke from a cigar. He glanced furtively to each side, as if looking for someone, and walked on.

Rain clattered like artillery shells on the corrugated aluminum roof. I kept two or three people between us. A burly man squiring an unruly boy lunged in front of me just as Samson was hurrying away. He had seen someone.

I scampered around the family that might or might not see better days and weaved between the groggy passengers. I knocked into a white-haired lady with my valise—she kept hold of her daisy-bedecked hat—and mumbled an apology. I hurried on, searching for Samson.

I left the din outside. The waiting room was gloomy and shockingly quiet, an omen of a world that no longer includes you. My footsteps echoed on the marble. The pews were empty at this hour; it must be too early to leave and too late to come home. The passengers from my train seemed to have gone up in smoke. Except for Samson. Through the far door I caught sight of him rushing out—into the ladies' waiting room next door. He was not alone. A tall, cloaked figure scuttled along at his side.

As I bolted across the main waiting room and into the ladies' haven, my valise bouncing into my ribs, I caught sight of the pair rushing through the exit door, onto Sixth street. I tore after them. I took pains to sidestep the golden star that marked Garfield's murder, but I glanced down as I ran by it. Lights bounced from the ceiling, and I noticed a heel print at the center of the star. It looked fresh in the surrounding dust. Its shape was unmistakable: a hexagon.

My eyes went wide. I had seen this shape before—Nellie Bly had pointed it out—in the heel print outside of William Turtle's door. The figure in the cloak was a woman. Maybe the woman the Willard desk clerk had seen rush by amid the chaos after Turtle was shot. And maybe the woman I had heard back in Turtle's bedroom.

"You!" Turtle had exclaimed.

How I hoped against hope it wasn't Lizzie. But I had a stomach-heavy feeling that it was.

I dashed through the Sixth street door and looked frantically in every direction, but they were nowhere in sight. The rain had eased to a drizzle but, judging by the smell, was soon to revive. It was deathly dark; either the gas lamps on the Mall had been extinguished at midnight or the city's budget had run dry. Other than a carriage nearing the corner of B street, all was still.

I stepped into the roadway. Which way should I search? Suddenly, I heard a rumble behind me, like a beast in a Jules Verne nightmare. I turned. The headlamps were blinding; the machine hurtled straight at me. I leapt out of the way just in time.

I swiveled. Filling the back window were two familiar silhouettes.

My breath heaved, but I gave chase. The effort was absurd. The horseless carriage reached B street long before my legs could. I watched helplessly as it sputtered for another short block, to Pennsylvania avenue. It turned left.

I stood in the middle of Sixth street and howled. Nobody heard me, and it served no useful purpose. I took two deep breaths and then got practical and ran into the middle of the avenue. The scene was lovely, had I time to admire it. The Capitol, its dome illuminated, was glowing through the mist.

I waved my arms at the first vehicle I saw. The one-horse dray veered to miss me, not slowing in the slightest. The driver shouted something I was pleased not to hear. The headlamps of the next carriage flickered a block to the east. I positioned myself in its path, albeit close to the curb. The driver was wielding a whip on a pair of white horses. Exactly what I needed. Maybe they could catch an automobile.

Theodore would have been proud of how I stood my ground, even as the carriage—a fine barouche, from the front view—kept coming at me. I stared up at the driver, who sat on the box in a knitted shawl and silk hat. Here, a street lantern was lit, and I felt sure he could see me. Sure enough to wager my life? Nope. But I still had time to—

I was about to spring out of the way when the driver shouted, "Whoa, gents! Whoa!" With an impressive suddenness, the horses slowed and came to a halt a few feet in front of me.

"Police business!" I shouted as I stepped up to the driver's box. "I need the use of your carriage."

"Yer badge?" He was a young man with sculpted cheeks and a whimsical brogue. Thatches of hair, presumably red, curled from beneath a woolen cap.

"I don't have one, I'm afraid." I introduced myself and offered a business card, which sounded silly—worse, implausible—even to me.

"I seen yer pitcher in the paper," the driver said. "My rig is yer'n."

I heard *urine* before I realized his generosity. "Thank you, thank you," I said. I climbed up onto the driver's box—this was where Big Bill Craig had sat. "We need to overtake an automobile."

His smile had a surprising delicacy. "A piece o' fun, sir. Ronan," the driver said, extending his hand, which I would have preferred remained on the reins.

"John," I replied, with a quick, firm handshake. "Turn here."

The side of the Central Market smelled of last night's rotting produce and leftover meat, its vendor stalls boarded up until dawn. Pennsylvania avenue was eerily quiet. The shuttered shops, the greasy restaurants and liquor outlets, the boardinghouse and shabby hotels, the second-hand furniture store, the Christian mission—the capital's most famous boulevard had grown too desolate to hold its ambitions.

I heard a horn toot, two or three blocks ahead of us. An automobile, all but certain. Ronan shook his fist and applied the whip with joy in his eyes. Two horses can run no faster than one, of course, but they can run longer at maximum speed. They surged along the avenue, kicking tar from the roadway into the air, intimidating any carriages that might be counting on north–south traffic's having the right-of-way. Thank the Lord, nobody else was on the road. The erratic wind, laced with raindrops, pricked my face.

Lizzie Cameron (God forbid!) and Frank Forney—what an incongruous pair! The political duchess and the liveryman's servant; the doyenne of Washington and Samson of the Berkshires. What on earth was their connection? Had she known him before? Not if her description of events at the Georgetown wharf was accurate. (If.) But didn't conspirators need to know one another? How had they ever become acquainted? Somebody must have introduced them.

"Still see it?" I said.

No reply but the whip.

I looked as hard as I could, and I, too, saw it. Heard it, more like: a metallic sputtering that kept threatening to die. What sounded like squeals of delight was probably the pistons or whatever the hell those parts were called.

"Not too close," I said. "I don't want them to—"

"I've done this before."

"Oh?"

"Over a beer someday, John."

I threw my head back and laughed. I was in capable hands.

Past Eleventh street, the new post office clock tower stood like a sentinel against the black sky. Only the Willard showed any signs of life—the lights inside, the unending hubbub at the curb. The automobile was nowhere in sight, but Ronan seemed to know where he was heading. He nodded his head toward the Treasury Building, straight ahead, at night a somber, unscalable wall. Ronan pulled on the reins, applying the whip with precision, mindful of the chase yet also of the turns to come. I marveled at his skill and at his willingness to be cruel and wondered if excellence required both. At Treasury, we turned right and then slowed for a left, to follow the avenue. I knew where we were heading.

Lafayette Square.

Where all roads in the capital led. Where I lived. Worse, where the president lived. Why not kill him in his bed? Easier than on a trolley track in Pittsfield. If a single guard was at the door, how hard would it be for assassins to shoot their way past him?

"Hurry!" I shouted—unnecessarily.

The turn back onto the avenue brought the machine smack into view. It was halted a short block ahead of us, at the closest corner of Lafayette Square.

I whispered fiercely, "Stop!"

Ronan tugged on the reins and the horses obeyed. *If only people did that*, I thought. I clasped Ronan's shoulder in admiration and shook his hand in thanks.

"I'm not going anywhere," he said.

I thanked him again and left my valise on the seat.

Would I be more noticeable in a top hat or in no hat? I decided on none. I climbed down from the barouche and checked for the derringer in my waistcoat pocket.

Two dark figures had emerged from the automobile. One was wide; both were tall.

Wait. Why would potential assassins want to approach the temporary White House from the opposite side of Lafayette Square? To cloak their presence, perhaps, or to check for an agent in the park. By the time I reached the corner, their machine had driven away and the two silhouettes had sidled into our heart of darkness. The statue of the Marquis de Lafayette, shunted to the corner of the park, rose like a fiery angel. I walked past.

The bower of trees shaped Lafayette Park into a funnel, pulling me in. The park was empty except for the two figures, side by side, pacing purposefully ahead. I tried not to scrape my boots on the gravel, and I kept to the side of the path; if one of my prey turned around, a tree could hide me. At the center of the park, Andy Jackson reared up on his horse, and the silhouettes circled around to the right of it. They took the radiating path, toward the northwestern corner of the park. The temporary White House was in the middle of the block. My prey either would reach Jackson Place and turn south or, more likely, would circle around to the west.

I considered trying to intercept them and then saw the folly. It would be two against one, and my two-shot derringer against Samson's . . . armory. Better, I could head them off. I veered off the path and headed across the grass toward the president's town house. If a Secret Service man *was* lurking and didn't shoot me first, he might help.

Later, I would feel proud of my lack of hesitation. Maybe I *was* as brave as Theodore would want me to be. But no one else, good or evil, was skulking in the park. My boots dragged through the twisted wet vines, and I looked across Jackson Place. No bodyguard stood on Theodore's porch; I hoped one was inside. Also no sign of a scraggly-haired giant or a woman in a cloak. I heard only crickets.

As I crossed the outer-ring path, I headed toward the president's residence, to warn the agent inside. A bulky man stepped from behind an oak. He wore a rough tweed overcoat and a military-style cap. He carried a gun—quite a large one, pointed at me.

"Halt!" he said.

I did not consider doing otherwise.

"Where are you going?" he said. His nose looked like it had been broken multiple times.

"To warn the president," I replied.

"About what?"

"You Secret Service?"

"Who are you?"

I told him. The man scrutinized my face and decided to believe me, apparently because my claim was too outlandish to be a lie. "What do you want?" he said gruffly.

"Two people are coming for—*might* be coming for . . ." I pointed toward the corner of the park. "Now! I need to talk to—" I started to pass him, and he blocked my way.

"You can talk to me," he said.

"I just did."

"We are aware of this already."

"Oh?"

"From a barouche driver, a couple of minutes ago."

Hurrah for Ronan. "Have you seen them?" I said.

"Only you."

"Shouldn't we warn—" I tried again to edge past him.

"You just did. Thank you."

"But they're still—"

"Thank you."

I turned back the way I had come. The rain had stopped. Behind Andy Jackson, the sky glowed. I turned north at the outer-ring path. Still no sight or sound of Samson and his hexagonally heeled companion. I was a predator who had lost my prey.

What else could I do but go home?

The naphtha lamp at the corner was lit. I glanced at Henry's house. A light was on behind his library's high windows. The screens were down. Two silhouettes bobbed behind them—the silhouettes I had seen in the back window of an automobile and then striding across Lafayette Square.

I gulped.

A third silhouette entered the frame. To my horror, I recognized this one, too. The sweeping forehead and the cultured nose, the pointed beard. It was Henry. The silhouette with the straggly hair was reaching for his neck.

I rushed across H street and under the low stone archway, and I pounded on Henry's door. I pressed the handle. The latch gave way.

The entrance hall was dark. Fortunately, I knew where everything was, and so I avoided the armoire and the umbrella stand and ventured down the hallway. I took care not to brush Clover's photographs along the walls. The staircase was near the rear. I got ready to mount, and then I became aware of a presence on the bottom step. A lamp at the top put the face in shadows.

The figure turned at my approach. The hood of the cloak had slipped.

The face was not Lizzie's.

It had the coarse, peasant-like features of Margaret Hanna.

I had an instant to take this in before she punched me in the mouth and kneed me in the groin. I went down. The lower pain radiated, and I opened my eyes in time to see a six-sided heel throttling toward my forehead. I slipped my head aside, grabbed at her ankle, and whipsawed it. She shrieked and fell back onto the staircase. Her head landed with a thump. She looked like a rag doll sprawled on the stairs, breathing in fits and snorts. Then she was quiet.

I heard a shout upstairs. It sounded like Henry. I forced myself to my feet, stepped over Margaret, and reached the landing as the quarreling grew louder. I reached the second floor and rushed toward the front of the house.

"You damn well better!" That was Frank Forney's voice.

"I can't. Not to-night . . . I simply . . . No! *No!*"

The library, on my right, was the center of Henry's universe. It was a large, comfortable room overflowing with books and Chinese bronzes and Henry's baubles from exotic lands. Frank Forney had backed Henry against the fireplace and was waving a black Oriental vase, which he smashed against the onyx mantel. The crash was as loud as a gunshot. A thousand pieces sprayed across the floor. I jumped, and Henry let loose a sob. I held my derringer in my right palm and pointed it at Forney. Like a character in Owen Wister's next Western, I announced, "Drop it."

Forney, to my surprise, didn't. He examined me as if I were a low-hanging fruit and started toward me, a gun in his hand. He glanced back at Henry and said, "You're coming, too."

"No, he isn't," I said, waving my derringer.

"Oh, he is," Forney growled. "He owes me another grand and he's gonna pay it. When does Riggs open—at eight?"

"You've been paid what you were promised."

"Paid for what?" I said.

If a face could fall, Henry's did. His vast forehead looked sickly in the gaslight. His sharp, graying beard pointed like a dagger at his chest.

"What you paid," Forney said, "didn't include the extras. Your rotten Mrs. Cameron and my dear dead Mr. Pratt."

Henry had sunk into the maroon leather chair, collapsed in on himself.

"Paid for what?" I said again.

But I knew.

That was the moment Frank Forney made his escape. He pushed me aside, swatting my hand with his gun, and careered out the door before I could react. His footsteps fled along the hallway and down the stairs.

The only sound was Henry's weeping. Until the first gunshot out-side. And the second. I braced for more, but all was silent.

+≡≡+

"It isn't easy being an Adams," I tried to explain, to myself as well as to Theodore. It was a quarter past nine, in his rear sanctuary at the temporary White House. Theodore was on his third tumbler of coffee; I marveled at his bladder. "Henry didn't put it exactly like that, but that's what he meant. His grandfather and great-grandfather *made* history, and he was just watching it."

I was hoping to remove the dreamy look from Theodore's face. If he had his way, the Roosevelts, too, would spawn a dynasty. Wasn't he grooming his sons for greatness? Alice was grooming herself.

"How can you live life as an Adams," I went on, aware of my des-perate tone, "and not want to *do* something, accomplish something— preferably, for the ages? It's what every old man wants, but for an Adams it's magnified, multiplied. That's no small burden to carry."

"And so he relieves his mighty burden by killing me?"

I could not tell him of Henry's contempt for his character—which, in Henry's eye, mattered most in a president. Why should I confirm what Theodore already suspected? Instead I said, "Henry wanted to be a kingmaker, to *make* a president, unknown to anyone else but him-self." This was also the truth.

"*You?*" Theodore replied.

That hurt a little, but I had to admit (not out loud) that there was truth to that, too. Theodore thought I was timid, and in a way he was right. I could step into the boxing ring against anyone roughly my size and live to tell the tale. But I didn't relish the fighting like Theodore did. More and more, the job seemed to require it, if it was to be done well. The world was getting nastier, and Theodore was changing the nature of the presidency. No longer was it a backwater, subservient to Congress and Wall street. The president could speak to the people—*for* the people. Maybe I wasn't the best man to run things, despite Henry's faith that I was. He told me I had won all the great prizes but one. I said I didn't want that one—that I never had—but he replied matter-

of-factly that anyone would kill for the chance. And he had tried to—
for me.

"I should have figured it out," I said to Theodore. "He said something he had no way of knowing: that Mrs. Madden was with child.
How could he have known that, unless somebody from Pittsfield had
told him? And he knew I had been attacked in Pittsfield, but I hadn't
told him that, either."

"Telling you too much of what he knew," Theodore marveled. He
sat back, flexed his injured leg, and added with a tone of devotion, "The
perfect flaw for a man of the mind."

"He let me use his own silk cravat to tie his wrists behind his back,"
I said. The sort of detail Theodore would savor. "A somber yellow with
stripes of mauve. But he claims he didn't really mean it."

"Didn't mean it? Nonsense! You try to kill the president of the United
States, but you don't really mean it? It just happened on its own? He
did admit there was an attempt, did he not?"

"Oh yes, and with a measure of pride, I must say." Which I had found
chilling. "He even admitted to opening that mystery account at Riggs
while wearing a ridiculous disguise. Of course, he insisted on using his
own pen—so *like* Henry—filled with the finest ink."

"Which he did not buy at Brentano's."

"No need to, when there's Paris and New York. He also admitted to
putting my name on the application. His idea of a joke."

"The humor escapes me," Theodore said.

"And me. But not Henry."

"No, I don't suppose it would. I thought I understood the man." Theodore *was* perceptive about how other people ticked. "I met him when
I was a boy, along the Nile. I was with my family; he was on his honey-
moon with Clover. How many meals have I shared with him since? He
isn't exactly my cup of tea. A little . . . unmanly, shall we say, for my
taste. But I can't honestly say that I know him at all."

"Me neither," I replied.

I had known Henry for forty-one years, since his father served in
Congress. And we had been friends from the start. Sympatico, in our
interests and instincts. But had I ever known the man? Obviously not.

Yes, he was a pessimist—whatever is, is wrong—but that was part of his pose. And of his charm, truth be told. His value as entertainment. And yes, he was brilliant and witty and kindhearted and tender and amusing—all of those—not to mention an intellectual of courage, in his freethinking ways. But the Henry I knew was the one that Henry wanted me to know. I must have been unaware of the roiling of lava underneath. At any rate, of its depth.

None of this would I tell Theodore.

"And I can't imagine," Theodore was saying, "that he committed any of these crimes on his own. He isn't capable. He had other people do them."

In Theodore's mind, that was a worse crime than the crime itself. I could see his point.

"It was his idea, that's true," I said, "but I'm not sure how serious he was. You know how Henry likes to talk. Things must have gotten out of hand. He had no intention of going that far. I'm convinced of that." I guess I had to be. "*That* was Margaret Hanna's doing."

Theodore was glaring at me. "He *is* your friend, I can see, and I admire a man who stands behind his friends. Even a murderer. But I have my limits, and I trust that you do, too, John. Tell me, who is this Margaret Hanna? She is related, I assume, to our friend Marcus Aurelius."

"Marcus Alonzo. Actually, she isn't, but she is definitely an acolyte. She wants nothing more in the world than to see the good senator from Ohio in the White House. She and Henry have different . . . preferences about who the next president ought to be, but they joined in common purpose in wanting a successor to . . ." I was unable to keep up the lighthearted tone.

"They did not get their wish, and they will not." Theodore's voice had dropped an octave. "Not if I have anything to do about it, and I do. Was the good senator aware of these goings-on, do you suppose?"

"My best guess is no." Did I detect disappointment in Theodore's brow? "But it seems his henchman was, at least a little bit. Elmer Dover, I mean. He ran the Senate's Canada committee for Hanna, and Margaret handles the correspondence with Canada at State."

"Under your very eye," Theodore pointed out.

"Afraid so," I conceded. "It was Elmer Dover who took Lizzie to

Mason's Island. They also know each other from Lafayette Square. She still owns Hanna's house, which Dover frequents. It was through him that Margaret found Frank Forney—the Canada connection. A brilliant idea, to hire a brute from the opposite side. Hanna salivates at the prospect of annexing Canada; all he sees is dollar signs. Forney's parents are from Quebec, and he feels more Canadian than any actual Canadian. An angry man in search of a cause. He would mount the barricades to block annexation."

"Or kill someone."

"Yes, or kill someone."

"Kill *me*," Theodore said.

"No accounting for taste," I replied.

Theodore laughed. It was a raucous laugh, possibly fueled by fear.

"Another confession," I said. "Miss Hanna met Henry Adams at my dinner table. It seems they hit it off over the plum pudding."

"A spinster and a widower," Theodore observed. "Destiny."

"And on that glorious evening, or sometime later, they began to keep company. She towered over him, but never mind. And they hatched an idea. Actually, Henry hatched it, and she . . . nursed it to life."

This piqued Theodore's interest. "*She* made it happen?"

"Oh yes," I said. Henry had confessed everything, between sobs. "A woman of many talents, she is. Efficient and intelligent and fluent in languages—these things we already knew. Also a sharpshooter, a lady wrestler—"

"Like on stage at Kernan's."

"Tennis, jousting, archery, shot put—you name it, she's good at it. In most things, can't be beat. A prominent member of the Columbia Athletic Club, which—"

Theodore finished for me. "Puts on events at Mason's Island."

"Exactly. She won a riflery prize there on Labor Day. She also . . ." I was wary of revealing this to Roosevelt. "It wasn't a man who put a knife to my throat in Lafayette Square. It was Margaret Hanna." Even now I could feel the strong hand at my neck, the assailant who was taller than I, the muffled voice, the theatrical accent. "And she killed William Turtle. The suite at the Willard has two doors. She was with him back in the bedroom, slipped out into the hallway, shot him dead at

the front door, then made her escape. I think she also was listening in
on my 'phone conversations at State, including with the police chief in
Pittsfield. Once, I noticed a late click on the line. She probably knew
whatever I knew."

"All men are created equal," Theodore declared, looking unaccountably pleased. "Bunkum! Mr. Jefferson forgot the womenfolk."

Edith was lucky to have a husband so devoted. I silently promised
the same for Clara.

"*She* was the Hanna in Turtle's pocket diary," I said. "He was to meet
with Margaret, not Mark."

Suddenly, Theodore became stern. "I don't want any of them pros-
ecuted. None of them."

"What do you mean? They're guilty of—" Though I did feel a flood
of relief. "Can you do that?"

"Of course I can." No reason to doubt him. The District of Columbia was a federal enclave. "Are they in custody?"

"Yes, both of them." I could picture the holding cells, Margaret Hanna
to the left, Henry Adams to the right, a baton-wielding guard stalking
the corridor between them. Frank Forney was dead, by Ronan's hand.
Elmer Dover was nowhere to be found.

"Then I want them released," Theodore said. "The authorities in Massachusetts may do whatever they must, *if* they must, given that the
apparent perpetrators—the carriage driver and his supposed servant—
are both dead. But I will not press charges or allow any federal court to
bring this to trial. I will not be made a fool of in public. Or a victim."
I wondered if he saw any difference. "I *will* not. As far as we are con-
cerned, your investigation is finished. In fact, it never happened. Life
will go on as before. Is that understood?"

It was. Not *understood* as in *comprehended* but as in *this wasn't up to
me*. Because it wasn't.

"I forbid you, John, to say a word about this to anyone," Theodore said.

Lincoln had asked (not ordered) me to do the same, and I had ac-
ceded. I was twenty-three and didn't know my own mind. That had
changed, but again I saw no choice.

"Even to Clara?" I said.

"You are free to tell Mrs. Hay anything and everything. But nobody else." Behind the pince-nez, his eyes glittered like diamonds, bright and hard. "Nobody."

I knew who he meant in particular. "You needn't worry," I replied. "I am done with her." My infatuation was about Del, not about Lizzie. I knew that now, and I was confident I could put it—and her—aside.

I had another confession that I would reserve for Clara, when I got home to sleep (and not alone, I hoped). I had not actually solved this mystery, these murders. They had solved themselves—quite literally, in front of my face. Frank Forney had popped up on the train. Silhouettes had appeared in Henry's window. Margaret Hanna was unveiled on Henry's staircase. Each time, I was in the right place to notice. There is some skill in that, I suppose. But how much had I truly learned in forty years?

Well, occasionally you just get lucky. Life works that way sometimes. Good luck has always pursued me like a shadow. I've lived a life beyond the dreams I had as a boy, and in almost precisely the shape I had dreamed of, even if it came late in my years. Here's another confession: I've been extraordinarily happy all of my life, and I've even had the luck to know it. Everything changed, of course, when Del died. I had never set things right with him, and now I never will. I had never told him I loved him. Clara kept urging me to, and I resisted, Lord knows why. Now I tell him so all the time, and can only hope that he's listening.

I know we're too old ever to recover, and I wonder if I'll ever be happy again. Though maybe, with Clara at my side, and if I do a good deed now and again, there's a chance.

AFTERWORD

This novel is based (as the movies say) on a true story. On September 3, 1902, after Theodore Roosevelt had been president for almost a year, he was finishing a thirteen-day tour of New England in advance of the midterm elections. As he rode from Pittsfield, at the western edge of Massachusetts, to neighboring Lenox, an electric streetcar hurtled down Howard's Hill and broadsided his open-air, horse-drawn carriage. His bodyguard was killed instantly. Roosevelt, thrown thirty or forty feet, was hurt more seriously than was clear at the time. His leg injuries may have contributed to his death seventeen years later, at age sixty, from a pulmonary blood clot.

Everything in the prologue, including the dialogue, is taken from contemporaneous accounts. The outlines of the ensuing events are also accurate. Berkshire County held an inquest into the bodyguard's death. The motorman pleaded guilty to a charge of manslaughter (charges against the conductor were dropped) and was sentenced to sixty days in jail; he was allowed to spend nights at home. His lawyer, William Turtle, a state legislator, was also the streetcar company's lawyer.

I have changed a single, central fact. The collision was assumed to be an accident. In my story, it was an attempted assassination.

Some of the coolest details in my tale are true. Emma Goldman was arrested in Omaha as an alleged threat to President Roosevelt eleven days before my story starts. John Hay once interviewed President McKinley's assassin, Charles Guiteau, for a job. While secretary of state, Hay

dispatched a letter urging European governments to help the Roma-
nian (then *Roumanian*) Jews. At four o'clock on weekday afternoons,
he took a stroll with Henry Adams, followed by tea. Adams once described Roosevelt as "a stupid, blundering, bolting bull calf"—though
to Lizzie Cameron, not to Hay. Both men, at one time or another, harbored romantic feelings, apparently unconsummated, for Mrs. Cameron. Her beloved sister was married to the army's commanding general,
Nelson Miles, the target of Roosevelt's tongue-lashing. David Pratt, the
carriage driver, worried aloud (to New York policemen, not to his son)
that the Pittsfield collision had been his fault. His unlikely story of
two men on the trolley aiming shotguns was recounted by a grandson seventy-one years later. Frank Forney, whose parents came from
Quebec, was Pratt's live-in servant. Massachusetts governor Crane was
president of the Agricultural National Bank of Pittsfield. All true.

I've tried to bring the time and places of my story to life. In 1902,
the world was roiling with technological advances, struggling between
capital and labor, and adjusting to a confident, even cocksure, America. The surge of U.S. imperialism revived interest, lingering since the
1870s, in annexing Canada. Trusts and tariffs were the issues of the
day. In Washington, the doctors defeated the lawyers, eight to two, in a
Labor Day baseball game. B street, which is now Constitution Avenue,
was no longer a smelly canal. Mason's Island, as locals called Analostan
Island until it was renamed for Theodore Roosevelt in 1933, had indeed
been home to a mansion, outbuildings, orchards, and athletic fields.

I've left anachronisms of style in place—the lower case for *street* and
avenue, a hyphen in *to-day* and *to-morrow*. The floor plan of the Willard Hotel is as it used to be, featuring, beyond the reception desk, a
staircase that no longer exists.

Except for the livery drivers, hotel clerks, elevator operators, and the
trolley yard worker in Pittsfield, all of the characters in this novel are
real. I have generally kept to what is known about the historically
prominent ones, although John Hay has seen a few changes. The facts
of his life are accurate, but I have no evidence that he was a boxer or a
detective, and he was in poorer health than I have him here. (He would
die of a heart attack in 1905, while still secretary of state.) When the

collision occurred in Pittsfield, Hay was at his summer home in New Hampshire, not in Washington.

I have taken a few other liberties to serve my story. President Roosevelt was in Oyster Bay or touring the South and the Midwest during most of the time my story has him in Washington. (He underwent emergency surgery on his injured leg, in Indianapolis, on September 23, and was confined for three weeks to a wheelchair.) General Miles, meantime, was in the Philippines. I have no reason to think that Nellie Bly visited Washington in the fall of 1902 (nor any reason to think that she didn't). William Turtle and David Pratt weren't murdered; they lived another twenty and fifteen years, respectively. I can't vouch for my description of Berkshire County's political machine. I made up Hay's memories of his late son, Del, but used his own letters in describing his grief and lifelong luck.

Minor changes, too. Alvey Adee's crack about "Grand Duke Bore-us" came in an August 26 letter to Hay, not in a September 4 telegram, and the luncheon for the tsar's cousin was held in the front hall at Sagamore Hill, not in the dining room. The scandal of the Austrian prince's arrest in London occurred in July, not in September. Saint John's Church was closed for repairs, and between pastors, in September 1902; the sermon that angered Roosevelt was actually delivered in front of him that day by his minister in Oyster Bay. I doubt that the door knocker at Mark Hanna's home was shaped like a lion's rump.

I've also imagined most of the scenes and almost all of the dialogue. But I've tried to portray the world of TR's presidency with factual and emotional accuracy, as it was changing into the world we can still recognize—or at least remember—today.

ACKNOWLEDGMENTS

My favorite quote about writing comes from Sinclair Lewis, who remembered being taught, by Mary Heaton Vorse, "The art of writing is the art of applying the seat of the pants to the seat of the chair." I spend long hours hunkered over my keyboard, flicking away. But I keep asking people for help and, to my surprise, they keep helping me.

Librarians and curators are simply the best. Especially helpful were Nancy Kervin at the U.S. Senate Library, Jerry McCoy at the Washingtoniana collection at the DC Library, and Don Warfield and his colleagues at the local history section of the Berkshire Athenaeum in Pittsfield, Massachusetts. Deborah Capeless, Berkshire County's clerk of courts, kindly showed me the room where the 1902 inquest took place. Susan Sarna, the curator at Sagamore Hill, couldn't have been more obliging in answering my queries and suggesting books to read. The Library of Congress, with its incredible holdings and resourceful librarians, is one of the rare government agencies that truly work.

Nonlibrarians were nicer still. Jim Hewes, the longtime bartender at the Willard's Round Robin Bar, was a font of knowledge about the hotel's glorious history. Mark Bergin, a retired policeman in Alexandria, Virginia, advised me on police procedures and on the sound and smell of gunfire. Paul Rosenberg suggested which guns to use. Other friends who helped include Bill O'Brian, Jim Brisbois, Harry Katz, Dan Shapiro, Mark Iwry, Tim Wendel, Glenn Davidson, and Dennis Quinn. I'm beholden to books about TR by Edmund Morris, Doris

Kearns Goodwin, David McCullough, Edward J. Renehan Jr., Louis Auchincloss, Jerome Charyn, Owen Wister, and Roosevelt himself for illuminating a complicated man. I found John Taliaferro's *All the Great Prizes: The Life of John Hay, from Lincoln to Roosevelt* invaluable in understanding my detective.

Tom O'Malley, chairman of the Treasury Historical Association, was a detective himself in tracking down the Secret Service chief's 1902-era office; the Treasury Department's Melissa Moye generously arranged a tour. Richard Grimmett tutored me on the history of Saint John's Church. National Park Service rangers—Geraldine Hawkins at TR's birthplace in Manhattan and Bradley A. Krueger at Theodore Roosevelt Island in DC—answered every question I could think of. Thanks also to Eric Madison at the National Capital Trolley Museum in Colesville, Maryland, and to Jill Reichenbach at the New-York Historical Society. Julie Smith, my "mentor" at the Mystery Writers of America, helped me anticipate, and I hope skirt, the pitfalls of writing a sequel.

At Macmillan's Tor/Forge, I can't thank Claire Eddy enough for her graceful and perceptive editing. Her assistant, Kristin Temple, has been a pleasure to work with. Kudos again to my agent, Ron Goldfarb, as well as Gerrie Sturman, for their legal—and moral—support.

Which brings me to the people who matter the most. I am incredibly fortunate (not to jinx anything) to have both of my children, Anna and Matt, living nearby, with their wonderful spouses, Jasyn and Cat, and two amazing little boys, Nolan and Jack, who run in opposite directions. As always, my greatest—and gravest—thanks goes to my wife, Nancy Tuholski, who keeps getting lovelier.